NAKED OR DEAD

A. E. MURPHY

XELA KNIGHT

Dogan Yildiz, my best friend. Thank you.

CHAPTER 1

"Name?" He slides the pointed nail of his forefinger down his roster, stopping at the empty row at the bottom of the page.

"Lilith Deville," I reply as I move to the only empty space in this dreary classroom.

My new classmates murmur around me, whispering questions of who I am, where I'm from, and why I'm here in their stupid preppy bullshit of a school.

"I wasn't aware I'd be getting a new student today," the teacher mutters, a frown marring his aged, yet handsome features. I wonder if he knows that his red tie clashes with his orange hair or if he simply doesn't care. "Where have you transferred from, Miss Deville?"

"A place where teachers couldn't wear ties," I respond loudly. "Ties became nooses in my old school."

"High rate of suicide?" he asks, sounding and looking concerned as his hand adjusts the clothing piece in question.

"Not suicide, no."

My meaning isn't lost on him, his polite smile falls. He clears his throat and those whispers around me become more desperate. Eyes level on me and glance away, others stick to me like glue, some don't even venture near me at all.

"Well, as I'm your first teacher of the day, welcome to Lakeside Preparatory Academy. I'm Mr. Bromley."

I nod and pull the shit I need from my bag.

"Do you have a buddy for your first day?"

"I'm good."

"It's a big school." He looks at a girl over in the back corner, I clocked her as soon as I walked in. "Perhaps Blair would..."

"I said I'm good," I repeat, clicking the end of my pen incessantly.

More whispering. Somebody calls me a bitch.

I don't care.

"Well, alright then. Everybody, eyes back on the board."

"Hey," the guy beside me whispers, tapping me on my bare shoulder with the eraser on the end of his pencil.

I look at him, his dark hair and pale skin, his stubble that he's likely super proud of despite the fact it's patchy, the trail of acne scars visible along his neck. He's cute, exactly the kind of guy my sister would have dated. I hate him already.

I catch my reflection in his glasses, a faceless outline with wild hair and a stiff posture, then take his pencil that is still suspended between us and snap it with both of my hands.

His lips part and his brows furrow.

"What the fuck?" he mouths, looking at the broken pencil that I just dropped to the floor. "You're not going to make any friends with that attitude."

"Good," I reply, smiling a fake-ass smile that I've perfected over the past few months. "I don't want friends."

"Psycho," a girl behind me whispers but she straightens nervously when I turn to look at her and the desk that separates us.

All I have to do is stare and her wide gray eyes almost pop out of her head as her body slowly slinks off her chair like a slug over an edge.

Satisfied, I turn back around and look at the board. Mr. Bromley's eyes are on me, his lips are a thin white line. I hold his gaze letting him know what I'm about.

I'm not here to learn. I'm not here to make friends. I'm here because I must be and here is where I'll stay until I've gotten what I need.

My dad always said you can say more with a single look at the right time than you can with a thousand words. Actions speak louder than words.

"Loki, right?" I ask the guy whose pencil I just snapped.

He keeps his gaze ahead as Bromley starts talking us through some local history but I know he heard me.

"Who is the most arrogant guy in school?"

He frowns and wets his lips. "Why should I tell you anything?"

"Because the longer it takes me to get answers, the longer I'm in this hell hole of a school."

He rolls his eyes. "Why do I care?"

I look at the girl behind me. "Clay eyes," I hiss, craning my neck and twisting my body in my seat.

"Me?" She points to herself, her eyes wide again.

"What's the punishment for sexual assault and harassment here?"

Her lips part, her eyes swim with confusion. "Why?"

"Just answer the question."

"Suspension pending investigation..."

Loki shifts in his seat, catching the gist of my threat. He's really annoyed. "Nok."

"Knock?"

"Yes," he huffs. "Nok is the most arrogant guy here."

"By far," the girl behind me agrees.

I don't remember seeing that name on the list of pupils here. I scour my brain but nothing comes to mind.

"Full name?" I ask abruptly and his hands squeeze into fists.

"Nokosi Locklear."

I know that name. It's exactly the person I was told about.

"He's like the only Native American that attends here, he's not hard to spot."

I rotate to look at her again and raise a brow. "This school is meant to be progressive and you're telling me there's only one Native American?"

"You have to be rich to get in."

"And white apparently," I mutter and then snort, "Well... fuck."

"What is it?" Loki asks cautiously.

I don't reply, instead I burn the name to memory and mentally curse that my first target is the only minority in the school. That's a racism charge if I ever saw one. Fuck.

Never mind. I have shit to do. I don't care who I upset.

"Did they teach you respect in your last school, Miss Deville?" Bromley barks at me, annoyed at my ignorance and chatter. "Because in our school we wait until we're on our own time to speak to our friends."

Silence is my answer. I put pen to paper and scribble my name all over the lines in different types of handwriting. It at least looks like I'm doing something.

"Anybody else you can think of that stands out as an arrogant asshole?" I ask just before the bell rings but neither of them answers.

Never mind, I have my starting point.

Nokosi Locklear.

His reputation precedes him.

Now to find him.

A task easier than I anticipated I discover, after second period during first break, when a small riot breaks out in the halls, right where one hall joins another.

Students charge past me, eager to follow the crowd, teachers blow whistles and an alarm sounds overhead as security tries to get to whatever is happening just before the next bend.

"NOK! NOK! NOK!" they all chant and the sound of something or somebody slamming against a metal locker echoes over their heads.

I can't be bothered to squeeze through so I toss a metal trash can upside down, letting the contents spill all over the floor and grab the shoulder of somebody nearby for leverage before standing on the flat bottom of the can.

I see a brown fist connect with a white cheek, and as though a filter of slow motion takes over my eyes, I watch a spray of blood fly through the air. White cheek guy hits the floor with a thud and does... not... move. Nobody steps forward, everybody freezes. But then he groans and tries to get up and the roar of the crowd is deafening.

The guy who I assume to be Nokosi grins at them all, making the cut on his lip bleed worse. He raises the fist he just KO'd the guy with and kisses his bulging bicep.

This guy is a piece of fucking work. He's also extremely beautiful. He also knows it.

I've never seen such a sharp jaw, and longer hair on a guy never once appealed to me. It does now.

Long, black hair, tied back with a single hair tie.

He has a tribal-looking tattoo on the arm he just kissed and it is almost as stunning as he is. So intricate, patterned, perfect. I pull out my phone and try to get a picture of it but it's grainy at best. There are too many bodies between us. Too much space.

As though sensing my eyes on him, or my camera, he looks up, his dark eyes narrow and land on mine, penetrating through my façade and startling me for just a second. His smile fades, his arm lowers. Nobody else seems to notice the exchange between us and that suits me just fine.

I almost shy away but I'm not that kind of person, not anymore.

I hold his eyes, reading him, seeing into him. My dad was right, eyes do communicate more than a thousand words and there's one word in particular that keeps repeating itself as our gazes remain locked.

Damaged.

Nokosi is damaged. Damaged people can always tell.

I need to make myself known to him, because if he's as arrogant as I believe him to be, he'll seek me out soon enough.

I have a feeling this school has a hierarchy and I have an even stronger feeling that this guy might be King.

Lakeside prep is the prettiest-looking shithole I have ever come across.

The teachers have sticks up their asses thinking they're some fucking privileged pricks because they work here. And I learned all that before lunch, first day.

Really this place is just an academy for stuck-up shits that have more money than sense and parents that don't give a fuck about them. I will admit the food is good. Normally I don't eat lunch, not because I'm worried about my figure but because the cafeteria is just not a place I want to be. But I need to be here today.

I need to study everybody and everything. This school is nothing like my last school. Or the school before that.

Its files are locked tight, its students watched closely.

I couldn't get much more than a list of names and seating charts before I arrived and fuck it if I didn't try. They've got some well-funded systems here.

I take my tray, surprised by the food choices. My last place served patties likely made from maggots and the tears of failing students, this place serves bagels with almond butter and organic jelly.

6

It's laughable how fancy this place is yet how rowdy the students are. There's no order, nobody keeping them in control. My last place wasn't as feral as this and that's saying something.

There are two girls from the cheer squad dancing on a table in the far corner, the jock-looking assholes at the table beside them throwing a football around, laughing when it hits Blair on the head and causes her to drop her tray.

Blair... maybe I should have agreed to ally with her. Not that she'll gain me any ranking, but I bet she has a lot of opinions on who are the shits and who are the not shits.

There's a girl sitting on the floor in the corner with paperwork spread out all around her. Clearly a kiss-ass. Maybe she's worth speaking to.

Meh.

I raise a brow and sit at the end of the closest table, pulling apart my lunch with my fingers and popping it onto my tongue. It tastes as good as it looks.

Fuck.

The people sitting at the other end of this table start whispering about me. Word has already travelled about the arrival of the new kid.

I find Loki two tables over, whose pencil I snapped this morning, and wink at him when he leans around the head of his friend to look at me. He scowls and looks away, making me laugh through my nose.

When lunch is over, I dump my tray and head out to the halls to explore and familiarize myself with the layout. I skip as I go, chewing on a wad of gum, headphones in one ear but not both. I like to be able to hear my surroundings.

"Miss Deville!" a booming voice calls, forcing me to stop.

"Principal Cooper," I respond, turning to face him as he waddles in his large legs to reach me. "Problem?"

He's almost wheezing when he reaches me. Dude needs to eat less pie and do more cardio.

"I spoke to Mr. Bromley." He wipes at the sweat on his brow with a folded handkerchief. It even has his initials on it and the school emblem. I bet they were a gift from one of his kiss-ass students.

I fold my arms over my chest and give him a settled look. "And?"

"He said you were very disruptive in your first lesson, talking about ties becoming nooses and disturbing your classmates."

I fight the urge to sigh and roll my eyes. "It was the excitement of my first class, Principal Cooper. I get anxious in social situations and say things I ordinarily wouldn't say."

"That's all well and good but..."

"It's a genuine thing, I can't help it. Surely I'm not about to be punished for something I can't help?"

"Disrupting your class can be *helped*. As in don't do it again."

I salute him. "I'll try harder to be a better student, Principal Cooper."

This seems to appease him. "And I'll try to better understand your anxieties. We want you to feel safe here at Lakeside. Not anxious."

"I appreciate that, Principal Cooper." I'm gritting my teeth and forcing a smile as my faux saccharine tone wins him over.

"Well, enjoy the rest of your first day, and remember to come knocking if you need anything."

I nod and continue my way, almost walking into somebody when I turn. I try to sidestep around the bitch but she does the same, staying in my path, putting us almost chest to chest.

"Who are you?" she asks, looking down her nose at me, brown eyes glittering with malice.

Here we go.

"Back up out of my space and maybe I'll tell you," I reply, wanting this day to be over.

She smirks, her thin lips stretch revealing long dimples that make her look a lot older than she is. "Feisty. I can respect that." I'm surprised when she steps back, giving me a better view of her as a whole. She's slender, but muscular, definitely sporty, a real knockout. I bet she's every guy's wet dream. Teachers included. "Again, who are you?"

"Lilith, I just transferred here."

"From?"

"None of your business." When I try to move around her, she steps in front of me again. I press my lips together. "If you're here to warn me off your boyfriend or tell me that you're queen bee, I don't give a fuck. I'm not here for long. I'd like to make it through my first day without having to imprint your pretty face into that locker over there."

She hesitates, her smirk fading. I've succeeded in intimidating her. "You'd resort to violence because I'm in your space?"

"What better reason is there to resort to violence, Barbie?"

One of her posse of three laughs under her breath, the other two who I'm only now getting a good look at seem to freeze. They don't want this conflict and they're not about to have their queen bitch's back.

Interesting.

"My name is Yasmine, not Barbie."

"Nice to meet you, Yasmine," I lie and smile at her in a way that has her taking an involuntary step back. "Can I pass? Or are we about to get you all ugly looking?"

"I don't take kindly to threats."

"She's a black belt in karate," the girl that laughed before states, looking proud.

"And I have a switchblade in my boot and fuck all to lose."

9

They all step back at my words. "I'm not here to cause any shit with y'all, but I will if I have to."

"Just stay out of my way." She's trying to be brave but failing, soon as I mentioned my knife, she lost her gumption and mentally pissed herself.

"You're the one blocking *my* path here."

She takes another step back and looks at her posse who look like they want to be anywhere but here. I'm glad to see they're a diverse group, it's a shame they don't look to have more than a handful of brain cells between them.

"Before you toddle on," I say, eyeing them all up. "Who would you say is the most arrogant guy in school?"

Barbie's brows furrow with confusion. "Why?"

"Just wondering who to avoid."

It's the girl who laughed that looks at her nail beds and responds, "Definitely Nok. He's super arrogant."

"But so hot," the girl to her left adds with a dreamy sigh.

"Don't get mixed up with Nok, he's not good people," Barbie surprisingly warns.

I give her a look. "Is that your way of telling me you're sleeping with him?"

Her posse look at her, a silent conversation passing between them. Not a good one from what I can tell too.

Barbie flips her blonde hair over her shoulder and raises her chin. "Hell no. I've been there and done that. He's... Nok is dangerous."

My skin prickles with excitement. "Dangerous how?"

"He's rough, gets into a lot of trouble," the girl who laughed says quietly as the others glance around them. "He's basically immune to the law too."

"Yeah," the final girl adds, her eyes wide. "He like totally doesn't care about anything and he *hates* white people."

Of course he does, that's not going to help my case much.

"The locals did try to sell his family's lands to push an oil pipe through, we did a fundraiser to stop that shit and it's protected lands now," Barbie adds, frowning at her friend. "But they're right, he's dangerous."

"If he hates white people why did he sleep with you?"

"That's why he slept with her."

Barbie nods her agreement. "He's not a nice guy."

"Thank you for the heads-up." I'm about to move around her when she steps in front of me again.

"This is Tish," Barbie says, pointing at the girl who laughed. "Mila, and Kim."

Why is she introducing them like I care?

"Pleasure," I murmur, looking at the girls from right to left. It's nice to see such a diverse group of friends, even if they are mega bitches. "May I get on with my day, Queen Barbie?"

"It's Yasmine."

I stick my thumb up and saunter past. This school is hell already.

"You need friends here if you want to survive," Barbie calls after me, her words echoing along the near-empty hall.

"She's right," Tish adds.

"Friends will just slow me down," I utter to myself and continue on my way.

Besides... I don't plan on surviving.

I explore some more but my aim now is the reception. I'm hoping I can sweet talk my way into getting more information on this Nokosi character. Such as where he lives.

The receptionist is a no go. The sour-faced bitch wouldn't even smile. There's no way I'm getting into the system this way.

I'll just have to do some good old-fashioned stalking.

Except Nokosi isn't here. He was sent home after his fight this morning. So was the guy he fought with. She told me that much at least.

Ugh.

Now I've got to wait until tomorrow.

I need to practice patience. I'm too eager.

I head back out to the halls and squeeze through the crowds of people, glaring at those who don't move.

CHAPTER 2

Columbia River is quite possibly the most beautiful place I have ever been. Truly. Oregon is incredible.

I drive my forest green Kurz pit bike, something we agreed I wouldn't ride to school because I would just stick out like a sore thumb wacked by a hammer. So, I take my dad's silver Prius to school and leave the bike out of sight. I hate this arrangement. I love my bike, I hate Dad's car.

I needed to get out of there, my new home, if I can call it that.

My sister is losing her fucking mind, so it's best to just stay out of her way. She doesn't like it here, but then again, she doesn't like it anywhere. She doesn't like much of anything, or anyone. We don't talk anymore, not like we used to. I'd shed a tear over it, but I don't really care anymore. I don't really care about anything, or anyone.

I burn rubber, one foot on the ground as the engine roars and my back wheel kicks up dirt and grass, creating a small ditch in the lumpy earth.

My bare hand feels on fire as I twist the throttle to full speed.

I shoot forward, taking the first hill with ease, landing with a jarring thud that almost throws me off and will give me some major monkey butt. I did not land it right so now I'm frustrated. I spin on the spot, creating a circular rivet and then line myself up with the next slope.

I fly at it and catch air again, performing a whip, though not a full one because the slope didn't give me enough height to work with. I land skewwhiff but correct it and keep going, ready for the next slope. This place is a biker's dream, so many rocky paths and slopes to catch. The dirt is solid beneath a thin layer of wet, and the grass isn't too long to maneuver through.

I rotate round, letting the sound of the engine overtake all my senses, and hit the biggest slope. But I snag, my chest feels tight as something hits me across the shoulders. The wind leaves my lungs and my bike goes forward as my body stays in the same place before slamming hard onto the ground on my back.

Can't breathe.

I've been clotheslined.

I roll onto my side, spluttering for air as the pain in my chest and back intensifies. That's going to hurt tomorrow. Fuck. It already does.

I can hardly breathe. I wasn't expecting it. I knew I should have found a place with less trees. Though I don't think a tree did this to me.

I look up at the sky through the dark shade of my helmet and try to steady my breathing.

I hear footsteps getting closer and voices getting louder.

"Howah!" one voice breathes. "It's like a chick, cri."

"You think she's dead?"

A foot taps my helmet.

I close my eyes when one of them flips my visor up, revealing my eyes.

"I think she is."

"F'reals?"

"I don't know, I'm not a doctor."

His fingers go to my wrist which I keep limp. "I can't feel a pulse, but her chest is moving."

When the second one crouches beside me and starts to unzip my leather jacket, I bring my booted foot up and kick the first one over, making them both scream with shock and terror. Then I bring my helmeted head up and into the nose of the one trying to unzip me.

I jump to my feet and race to where my bike landed in the dirt just a few meters ahead, ignoring the pain in my ribs and back. They both scramble around each other, taken by surprise at my quick movements.

"Hey! You're not supposed to be here; this is private land!"

"You could have just told me that, you fucking assholes!" I shriek back but don't stop.

I pick up my bike and sling a leg over it. I start the engine just as one of them reaches me and grabs my arm but it's too late, I sail forward, dragging him with me for half a meter before he lets me go.

I power shift, almost fucking up my clutch, and put them as far behind me as I can.

That wasn't supposed to happen. Those absolute fucktards. They could have killed me. I'm lucky they didn't.

I ride home, swerving around cars, lorries, whatever the fuck is in my way.

"You're back earlier than expected," Mom says when I walk through the door, rage in every step I take. "And dirtier."

I kick off my boots and drop my jacket on the floor. "I fucking hate it here."

"Language," she admonishes, her pale blue eyes narrowing with anger.

I say nothing else and stomp up the stairs and to my room. I haven't unpacked. I don't see the point. Everywhere we go is temporary. Mom's job makes it so.

I pass my sister's room where music hums through the door and wall. It's shit music too so I play mine louder to drown it out, then I have a bath and wipe myself out with some extreme pain killers.

Those absolute dicks.

Who the fuck clotheslines somebody to get them off a bike? If they'd flagged me down, I'd have gone elsewhere. I'm not looking to start debating over who owns what land. I don't really care. We're on the banks of Columbia River, there's nothing but land out here, not gonna be hard to find somewhere else to ride my bike.

Absolute dicks.

Gah.

I'm so mad.

I'm also sleepy.

I crash butt naked on the top of my covers and close my eyes. I'm going to feel so fucking groggy tomorrow, but I don't care about that either.

CHAPTER 3

A russet brown hand slams my locker closed, almost catching my fingers in the process. The hall around me stills and people move away but stay to watch the exchange.

I can smell him, smoky, powerful, masculine. It makes me want to inhale deeply.

His breathing is steady, his chest almost brushing against my back. I feel shadowed, completely covered by his athletic body. His forearm is as powerful as the bicep he kissed yesterday. His nails are trimmed neat and his hands are clean.

There's something to be said about a man-slash-boy with good hand hygiene. My dad always said that if somebody displays good hand hygiene, they likely have good other hygiene too.

"You're new," Nokosi growls, his tone rough and deep. This is the first time I've heard him speak. His voice is... wow.

"And?" I respond, my tone strong as I keep my eyes on my matte black locker.

"And that doesn't just give you a free pass to wander wherever the fuck you like, belegana."

I close my eyes for a moment when he wraps my thick braid around his hand and yanks my head back. It pulls on my scalp and makes my already sore neck ache. My heart is hammering in my chest so rapidly I'm surprised it hasn't chiseled a hole through my ribs.

"Fair warning," he whispers in my ear, his lips almost touching the shell. It sends prickles of fear and arousal down my spine. My ears are one of my most erogenous zones. "If you tread where you're not welcome again, you'll get more than just a hand in your hair."

I don't say anything, but oh I want to. I want to cuss and spit and press my knife against his throat so hard that he bleeds. But instead keep my lips a thin line and stare at a mark on my locker door. I would never have noticed it had I not been forced to look for it. That's how clean and well-kempt these lockers are.

"Am I understood?"

"Perhaps you can draw me a map?" I bite back and my bruised front hits the lockers. I bite on my tongue to stop me from crying out. That really fucking hurts. "Let me go."

"Am I understood?"

"Yes," I breathe, needing him to just let go of my hair so I can regain control of the situation.

"Remember this moment and imagine how much worse it can be," he hisses, pulling even harder on my hair before finally releasing me and stalking away with his equally tall and muscular tanned and dark friends at his sides. One of them slaps my ass as he passes.

Dick.

That's sexual harassment, he's lucky I'm not a snitch. Though something tells me in a school like this, shit like that gets swept under a very heavy rug.

I stare at Nokosi's back as he walks away, a stride in his step like he owns this fucking place and the fact that there are two teachers walking by who definitely saw the exchange and did nothing, just further proves that he's King of this castle.

But why?

Loki was right, he really is the most arrogant prick here. Somebody needs to bring him down a peg or two. I'm not sure that I care enough anymore to try.

This place will not cut me a break.

Lilith: I hate it here.

Willow: So you've said.

Lilith: It's the worst place we've been so far.

Willow: And the most prestigious, so it should be the best.

Lilith: Right?! Wish you were here.

Willow: Glad I'm not.

I laugh and stuff my phone into my pocket. My sister can be okay sometimes. We used to be a lot closer.

"Lilith?"

I look at Loki who is sitting to my right again in this class. "Mm?"

"Are you okay?"

I'm surprised by his concern. "Fine, why?"

"I saw what happened with Nok. I just thought..." He shrugs his shoulders. "I've been on the receiving end of his shit before, it's not nice."

"Oh, that." I smile genuinely, to reassure him and because it just seems the right thing to do with my face at this point. "I'd already forgotten about it."

"Oh... well, good." His brows draw together from the confusion. "What did you do to get his attention?"

I contemplate not telling him but then that'd just be petty. "Drove my pit bike through his lands... apparently."

He rolls his eyes. "Oh yeah, Nok's tribe are like worse than the Canadian border. Be careful. They rule the roost around here."

"I'm starting to gather that."

He shifts in his seat and opens the textbook on his desk. "Why did you want to know who the most arrogant guy in the school is?"

I tap my nose and look at my own books. Then I look up at the board and do the work I'm supposed to be doing. It gets rid of the humming noise in my head for long enough. Thankfully.

I get bored after all of ten minutes and go back to texting my sister. She doesn't respond.

Cunt-bitch that she is.

This is so fucking dull.

"Does your hair color fade quickly?" questions Mackenzie, who is sitting to my left. She's the same girl who was sitting in the corner alone surrounded by paper the other day.

Lifting a shoulder, I glance at her, meeting her silver eyes for a second and reply, "Not if I use color protection shampoos and conditioner."

"Brilliant!" She holds out a lock of her auburn hair. "Reckon it would take?"

I snort. "Umm, definitely not. You'd need to either gradually go to a platinum shade like I did and then apply a pink, or nuke it with bleach, apply a pink and have pink hair for two weeks before it all snaps off.

She looks disheartened. "What's your natural shade?"

Why do these people ask dumb fucking questions? "Pink."

"No, seriously."

I deadpan, "Pink."

It's obviously not pink, but it's also none of her business. I lift my braid into the light and admire the pastel pink sheen. I honestly thought they'd make me change my hair to fit their image at this school, but they haven't said a thing about it. So long as I roll up in their plaid skirt and navy blazer, they seem content with anything else as it is.

"A woman of mystery, I like it," she mutters to herself and I find myself smiling for real this time. She's funny, in a natural way, not the attention-seeking kind of way. Then, just when I think she's done talking to me she adds, "I'm Mack, by the way, short for Mackenzie."

I look at her outstretched hand and clasp mine together, letting her know I don't want to touch her. "I'm Lilith."

She retracts her hand, still smiling at me. "Lilith Deville, right? Very biblical and kinda creepy, no offence."

"None taken."

"Good, I got worried you'd snap my prized pencil," she holds up a metallic rose gold pencil with her name inscribed in the side in black lettering. "Isn't she a beauty?"

"If you don't poke me with it I'm sure it will survive the semester."

"Awesome," she whispers as the teacher walks back into class, having stepped out five minutes ago for something. I don't know what thing. "So that's why you snapped Loki's pencil?"

"Does it really matter? It's just a pencil."

"It was rude," Loki hisses.

I spin and glare at him. "Rude is poking somebody you don't know with a pencil."

"Wasn't like it was the pointy end," he grumbles to himself.

"Settle down, class." The teacher's voice sounds as mundane as I'm feeling. "Ah, we have fresh meat. Welcome to Lakeside Preparatory, Miss..."

"Lilith Deville," I reply for the millionth time since yesterday.

"Ah yes, I have you here..." She presses something on her tablet, and I wonder why all of the teachers but Mr. Bromley have high-tech gadgets to take the roll call. "So where do you hail from?"

"Everywhere. Mom's an environmentalist so we travel," I answer robotically, also for the millionth time since yesterday.

"Wow, that's interesting. What kind of things does she do?"

I sigh and shrug my shoulders. "Environmental stuff."

The class snickers as the teacher frowns but she doesn't comment on my reluctance to respond with genuine answers to her prying. "Okay, well, I'm Ms. Bacon, it's nice to have you in my class."

"Thanks." I look away, out of the window, hoping to daydream my way through the rest of the day. I blink twice when I catch sight of somebody by a big tree across a staggered stepped walkway that leads to the main entrance.

It's Nokosi in his uniform, and some girl in a white top, standing in the rain beneath the budding leaves of the tree. He has her caged in, his hands on the bark either side of her head, she's smiling at him. He smiles back, leans in, and kisses her lips, then deepens it, making her cheeks hollow and her body relax. Her hands grip his blazer-clad waist until he pulls her leg over his hip. The dark skin of her bare navel makes his bare arms look almost red in comparison. Hers bronze, his umber. Both so attractive. But I can guarantee she's not his girlfriend. Nokosi doesn't have girlfriends, I can tell that about him already.

I can't tear my eyes away, the way he commands her body with just his tongue in her mouth. I've never been kissed like that. Sure, I've been kissed but he's not just kissing her, he's possessing her.

She's bending her body to meet his like she's desperate for more of a taste. How much more of a taste can she get with her tongue in his mouth already?

I've never seen anybody kiss like this, let alone be kissed like that myself.

I touch my lips, imagining a tingle there that will probably never be there.

Principal Cooper appears out of nowhere waving a finger at them, pointing towards the parking lot while his lips form words I can't hear. Nokosi peels himself away from the girl and pushes his wet hair from his eyes before sauntering back into the school. The girl walks away from the school entirely. Her lack of uniform just shows that she doesn't go here. I'm pretty sure she's native, maybe half and half because her skin is darker, and her hair is poker straight but is starting to frizz where the rain has been wetting it

Fuck.

I need to get me some of that. That was hot.

My sister wouldn't approve.

I look around me at all the boys in this class, considering my options. None of them will do. Not now. Though I'll be damned if I ever sleep with a guy like Nokosi. Not a chance in hell.

Still, *that kiss.*

I get to lunch still thinking about it, still consumed by it. How can such a douchebag be so passionate with a girl? Normally they're out for what they can get and never for what they can give. Does he get off on pleasing women because the way she was rubbing against him meant she was genuinely enjoying herself.

I head outside to the same tree he was at with my phone in

hand. I walk around it once checking for spiders and bugs. I come across a plaque at the base facing the entrance, it's dedicated to some kid that died a couple of years ago. Sad.

I move away from that and rest my head back against the bark and scan the grounds. I should be exploring the school to become more familiar with its layout and people, but I just need this moment to understand a moment that I've never witnessed outside of staged porn.

It has blown my mind.

I try to think of other things but it's near impossible. I need to go for a ride. That'll get my mind set on the right path.

Lilith: Did Mom clean my jacket?

Willow: I did, last night. You should really take better care of it.

Lilith: You know I didn't have any control over what they did.

Willow: Just check that you're not on the res before you tread dirt. Okay?

Lilith: I should make them pay for what they did to me.

. . .

Willow: Good luck finding them... on their own land... Miss Brainiac.

Lilith: Even through text message your sarcasm is strong.

Willow: I learned from the best. Be nice to your peers. Blend in. Or try to.

Lilith: Whatever...

I see Nok with two male friends exiting the main entrance to the right. I watch him out of the corner of my eye as they throw each other around, playfighting and showing off like little boys. I stand, ready to follow from a safe distance when he suddenly clocks me and stops in his tracks.

His black hair is piled up on his head in a messy knot, his eyes are tense and dangerous. He glares at me, trying to intimidate me and I glare back, unphased by his tactic.

"Come on, Nok," one of his buddies urges, still smiling from the playfighting. "I'm fucking starved."

Nok tears his eyes away and I wait a moment before following, ignoring the bustle of the students. I just need to know what he's driving.

I swing my keys around my finger, making it look like I'm headed to my own car, and hasten my steps when they all climb into a large four-by-four truck with a covered bed. I memorize the license plate and brand as it peels out of the lot, and then, smiling to myself, I climb into my own car and type it into my phone.

Got him.

They return forty minutes later, and I follow them inside, not because I have to, but just because I want to appreciate his rear for just a bit longer. It's a nice, firm, round, athletic rear. It's just a shame it's attached to such a douchebag.

I do love though how he automatically has an issue with me. Like he just knows I'm about to make his life hell. He's obviously very perceptive.

But so am I.

He obviously has good instincts.

But so do I.

I notice him glance over his shoulder at me as we both stroll down the hall in the same direction. I notice his lips purse and his eyes narrow. I notice him whisper to the guy on his right.

They keep going, but so do I. I quicken my pace to get even closer, shouldering past coeds and even teachers. I get so close at one point I'm a nose breadth away from his back. I could kiss his spine if I wanted to; that dip that rests perfectly center to both sides of his body.

God, he smells good.

Then I drop back, just in time for him to check again without seeing how close I was. Though he felt me for the most part, I was too quick for him to catch.

He glances behind him again and I smirk at him.

He takes the bait, stops, and turns so suddenly it takes his friends another two steps to realize he's no longer walking with them.

"What the fuck do you want, maggot?"

The people around us still like before, a few laugh, the boys with him share excited glances.

"Your attention," I state boldly, still smirking.

He scoffs and looks around him with a fake smile on his face. He's assessing his peers. Checking they're listening to him for when he roasts me.

I beat him to the punch and hold up the black leather square, full of bank cards and cash and likely his ID. His smile fades and his eyes go to the wallet. It really is quite full of some serious dollar. I should have snuck a few out of it.

"You dropped your wallet." I hold his gaze and his dark eyes lose the hardness they had.

He tries to snatch it from my hand while sneering at me. "Don't touch anything that belongs to me, belegana." I move my hand away, keeping it out of reach.

"Okay, so I should have just let somebody else pick it up and steal your cash? I'll do that the next time your irresponsible ass can't keep track of your shit in my path." I slap it against his chest so hard the sound echoes around the hall and his chest muscle twitches under the force. He grits his teeth. "You're welcome."

He catches it before it falls past his waistline and watches me saunter away, flipping him off over my shoulder as I go. I catch the eyes of Barbie and her squad; she surprisingly gives me a sympathetic smile.

Sympathy over what?

I've got Nok exactly where I want him.

CHAPTER 4

"We have to make our own luck," my sister says, picking at the food on her plate. She's not been eating much of anything lately. "You've got to stop picking so many fights."

"I enjoy it. It gives me something to focus on before Mom makes us leave again."

She laughs under her breath, her pink lips stretching and showing a slight tinge of blue around the edges.

"You're cold," I say, frowning.

She nods so I race into the den to grab her favorite mustard yellow throw. I drape it over her shoulders and pull free her dark brown braid. "I'm feeling a lot weaker than usual today."

"That's the drugs," I respond. "You need to take them earlier and eat more."

"Whatever," she grumbles, casting her sad hazel eyes to her plate again where she proceeds to push it around with her fork some more. "Do you want this?"

"No, I'll put it in the oven, it'll keep for Mom."

"If she ever gets home."

We laugh gently together. Mom is struggling with Willow's decline, so she finds any excuse to work out of the house. And when she's home, Willow finds any excuse to be in her room.

"Thanks for cleaning my jacket for me."

She smiles again and shivers again.

Fuck. I hate this. I hate seeing her this fragile.

"Why were you so late coming home after school?" she asks, coughing violently the moment the question ends. She sounds terrible. I wait for her to start breathing again, letting her squeeze my hand as the coughing takes over her entire body.

I take her arm and guide her to the stairs while replying, "I just had a couple of errands to run."

I followed Nokosi home as discreetly as possible, not easy through the res where every road is essentially private, I had to hang back so far I almost lost him a few times.

I was... *surprised* by what I saw. By the amount of cash that was in his wallet and the type of truck he owns I expected to see him living by some fancy casino in a mansion with a butler. *An exaggeration of course.* Instead he lives in what can only be described as a modernized log cabin, big enough for a very small family. There were others in the distance and even a couple of tiki huts from what I could see using my binoculars through the thick trees.

But at least now I know where he lives.

"And how much longer until we move again?"

The million-dollar question. "Hopefully not too soon, it's real pretty here."

"I might go out later—" She stumbles and starts coughing again.

"Don't be stupid, you're a walking corpse."

She tries to laugh but it makes her choking worse.

We wait for it to pass before she croaks a husky, "Okay, I'm going to sleep. Is that cool?"

I nod, taking a lot of her weight as we make our way up the staircase. My body aches still but it's nothing compared to how she's feeling. "So long as it's cool with you that I go out on my bike."

"Your jacket is behind your bedroom door."

"Thanks, sis."

"You owe me."

I roll my eyes. "I think I do enough for you already."

Grinning, she pads into her bedroom, blows me a kiss, and shuts the door. I race to my own and grab my jacket before pulling it on, feeling confident that I know the layout of the reservation now. I know where it ends, and I know where to avoid.

I'm not sure I should even be going back out, not with the state my body is in right now, but I need to. I need to get my head on straight and this is how I do it. Not in Dad's shitty Prius.

I take to the road again, gloveless, jacket on, helmet tight, and navigate through the small amount of traffic.

I go up and down and around before hitting the dirt path I took yesterday, but this time I turn right instead of left and follow it to a point I marked on my phone map. It's not too far from the reservation but I don't care. I like playing with fire, I like the burn, I love the chase, I envy the power.

Plus, it's the only place close enough to home that looks bumpy enough to ride around and it's clear, so I won't get any little fucktards with rope trying to snap my neck from behind the trees.

Pussies.

My anger at them comes forward and I pick up speed, skidding around a sharp bend on the footpath before careening off course and almost losing myself over the edge of a fucking cliff.

"SHIT!" I curse, breathing heavily as my heart rapidly beats behind my ribs.

That was way too close.

I need to control my fucking temper, but God I want to hammer them into the ground so hard for what they did. It remains prevalent even as I try to figure out where I went wrong and how I got so off course.

I rip my helmet off and look over the cliff edge, the tip of my toe hanging over the edge. I get a delirious jolt of adrenaline from being so close to the edge of death, a good hundred-foot drop between me and the coarse ground below.

What a thrill.

I sit, letting my legs dangle, digging my fingers into the moss that is covering the smooth rocky surface.

This place truly is beautiful. I can see a branch of water coming from the Columbia River which is miles to the west.

I take out my phone and snap a picture to send to Willow. I wish she could sit here with me.

Willow: Wow. Amazing. But foggy. You should be careful.

Smiling, I tuck my phone back into my zip pocket and stand on the edge again, spreading my arms to feel the gentle wind flow around my body and through my hair.

I count the tops of the trees and the rocks and count my heart-beat against the sound of the water as it flows.

Its tempo is now faster than my heartbeat.

So soothing. So wonderful.

"If you jump, there's a high chance you'll survive and break every bone in your body," an unfamiliar male voice calls from the tree line behind me.

I turn to face the intruder, spotting a man not much older than me watching me carefully. He's leaning against a big leaf maple, his arms folded over his chest, his biceps bulging against the fabric of his short-sleeve blue shirt that's wide open at the front. His chest is bare, hairless, muscular.

He looks like Nokosi, but I won't say that for fear of them not being related and then I'm just low-key racist.

"I'm not on the res. I got a local map and marked it off."

"Didn't say you were," he replies, smiling now. "Nice bike."

I step away from the cliff edge and move to my discarded green pit bike. When he lifts it off its side to an upright position, I'm sad to see the paintwork has scratched on the rocky ground when I skidded to a stop. I'm lucky I didn't tear my leg up though these jeans aren't faring much better than the paintwork of my bike.

"How is it?" He motions to the leg I'm checking over by peeling back the torn flaps of my pants.

I rub it down and peel apart the small rips to check for damage to my skin. I got off lightly. "This place is trying to kill me."

"Is that so?" He pushes a hand through his short black hair. "Or maybe you're taking unnecessary risks riding your bike like a lunatic through forests you don't know?"

"We've all got to die sometime right?"

"Doesn't mean we can't try to delay it for a while."

I grin at him, figuring this dude isn't so bad, I don't completely feel like I want to avoid him. "But where's the fun in that?"

Laughing gently, he swings his leg over my bike and kick starts it with a powerful push of his foot. I tense, wondering if he's about to leave me out here but he just makes it roar, startling birds from the trees and other creatures into deeper woods.

"You going to steal my bike?" I ask and he pats the space behind him. "You're kidding? I'm not riding off into the sunset with my friendly neighborhood native."

He laughs louder this time and holds his smile as he pats the seat again and assures me, "I'm not about to kidnap you, but I will take you some place better than this part of the forest. Somewhere you'll appreciate."

I hesitate, wishing he'd just get off my bike and fuck off back to his hut or whatever.

Now that was definite racism.

But then he taunts, "What's more thrilling than something as random as climbing onto a bike with a complete stranger?"

And I conclude that he has a point. "Fine." I grab my helmet and yank it on my head, he watches me click it into place. "You ever ridden one of these before?"

"Best rider in Oregon."

I roll my eyes and swing my leg over. I've not done this since my dad used to take me out on his as a little girl. I don't know what to do with my hands.

"What's your name?" he calls, his voice deep and gravelly.

"Lilith," I reply. "Yours?"

"Nash," he answers and waits for me to grip the seat. I'm not about to wrap my arms around him.

"Where are you taking me, Nash?"

He smirks at me over his shoulder. "You'll see."

We jet forward, taking the path that I skidded off. I squeak, not used to the feeling of not being in control of my own bike and very soon my hands leave the seat and grip his bare waist. I feel him laugh at me and resist the urge to pinch his skin.

We whip through the trees, zigzagging on rocky paths that completely batter my parted thighs and rear. I slip forward without meaning to, my chest against his back. It's so uncomfortable in a really comfortable way.

Maybe this guy can scratch my itch?

We ride for another ten minutes, I try to pay close attention to where I am but after a while all the trees, rocks, green bits, and streams become the same.

Finally, the trees break apart and we enter a massive clearing, this one mostly dirt and there are a few people on quad bikes and a dirt bike flying over steep inclines into watery, shallow trenches.

"No fucking way," I squeak as indigenous people look our way. "We are definitely on the res now."

"It's okay, we're not white-people-hating devils out for your blood," he retorts in jest as I yank my helmet from my head. "You're welcome to come here whenever you like."

I push back the hair that has escaped my braid and hook it around my ears, watching dirt bike guy get squirrelly for a second as he tries to land a move beyond his capabilities. Yikes.

"You don't know me, why are you being so kind?"

He ignores my question and climbs from my bike after securing its standing position.

I change my question. "How did you know I was there anyway?"

"Fate? I don't know. I was planning on going for a swim, there's a lake near where you were."

"So that's why you're topless," I point out. "Isn't it too cold to swim?"

He laughs and shakes his head. "Not for me."

"Well... whatever... thanks for bringing me here. Why is this even here?"

"Where else am I going to practice?"

"Yeah, you need it," I joke, making him laugh because we both know he doesn't need it. He handled my unfamiliar ride like a fucking dream, he made me feel amateur and it's my fucking bike. "Thanks for the offer."

"Nash, who's she?" one of the girls from a small group of friends asks as they make their way over. She sounds curious, not threatened. This is good, I think.

"Just a lost puppy I found in the woods."

I don't like that one bit and I let him know I don't like it with a glare that does nothing to shift his smile.

She struts towards me, legs bared in denim shorts, thick black hair in a ponytail to her mid-back, skin a dark, golden, reddish brown like Nash's and Nok's. Her friends stay behind, one of them seems to be recording the others on their rides.

She looks at Nash, a recognizable glint in her eye, disappointment, jealousy, lust. She wants this guy and he just rolled up with me.

I take a step to the side to let her know I'm not interested in him, at all, in any way. I'm just here to ride.

"Can I?" I ask him before I'm forced through introductions I don't care about.

When he nods, I pull on my helmet and reclaim my scratched bike. I am so looking forward to this.

I do a couple of basic laps, getting used to the terrain before rejoining Nash for a short break.

"Can you mark where I'm at on my phone so I can find my way home?"

"It's cool," he says politely, lifting and dropping his shoulders. "I'll show you."

"I'm sure she'll be fine on her own, Nash," the girl puts in, annoyed that his attention isn't on her.

"Lilith, this is Winona," Nash states and she holds out her hand.

I show her the dirt splattered on mine and she yanks back her own. Grinning, I wipe mine on my ripped jeans and look at Nash. "You got time for me to squeeze in another two?"

"Go for it, I'm good here."

Woohoo!

I kick up dirt behind me and hit the first hill, catching air for two seconds before landing it perfectly. Fuck yes.

I hit the next one, going a bit faster this time and catch the air for long enough to do a whip. Then I go around and around, hitting the hills, landing my bike... two perfect runs. On the second run I notice more people have arrived and are watching me sail past the quads and the other pit bike. I love riding, I

36

love trails, it's the only thing I do these days that is purely for me.

My dad taught me, and he taught me well. So well I out-skilled him by age fourteen.

I skid to a stop in front of Nash, unable to stop the beaming smile from stretching across my face, totally not realizing who he's standing with.

"That was a killer run," Nash grins, and Nokosi, who must be his brother, just sneers at me. Nash, noticing his brother's glare, slings an arm around my leather-clad shoulders. "Don't mind him, he's had a stick up his ass for years."

"It's really jammed up in there," I reply, and he laughs.

Nokosi narrows his eyes on me but doesn't say anything. Likely so he doesn't look like a bigger ass than he is already.

"So, what brings you to Westoria, Oregon?"

"Mom's work, as always, we'll be gone again in a month or so."

His brows pulled in. "Sounds like hell to me. I'm a homebody, couldn't imagine living anywhere else."

I shrug my shoulders, not showing that it does affect me, it fucking sucks when I get used to a place and have to leave. "I don't complain about what I can't change."

"That's smart, peaceful even. Learning to just accept the inevitable instead of trying to fight it."

Nokosi snorts and I wonder if Nash's words are also referring to something going on with them.

"Thanks for bringing me here," I tell him, wanting to get out of here now, get home and eat some grub.

"Yeah, Nash, *thanks*," Nokosi grits, putting extra sarcastic emphasis on the *thanks*.

"I meant when I said you can come here any time; my people won't mind."

His people? Is he their chief or something? I doubt it, he's so young. He must just know them all really well.

"Speak for yourself," Nokosi adds, glaring at his brother now.

"I don't want to intrude."

"You're not," Winona assures me, smiling kindly. "Ignore him." She shoves Nokosi, or tries to, he doesn't budge an inch, he's a solid mass of body and muscle and attitude.

He sneers at me one more time and then walks away, stopping at a quadbike that has been parked haphazardly at the edge of the dirt track.

"It's not you," Nash explains.

I raise my brows. "Oh, I don't care, to be honest. He doesn't scare me."

"Good," Nash replies softly. He smiles gently and taps his knuckles against the helmet that I'm holding under one arm. I'm such a sweaty mess right now. "I'll let you drive us back, so you get a feel for the way here."

"You sure I'm okay to come back here?"

"Any time you want, Anetúte..." He sees my confusion at the word. "Meaning *my father*, will be happy. He wants us to mingle more with you pale faces."

"Is that why Nokosi is the only native in school?" I had to ask because I've wondered about it since I started.

He sighs gravely. "Kind of, Nokosi was made to join Lakeside last year because of his hatred towards your people."

"Not my people," I correct, and he smiles again. He has such a nice smile. It's so calming.

"Anetúte wanted him to learn to love them and forgive them."

"Forgive them for what?"

He sighs again and looks up at the graying sky. "If only we knew."

I look over at Nokosi who is riding the quad over a slope. He's not bad himself, navigating the bike with ease and strength. I can't help but watch him and wonder why he hates white people so much when, if what Nash is saying is true, he's been raised to be tolerant despite our history.

I often find that people don't hate for no reason, if it's not the way they were raised or the influence of their peers, then it's usually something in particular that has flipped that switch.

"Just stay away from him and he won't bother you."

"Noted." I climb on the bike before patting the seat like he did to me before. "Thanks for showing me the way back."

"It's no problem."

He climbs on behind me, eliciting cheers from his friends who are supposed to be watching Nokosi. His chest presses against my back and his thighs grip mine.

"Don't crash, my brain will scramble, and my people will miss me."

I laugh under my breath. "I'll do my best."

We ride forward, him holding on to my waist with a tight arm banding around me, his other hand points to direct us out of the forest and back to the main road.

It doesn't take too much time which I'm grateful for because my butt is hurting and it's disconcerting having a guy so close to me like this. It makes me nervous and uncomfortable. I don't like being this close to people, especially men. It's not so bad if I'm at the back and in control, but right now I'm in control of nothing but the bike.

I stop at the mouth of the forest and grip the handles after pulling up my visor. "Are you sure you don't want me to give you a ride home?"

"Nah, it's cool, it's not far."

I know for a fact that's not true, but I don't admit it because then he'd wonder how I know where he lives. Stalkers don't make for good company.

He shines another charming smile my way. "Same time tomorrow?"

I eye him warily and make my bike rev. "I'll think about it."

Truth be told the track is exactly where I'll be going because it is exactly where I need to be.

CHAPTER 5

I take gas money from the jar on the kitchen windowsill. It looks like an ordinary vase to any unsuspecting burglars. Mom keeps it mostly full so we can grab what we need while she's not around. Tonight, it's for gas money. She told me to help myself right before she walked out of the back door and out of my life for another three days. Leaving me to deal with my sister, the house, and school.

I can't remember the last time she asked me about my day.

Fuck her for that.

"Going to see Nok again?" Willow asks.

"No, just off to feed my bike."

"And to see Nok again."

I shrug, no point in denying it. "I have to try. He wasn't at the track today."

"Why do you always do this?" she snaps, her tired eyes weary. "Why play these games? What's the point in any of this?"

"You ask me this every time."

Her voice gets so loud my head feels like it's splitting open for a moment. "Because you do this every time!"

"I have to!" I yell back, wishing she'd stop fighting with me on this. "It's the right thing to do."

"You're insane if you think that."

I laugh sardonically and slam the door in her face on my way out of the kitchen and then out of the house.

I went to the res again after school today once I'd finished dealing with Willow and getting her comfortable. I raced a few laps against Nash and two of his buddies and then sat and ate amazing sandwiches prepared by his grandmother who I haven't met. He used a different word for her, but I can't remember what it was.

He told me his nan is an elder and she doesn't leave the immediate vicinity. Apparently, she's sensitive to the emotions and troubles of others so she doesn't like huge crowds of people.

She just makes them all sandwiches and snacks when they ask. A lot of it is freshly caught and cooked. I'll never look at store-bought fish the same way again after such amazing sandwiches.

They are such welcoming people. Even Winona who is totally vying after Nash's affections. She should hate me and she probably does but it's ingrained in her to be polite. Unlike Nok who took one look at me, spat on the ground by my feet, and rode away with his own group of friends to location unknown. He's hard to get near. I had two classes with him today and I couldn't even entice him to look my way. He just did his work with his head down, not saying a thing to anyone.

Though I did get some info on his relationship with Barbie and I was shocked by what I heard. Apparently, rumor has it, he had sex with her in the back of his truck and then left her at a truck stop because he was done. That's all he wanted. To humiliate her.

But I don't know if that's true as it didn't come from Barbie herself and rumors in school spread like cancer.

Still... he gets worse and worse the more I hear and see of him.

I mount my bike and make the long drive to the gas station. Nash shouted at Nok earlier to remember to pick up a few gallons of gas for the quads. Of course, I low-key enquired about where he'd be getting it from on the lie that I was looking for the cheapest fuel prices around here, but whether he'll be there or not when I get there is another thing entirely. Knowing my luck... he won't be.

I fill up my tank in the empty station, lifting up my visor so I can see better in the dark. The only light comes through the glass windows of the gas station. I put the nozzle back and head inside, readying my wallet to pay.

One of the truckers loitering around with two others to the right of the building wolf whistles. "Walk on over here, pretty lady, if you want a good time."

They laugh as though he's so fucking hilarious which he's not.

I ignore them and push on the store door; it beeps when it reaches a thirty-degree angle and drags on the tiles the rest of the way.

"We'll pay you!"

"With my massive dick!"

I keep ignoring them and head inside, letting the door close behind me. I'm not scared of them, but I am aware of where my sharpened switchblade is tucked into my boot just in case I need it.

A TV in the corner by the counter fills the space with sound. I vaguely listen as I search for where they keep the cold drinks.

"Such a nice, loving young man... didn't deserve this... family distraught... miss him... inhumane..."

I roll my eyes. People always lie when people die, they tell about how nice they are and how loved when really they were a complete dick while alive. It's such a joke. People are pussies. When I die I want the world to know what a cunt I was while alive. Don't do me a disservice by pretending I was anything other than what I am.

I grab a bottle of water from the refrigerator and almost squeak with glee when I hear another car pull up outside. It's Nok's truck.

FUCK YES!

I didn't think I'd get so lucky.

Somebody climbs out with him; I think his name is Joseph but I'm not completely certain. I saw him on the track today riding a quad before leaving with Nok as I sat with Nash. So many names. I'm usually good at this but I'm tired and too eager.

I've never struggled to entice a bad boy before, ever. Nok is too much of a fucking challenge, I might just not bother with any of this at all. Maybe my sister is right? Maybe I am insane for doing this but it's just... he's not a nice guy. I know that. There's no redeeming him in my eyes. But whatever.

I've got to do what I've got to do to make this hell a little bit more bearable.

This is perfect though. I am buzzing with electric excitement at how well this has panned out.

I quickly pay for my water and gas and mutter a curse under my breath. "Do you have a restroom?"

"Over there," the bored-looking cashier says, pointing to the far corner.

I don't actually need to pee, but I need a reason to hang back and make my play. I head inside, careful not to touch anything and wait approximately three minutes until the beep above the door sounds across the store.

I make my exit and as I'm doing so the beep sounds again.

"Don't you fucking ignore me, bush nigger," snarls the voice of the trucker that catcalled me outside.

Oh man. Come on. Give me a break, Satan.

"Don't, Nokosi," Joseph pleads. "He's not worth it."

"No, niggers like you ain't worth it. Ain't worth shit. Fuck off back to your hovels and grill a salmon." The trucker and his pals start laughing, I creep around the shelving unit and watch them all high-five like children. Nok is livid, his hands are balled into fists, but he's outnumbered, and these guys are packing. Or at least the greasy-looking white guy with a red cap is.

I see the handle of his Glock when he flips his leather vest back to put a hand on his hip. It's in a holster on his belt. This is bad.

Nok and Joseph see it too and their demeanors visibly change.

"We're not looking for any trouble," Joseph says calmly, raising his hands as I check out the dome mirrors on the ceiling to get a better look of all three men. I don't see any guns on the rest of them. "We just want to pay for our gas and go back to the res where we belong."

"A lot of gas you got in your trunk," one trucker comments, this one in a denim jacket and loose-fitting jeans. "Paying in cash?"

The guy behind the desk tenses but says nothing. He's about to lose a sale and a lot of gas if these guys take Nok's money.

Nobody moves, they're at a standstill, waiting for Nok to retrieve his wallet. He doesn't. He's boiling with anger; I can see it in his eyes. No wonder he hates white people if this is how we've treated him all his life. He's not surprised by the racism and neither is Joseph, in fact Joseph knows exactly how to react to deescalate this situation. They probably get more of this than most would like to admit.

"Hand over what you've got, we'll cover the bill and take the rest, how's that sound?" red cap asks, a twisted smile on his face.

"Sounds about right to me," his friend adds, grinning just as twisted.

"Whatever, just don't start fighting," the cashier, still looking tired, says. He even finishes it with a yawn. "I'm not in the mood to clean your blood off the shelves."

"You're not having shit," Nok barks, his voice deep, angry, and gravelly.

Joseph puts his hand on Nok's shoulder. "Nokosi maybe we should—"

"I didn't say this was open to negotiation. Ain't no cameras in here, boy. Give me your money and we'll be on our way." He looks at the shaggy-haired cashier. "You seen us in here, kid? Seen what we done?"

The cashier shakes his head. "Not my problem, don't care."

Nok is going to blow. I can see and feel it. And he will lose. This isn't how it's supposed to be.

Fuck. What do I do? Why do I care? There are plenty of other assholes in that school to taunt. There will be another just like him.

I hide behind the shelves and assess my options. I have my switchblade which will be useless against a gun so really... I need to get the gun. Or I could just let them take the money and leave, but then where's the fun in that?

"No sudden movements, just hand over the wallet and we'll be done here."

I pull my helmet back on, having taken it off in the bathroom to breathe for a moment, and flip down the visor.

Then I clear my throat, raise my hands and utter in a polite, Southern accent, "Can I just meander on by? I ain't seen nothin' here but I'm tired and lookin' to get back to my motel."

"It's the girl," the third trucker whispers and all eyes come to me as I walk down the side aisle towards them, hands up, fingers splayed either side of my shoulders. He has what looks like a dead beaver on his head.

I mentally name them for ease, this one is Beaver, his buddy is Butthead and the guy with the gun is Grease or Trucker... whichever.

Nok looks at me, his eyes widening in question. He flickers them back to the bathroom, communicating with me to go back. I'm surprised by this, to be honest. He's the last person I expected to tell me to get the hell out of Dodge.

"Sure, you can squeeze on by," the trucker with the gun says with a grin. "Did not realize you're a Texan girl yourself. If I'm right in sayin'?"

"You are. But I'm just passin' through."

"Long way away to pass through."

I shrug, lowering my hands and flipping up my visor so as to meet his eyes. "I pass through a lot of places."

He shows his yellowing teeth. "Well, why don't you hang with us three gents for a while? We'll show you a nice time local, buy you dinner, coupla drinks."

The fact he called himself a *"gent"* is almost laughable.

I glance at Nok ignoring the stiffness of his jaw and fury in his eyes. "Don't he need to give you money for that?"

"Nah, I just don't like my good American dollar in the hands of a prairie nigger."

I grit my teeth at that insult and smile like I agree with him which I absolutely don't. "Right? Fuck them. Throw them over the wall with the rest of those brownies."

"Knew it," Nok mutters and Joseph sneers at me too. Neither of them knows what I'm doing, that's how convincing I'm being. Or at least I hope I'm being convincing.

Trucker's friends laugh so hard at that, giving me opportunity to sidle closer. "Actually, it'd be nice hanging with some Southern men, drinkin' beer and eating wings. I've had a cravin' for some chicken wings in I don't know how long." I'm close enough now to do what I need to do, I put my hand on his chest. My heart is a blur in my chest. I can hardly breathe. "Give him the money he asked for and we'll be on our way."

Joseph pulls the wallet from Nok's pocket who is glaring at the man so hard his eyes are bloodshot. He's mad. Really fucking mad.

"You'll pay for this," Nok says to me, his eyes on mine.

I grin at him. "Only person payin' here is you, darlin'."

Trucker's friends laugh again and watch as Joseph pays for the fuel and then starts to hand over the wallet. I snatch it from between them making them all look at me, confusion marring each of their very different faces.

I flip it open with one hand while backing out of reach. "Whoa, there's gotta be at least eight hundred bucks in here."

"That's mine, kitten," Trucker breathes, his tone warning. He doesn't trust me or my intentions anymore.

I shove it into my jacket where it gets trapped between my breasts and the tight protective material. "Nope, pretty sure it's mine now."

Trucker's friend Beaver barks, "Her accent is gone. She fucking played you."

"Give me the wallet, I ain't playin' back."

"What you gonna do?" I taunt, laughing when he steps towards me. "Shoot me?"

He glances at me with wild brown eyes, then at Nok and then back again. "That's exactly what I'm gonna do."

When he reaches for his gun and finds the holster empty, I pull it from around my back, then point it at his chest and smirk. "Looking for this?" So fucking cliché but I am so fucking proud of myself. I feel extremely powerful right now.

Everybody falls silent again and this time I'm in charge.

"Sweetie, do you even know how to use that gun?"

I drop the clip, check the chamber, estimate there to be at least six bullets in total, replace the clip, click off the safety, and my smirk becomes an evil grin. "Do y'all know how to run from a bullet?"

"Holy shit," Joseph hisses, his tone awed.

Nokosi has a brow raised, but he also has his hands raised, so do the truckers when I slowly point the gun at them one by one, letting it drift back and forth like the gentle waves on an ocean shore.

"The rest of you got any weapons?" I ask, keeping them

pinned to the counter. If they separate, I don't much fancy my chances of winning, even with the gun.

They shake their heads.

"Check them," I tell Nok.

"Don't you fucking touch me, you buffalo jockey."

"I can't see any," Joseph states, leaning around them. "I'm not getting close enough to find out for sure."

I raise the gun higher, pointing it at Greasy's face and take a step closer.

"Good," I answer and relax my shoulders. "Now... hand over your money."

Greasy laughs, throwing his head back with it.

I pull the trigger, and everybody yells and ducks, sounding panicked. My ears ring for a second but the space isn't compact so it's not too bad. My head feels a bit hollow from it and my hand aches but nothing enough to make me flinch.

"What the fuck? You crazy bitch!" Butthead yells and now they all have their hands up as dust flutters and swirls around us from the hole in the ceiling.

"This is a gas station!" the cashier shrieks, sounding seven pitches higher than before as he hides under the counter. "Are you trying to kill us all?"

I shrug. "Always said I'd go out with a bang, may as well be this kinda bang. Quick, painless, *hopefully*." I wink at Nok, dipping my head back so he can see it. "But then again, I like a bit of pain from time to time."

Nok's eyes flare, I saw it, I fucking felt it between my thighs.

I quickly look away and stare down Greasy instead, feeling wave after exhilarating wave of adrenaline pulse through my body.

"Now hand over your *fucking* money," I bellow at them, pointing the trigger at his head now.

The truckers behind him scramble for their wallets. I look at Nok. "Take every penny they have. Snap their cards."

He smirks, his brow still raised in that alluring way, but he does it. Quickly too.

"You're going to regret this, bitch."

"Just get the fucking gun, Bill, she doesn't have it in her to shoot anyone!" one of the truckers hisses. I point the gun at his face and pull the trigger without hesitation.

It clicks a hollow sound and he shrieks like a child and drops to his knees with his hands over his face.

"Silly me," I sigh, dramatizing my tone, "I forgot to crank it after my last shot." I look at Nok and Joseph. "Isn't that lucky?"

Nok's lips thin to a white line, he's fighting back his laughter and almost failing.

"Now now, stop crying." I check the chamber and point the gun at them again, keeping my finger off the trigger just in case I accidentally pull it. It's tempting. "You have the money?"

Nok nods and holds up a roll of cash.

I unzip my protective jacket pocket and motion for him to put it inside. He does so and I try to inhale deeply to catch his scent, but my helmet is all I can smell. Shame. He always smells good. I could smell him in class today too. So earthy and manly and masculine. Ugh. I almost feel bad for doing what I'm doing to him.

When he zips me up, I look at the truckers again. "Get in the bathroom."

They surprisingly comply, two of them grabbing the one that's on the floor and drag him to the back of the store, over the white tiles that could use a clean.

"Phones," I demand and Nok takes those too as Joseph stays as a lookout.

"Thank you kindly, my good native sir," I jest, putting my thick Southern accent back on.

He laughs under his breath and can't wipe his smile. I think I've impressed him.

When they're backed into the corner of the bathroom I can't just stop here. I'm having too much fun. This is exhilarating.

"Now, get on your knees."

They do so, grumbling and cursing, looking humiliated.

"Kick him in the face," I insist.

Nok hesitates, giving me the side eye. "He's down."

"So?"

"So... he's down."

"He called you a prairie nigger."

He tenses. "He's down. I'm not kicking a man while he's down."

"He'd do it to you, to your brother, your dad, your gran... he doesn't give a fuck. Teach him a lesson."

He turns to face me fully and waves a hand at them. "You want me to be as bad as he is?" Despite his protests I see the glint in his eyes, the thirst for violence and vengeance.

"I want you to get a good kick in before we lock them in this bathroom."

"He's fucking down. I'm not about to kick a man while he's down."

I raise a brow, wanting to push him more but I can't risk sticking around. The last thing I want is the cops on my case, Mom would kill me and Willow is too weak to move again right now. I'm lucky nobody has walked in yet but then again this is a small town and we are on the edge of it. If these are the kind of people this gas stop attracts then it's no wonder it's so dead here.

"Pussy." When I look at the truckers, I flip down my visor. "It was nice meeting you, *gentlemen*."

"Fuck off," Butthead snarls and Greasy spits at my feet. "Nigger-fucking bitch."

I smile when Nok spins, his temper maxed out. His booted foot flies out and connects with Greasy's jaw. I see it snap to the side, probably breaking when it does. Blood sprays across the tiles in a pretty pattern and he hits them cheek first with a jarring thud. The sound it makes... fuck. So nice. You just can't replicate that sound. No movie has ever done it justice.

"Fuck yeah," I breathe and swallow to make my mouth moisten. "Nice hit."

"You absolute cunt! You broke his jaw!"

I raise the gun to the man who starts to stand, and he quickly gets back on his knees. I smirk at him, not that he can see it through the helmet.

"Maybe you'll think about that the next time you mess with a *nigger-fucking bitch* and her band of merry natives."

"I want to laugh, but it's not really appropriate," Joseph calls from the gas station.

I back out of the room, using my hand on Nok's chest to push him with me. Then I slam the door shut and lean around the shelf to look at Joseph. "Get me the key for this fucking thing."

The cashier hands them over and Joseph tosses them to Nok who uses them to lock the door and then tosses them back to Joseph. I won't admit aloud that I watched his shoulders and arms as he moved and enjoyed every second.

"Well, it's been fun, boys, but I've got places to be and shit to do." I put the safety back on the gun and tuck it into the front of my pants.

"My wallet," Nok demands, sounding gruff.

He holds out his hand but I thrust my chest forward slightly, making my play.

"Get it yourself."

He laughs once and wets his lips. "Oh, it's like that, is it?"

I step closer to him and walk two fingers up his chest. "Either you get it, or I leave with it."

Smirking, he holds my eyes as he lowers his hand into the V of my jacket. He could just unzip it a little more for better access but where's the fun in that? He wets his lips and slides his fingers between the stiff material of my jacket and my shirt, grazing and brushing my heaving breasts with his hand as he searches for his wallet.

I turn, putting my back to him, the back of my helmet thumps against his shoulder as his hand dips further into my jacket. I hum happily, enjoying his touch which is rare for me because normally I hate the touch of anybody.

"Take your time," I whisper just as his hand grasps it and slowly starts to drag it to freedom.

He stops at my breasts again but then one of the truckers starts kicking and screaming at the door.

"SHUT THE FUCK UP!" I yell back and he stops.

Nok moves away much to my disappointment.

"Time to go," I say brushing past him, putting an exaggerated sway to my hips. "Have a good evening, boys." I look at the cashier. "If I catch wind of the cops sniffing around, I'll come back."

He audibly gulps. "But what if *they* call them?"

I laugh because I know that those greasy fucks have got more to lose than a gun and couple of grand if the cops get involved. "Truckers aren't snitches. Are you?"

"I didn't see anything."

"Attaboy," I cheer and exit, the door beeps on my way out.

I go to my bike and get the fuck out of here before anybody can stop me to talk. That was so wild. I can hardly breathe.

So fucking wild and so fucking dangerous.

Twenty minutes later when I walk into my house still buzzing with adrenaline, my sister greets me. She recognizes the glint in my eye immediately.

"What happened? Something happened."

I fluff out my hair and dump my helmet onto the windowsill. "You wouldn't believe me if I told you."

She taps her foot on the ground. "Is he the guy?"

I hesitate, still panting. "Jury's still out on that one."

She huffs and stomps upstairs as fast as her frail legs will carry her.

I wish she could have felt what I just felt. We both have completely different tastes in fun these days, but I suppose that's to be expected.

CHAPTER 6

I let my hair fall wild around my shoulders and face for school today. It looks like soft cotton candy on my head, a cloud of it framing my face. My eye makeup is darker today and I leave a few buttons of my shirt undone.

I feel alive for the first time in so long. I'm still reeling after the events last night. My body is still vibrating with excitement. I was so fucking horny last night I can't even begin to explain it.

I make my way to first period, a skip in my step, my bag hanging from my arm. I even smile and wave at my peers. So much has happened and it's not even the end of my first school week yet. This is good though; this is fast paced. I need fast paced. I need to get this done.

The sooner I get Nok where I want him the better.

Speaking of Nok, the second the bell rings I exit the classroom and almost bump into him in the hall. He's waiting for me, leaning against the wall, a smirk on his lips. People stop, likely waiting for an altercation like the last time we met at the lockers.

His dark eyes scan my face and his thick diamond-heart lips smirk when I mirror his stance and hold his eyes. We stand, staring at each other, just breathing for the longest time.

"You coming, Lilith?" Loki asks and I'm surprised that he's trying to rescue me.

"Track tonight?" Nok asks.

"No can do, bike's clutch is fucked. I need to fix it."

He stares at me again, still smirking but now he's thinking too. He has such a naturally devious look about him. It would deter most but I find it intriguing. It's as though he's trying to figure me out, find my weaknesses and then use them against me.

"All right."

His eyes drag down my body one last time, so slow I can feel them caressing my curves like hands. My womb shivers.

Pushing from the wall, he walks away, his hair a long tail down his back. I want to feel how soft it is. I bet it's like satin threads.

"What was that all about?" Loki asks as we both watch Nok catch up with his friends.

"I made friendly with his brother."

Loki forms an O with his mouth before asking, "You mean Nashoba?"

I nod. "He's cool."

"Oh yeah, from what I've seen of him he's great. He does a lot of volunteering in Westoria, Astoria, and Knappa."

This doesn't surprise me. "What do you need, Loki?"

"I just wanted to check that you're okay?"

Why'd he have to go and be nice to me? "I'm fucking peachy." I shove off the locker with less grace and more aggression than Nok did, and check my watch as students sluggishly move to their next class. Loki follows, and I wonder if he has many friends. I've never really seen him with anyone but then I've never really paid attention.

He's a good-looking guy and seems nice enough.

Maybe it wouldn't be so bad having just one person I can relate to here.

I look at him while chewing on my lip just as he reaches out to tap me on the arm but thinks better of it.

"Do you want to get high?" he asks quietly, and my eyebrows hit my hairline.

My lips stretch into a wide smile. "Fuck yeah."

He shares my excitement and we skip school to sit in my dad's shit car down an old dirt road, a joint filling the car with delicious smoke. Then we nap until three and I drive him back to his house.

I almost feel bad for snapping his pencil.

Kidding.

As I'm working on my bike in my driveway, wearing waist-high shorts and a black lace bralette, hair in braids and sunglasses perched on my nose, a familiar truck pulls up on my side of the street.

"Hey, snowflake," Joseph calls, dropping from the passenger side of the truck.

I look at him over my sunglasses and watch Nok round the front of the truck, showing off by sliding across the hood.

"Aren't you cold?"

"How'd you know where I live?" I ask, frowning as Nok gets up close to my naked bike and starts prodding around.

"Small town, new kid, not hard."

"Do you always talk in unfinished sentences?" I ask him but he doesn't respond. "I'll take that as a yes then." Clearing my throat, I drop the bolt into the tray with the others and wipe my forehead on my arm. My hands are covered in brown grease. If you turn out the lights it looks like drying blood. It's mesmerizing in a really twisted way.

I flex my fingers and sit back on my butt when Nok takes over tweaking my bike.

"You know how to fix bikes?"

"He doesn't," Joseph states and then laughs when Nok glares at him. "But I do. My pa runs the garage where you bought your part this morning."

Fucking small towns.

Nok rolls his shoulders, stands, and flexes his neck. "I know a bit."

"Have at it," I say, waving my oil-slick hand at my machine. "I'm too fucking high for this shit right now anyway."

"You been on the ganja?" Joseph asks, looking surprised as I start scrubbing the grease from my hands with a damp towel.

"Needed something to bring me down after last night," I reply and look at Nok who is now sitting on my bike as Joseph works on it. His eyes look at my house.

"Your parents home?" Joseph asks, noticing Nok's eyes. "'Cause we can't be here and not introduce ourselves."

I shake my head. "Mom's at work, will be until tomorrow."

"Dad?"

My cheeks puff out as I blow into them. People in this town ask so many fucking questions.

"Is he working too?"

"Joseph," Nok warns and they share a look between them. Brown eyes clash as Nok silently tells him to shut up and Joseph silently replies that he's not doing anything wrong.

I alter the conversation. Something I'm good at. "You want a beer?"

"Nah, I'm good."

"I'm good. Thanks."

I lick my lips and look at my bike. "Is this your way of saying thanks for saving your asses last night?"

"I had it handled," Nok retorts, as firm and as harsh as always. I respect that about him, he doesn't feel the need to kiss ass with a changing tide. He stays true to himself.

Still, I laugh while shaking my head. "I know. I just gave it a new angle."

Joseph snorts and looks at his friend. "I like her."

"I don't," Nok states and looks down his nose at me. "What did you do with the gun?"

I tap my nose. "Why would I tell you? You don't like me."

"Guns in the wrong hands are dangerous."

I quirk a brow. "I took it out of the wrong hands."

"Let me have it. I'll get rid of it." He sounds and looks genuine. "Let it be my burden. You'll get into serious shit with somebody else's gun in your possession."

With flat lips and an even flatter stare, I click my tongue against my palate and curb my temper.

I'm no damsel. I take care of business myself.

"Why are you here, Nok?"

"This is me paying you back for last night."

"By fixing my bike?" I ask incredulously. "No, this is you inserting yourself into my life when I didn't ask for your help."

A muscle in his jaw flexes.

"I'm not sure that you've noticed, but Justin is doing all the leg work." I grin a genuinely sadistic grin and stand so we're almost at equal height, putting my weight onto the tips of my toes, brushing my chest against his.

"It's Joseph," Joseph replies but we both ignore him.

"From what I've heard, you natives like to owe favors when people do things for you. And I did some pretty big things for you last night." I walk my fingers up his chest like I did last night and tap him on the tip of his perfect nose. "You owe me. Like it or not. And I will cash that in eventually. You do not get to say when."

"What about me? Do I owe you?" Joseph asks, looking way too excited as Nokosi glares so intently at me I feel the heat burning my profile.

"Yep."

"Awesome."

I laugh but then stop, worried my sister might hear. I look up at her bedroom window, but the drapes are drawn shut.

"Who's upstairs?" Nok asks, following my line of sight.

"None of your business, that's who."

He stares at the window for the longest time, until I feel like pushing his face away.

Joseph with his cute dimples and shining hazel eyes pulls a face behind Nok's back. I snigger to myself and walk towards the truck. I open the passenger side and climb up without permission, surprised when Nok charges at me, grabs my hips, and yanks me back down so hard my entire body collides with his.

Unfortunately for him I really don't like it when people sneak up on me, especially not after he got the drop on me in school. I react instinctively by bringing my elbow up and jabbing him in his throat. He moved in time for me to not accidentally collapse his esophagus, but he still chokes and cups his neck.

"Don't sneak up on me," I snap, pressing my back to his truck and holding myself.

He continues to act like he can breathe despite the fact he clearly can't.

"Dude," Joseph mutters, looking concerned. "You okay?"

With red eyes Nok nods and looks at his friend. "Fine," he husks, his voice breathy and hardly there.

"You both need to go," I snap, feeling edgy and irritated. My anxiety has been triggered.

They don't move.

"Now," I snarl. "Go. I can fix my own damn bike."

"I'm almost done."

"Go," I yell, tucking my trembling hands into my pockets.

Nokosi grabs Joseph by the collar and yanks him to standing.

"Don't come back here," I shout after them, looking around me to double check that nobody is listening in. I'm not in the mood for any more invasions of privacy and personal space today.

"She's a bit loco," Joseph mutters as he climbs into the car and I resist throwing a wrench at his head.

I look at my phone in my stained hand when a text comes through. It helps to take my mind off everything that just happened.

But when I see it's from my sister, I glare up at her bedroom window, directly at the part where the curtain is twitching.

Willow: Why do you put yourself through this?

Lilith: Go back to sleep. You need your rest.

Willow: *Insert middle finger here*

I laugh through my nose and look at the road where the truck no longer is.

Then I finish my bike myself.

I can breathe again now that they're gone.

I can't say the same for Nokosi, however. I bet he won't sneak up on me again.

CHAPTER 7

"Heyyyy!" Winona calls when she sees me exit the tree line. I wave back and hit the track. This place is contagious, the weather is perfect, the views are beautiful, and the school isn't terrible, it's making me almost wish I didn't have to leave.

My bike is fixed so all is right with the world again. It took me less time than expected. So much so that I got to sit and watch my sister pick her food, dose herself, and pass out. Mom didn't come home either, but she did text me telling me she'd be home later and not to wait up.

I don't plan on waiting up for her but chances are I'll get home later than she does.

About twenty minutes and two sweet runs later, I stop and head over to where Nash is.

"Watched you clear that double, that was sweet," Nash says as he raises his knuckles for a fist bump that I reciprocate. "You've been watching and learning."

"That and I've memorized the track," I pant after ripping my helmet from my head. "And I fixed my bike."

"She sounds a lot healthier."

I grin and sit beside him on a log with a mat tossed over it. "She does, doesn't she?"

"So..." He bumps his shoulder against mine. "How are you liking Lakeside and Westoria?"

"Beautiful places, if not a bit lackluster."

He chuckles and digs his heel into the muddy ground, making a rivet in the earth. "I feel you. There's not much to do around these parts. Though we do have a drive-in."

I blink with surprise and slight excitement. "You do?"

"It plays mostly crappy movies. Older horrors. But they do amazing fries and popcorn." He bumps me again. "Maybe you'd like to—"

We both startle when Nok suddenly slams his booted foot into the narrow space between us. He nudges his brother, forcing him to move and stands fully on the log, cups his hands around his mouth and howls at the sky like a wolf.

Everyone stops what they're doing to join in. Everyone but me.

Howl upon howl sound around us. It's amazing, but also crazy.

Then he just stops and sits between us, his hip against mine. He rests forward, arms on his knees, hands clasped, biceps bulging, eyes on the track.

"Why do you smell so good?" I ask, scowling at him. I don't know why I verbalized my inner musings, but I did and now I really fucking regret it.

Nash looks over his brother's shoulders at me, realization in his eyes though what that realization is goes beyond my mind-reading capabilities and Nok smirks sideways at me. He looks as smug as ever.

I need to fix this.

"You should smell like ass and brimstone to match your soul."

Nash laughs, Nok's smirk vanishes.

He keeps his eyes on the track and I take this moment to look over his forward leaning body to seek out Nash.

"Nash? You were saying?"

He glances at Nok and then clicks his tongue against his palate. "Just that there's a movie on tomorrow night."

"What movie?"

"Zombie Warrior or something like that."

I hum and think about it before replying, "I do love a bad zombie film."

His brown eyes light up with a small amount of excitement. He seems to be fighting a smile. "So maybe I can pick you up at around seven?"

Oh shit. I wasn't ready for that. Not at all. "Umm..."

Nok looks at me sideways again, his smirk has gone. Is he waiting for my answer? This is so fucking awkward. I don't know what to say. If we were alone, I'd just tell Nash no, but we're not and for some reason I care about Nok's reaction.

Not to mention I have a goal and dating Nash would mess with that.

I blow a breath through my nose and bite hard on my lip for a moment before replying honestly, "I'm not a good person, Nash, and you are."

"Maybe I could be a good influence?" He hasn't fully lost hope, but the excitement has left his eyes.

"I don't wanna be good." I stand and stretch and put my helmet back on my head before he can question me further. "I'm not your type." I throw my leg over my bike and kickstart it.

It seems I've inadvertently attracted the wrong brother.

Fuck.

"Hey, Mom," I say around a yawn the next morning when I find her standing at the sink, having just finished cleaning our dishes from the day. Saves me doing them.

"Hey, sweet girl," she replies, her eyes tired and sad. "I miss you."

"I miss you too." I move to the refrigerator and drink some OJ straight from the carton.

"Can you pick up the groceries for me today?" she asks, smoothing back her dark hair and yanking her ponytail tighter.

I close the refrigerator and look at the list on the door. "Sure. Is there enough money in the jar?"

"Seems to be a little bit extra," she comments, wiping her hands on her white apron.

"Oh, yeah, I did a job for a neighbor and they paid me." I'm so good at lying. I hate how good I am at it, but I can hardly admit I robbed men at gunpoint in a local gas station.

She smiles with so much love it makes my heart ache. "That's so good of you, sweetie. I knew you'd be helpful. We have to look after each other in this life."

I grab the list and stuff it into a pocket on the outside of my bag.

"Are you going back to work?"

"Not yet." She cups my cheek with her cold hand, her skin so soft her touch is but a whisper. "I'll be here when you get home."

"How much time do we have until we leave again?"

She shrugs, her dull gray eyes look sympathetic for a moment. "That all depends."

"It always does."

"But a maximum of four weeks I'd say."

"Of course," I grit and adjust the strap of my bag so it's comfier. "Not long then."

"Our little world is changing at such a rapid pace," she replies, following me to the door.

"I know. I'm just tired of moving."

"It won't be for much longer."

I've heard that before but there's always just one more place, one more thing *she* needs to do.

Grumbling under my breath, I leave, pulling the door closed behind me and then turning to lock it. Mom could do it, but I like to be in the habit.

I make my way to school, taking my dad's car as always, wondering if the police will ever come asking about the truckers and that night. I've not been worried about it because I know they'd never tell, but that cashier kid might have, though I'm certain I put the fear of Satan into him.

It is what it is. If I get ratted out, I get ratted out.

When lunchtime comes, I sit under the tree and text my sister. It's peaceful here. Nobody notices me, everybody is too busy doing their own thing. I don't know what it is about this tree that makes me feel more grounded. This place is full of trees and beautiful serene places. But at school, this is my safe space.

"Belegana," Nokosi says, looking down at me.

"I know what that means," I say, still looking at my phone. "Nash told me."

Chuckling, he sits too, resting his back against the tree with just inches of the rough, curved bark separating us. "I don't like you."

I smile at my sneakers, unoffended and amused. "I don't like you either."

"But you're strong, and brave, and honest. I respect that."

I look at him and he looks at me, a moment passes between us. One of understanding. A sinking feeling of dread soaks up the warmth I feel from the monumental moment.

"And you turned my brother down."

I look away, scowling at those who are staring at us as though they have any right to this private moment.

"Why?"

I turn and so does he, he rests his head back slightly, so his cheek is level with the tree. He's so cleanly shaven. So handsome.

"He's not my type," I reply, going for honesty, still scanning his face, following the shallow dips beneath his cheekbones and the sharp edge of his jaw. His eyes are hooded, relaxed, an acorn brown ringed by a striking dark chocolate.

"I'm your type," he states boldly, his soft-looking lips twitch into that familiar, arrogant smirk.

Laughing, I shake my head at him. "No, you're not."

"Why not? Every girl I've ever met wants to sleep with me."

I look him directly in the eyes, he really is so fucking arrogant. "Not me."

He narrows his gaze. "I don't believe you."

"It's true, Nok. I'm not into you. I'm not into anyone."

He shifts and I know I've frustrated him. He doesn't like not being wanted, he's so used to being fawned over and he's probably not afraid to admit it. "Is it just dating you're not into? Because I'm not about to try and take you to the movies."

That's an admission that he wants to fuck me, it's backwards but it's there.

This is it. I have him.

"It's not that either. I just..." I look up at the sky and squint against the sun. "It's not you, it's me."

"What about you makes you not want to date?"

"Not just date, I don't fuck either."

"Are you a virgin?"

I shake my head. "No. Nothing like that."

His breath leaves him and then he asks on a whisper, "Are you into girls?" His thick brows furrow with curiosity and intrigue.

"No."

"Then why don't you want to sleep with me? Everyone wants to sleep with me." He grins, only half joking in a smug way.

Because just not being into him can't be a possibility, I'd have to be a lesbian or a prude.

"Not me," I respond, folding my arms and raising my chin.

He looks so entirely perplexed. "And why not?"

Hook. "Because."

"Because...?"

Line. "I've heard how big you are."

His lips stretch into a smile, uncovering his perfect teeth. I just batted his ego out of the ballpark. "And that's a problem because?"

Sinker. "Because I'm *really* tight. Extremely."

He laughs once, a quick, startled sound but then he sees I'm not joking. His smile fades and his eyes lose all arrogance and harshness. I just killed his brain.

"How tight?" His voice is hoarse. He swallows audibly.

I take his hand in mine and uncurl his forefinger from his fist. Then I wrap my hand around it and squeeze. "That tight."

When I'm thoroughly convinced that all he can now think about is wrapping my legs around his waist, I release him and stand. The bell will ring soon anyway, and I need to use the facilities. All this talk of sleeping with him has gotten me worked up too.

"See you later, Nokosi Locklear."

He doesn't respond, he just remains under the tree, staring after me as I all but skip away.

I almost have him where I want him.

Almost.

Now I've just got to figure out my next step. Nokosi Locklear is going down.

"Miss Deville," a voice calls from the reception as I pass.

I stop and look at the sour-faced secretary.

"Can you come here for a moment?"

I nod and follow her, listening to the sound of her kitten heels clicking on the wooden floor.

I stop at this side of her desk as she goes around the other side and shuffles a few papers around.

"I'm struggling to locate your schoolwork from your prior schools. I know you've already done most of your finals, but in order for you to finish the year and graduate I really need a record of them."

I sigh heavily. "We have this same problem everywhere I go."

"Is it something you can chase up yourself? You might have more luck."

Smiling, I nod and tap my fingers on the desk. "I was just going to suggest that exact thing. Give me a couple of weeks, is that okay?"

"That's fine, if not you'll have to redo the year so far."

I nod again and turn towards the door.

"Also," she adds softly. "There's no record of you at the last two schools you listed."

Fuck.

"Yeah, that happens too. We move so much that a lot of time I get into a school and then straight out of it again. I'll be out of here in a few weeks too. Don't worry yourself about it."

She looks unsure. "What about your mom? Is it something she can handle?"

"She's busy working."

She clucks, unhappy about that but doesn't argue.

"Okay. Enjoy the rest of your day, Miss Deville." She nods for me to go and clicks away on her computer. I leave, letting my chest deflate from the relief that the encounter is over. She looks so bitter with her pursed lips and scowling eyes.

"Jesus," I snap when I almost walk into Nokosi who is standing to the right of the door. "Don't do that."

"Which school did you go to last?" he asks, falling into step beside me.

"Why?"

"Just curious."

"Salt Lake High."

He looks surprised. "Nevada?"

I nod and tuck my pink hair behind my ears.

"How long were you there?"

"I don't know, a few weeks, maybe?"

"So how long are you here?"

Grinning, I peer up at him. "A few weeks, maybe? I don't know, Nok. Why are you so interested?"

"Wait... Salt Lake High?" He looks lost in thought for a moment. "A girl died there, right?"

I stop and think back to my time there. "I don't know. Lots of people die in lots of places."

"Yeah, but this was different. She was murdered. I think. Is it the same place?"

"Maybe, I don't know, I didn't do a history check while I was there." To be honest, Salt Lake High isn't my last school, it's one of the first ones I attended, but I don't ever remember a girl being murdered there. He's probably remembering wrong. "Anything else?"

"Nope."

"Then why are you following me?"

His answering smile is devious and makes my core give a painful ache of arousal. He ducks into a classroom and I hear somebody yell his name.

Maybe he was just walking with me, but then why was he waiting for me outside of the office?

He's so weird, but in a hot way.

I enter my own class and look behind me when Barbie waves my way. She pats the desk beside her so I look around the room frantically for another.

"Come here, Lily."

I fucking hate being called Lily. I pad to her and slide into my seat.

"You and Nok?"

I knew it would be about that.

I groan. "Don't... don't make it about that. I'm not dating him, I don't want to date him."

She frowns. "No, you've got me all wrong. That's not... I'm not jealous. I just thought well... I wanted to make sure you know what you're doing."

My teeth trap my lips for a moment. "Oh, I do."

"He was vile to me, that's all. If I can save somebody else the same treatment, I'll try."

I look at her and place my hand on her arm. "He's not going to get away with anything he's done. Okay?"

Fear flashes in her eyes. "Why? What are you going to do?"

"Nothing, I just believe in karma is all."

"Eyes front, please, girls!" the teacher calls, tapping the white-board with her fingers.

We look up front for a while until I whisper, "Is it true? Did he really sleep with you and then abandon you at a gas stop?"

She nods, her eyes watery at the memory. "I was a virgin too. I really thought he liked me."

"What a monster," I breathe, looking back at the board.

"He's very convincing so be careful, okay?"

I nod. Oh, I'll be careful all right.

"Thanks for telling me, it can't be easy to talk about."

"It's not, but anything I can do to help a sister."

She's so fake. I hate that about her. Even while being honest she's just so insincere, it rubs me the wrong way. I want to tell her that I don't like her and to stop talking to me, but I've got bigger fish to fry.

CHAPTER

8

"I saw something on the news earlier," Willow tells me as I thread my fingers through her hair. She's on the floor between my knees, her head resting back on my thighs. "They found a body off the I-5."

"Eww." What is it with everybody's obsession with death today?

She snorts. "Not eww. It's sad."

I blink. "I don't want to talk about death and murder and anything else. Okay?"

"But..."

"No," I snap. "You know I don't like it."

She pushes away and glares at me. "You're such a bitch these days."

"Well, I'm under a lot of pressure, what do you expect?"

"You mean taking care of me?"

"No." I soften my features. "Never because of you... just... All the moving and I don't have a fucking clue what they're talking about in classes. I feel like an idiot."

"I've been doing your homework."

"I know and I appreciate it." I mutter and hug her. She's so frail. I can feel her slipping from me and I can't cope with it. I have to do something to make her stronger again. "Did you take your medication?"

"It makes me woozy."

"You're already woozy," I grumble and pull her back to me so I can braid her hair.

She laughs gently, breathily. "Yeah, you're right."

"We need to get you out and get you some sunshine, you look awful."

"Thanks, sis," she grumbles and curls under my arm on the couch.

Approximately ten minutes later there's a knock at my door. An odd occurrence seeing as our neighbors did the welcome wagon already and we haven't given out our address to anybody in town.

"I'll get it," I say to Willow who is almost asleep. She hums and curls into a ball, remaining where she is. As bad as it sounds to an outsider, sometimes I envy her illness. To have a constant excuse to not deal with people and a quick exit out of life without having to bring it upon yourself.

I pad through the hall and to the door, my freshly painted toes are bloodred. A contrast to the cream carpets that run through the hall.

Whoever it is knocks again, louder this time, more insistent.

"Just a sec," I snap and look through the peephole. When I see his elongated profile through the domed spyglass, I let my forehead thud against the door for a second before yanking it open. "Nash... what are you doing here?"

"I said seven."

"I said no."

"Well..." He points to Nok's truck on the street and smiles a triumphant smile. "We're all going so you have to."

Looking sheepish and hopeful with eyes so much like his brother's, he stuffs his hands into his jeans and waits.

"Who is *we?*"

"Huh?"

I snort and roll my eyes at his obliviousness. "You said *we're* all going?"

"Oh, right, me, Nok, Joseph. A couple of Nok's friends from school are meeting us there."

"And Joseph is where? I only see your brother in the truck."

His smile broadens. "We're getting him on the way. Don't trust me?"

"I don't trust anyone." I look between him and the truck again and can't think of a good reason to not go. In fact, I can think of about ten reasons why I want to.

One of them is that I love movies, another is because Nokosi is driving, which means alone time with him, which means progress.

"Give me five minutes, I need to..." I glance back at the room where my sister is on the sofa out of sight. "Get my shoes and stuff."

"You're coming?"

I close the door in his face and puff out my cheeks. I *was* looking forward to just a night in alone with my favorite person in the whole world. But plans change and this is good.

When I enter the room she's gone, and then I hear her bedroom door close upstairs right before my phone vibrates.

Willow: Have fun. The sooner you get this out of your system the better.

I slip my sandals on because I can't be bothered to find my sneakers, and then exit my house with my bag over one shoulder.

"Shotgun!" I yell with a smirk and race towards the truck

75

where Nok is sitting behind the wheel, eyes ahead. He looks annoyed about something, could it be because I'm joining them?

Not that I care or even feel apologetic about that in the slightest. I'm just curious.

Nash races me, beating me to the door by a millisecond, but only to pull it open and motion for me to climb in. I do so, admiring the cream leather interior and decked-out dash. No wonder Nok yanked me out of his truck. I was covered in grease. I get it now.

"Your truck is ballin'," I mutter as I squeeze into the middle seat, careful not to sit too close to Nok. Nash sits to my right and I jolt when Nok reaches across me for my seatbelt and clicks me in. I swear he inhales my hair as he passes. I almost do the same, but I need my panties dry. "Can we listen to the radio?"

He turns the knobs and presses the small screen as Nash smiles apologetically at me. Likely because his brother is being rude. Or he thinks he's being rude. I don't mind that he doesn't want to talk. It makes it easier to dislike him. Although when he does talk it's not usually very nice so even then I still don't like him. He just rubs me the wrong way, all the while rubbing me all the right ways. Metaphorically speaking. He hasn't properly touched me yet and I hate how much I want him to.

"So, popcorn or fries?" Nash asks.

Raising my brows, I snap playfully, "You're gonna force me out here and then make me choose?"

"So... both?"

"Duh."

"And your popcorn, how do you like it, salted or sweet?"

"Both mixed together."

Nash grimaces. "You two can share then. I'm getting sweet. Nobody likes salted and sweet mixed together."

"Nobody but us," Nok retorts, his eyes on the road so I'm extremely surprised when he flicks a bug off my bare thigh. A bug

I didn't notice, and he did, despite the fact he's driving and paying attention. How? Is he always watching me, and I just don't notice?

We drive through Westoria, collecting Joseph from a grocery store on the way. He has a crate of beer and a bag full of snacks. How old is Joseph? I put him at around nineteen because of how cute he is, but I guess he must be at least twenty-one if he can buy beer.

My phone vibrates, alerting me to a text so I pull it out of my bag.

Willow: Miss you.

"That your mom?"

I shake my head. "It's my sister."

Nok's hands tighten on the steering wheel.

Nash sounds surprised. "You have a sister? How old is she?"

"My age, she's my twin."

"Twin? There's another one of you? God help us all," Joseph jests and I find myself smiling with him.

"You should have said," Nash puts in. "We'd have brought her too."

I shift uncomfortably, I don't like it when I'm the focus point of the conversation, or my sister. "She wouldn't have come."

"We can go back for her?" Nok suggests.

"She's sick," I respond shakily, trying to keep my voice steady.

"Is that why she doesn't go to school?"

Nodding, I chew on my lip and stop talking.

It's Nash who asks, "How sick is she?"

"It's terminal."

"Cancer?"

I turn up the radio. "I don't want to talk about it."

Nash puts his hand on my thigh, over the fabric of my lace black skirt but I shift so he removes it. "If you change your mind."

He and Nok share a look. I know they're concerned now, even Nok. Though he's probably just worried I'll bring the mood down.

"Are you sharing those beers, Joseph?" I ask, putting on a cheery façade to lighten things up a bit.

He breaks open the box under his feet and grabs two beers, using one to open the other. I take a long pull and nudge Nok with my elbow.

"Sucks to be you tonight."

He smiles and surprisingly nudges me back. "Puke in my car and I'll throw you in Columbia River."

Laughing, I take another pull, smack my lips, and flex my neck from side to side. "I almost wish I didn't have to leave if this is what the rest of my senior year is gonna be like."

"No chance your mom will stay?"

"What is it that she even does?"

"Can we just not talk about my family tonight?" I ask, frowning at them. "Why are you so fascinated?"

"You're a mystery that's why," Nash answers.

"You roll into town all cool on your bike, with major attitude, no prior history to mention, family as private as you are, and you have pink hair and great tits," Joseph explains, smiling his cute, dimpled smile.

"Really great tits," Nok mutters so only I can hear.

My breath catches in my throat and I look at him, forgetting how close we are. Luckily my attention is diverted to the half-full gravel lot that resides in front of a huge screen. People are already here, parked by individual meters.

"I've never been to a drive-in movie," I admit, leaning forward to look out the windscreen as Nok navigates us past people and smaller vehicles. When he finally decided on a spot near the back, he reverses into it. "How are we going to see the screen if we're facing the wrong way?"

"Truck bed," he replies and offers me a hand when he climbs out.

I don't take it, I'm no delicate flower. Instead I put my hand on his head just because I think it's funny. Oh my God his hair is so soft.

We move around the back and Nok tugs the cover off, revealing a padded truck bed covered in a dark blue sheet and multiple pillows. I gasp when he grabs me by the hips and lifts me over the side of the truck.

I almost stumble forward as my body tips but I right myself at the right moment.

"Don't do that," I snap at his smug face, hands on my hips as I glare down at him from my towering height.

"Lift you?"

"Sneak up behind me."

"You knew I was behind you," he argues, not caring that I'm irritated in the slightest.

"I didn't know you were about to manhandle me!" I sit on the makeshift mattress, fluffing up the pillows behind my back. This is so comfortable. It smells good too, so I know they've used clean sheets and cases.

I look around for Nash but he's with Joseph, pointing to a food truck about forty yards away so I settle again and wait.

Nok climbs in after me and motions for me to shift up to the middle. I do so, fluffing those pillows too seeing as he took the ones I already organized.

It's getting darker now.

I listen to Joseph and Nash argue over Joseph's snack choices when Nok suddenly starts to howl again, like he did at the track that night. His reservation buddies all join in, I'm surprised by how many are here and laugh when the howling is the only thing that can be heard likely for miles and miles.

He then sits next to me and passes me a new beer. His shoulder is touching mine. This guy does not care about boundaries. This is good. This is what I need. Though not when it's from behind. Nobody needs that.

"What time does the movie start?" I ask and look up at the darkening sky. It'll be pitch-black soon. I'm really looking forward to this. I'm getting this feeling of excitement that I haven't had for such a long time. I try not to let it take hold because I need to remain impartial. I'm leaving in a few weeks and when I feel things, it's hard to leave. It's so fucking hard.

"In about forty minutes." He catches a lock of my hair and brings it to his nose. "You smell like..." He sniffs twice. "Apricots and vanilla."

I move my head to get him to free my hair and look at the large rusting screen which is now holding an odd glow to it. It slowly gets brighter and brighter until a faded image takes shape. It's a soap commercial, complete with sexism in a bottle.

"You got into a fight on my first day."

"Yep."

"Why?"

Fiery eyes roam over my face as I look at him expectantly. "He said something I didn't like."

"Do you fight everyone who says something you don't like?"

"Yep."

I can't fight my smile. "Me too."

We laugh together gently, and he edges closer, just enough that I can feel his body heat.

His eyes flicker to my lips as that familiar smug grin plays at his. "Do you want to kiss me, Lilith?"

"Oh God," I groan and push his face away. "You really love yourself."

80

"You were tempted."

I shake my head. "You're incorrigible."

"You were still tempted."

Narrowing my eyes, I slap his chest and shift away slightly. Being cautious about my skirt and legs. "You can stop staring at me now."

"You. Were. Tempted."

"If I kiss you will you leave me alone?"

"No."

I grin and try to unsnap my gaze from his but it's impossible. He's a magnet and I'm his opposite, we're always going to be drawn together. "I thought you don't date white chicks, anyway?"

"I don't."

"So why are you trying to kiss me?"

His eyes glint with humor. "You're not white in the dark."

I laugh, unable to stop myself, and then shiver as cold seeps into my bones.

"Cold?" Nash asks, appearing out of nowhere, his eyes round with concern. Nok moves to grab the popcorn and drinks as Nash climbs into the truck bed, making it a tighter squeeze. He grabs a rolled-up blanket and shakes it out over the side. Dust sprinkles into the air.

Joseph helps but doesn't climb in after him, he grabs a couple of beers from the crate by Nok's feet and moves to a car that pulled up at the right of us.

I sip my beer and listen as Nash and Nok converse in another language. Nash seems mad about something or maybe it's just familial ire. Satan knows my sister and I have enough of that between us. They both settle either side of me, seeming perfectly comfortable. Whereas I feel flanked.

Though I feel a lot warmer and less exposed when the blanket is draped over the three of us. I'm not so worried about anyone being able to see my panties, not that anybody is even looking this way.

"This is really cool," I tell them both as the sound of the advertisements get louder. People are still rowdy, but Nash already said they'll settle down when the movie starts.

The beer gives me a warming buzz and the two bodies either side of me add to that warmth.

"Nok, I thought you were going to sit with Vienna in her car?"

My body solidifies in a split second. I don't want Nok to go.

"She cancelled, had to work."

"Vienna is Nok's girlfriend," Nash explains, leaning closer to my ear.

"She's not my girlfriend. She's just somebody I fool around with from time to time."

I keep my eyes on the screen and remain silent. I don't care who is with who.

"My brother likes to fool around with girls," Nash whispers and Nok hears him.

"Means he's probably good at it," I mutter and grab a handful of Nok's popcorn from his lap. Nash falls quiet and Nok laughs silently but I feel it shaking his side of the truck. I bet Nash can feel it too.

Nok says something to him and whatever Nash says back has Nok laughing even louder; something I can tell he rarely does.

"Sitting right here," I murmur, feeling like a fucking doorstop between them.

"Sorry." Nash gets comfy and puts his own popcorn on his lap as I finish off my beer and look for a place to put the empty bottle.

Nok tosses it out of the truck bed. It lands on the gravel with a thud.

"Don't litter," I admonish. "It's bad for the environment."

He laughs again as though I'm hilarious when I was being serious.

"An animal could cut itself on the fragments, or a mouse could get stuck inside. Don't be an ass."

He stops laughing. "You're serious?"

"Deadly."

"You care about mice?"

"All life is precious," I murmur, feeling petulant and stupid all of a sudden.

Nok stands and jumps out of the truck bed, landing with grace and ease. I bet he does free running; he has the body for it.

Shit. I think I pissed him off. "Dude, I didn't mean to—"

He grabs the bottle and dumps it by the crate of beer in the truck bed.

Nash's jaw hits his chest, he looks as dumbfounded by Nok's act as I feel.

When he climbs back under the covers and presses his arm against mine, I wonder if I've been entirely wrong about this guy the whole time. That makes me feel even more dread than ever.

No. Just because he did one nice thing doesn't mean he's suddenly a nice guy. There are so many horror stories floating around about him. He's violent, full of hatred, treats women like objects... the list goes on. In fact, I've never heard anybody say a single positive thing about him.

But then, I could say the same about myself. Who am I to be judge and juror?

"You really think all life is precious?" Nash asks softly, his voice a whisper in the cool air.

"Yeah. I do."

The movie starts off strong, with some good zombie-eating-human-face action. I don't enjoy gore, but zombie gore is awesome.

We're fifteen minutes in when a woman shoots a soldier zombie in the face.

Nok leans in and whispers, "Where'd you learn how to shoot?" I love how I came to his mind in this moment.

83

Licking my lips, I pop a kernel between them and then grin in the darkness. "The Walking Dead TV show."

He chuckles, a whispered sound that comes with the most handsome smile I have ever seen from anyone.

I drop my leg that's closest to him and mutter an apology when it lands on his hand. His hand that's under the covers for some reason.

I tense when he places the popcorn on my lap between the crook of my other thigh and my stomach. His hand goes back under the covers and grasps my skirt. I shiver and my breathing stops as he pulls it away from my hip.

His eyes stay on the screen, so do mine. His hand however... it starts to trail a light path, using the tips of his fingers over the soft skin of the outside of my thigh.

When I look at him, he brings his other finger to his lips, telling me to shush.

I do as I'm told for the first time in my life. Too invested in the tingles that are coiling from my thigh to my core. I stuff more popcorn into my mouth, trying to act natural.

He grips my thigh with his entire hand, massaging up and down, careful to not manipulate the blanket so Nash doesn't see. Poor Nash... but I'm too wired to feel bad.

I hold my breath when he drags his hand up until he's covering my sex. I almost jump out of the fucking truck bed.

Dear Satan... *fuck.*

But then he goes back to my thigh again, digging his fingers in as I shift my other leg to make a hollow space over his hand with the blanket so nobody can see his movements.

He does it over and over, going up and over my panties and then back down my thigh, teasing every inch of flesh that he can reach while barely whispering the tips of his fingers over my heated sex.

I spread my leg outward, giving him permission. I no longer

know what's going on with the movie. I don't care. This feels amazing. I've never been touched like this. I've never felt like this.

My clit is throbbing, my core pulsing, I'm soaked between my thighs. He's not going there though. He just keeps breezing over it, rubbing my leg softly and that's it... nothing more.

I want to cry. I'm writhing inside with need.

I feel Nash shift to my right and Nok stills until he's satisfied Nash isn't paying attention.

"Hold still," Nok whispers in my ear and flicks his tongue at my lobe which is a mini fucking orgasm in itself. His fingers pull my panties to the side and his head thuds back against the truck when he slides one into the wetness. I hear him mutter something in his own language and wish I could repeat it because it sounded perfect for the moment.

He rolls my clit, rubs it with two fingers. Burning starts to rage through me. An inferno that's making it near impossible to sit still consumes me.

I whimper and shift in my seat but immediately stop when Nash looks at me and asks a quiet, "You okay?"

I nod but dare not speak.

Nok touches my ear again with his tongue. My eyes roll into the back of my head.

His fingers keep rolling, getting a little bit quicker, just enough to give me a nudge closer to the edge. It is getting so hard to sit still. Impossible even. Yet I manage it, until he pushes a slick finger into me. His head thuds again when I clench down on his finger, squeezing him as tightly as I said I would when we were under the tree.

I unravel. My orgasm crashes through my body. My sex pulses and grips his middle finger in waves. I stop breathing which only seems to make it more intense.

I don't know how I manage to stay silent, but my head feels like it's about to explode. I grip his wrist under the blanket, holding him still as my orgasm slips away and I finally inhale sharply and then swallow.

Nash must think it's because of whatever is going on in the movie I'm not watching because he just grins at me.

Nok places his hand on my thigh but stays silent. His fingers are wet. I'm wet. I'd be surprised if the mattress beneath my ass wasn't wet.

I should return the favor, but when I reach for the button of his jeans, he gently guides my hand away and holds it for a moment between us. When he releases me, his hand goes back to my thigh for a while. I don't push it. Why would I? He said no.

We continue watching the movie like nothing happened while I sit uncomfortably in sodden panties.

Ugh.

After twenty minutes I have to get up to use the bathroom. I can't take it anymore. It's too uncomfortable.

"I'll be right back," I say quietly and look for which side to climb from. Either way I've got to climb over a guy if neither of them move.

Nok moves his legs and I feel his eyes on me as I grip the side of the truck bed and hop out. Landing well enough but with nowhere near as much grace as Nok had when he did it.

I make my way to the food truck and head to the bathrooms around back to do my business. I clean myself up, wash my hands and look at my reflection in the mirror. Jade green eyes stare back at me shadowed by black lashes, coated with mascara. My makeup is usually always minimal. I don't typically wear foundations and such because it rubs off on the inside of my bike helmet.

"What are you doing?" I hiss at myself in the mirror. This wasn't part of the plan. I'm not supposed to enjoy his touch. I tap my cheek and shake my head. "Focus. Don't get attached. It hurts to get attached."

Fuck.

I exit the bathroom and the light from within spills across the gravel and the trees in the distance.

"Good evening, little lady," comes an unfamiliar male voice from my right.

I look at the sheriff in his beige uniform, a flashlight in hand pointed at my legs, likely so it doesn't blind me. "Evening, officer."

My heart is racing.

"You're new in town."

"Just moved here with my mom and sister, sir."

"Like your manners, you were raised correct. Bet your mom is proud." He takes a step closer to me and instinctively I take one back. My skin crawls. I don't like cops as it is but this one... he feels dangerous to me. There's something about him. His pale eyes and the sallowness of his white skin. His eyebrows look like two skunks across his forehead, thick and bushy, start black and end white. I wonder if his hair is the same.

"Name's Officer Deacon, know what number to call if you ever need anything."

I nod but don't speak or offer up my own name.

"Well, you run along now and enjoy your movie," he shines his flashlight towards the path that leads back to the cars. "Stay safe out there, little mud shark."

Mud shark?

His light gets higher suddenly and his smile fades. "Nokosi."

Nok glares at the man, his hands balled into fists by his sides and both are trembling, with fury or fear I can't be sure. They have history. I immediately want to know what.

"How's school?"

"Have a great night, officer," I say, placing my hand on Nok's shoulder to try and guide him away. No good will come from whatever Nokosi desperately wants to say to this man.

"Don't fucking touch me," Nok growls at me, shrugging my hand off him.

I let it drop to my side and watch him stalk away, back to his car, every step showing how angry he is.

"Be careful with that one," Officer Deacon warns, his brows pulled together. "He's got anger issues. He's done some nasty things in his time."

"Thanks for the heads-up," I mutter and skulk back to the truck where Nok is nowhere to be found.

I climb into the truck bed, using the wheel as a boost, and snuggle back under the covers leaving a gap between Nash and me.

"Where's Nok?" he asks quietly.

"Haven't seen him," I lie and take some of the cola that he offers.

When he moves closer and tries to snake an arm around my shoulders, I shake my head and move further away. He looks dejected and I should feel bad, but I don't owe him anything.

"Is it because I don't smell as good as my younger brother?" he jests but I can hear the animosity there.

I shake my head again. "You're too good for me, Nash. I'd only drag you down."

"The scary part about that is, you actually believe that."

"Because I'm honest and it's true." I look into his warm eyes. "You don't know me. You don't know the shit I've done."

"I don't care about your past. I want to get to know you."

"I leave in a few weeks, what's the point?"

He grins playfully. "Maybe I can convince you to stay?"

"I have to leave; I don't have the luxury of choice..."

"You're eighteen. You don't *have* to do anything."

"I can't leave my sister," I admit sadly. "She won't make it without me."

"Right." He places his hand over mine. "I forgot about your sister, I'm sorry, I'm being insensitive."

I wave him off and look at the screen. "I am flattered though. You know?"

"You are?"

"A hot, smart, college-age guy wants to kiss me. Of course, I'm flattered. Maybe if things were different. Maybe if I were a different person—"

"This movie is shit," Nok declares and yanks open the door to the truck with us still in the bed. "Let's go."

"Nokosi," Nash snaps but Nokosi is already turning on the engine. We pull away from our spot, lights full, both Nash and I rolling around in the back as we go over the bumpy gravel lot. "Stop! What is wrong with you?"

I move to the side and hold on tight as we careen around a corner and over a speed bump.

"What's wrong with him?" Nash asks me.

"How should I know?" I yell back over the sound of the wind and the engine battling for decibel supremacy. I don't like this. I hit my head on the truck side as we go over a bump at a ridiculously high speed. Burning pain pops along my temple and cheekbone.

My mind starts to conjure images, irrational fears of events that never happened but suddenly feel so real. I feel dizzy, like when a car flips over and rolls down a steep hill, hitting trees and shit along the way. I can't breathe.

My head hurts. I want to vomit.

The faces of the people I love hold lifeless glassy eyes. My limbs won't move. I'm broken.

I'm having a panic attack.

My head really fucking hurts right now.

Nash slams his hand against the window that overlooks the cab of the truck. "NOK!"

We hit a smoother terrain and stop at a junction leading to the main road that takes us back into Westoria.

I take this moment to dive over the side of the truck. I land on my hands and knees and gasp for air. I feel something warm hit my hand and at first I think it's a tear but then I realize that it's too dark to be a tear. It's blood from my nose.

My head is throbbing.

"Lilith, loca, are you okay?" Nash asks, skidding to a stop beside me.

"Don't fucking touch me," I shout, wiping my bloody nose on my bare wrist. Dark red smears up my arm. It reminds me that I'm alive. I'm okay. I can breathe... it's okay.

He hands me a rag of some sort, I take it and hold it against my face, pinching my nostrils closed through the material.

"Is he insane?" I yell at Nash but Nok finally climbs out of the vehicle. When he opens his mouth to speak I repeat my question but change the direction, "Are you fucking insane?"

"Let me see," he insists, stepping closer to me but I hold up my blood-stained hand.

"You could have killed us. You could have killed your brother. Does he mean nothing to you?"

"You're being really dramatic."

Even Nash blinks at him for that one.

I show him the bloodied rag and let my nose leak more of my life fluid. "Dramatic? This is dramatic?" When he doesn't react, my rage fills my eyes with a red blur. I reach into my bag and pull out my switchblade, then press the little silver button and let the sharpened end flip free. "I'll show you fucking dramatic."

"Whoa, okay, let's calm down," Nash tries, raising his hands and taking a step backwards. "I know he scared you and hurt you but..."

Nok stares me down, his eyes flick to the blade. "You won't stab me."

"Are you so sure about that?" I ask, taking a step towards him, feeling angry and powerful. My head is throbbing, my nose has stopped leaking blood, so I wipe away the excess with the rag and throw it on the floor. "You're an arrogant prick."

"You're right, he so is. He's not worth going to jail for."

"Shut up, Nash," Nok and I say at the exact same time.

"What do you want from me?" Nok snaps, glaring me down, just a meter between us. "An apology?"

"Don't," Nash warns, looking at his brother.

"Just get back in the truck, I'll take you home, and you can sleep off this tantrum you're having."

"Tantrum?" I hiss. "You fucking threw me around in the bed of your truck!"

When he rolls his eyes, completely disregarding my feelings and how he hurt me I walk over to the passenger door.

"Good girl," he murmurs, that smug lilt in his voice.

I raise the knife and bring it down, jabbing it straight through his tire. The tire makes a pleasant hissing sound and Nok... well, he doesn't make a great sound at all.

"WHAT THE FUUUUCKKK?" he screams and charges towards me but I'm already at his back tire. I manage to stick it through the stiff rubber just as he reaches me, grabs me by the throat, and pins me against the side of the vehicle, bending my top half over the truck bed slightly. The knife drops from my hand and I smile up at him, feeling much better now. "You psychotic bitch!" Oh he's furious. "This is why I hate white bitches. You're all fucking... AAARRGHHH! HOW THE FUCK ARE WE GOING TO GET HOME NOW, HUH?"

"NOK!" Nash pulls his brother from me and my hand instinctively goes to my throat to rub away the ache. He didn't squeeze so hard that I couldn't breathe but I could see how badly he wanted to.

"You stupid, crazy fucking whore!" he yells, struggling against his brother's hold. "You'll pay for this."

I pick up my switchblade, close it, and put it back in my bag.

Then I flip him the bird over my shoulder and start the long walk home.

I don't mind walking, but I didn't think this through. I don't know where the fuck I am and my head is pounding something fierce.

Trees line the road and metal railings stop cars from crashing into them. There are no signs, just stars in the sky. So many stars.

"Lilith!" Nash calls and his footsteps follow me. "What the hell happened back there? You know that's not my brother's truck, right? He only has it because of his job. You think we can afford a truck like that?"

"Didn't know, don't care."

"Lil—"

"Leave me be, Nash. I told you I'm not a good person."

He hesitates but stops and I stroll on ahead of him. "I can see that now."

"Lucky you," I reply and pick up the pace. The straps of my sandals are cutting into my feet already.

That's what he gets. That's what they will all get.

CHAPTER 9

"Stop feeling bad, he deserved it," Willow snaps, prancing around the kitchen as I slump over the counter, tired and achy. It took me two hours to walk home last night. "Look at your face."

I prod the side of my temple where the swelling begins and stops under my cheekbone.

"I still think you should get it checked out," she murmurs, and I might actually agree with her.

I don't feel great.

"What if you've fractured your skull or something?"

It's a possibility, my nose bled again on the way home and I woke up with a pillow covered in it this morning.

"I'll be fine." Then I smile up at her, feeling relief despite the pain in my head. "You look great."

"I feel great. Today is a good day."

"Good, then maybe you can do breakfast." I fall to my knees when I try to stand.

"Right," she snaps. "I'm calling an ambulance. You're seriously fucking hurt."

"No!" I blurt. "I just... I'll call a friend. No ambulances."

She raises a brow. "You have friends?"

"I'll call..." I think about it and the only person who comes to mind is Loki. He drives... I think.

My sister helps me to my feet, and I pick up my phone. I don't have his number, so I find him on Twitter, logging in to my old account. I send him a message asking him to call me, then I sit on the floor again and rest my head back against the wall.

"You'll need cash."

I sigh and move to the jar. I take everything out of it because I don't know how much this is going to cost, and stuff it into my bag.

"Can you pay cash? Going to a hospital isn't like going to the grocery store."

"I don't know. Call Mom?"

"NO!" I blurt and the noise makes my head hurt. "Don't bug her with this. She'll panic and then ask questions and then we'll leave again, and I really don't want to leave yet."

"Good point." She worries her lip. "Maybe I should take you."

"And risk a seizure, or worse? Plus you're way doped up right now."

She blows a raspberry until her attention is diverted. "Your phone."

I answer the number I don't recognize and put the phone to my ear. "Hello?"

"It's me, Loki. You asked me to call?"

I blow out a breath and smile at my sister who looks as relieved as I feel. "Can you take me to the hospital? It's kind of an emergency."

Loki came and drove me to the hospital in near silence. He asked me what happened, but I didn't tell him, I almost feel ashamed to admit that I slashed Nok's tires last night. Also, I'm worried he'll throw me out of his car and never talk to me again.

He did tell me how bad my head looks though. So nice of him. He made it a point to tell me I look like a zombie.

"Can she pay cash?" Loki asks the receptionist as I sit in the corner and rest my eyes. "She doesn't have health insurance and her mom has gone away."

"I'd have to speak to the doctor," the receptionist replies, and I drift away for a bit, listening to the radio in the background.

"*Another victim has been found but sources can't confirm if this death is linked in any way to the deaths of the three young men from surrounding states.*"

"*It's terrifying, Cheryl, could this be the work of the person in question? If we can call them a person... Will the police ever notify us if it is?*"

"*Probably not, though I'll be telling my loved ones to stay safe and avoid strangers at all costs.*"

I shut off and fight the urge to vomit.

"Miss Deville?"

"Come on," Loki takes my arm and helps me to my feet.

I walk unsteadily towards the kind-looking male doctor.

"That's a nasty bump you've had there," he comments softly and sits me on the bed in the sterile room. He presses it with two fingers and shines a light in my eyes. We go through my symptoms and he clucks with displeasure. "You should have called an ambulance and come in immediately."

"Is it bad?" Loki asks, looking more concerned than I feel.

"I suspect it's just a concussion, nothing too major but if you'd tell me how it occurred and on what object I might get a better idea."

Sighing, I finally admit, "I was in the back of a friend's truck last night when he decided to take me on a bumpy ride. I hit my head against the inside of the truck bed."

"Nok?" Loki grits and shakes his head. "I told you he was dangerous."

"I slashed his tires, it's all good," I reply and look at the doctor who only raises his brows at my admission of guilt. "What drugs will I need?"

"I'd like to send you for a CT scan, just to rule out any brain bleeds. I'm sure you're fine, you're responsive and your eyes look great, but it would make me feel more comfortable."

I pinch my lips together. "How much are they? I only have cash."

"We'll worry about that later."

I nod and rest back, feeling woozy. "I feel sick."

"You've got a definite concussion, let's hope that's all it is."

"How long will the results be?"

"A few days, like I said, I'm not too worried."

I blow out a breath. "And it's necessary?"

"Definitely. My professional opinion says so. In fact, if you agree to one, I'll cut the price in half."

Narrowing my eyes, I ask sardonically, "I thought you weren't worried."

"I'm not, but I do like to be sure."

"She'll have it done," Loki replies for me, his dark blue eyes round with concern. "And what do we do about her concussion in the meantime?"

"Rest, plenty of it, and keep yourself hydrated," he explains and starts to scribble on a piece of paper. "I'll prescribe you something for the pain."

"Thank you," Loki says on my behalf and takes the prescription note.

"*Plenty of rest*, you need at least a week."

I smile a flat-lipped smile but don't confirm that I'll do that. I don't have fucking time to do that. I've got to take care of my sister.

I'll sleep today and maybe all day tomorrow, but after that, I'm done.

We leave two hours later, after a CT scan that didn't take long but the wait for it was ridiculous. My wallet is a lot lighter than it was, but it wasn't as expensive as I thought it might be. I'm just glad to be rid of that place.

"Can we take a detour?" I ask Loki who looks at me incredulously. "I just want to go to Sander's garage real quick."

"Are you serious?"

"Please?"

He bites his tongue and takes me where I asked to go.

I instantly spy Nok's truck when we pull in and so does Loki. Hopefully Nok isn't anywhere in sight. My head is hurting too much to handle him yelling at me today.

"What are you doing?" Loki asks as I make my way to Joseph's father who sold me the part I needed to fix my bike not long ago.

"How much do you think two new truck tires cost?" I ask him, ignoring his gaping stare.

"Are you fucking serious? You just paid over a thousand dollars for an injury he caused."

"I know, it doesn't make sense," I say and smile at Joseph's dad. He looks at my bruised face and his smile fades. "Mr. Sanders."

"Lilith, been keeping out of trouble?"

I shrug. "Nope."

He smiles again but it's cautious. "Joseph said you had a bit of a run-in with Nokosi?"

"He did that to her face," Loki snitches and my eyes fly to him, telling him to shut his mouth. "Well, he did, and now she wants to pay for his tires, even though she's a grand out of pocket for her hospital bill."

Mr. Sanders isn't smiling anymore. "Nokosi hit you?"

"No. It was a misunderstanding."

"You're defending him?"

"Loki, please, your voice is pissing me off." I pull out my wallet and start counting bills. "How much are the tires costing him?"

Sanders doesn't know what to do, he looks torn but when I ask again and explain that I need rest, he shows me the invoice and I pay it in full.

"Now we can go."

"I can't believe you just did that."

I stop and look at Loki. "I'm grateful for what you've done today but stop. What I do and why I do it is none of your business. I know you don't understand, and I know you never will, but it's done. Now drop it."

He looks like he wants to argue some more but then his eyes drift to my temple and he resigns himself to the silence I've asked for. We make the journey back to my house and I leave a hundred on the seat before he walks me to my door.

"Thanks for being there today."

"It's no problem. Truth be told it's not even because I like you. It's because I'm nosy."

I laugh at that despite the pain it causes me. I need to lie down.

He drops me off and my sister for once takes care of me while I slowly die in bed.

CHAPTER 10

I go to school on Monday, wearing my sister's lumpy-ass foundation and other makeup that she helped me apply. I need to buy her some new ones, although she's perfectly capable of shopping online. I need to find a wheelchair and take her out. I keep saying I'm going to but I never get around to it. Truth be told she's become a bit of a hermit. She doesn't want anybody to see her looking so frail and I don't blame her. So she only goes out on days she's feeling good and looking good. Which these days isn't often enough.

I wear sunglasses and keep my hair around my face. People look at me as I enter. No, they don't just look, they fucking stare.

Loki.

I bet he's told everybody. I never should have trusted him. Though a niggling voice in my head is reminding me I never told him to keep it quiet. He's obviously the type that loves to gossip and feed the drama.

Plus the bruise is pretty fucking obvious.

I get to the door, say, "Fuck it." Then turn around and head back to my car.

I'm not doing this.

Why am I still trying with Nok? Why? He's a lost fucking cause.

Why do I care?

Or maybe I'm being paranoid, and they don't know anything.

I yank open the silver door and sit inside, pulling off my glasses and dumping my bag on the back seat. My forehead rolls along the steering wheel as I try to gather my thoughts and shut my eyes for a moment. The passenger door opens, I smell who it is before I see who it is.

"Get out of my car, Nok," I demand tiredly.

"Drive," he clips, his eyes front and center.

"Are you kidding?"

He levels me with a flat gaze, one void of happiness and full of frustration. His acorn-colored eyes hold the reality that he wants to be anywhere but here. "I'm not getting out of this car until you drive us to where we need to be."

"And where's that exactly?" He snatches my bag off the back seat and rummages through it. "Hey. Don't touch my stuff."

"Just checking you don't have a knife, or a gun stashed away."

"Oh, I do," I respond, raising a brow at him, not that he can see it beyond my large glasses.

"Course you do. You're a fucking psychopath, you know that?"

"Yep."

He sighs and rests his head back. We both look at the students watching us, or making it look like they're not when really, they are.

"Where are we going?" I ask quietly.

"Back out. I'll guide you."

"Okay, Sacagawea."

He starts shaking, first it's small, but then it gets more prominent, and then he's laughing so hard he starts choking for breath.

I smile with him, he has a nice laugh. It's gentle, not booming, almost cute. It makes him seem less harsh than his eyes constantly emit.

"That's probably racist," he comments, still grinning from ear to ear. "Next right."

"So is calling me a white whore." We keep smiling, neither offended because even though we have beef, we also understand each other.

"I'm sorry about that."

"No, you're not."

He laughs again and shrugs. "You're right, I'm not."

We don't talk as he guides me around a winding path, past trees and around rocks and down a steep hill. In my dad's fucking Prius no less. Not a 4x4 like his truck.

If we get stuck here, I'll hurt him as payback.

"Stop here," he instructs, and I do so, grabbing my bag and hooking it over my shoulder.

"Is this where you kill me and bury my body?" I follow him down another path on foot but have to stop when I get dizzy. I grip a tree trunk for support as he goes on ahead, only noticing I'm not there when he says something I can't make out from back where I'm at.

"I'm not going to kill you if that's why you're—" He reappears but stops when he sees me. "What's wrong?"

"My head." I stand upright and brush it off. "I'm okay. Just need a sec."

He reaches for my massive shades and slowly pulls them from my face. I hum a grunt of pain when the arms of my glasses scrape my temples. The sore one really fucking hurts.

I hear his intake of breath when he sees the swelling. I don't have a black eye but my temple and cheek are really tight, bruised, and swollen.

He stares, his body tight and his diamond-heart lips dry. "I did that to you?"

"That night was wild, huh?" I joke but then the truth of the situation registers with his confused expression. "You didn't know?"

"Why would I know?"

"Because Loki..." I trail my words off and look around, wondering why I'm here if not for his guilt. "Look, it doesn't matter. It's done."

"Doesn't matter?" When he steps back, he looks almost distressed. "You told me I'd hurt you and I called you dramatic. I thought it was just your nose." He shakes his head and raises his shaking hand to my face. "I don't like that you wear a mark and have pain caused by me."

I didn't expect him to be so upset by it. But then I honestly thought he knew already. "Loki took me to the hospital, so I just assumed you knew."

"You went to the hospital?"

"I had to have a CT scan."

He blanches. "A fucking CT scan?"

"Yes, Nok," I snap, snatching my sunglasses back. "I was really bad. I collapsed and everything." Now I'm just milking it. "I get my results in a few days."

He scowls at the ground. "And you came to school?"

"I wanted to see you," I admit before I can stop myself.

"Because of my truck?"

"No," I scoff. "I'm not sorry, I'd do it again but this time I'd go for the body if you ever put me in a position where I feel unsafe."

He nods and some of his long hair escapes the tie that holds it, my fingers twitch, aching to reach up and push it back. "Is that why you paid for the repairs?"

"Who says I did?"

"Sanders."

I put the glasses back on and stomp past him. "Sanders is a dirty rotten liar."

He chuckles and catches up with me. "We both fucked up that night, but what I did was worse."

"Why did you do what you did?" I ask, glancing at him through the corner of my eye.

He grips my arm with a firm hand and guides me over a fallen tree. "It doesn't matter the reason behind it."

"You mean like when you slammed me up against the lockers for trespassing?"

Stopping, he turns me to face him and glares at me. "You shouldn't have been there, you had no right."

"Yes, forgive me for riding my bike over grass and earth in a place with no fences lining their border."

"Those are sacred grounds you were tearing up. Did you ever ask? Did Nash never tell you?"

I roll my eyes and keep walking; despite the fact I don't know where I'm going. "I said I was sorry and never went back. What more do you want from me?"

"I don't..." He stops himself and growls, gripping my bicep again to turn me to face him. His light brown eyes are glowing. He's so handsome. "Look, I don't know if I like you, but out of every white chick I've ever met, you're the most genuine, and psychotic. It makes you interesting and I like figuring out interesting things."

I bark out a laugh. "That's fucking weird, man. Can we just get to where we are..." I trail off when I adjust my eyes to something or someone in the distance. I step around Nokosi for a clearer view and push up the leaves of a low-hanging branch.

I spy a figure in the distance, in the thick of the trees. Goosepimples break out over my arms. He's looking our way, his legs spaced but the entire form of his body is shrouded in shadows. I squint to make out his face but it's impossible. "There's a man over there."

Nok swings around, looking where I'm pointing, and the rest of his hair falls from the tie. I'm mesmerized by it for a moment.

"Probably a hiker."

I look around his bulking frame and scan the spot where the man shrouded by shadows was standing but no longer is.

When he sees my frown he checks again, walking away from me a few steps. He cups his hands to his mouth and howls, but nobody howls back. His howl lingers in the trees and space around us. It's eerie.

"Definitely not one of my people."

"Is that like a tribe thing?"

"The howling?" he asks, still looking around the area.

I nod.

He smiles that seriously attractive happy smile that only he can pull off. When I smile like that I look like a grimacing hairless cat.

My sister always had a nice smile, I had the creepy version of it. It's because my eyes hold secrets, or at least that's what my mom says.

"No. It's just something I started with my brother when we were kids. It became our thing and then others joined in."

"That's really cool."

"You should do it. If you ever hear me howl, howl back. Then I'll always know where you are."

I smile my creepy smile. "Okay. Do it."

With eyes lit from the excitement, he cups his hands to his mouth again and starts to howl a long high note.

I watch his lips make a perfect O and recall the time he kissed that girl against the tree.

I don't want to kiss him.

Okay, that was a lie.

I do want to kiss him, but I can't.

Maybe just once.

But not today.

After daydreaming for a couple of seconds I finally join him, cupping my hands around my own mouth and howling into the air as loud as I can be.

Our voices echo for what seems like miles and eventually, somewhere out there, somebody howls back. It's faint, so quiet the forest almost swallows it.

Though I just know it doesn't belong to the man I swear I saw staring at us. It's too far away and I just have a feeling.

Either that or I'm losing my mind.

"Where are we going?" I ask when he takes my arm again and leads me to the sound of rushing water. I don't know if he has noticed his poker-straight near-black hair falling over the curve of his amazing biceps.

He doesn't have to answer because we arrive at a branch of the Columbia River, a gushing stream of water in the middle. It's crystal clear and gorgeous but so fast the water bounces over rocks and sprays a fine mist into the air. It's not even particularly steep here so I don't know why it's so fast.

I squeak when a fish jumps from the water and bounces on the bank before rolling back in.

There's a shack of sorts across the flowing stream that for how shallow it seems, looks extremely dangerous.

"I have vertigo, I'm not getting across that," I admit when he motions to a path of small, slippery-looking rocks in the water. They form a gapped, zigzagged bridge. "I'm almost ashamed to say it."

"Your head hurts?"

I look at him incredulously. "Have you seen it?"

"I don't want to look at it."

"Well, you should." I yank off my shades and tilt that side of my head towards him. "What I did to your tires can be fixed, what you did to my face with your truck can't. Your actions towards others, your attitude, it has an effect on them."

"You think I don't know that? I'm not stupid."

"Then stop acting like a bad guy all the time. Your reputation at school is abysmal."

He laughs harshly. "You think I care about what people think of me?"

"No, I don't, and I don't care what people think about you. But I care what they say."

"About me or you?"

"Does it matter?"

He raises his hands. "What talk are you talking about?"

"NOTHING!" I yell, stomping to the water. "I don't know. *Fuck.* Barbie."

"Fuck Barbie?" He smirks.

"I've forgotten her name. The blonde one. She said you fucked her and took her V card then dumped her at a gas station."

He shuts down again like before, all emotion leaves his eyes and his smile vanishes entirely. "If you really think I'd do something like that then why would you follow me into the woods."

"You overestimate my intelligence."

"Clearly."

"Or maybe I'm just not scared of you." I step into his body, the toes of my boots against his. He towers over me like a bear of the sexy variety.

"I think you're scared of how I make you feel." His hand snakes around my back as the other cups my groin over my jeans, eliciting a whimper from me. "Because you know me, somehow, and you know what I'm capable of."

I do, or at least I think I do. Deep down. I know exactly what he's like and exactly what he's capable of.

"What happened on Friday night? Why'd you freak?"

Sighing, he turns after releasing me and crouches in front of me, hooking his arms behind him.

"Hop on."

I want to tell him that there's no way he can get us across safely, but I know he can. I trust that much about him.

I perch myself on his back, wrapping my thighs around his waist and then my arms around his neck. I rest my cheek against his ear and grip him tight, but not so tight that he can't breathe.

"Why do you always smell so good?"

"Why are you always smelling me?" He takes the first step and then the second, his body is graceful and poised. I wonder how many times he's done this.

When we reach the other side, he doesn't let me go, not until we reach the shack that looks to have been handmade out of materials found across the forest floor and some parts from a hardware store.

He places me on the soft grass and yanks open the shack door. I wait for him to bring out two dark green fishing chairs, the kind that fold up to near umbrella size.

I watch him adjust them at the water edge for a moment before peeking into the shack to see what's inside.

Tools, a couple of fishing rods, a net, buckets. Typical tools that you'd find in a shack in the forest by the river.

"Why are we here?" I ask softly, not wanting to ruin the moment.

He pats the seat. "Originally I was going to kill you and bury you out here but then I saw your face and figured I probably deserve worse than what you did in retaliation." When I sit, he relaxes into his seat and I follow suit. This is nice, it's so quiet in a peaceful way.

"You're not a good liar, Nok. Why did you bring me out here?"

I follow the line of his soft, full lips with my eyes. He notices and raises a brow. It's so obvious when somebody is staring at your lips.

"I didn't go after you on Friday night. Regardless of what you did, you were my guest in a location you don't know."

I laugh lightly. "Since when do you care?"

"I don't, but my father and Nash do. I've disappointed them enough over the years."

Now that is something I can definitely relate to.

"They told me to make amends."

I laugh louder this time. "Of course. And that's why you haven't apologized, because you're not sorry."

He shrugs his broad shoulders. "I feel bad for hurting you, but I'm not sorry for getting us the hell out of there." His eyes cloud over with sorrow and confliction, and then pain. I see it all roll through him and I want to prompt but I don't want him to close down.

But then he admits it himself and my lips part.

His tone is soft and quiet when he says, "I just... I *couldn't* be there anymore."

"Okay," I whisper, placing my hand on his because I understand him in this moment and understand that there's more to this that he's not saying. "You know, every time I try to find a reason to hate you, you just... pull me deeper."

"Why would you want a reason to hate me?"

I wet my lips and look up at the sky. The sun is shining today, a rare occurrence for this area at this time of year. "I have to hate you. I have to hate someone."

We share a lapse of silence until he utters, "You really are crazy."

"Oh... you have no idea."

CHAPTER 11

"Why do you go to mainstream when all of your res buddies go to school on the res?" I ask as he gently dips a hook into the water. He's caught three fish already with his dilapidated-looking fishing rod that is more duct tape than wood at this point. Still, he caught three fish.

I look at them swimming in circles in the bucket. They're steelheads, or rainbow trout, I'm not sure the exact name. They have a rainbow sheen over their scales. It's beautiful really. It's a shame he's going to kill them and cook them later.

"Because I don't know any good white people."

My lips part. "Seriously?"

He doesn't elaborate, he looks uncomfortable with the conversation.

"And then the first white chick you decided to befriend was me?" I start to snigger. "Oh, you poor thing."

"Exactly. I thought you're new, you might be different to the sheeple at Lakeside."

"And?"

He pushes his hair out of his face. "And you are definitely different."

I stand and move behind him, being careful not to kick the bucket of fish over.

He tenses when I stand behind him and lift a lock of his silky, dark hair. "What are you doing?"

I thread my fingers through his hair, surprised by how soft it is. He shivers when I gently tease the snags free, and groans when I scrape my fingertips over his scalp.

"I've wanted to do this all day," I admit, continuously brushing to the ends with my fingers. "I love playing with hair."

"I love having my hair played with... as of this moment. But that stays between us." He leans his head back and reaches up to remove my glasses. When he sees my bruised face, he frowns. "I hate that I did that. I'm not a violent person."

I crook a skeptical brow.

He grins, still leaning back to look at me as I gently rub his scalp with my fingers and thumbs. "Okay, I'm not a violent person when it comes to women."

"You slammed me up against a locker."

"You liked it." He stands, letting my hands fall from his hair, and drops the fishing rod. "You're as fucked up as I am. So I know you definitely liked it."

"I admit nothing."

He stalks towards me and I walk backwards, careful not to trip and fall. "Right this second, your heart is racing, wondering if I'm finally going to kiss you, or make you come all over my hand like you did Friday night."

My breath catches in my throat. "I didn't think we were talking about that."

"That's the only good thing that came out of that night. It's the only part that I want to focus on."

My back hits the tree, and my mind conjures an image of the way he kissed that girl at school. I want that.

The breeze whips through his hair, sending it across his face. I push it back behind him and then hold the sides of his smooth neck, letting my thumb feel for his pulse. It throbs against me, synchronizing with my own.

"You always look at me like that."

"Like what?" I breathe.

"Like you can't decide if you want to see me naked, or dead."

I blanche and then I start laughing hysterically because he has no idea how hard he just hit that nail on the head. "Something like that. Maybe both together."

"That so?"

He lifts his shirt over his head, pulling it off in one swift move that flexes every muscle of his abdomen, making each pec tighten while accentuating every strong, deep groove.

Oh... wow.

I place my hand over his heart, and he puts his over mine. He's so warm.

So tanned compared to me.

"I want to kiss you, but I don't want to hurt you," he breathes, letting his fingers drift over the swollen part of my face.

He kisses my temple, the swollen side. I close my eyes. His lips are softer than I thought they'd be and his touch sends lust and tingles spiraling through my body.

I gulp. "Why did you have to be shirtless for a kiss?"

"I wanted to give you more of a reason to say yes."

I laugh and bite my lip. "You're so arrogant."

"Is it endearing?"

Shaking my head, I stand on my tiptoes, the bark of the tree grazing the soft skin of my back. "Not in the slightest."

Our lips meet... at last.

I allow myself this thing that I will never allow myself again, and deepen it, pressing my tongue to his. He's gentle, frustratingly so. Too gentle. I need more. I need harder. I need him to consume me.

I pull back and search his eyes. "I'm not a delicate flower. Kiss me harder than you've ever kissed anyone in your entire life."

His brows rise and his eyes flare with arousal that he's now pressing against me.

He says nothing, he just grabs me and pulls me into his body. Mine slots perfectly against his, like two human puzzle pieces now a complete picture.

I moan when he assaults my mouth with his tongue, stealing my air and making it impossible to get more. But he knows when to pull back, when to let me breathe and I almost hate my need for air because it means I must separate from him which is something I don't want to do at all.

His hands wander to my hips and then sneak around to grasp my rear. We both groan, a rough harmonious note of wanting more, but more is where I have to draw the line. Or is it? Maybe I don't have to stop. Maybe we can keep going. Maybe I can try.

Something is watching you.

My mind screams it at me, but I don't want to stop. I loathe the idea that this has to end. It's the most I've felt since... since...

I can feel the prickles of distant eyes on my skin. A flash of paranoia lights up my hazy brain like lightning through a gray cloud.

I open an eye, expecting it to simply be paranoia, but dread twists my gut, and a humming sounds through my head when I put a body to the eyes I felt on me mid-kiss. He's back. The man from before.

Dark clothes, dark hair, heavy jacket.

No face.

"Nok," I breathe, pushing against him and pointing to the shade of the trees across the stream.

He turns, sensing a change in me as I look at the faceless man watching us from the shadows. I point and the man ducks down behind a bush. "What is it?"

"He's back, right there. Just staring at us."

Nok pulls away, keeping me behind him as he surveys the area. "I can't see anyone."

"He dropped down when I saw him."

He looks at me like he doesn't believe me and why would he?

"I'm serious," I admonish, slapping his chest. "He was standing right there."

Sighing, he peels away from me with clear reluctance. "Wait here." I reach down for my knife and pull it from my boot, but he immediately takes it from my hand. "You don't need to be playing with that today."

I'm not a delicate fucking wet paper towel that needs protecting but something tells me not to let him cross that stream alone without it.

He holds it as he hops across the rocks in the water, peering over and around all of the mossy obstacles that separate him from the creep.

"Hurry back," I call after him on a hushed note. "Knowing my luck, a bear or a wolf will come along and eat me while I don't have a weapon."

He laughs through his nose but sobers and stops in his tracks when we hear the cracking of a stick and the rustle of a tree. It's insane how instincts can force us to drown out all sounds but the ones we deem most dangerous during moments like this.

"Come out and I won't hurt you," Nok warns, yelling so loudly it echoes through the near silence, piercing it like a pin in a balloon. Birds fly and animals that lie sleeping now run away, startled.

My ears stay tuned in to anything out of the ordinary.

"Can you see anything?" I ask as he kicks at the ground.

"Nope. Nothing. Are you sure you saw someone?"

"You think I'd interrupt that make-out session for nothing?"

He grins at me over his shoulder for a brief second before

returning to his manhunt. After searching for another minute, he returns to me and shrugs. "We'll go, just to be safe." He peers around again, a crease in his brows. "What did he look like?"

"I don't know..."

"What do you mean you don't know?"

"Like... he kind of reminded me of my dad, I guess. Broad shoulders, dark clothes..."

He looks around one more time. "You don't think he followed us out here?"

I shake my head.

"Are you sure? It wouldn't be the first time a girl's dad has chased me with a shotgun."

"My dad's dead, Nok. I'm sure."

His eyes inherit an understanding sadness that one only gets when they've felt the loss of a parent.

"Your mom?" I ask and he nods grimly. "How old were you?"

"Seconds old. You?"

That's a tragedy.

"I was..." I want to answer; the age is on the tip of my tongue, but I can't think of it. It's not that I don't remember I just can't seem to get my head to work for long enough to conjure the moment my dad died. Or how he died.

"Nokosi," an unfamiliar male voice calls from somewhere to our right. It's distant, too distant to have been the man hiding, just like that howl before.

Nokosi mutters a curse and quickly pulls his shirt back on. "It's Anetúte."

"Your dad?"

He nods, his lips a thin line. "He's checking to make sure I'm being nice to you."

I raise a brow. "You know, I can switch on tears like that." When I click my fingers, he glares at me. "What's it worth to you that I don't make up shit for attention?"

"You wouldn't dare…"

I drop my features and inhale sharply. "How could you say that? Why do you have to be so mean?"

"What are you doing?" he asks, looking and sounding panicked.

I sniff dramatically as tears well in my eyes. "You think I'm fat?"

"You better stop it."

"Nokosi?" the voice shouts again, getting closer this time.

"What do you want from me?" Nok hisses and I realize in this moment that he respects his dad. I can see it in the panic of his eyes.

"Nothing, just figuring you out," I mutter, smiling wryly. Then I lean into him, pressing my shoulder against his arm.

"And what have you figured out?"

I lower my voice as I speak through the side of my mouth, "You're a daddy's boy."

"I will throw you in that river."

"I'm telling everyone that Nokosi Locklear loves his daddy."

"Nokosi," the voice yells once more.

This time Nok replies, his eyes still on me, both glittering with humor and curiosity, "Over here."

I hear footsteps come closer, more than one set. Two men appear, both look so much like Nokosi it is unreal. It's like looking at his future, plus twenty years then plus another twenty. They must be related.

"Dad," Nok says softly and bows his head with his hand raised.

"Son," the younger of the two men say, both with acorn-colored eyes lined by a sharp ring of darker brown just like Nokosi. They look at me, assessing me, figuring me out.

"Lilith, this is my dad, Dasan, and my grandfather, Peter."

I want to ask why they all have a mixture of Native names, yet

Peter seems to have a *normal* name. But that's probably rude so I don't ask.

"It's a pleasure to meet you," I say stupidly because I don't know how to greet them beyond that.

"Likewise, young lady," Peter says, smiling kindly at me. "I trust my grandson is being a gracious host?"

They all stare at me expectantly waiting for my answer. I look at Nok and consider telling them he's an ass, but he hasn't been, not today anyway.

"He's been teaching me some new life skills," I reply, nudging him with my arm. "Though I don't think I'll be able to survive in the wild for more than a few hours without heading back in search of a Starbucks."

They laugh and I feel a pleasant tingle in my chest that I'm the one who elicited such a response from them.

"This brings me happiness." Dasan places his hand on his son's shoulder and then looks at the discarded fishing rod. "Was your morning out here fruitful?"

"I caught three, but they're big," Nok explains and points to the bucket, his chest swelling with pride.

Dasan peers inside and beams with pride at his son. It makes me ache for my own dad. He looked at me like that... sometimes.

"Did you catch anything, young lady?" Peter asks me.

I shake my head. "No. I'm sorry."

"Maybe next time."

I look at Nok who looks at me and crosses his eyes, making me giggle under my breath.

"Perhaps you can bring her back on Wednesday and help her catch her own?"

Nok pulls his lips in and clears his throat. "You're inviting her to the thing?"

"What thing?" I ask and Nok stares at his dad unblinking.

"We're having a cookout on Wednesday; you're welcome to

join us." Peter grabs the bucket of fish and whistles with appreciation. "Nice size."

"Everybody brings a little something they caught," Dasan
explains. "Say you'll join us?"

I look at Nok for confirmation, but he won't give me his eyes.
"I don't want to intrude."

Dasan snaps at Nok in another language and Nok turns his
thin-lipped look to me and grits, "You wouldn't be intruding."

"Convincing," I comment and smile when Peter breaks out his
deep laughter, making his wrinkled face crease further.

But then he leans around the side, getting a better look at my
face. "You are injured."

My fingers touch my temple where the swelling is. "I'm okay."

"What happened?"

Dasan and Nok share a look but I can't work it out.

"I had a fight with the back of a truck and lost," I say, it's not
the full truth but I'm not about to rat on Nok. He'll get what's
coming to him eventually. Karma is a beautiful thing. Even when
forced.

"You are okay?"

I nod and he seems appeased for the most part, though Nok
can't meet his eyes when he looks his way.

"So we will see you there?" Dasan asks.

Nodding, I tug on my lip with my teeth. "What if I don't catch
anything?"

"You will. I have faith in my son's teaching abilities."

"You overestimate my ability to learn," I mumble and kick
my boot into the dirt beneath our feet. A pebble rolls towards
the powerful stream and stops just before the edge. Lucky
pebble.

Nok and his father exchange more words before they say their
goodbyes.

But then Dasan stops and looks at me, his body turned back

towards the way he came. His eyes scan me up and down and a frown worries his brow.

I wait for him to speak, I can see he wants to, but he doesn't. He nods and goes on his way with Peter following closely behind.

"If you don't want me to go I won't."

Nok clicks his tongue against his palate. "Too late now."

And he's gone cold on me again.

"What should I wear?"

His cool demeanor flashes with a brief warmth, I guess he hasn't totally frosted over. "The skirt you wore on Friday."

Rolling my eyes, I pick up the fishing rod and glance at the chairs. "We should get back."

"Scared I'll seduce you?"

At that I laugh loudly, I can see his ego is bruised but I don't care. "There's no way in hell I'm having sex with you, Nok. You made one thing clear back there with your family, I'm nothing more than a conquest to you." I'm not insulted by it. Not much anyway. "I get it. You don't like me. I slashed your tires. But I'll warn you that I hate fake people. You're either lying to me, or you're lying to them, either way you're lying. I'm done with you."

He laughs once. "You're done with me?"

"Yes."

"I just had my tongue down your throat."

I move towards the rocks that create a slippery path across the stream and inhale a calming breath. I'm not scared per se, but I've got consistent, mild vertigo which is making me woozy and off-balance.

"And you think I don't like you?"

I shrug and step onto the first rock, breathing with relief and smiling at myself when both feet rest on its slippery surface without death. "I know how this goes. We sleep together and you ditch me and brag to all your friends about how you had me, and I was a shit lay. Leaving me the sad, pathetic new girl that you destroyed to fulfill your own psychotic agenda."

I step onto the next rock and wobble a little.

"Do you really believe I would do something like that?"

"I believe anybody to be capable of anything. Also, I trust nobody." I leap over the final two and land wonky on the bank but straighten myself before I step in backwards and get swept away by the undercurrent. That would so happen to me. I just know it. "Because then nobody can hurt me."

"If you really think I'd do that, then what kind of person are you that you'd kiss me and let me touch you?"

I grin at him and wag my brows. "A horny one."

"You're so confusing." He's behind me now, his hands tucked into his jeans.

"You're only here with me because your family made you. You only took us to the movie because your brother made you. In fact, every interaction up until this point hasn't been because you wanted to spend time with me at all. Admit it. Tell me what you really want because you've made it and said it plainly that you don't like me."

"Doesn't mean we can't have amazing sex."

I laugh at his crassness. "I'm not having sex, not with you or anyone."

"We could try, I'm really fucking good." He falls into step beside me and raises a challenging brow when I look at him. "Don't believe me? Try me."

"I'm not having sex with you. Legit it's not happening."

"Legit it's not happening," he copies, making his tone sound high-pitched and whiny. "Why don't you admit it?"

"Admit what?"

"You won't fuck me because you're shit in bed."

I find his attempt at riling me up laughable. But this is what I want. What I need to see. He's not a good person but I respect that he doesn't pretend to be. Kind of like me. "Probably. I doubt being this tight could be pleasurable for anybody."

He groans, sounding pained. I smirk to myself.

"You need to stop saying that."

"You've had a finger inside of me, you know it's true."

He groans again and adjusts his pants. "What if I say please?"

"Are you saying please?"

"Not until I know it will get me the answer I want."

"It won't. Sorry."

"Such a tease," he murmurs and slings his arm around my shoulder. "What if I tell you the truth about what happened with Yasmine?"

This time I raise a challenging brow and hold on to his wrist so we can more comfortably walk in step with each other.

"Go on then. Tell me the truth."

He blows a raspberry and we walk in silence for a minute.

"Whatever I tell you now, it's her word V mine so what's the point? You're just going to think I'm telling you a tale to get laid."

I nod. "Probably. But I *know* and *you know* that you have no trouble getting laid. So why do you want to fuck me so bad?"

"Because you're hot," he answers simply. "And really interesting, in a psychotic 'don't ever want her to be my baby mama' kind of way."

"You just want to see if my psycho translates to my sex life."

"Does it?"

I stop us both and turn into his chest, placing my hand on his twitching pec. "I can deep-throat."

"No fucking way." He looks dazed, almost high, definitely excited. "Never had a girl who can deep-throat."

My hand wraps around his neck, under his silky hair. "I swallow too... while deep-throating."

He grabs my hips and pulls me into his body. "Prove it."

"Tell me the truth about Yasmine and I will. The truth. I'll know if you're lying."

He groans for an entirely different reason this time. "Seriously? What if you don't like the truth?"

"I'll still suck your dick."

"You're so fucking blunt."

I smile with pride. "I know."

"Fuck..." He releases me and grips my chin between his finger and thumb. "You're driving me insane."

"Already there," I quip and raise a hand.

Humming out a growl, he presses his lips to mine and looks into my eyes for the longest moment. It sends happy little flutters from my lips to the ends of my nipples. Nobody kisses like him. It's as consuming as I thought it would be.

"I have never put my dick anywhere near that girl."

I wait for it, the tell that he's lying, I'm not brilliant but I'm usually pretty fucking good at figuring people out. It doesn't come. Is he telling the truth?

He continues, looking bitter, and sneering in a way he never has, "She fucking hates me because I rejected her."

"So... how'd you end up leaving her at a gas station?"

His hands rise, signaling his confusion and anger. "I offered her a ride home after she showed up at my house absolutely wasted. She was falling all over herself."

"Doesn't surprise me."

"She tried her luck, I shot her down and she went fucking crazy. Scratched my face, punched me, started ripping at the interior of my car, pulled the wheel while I was driving. We almost crashed. I called her dad and he picked her up. But she was embarrassed. She told him I'd put my hands on her. She told everybody else I coerced her into handing over her virginity and dumped her because of my hatred for white bitches." He laughs humorlessly and picks up a stone to throw it as far as the trees will allow. "I

121

didn't rape her or fuck her or any of that. I don't fuck white chicks."

I blink once. That was a lie.

"Well... you're different." He corrected himself before I could call him out. I like that.

I roll my eyes at his line though. "Right. *Different*."

"Whatever. Just..." He laughs coldly under his breath and I can see now how much this has affected him. "What's worse is it made girls just want me more. Want to tame me. I got more pussy offers after that than I did before."

"But?"

"No buts. I just did. I suppose everybody hated me even more after that. I'd only been at the school a month and suddenly I was this villain that I never wanted to be."

I almost feel bad for him. Almost. Not quite. For all I know he could be spinning me a well-crafted lie. He's had plenty of time to think this over. But then the earnestness beyond his harsh exterior is calling for my pity and my support.

Ugh.

"That's the truth?"

"Pretty much." He smirks at me in challenge.

"Well, a deal is a deal I guess." I grab the button of his jeans and pop it open.

"I want to tell you that you don't have to, but I don't have the strength."

I look around, ensuring the coast is clear, and back him into a tree like he likes to do to girls. I give him a chaste peck on his lips and drop to my knees before him, yanking down his zipper as I go.

If that man is nearby, he's about to get a show.

He helps me adjust his jeans, helps me push them down just enough to free him from the confines.

He's hard already. Hard, thick, clean, cut, trimmed...

This is a guy that knows how to take care of himself. He's big, but I knew he would be. You can tell by a man's arrogance what kind of cock he's going to have.

His is for lack of better wording, fucking gorgeous.

It's solid, straight, powerful, and his girth is impressive to say the least.

I waste no time. I place him on my tongue and swallow him in one. It takes two tries, but I get there. This is not my first rodeo, not by far, but it is the best penis I've ever had in my mouth.

I don't do the teasing foreplay before; I've found men enjoy it more when you just put it in and fuck it all up in a good way.

He moans so loudly it echoes in the forest around us. His hand goes to my hair and grips it in a tight fist. He appreciates it all. I take my cues from him. Swallowing around him, making my eyes water and my nose tingle but it's worth it. I know exactly what I'm doing.

My head bobs as my hands grip his hips that thrust against my face.

"Lilith," he bites out, sounding strained.

I want to smile my satisfaction, but I cannot stretch my face anymore. It's physically impossible.

His groans get louder, his thrusts get rapid and uneven, his breathing is shallow, and his cock, it thickens even more. I'm wet, normally I don't get affected by the pleasure of a guy, but Nok is something else.

When I feel him tighten and sense the change that comes when one is about to climax, I release him from my mouth and push away from him, bating the bear.

His eyes that popped open the second I pulled away are wild with lust and confusion and a dash of desperation. His body is shaking. I did that.

All hail Satan and the bounties he gifted me.

I bite my swollen lip and grin a smug grin to rival the one he's so well known for.

"Why have you stopped?"

"I said I'd suck your dick; I didn't say I'd make you come."

"No," he insists, shaking his head slightly but quickly. "Don't do this."

I tap him on the end of his nose. "I'm bored. And hungry. It's past lunch."

"I have something you can eat."

I laugh and go on my merry fucking way, kind of remembering the way back to the car.

Kind of.

"This is so unfair."

"It is what it is."

He grabs the front of my T-shirt in a tight fist, making me tense with an unadulterated thrill. When he yanks me to him, I accept his kiss and bite hard onto his thick lower lip.

He answers it by bending at the waist, hitching my leg up his thigh and grinding against me. His cock which is still hard though confined is pressing against my own heated sex.

I gasp as I wasn't expecting it.

I hum because it feels amazing and I find myself rocking against him.

He turns us until my back is against the tree I had him against moments ago.

We really do a lot of stuff around trees.

He buries his face in my neck and grinds against me, desperate for entry I can tell.

He confirms this when he kisses me again and then down my neck, making me feel wild with arousal as his hand flicks open the button of my jeans and yanks the front of them down. My lips part, my head falls back. I want to curse, I want to give in. I've never wanted anyone this badly.

"Stop," I whisper, it's weak, I'm not sure he heard me.

He pushes a finger into my slick sex, rolling it over my clitoris and making me almost scream with the pleasure it inscribes onto my very soul.

His large hands push down my pants, getting them halfway over my curved rear. The denim is tight and traps my legs together.

For a moment I panic, feeling an urge to run wash over me more powerful than my lust for Nokosi.

"Stop," I demand, firmer this time.

He stops his frantic undressing of me and instead cages me in, his chest heaving. "Please... don't make me stop."

I tug up my jeans and fasten them before I can convince myself to keep going. I really want to keep going. "Use your hand later."

"No hand of mine can cure how I'm feeling right now."

I kind of like that. I want him to pine over me. I want him to feel desperate for me. I want to push him and watch him unravel with his need for me.

I guide him backwards with my own hand to his chest and shrug my shoulders. "Sorry, bro. Maybe next time."

With blazing eyes, he storms away from me, acting every bit the petulant child that he is.

I smile, knowing I have him right where I want him. I'll always have him right where I want him.

Hook, line, and sinker.

CHAPTER 12

I hadn't planned on using Loki as bait for Nok but it is working out quite nicely. It's Tuesday lunch break and Loki, bless his heart, insisted I sit with him. Now, I was going to say no because I'm still mad at Loki for talking about my business. But... he asked me before school, by my car, right after Nok pulled up in his truck.

He didn't just ask me; he also picked a bug off my collar and I saw Nok's eyes find us and slowly change from normal to angry.

Nok had stared, glared, foamed at the mouth. I swear I even heard him growl when I looped my arm through Loki's and let him guide me inside.

He's possessive but in a really sexy way. Or maybe it's just because I'm attracted to him, because in other men I'd find it irritating.

Loki slides his tray closer to me. "Want anything?"

I take a grape. They have those here.

"How are you feeling?"

"You asked me that this morning."

He smiles sheepishly. "Maybe you've changed your mind since then."

The look I level him with is flat.

"Or not."

I look around the cafeteria, wondering why I even bother with this place. It's boring and typical as fuck. I'm not learning anything worthwhile here. Not anything I need anyway. I'm just wasting precious time.

Yet I can't help but find this place intriguing and endearing. The way people are with each other. How they help each other. It's not as stuck-up as I thought.

Bullying here is at an all-time low from what I've seen. Girls who wouldn't normally interact are hanging together in little bubbles. There's no jock worship for the most part.

I'm going to be sad to see it in life's rearview mirror.

All except one.

One whom I've seen today laughing and joking amongst their peers. I hate them by default, but they deserve it.

"I'll be back," I murmur to Loki who was talking about something I wasn't listening to.

He huffs, but he won't take it personally. He wants in my pants too much.

"Where are you going?" Nok asks me as I pass him and his group of friends. I know their names, but we've never spoken.

"Nonya."

They look amongst themselves, confused, waiting to see if anybody knows what I said.

"Nonya?" Nok's lips twitch.

"Yep. Nonya business."

His friends laugh as I saunter past, one of them makes a comment about what a great ass I have. I give it a bit of extra sway until I'm out of the door. Gunning for one person in particular.

"Barbie," I say, making my voice high and welcoming.

"Hi, Lilith," she replies, making her voice equally as high and welcoming. Her eyes move to my swollen temple as students move around us at her locker.

Tish is looking at her phone, disinterested in this exchange.

"How are you? I heard you got into it with Nokosi?" Barbie winces when she sees the yellowing bruise. "What happened?"

"Can I talk to you?" I whisper, swallowing dramatically as my eyes fill with tears. "I just... I need to vent."

She places her hand over her heart. "Oh wow, of course."

When she clicks her fingers at Tish, the girl looks up at last and smiles. "Hey, Lilith."

"Hey, Tish."

"We'll be back." Barbie links her arm through mine. "I'm so glad you came to me. I know exactly how you're feeling."

"I know." We enter the girls' bathroom around the next corner, only unlinking arms to get through the door. It smells like peaches. Even the bathrooms in this place are fucking insanely clean.

"Talk to me," she instructs and moves to the mirror to check her purple lipstick. I have to admit the girl chooses a great lip color.

"I should never have gone with him," I mutter, shaking my head as though I'm the stupid one. "He told me you're a liar and that you came on to him."

With a dramatic roll of my eyes I move to stand beside her and we look at each other in the mirror. She's soft and pretty in a way I'm not. I'm gritty and real, and I have a dead silence to my eyes that creeps people out. Barbie is way more dangerous than me because people don't expect evil from her. Whereas that shit emanates from me like a fever.

"What a dick," she grumbles, but her eyes flicker to the left.

"He's so charming." Now I'm the liar. "He gave me this spiel about how I'm different and blah blah..." We both laugh, a gentle lilt in the empty bathroom. It bounces around the cubicles and lingers for a moment with our shared smiles. "Said you attacked him in his car."

"Of course he said that. I'm a black belt. If I'd attacked him, he'd know about it." She's lying again.

Or maybe I'm wishful thinking so I don't get my ass kicked?

Nah. She's definitely lying.

But about what? Being a black belt or about everything she said about him?

"I heard he tossed you around in the back of his truck?"

"Kind of," I place my bag on the water-splattered counter between the sinks. "Have you seen my face? I'm hideous."

"Want me to kick him in his dick for you?"

I shake my head, letting her brown eyes hold mine when I turn and rest back against the counter. Taking a casual nonthreatening stance. "Nah. I want you to tell me the truth."

She blanches, pulling her head in so her chin touches her neck. "The truth?"

"About what happened that night with Nok."

"I told you what happened. You've witnessed firsthand his aggression; you know it's true."

I hum thoughtfully. "Yeah. Maybe you're right."

"Of course I am."

"But you're not though. Are you?"

Her lips part. She's offended and gasping and spluttering for something to say. I love that I've trapped her.

My fingers tap against the counter side, curling over the soft, curved edge. It's cold like my soul. "You wanted him, and he turned you down, didn't he?"

Her jaw hits the floor. "Are you kidding me? How dare you?"

"I dare do a lot of things."

The bathroom door opens and a girl I don't recognized steps inside.

"Pick another bathroom," I bark and her eyes round with surprise. She slowly backs away and I turn back to a panicked-looking Barbie.

"Why are you doing this? Why are you picking a fight?"

"Meh..." I shrug my shoulders. "Boredom probably."

Her brown eyes narrow. "Boredom? Or is it because you like Nok?"

"Mixture of both I guess."

I bring up my booted foot and kick her in the stomach before she even knows what's happening. The trick to winning a fight is to always have the element of surprise. Fuck that *"don't hit first"* bullshit. If you know they're gunning for you, get your scope on them first and do not fucking hesitate.

She heaves and drops onto her hands and knees, looking about ready to vomit. "Thought you were a black belt?"

She wheezes, unable to talk or do much of anything really.

Saliva drips from her lips to the floor. I hit her really hard. I wonder if I broke a rib.

"Tell the truth," I demand, putting my phone on the counter.

"I am," she rasps, her voice a fraction of the tone that it was before.

I grab her hair and yank her up onto her knees.

"Stop," she begs, and a thrill courses through me.

I love this feeling. I love this power.

Dragging her to the middle stall, ignoring her shrieks, I kick it open and show her the toilet. She very quickly goes quiet.

"I'm gonna dunk you and I don't think it's been flushed yet." I peek over the basin and sure enough, there's an oily sheen of yellow resting on the water surface.

I kick up the toilet seat, but it clatters back down, so I do it again but slowly this time, with more patience. "Last chance. Tell the truth."

"Somebody is going to come in here and stop you."

"I wouldn't count on it." Her hands claw at my wrist, her nails dig into the skin drawing blood, so I step on the back of her ankle until she screams in pain and sheathes her claws. And then I force her face into the toilet, stopping only an inch from the water. It is so much easier to manipulate a person's body when you're pressing against one of their most painful places. Her forehead is against the basin. So gross. "Tell the fucking truth!"

"I am!"

I step on her ankle harder and push her face closer, so close the tip of her nose is also touching the basin. My hand in her hair is starting to ache but the thrill of this torture overrides that feeling. She sobs uncontrollably.

"Please."

"If you want it to stop, tell the truth!"

"OKAY! Okay..." I allow her some slack by bringing her head out a bit. "I lied. Okay? I was embarrassed and my dad was about to ground me so hard. I panicked."

"And you came on to him?"

"Yes."

"And you showed up at his house?"

She nods.

"FUCKING SAY IT!"

"YES!" she shrieks when I thrust her back into the toilet. "Yes, I showed up at his house."

My hands are shaking. I feel so fucking alive right now. Does that make me a sick person? Do I care?

Fuck no.

I pull my switchblade from the inside of my boot and raise her head so she can see it. I don't unleash the blade, I just need her to see it and know that it's there.

"Little miss black belt bullshitter. When you leave this bathroom, you're going to apologize to Nok. You're going to start telling the truth about what you did to clear his name." I whisper the last part for added effect and so the voice recorder doesn't catch it. "This right here is child's play in comparison to some of the shit I've done. Do you understand?"

"Please," she begs, sobbing. "It's over for him now. It's done. I'll be persecuted."

"You mean like he was and is?"

"Hardly, he got to stay in school."

This bitch. "Are you fucking deluded? You almost ruined his life!"

"I know. I'm sorry. But admitting it won't change anything."

I release the blade, unable to control my shaking rage, and she shrieks with panic and fright. I can feel her trembling, worse than jelly in an earthquake. If I wasn't holding her up, she'd be a puddle on the tiled floor beneath my feet where she fucking belongs.

"For every word you say to argue from this point, I'll carve a line into your neck. Do you understand?"

She nods, pressing her lips together as her breath comes out in staggered gasps.

"You're going to tell the truth, aren't you?"

"Yes," she sniffles, her breathing uncontrollable now.

I put my booted foot on the toilet rim and tuck the knife away. "Good girl. Let's keep this between you and me, huh? Your word against mine after all and I'm the one with nothing to lose when I creep into your room at night and cut your face from ear to ear."

"You're a psycho," she whimpers.

"At least I'm an honest psycho. I don't just ruin people's lives because they rejected me." I throw her face-first into the side of the stall, leaving her dazed and crying. Then I wash my hands at the sink, put my phone away and zip up my bag. "Good talk, Barbie. We should do this more often."

I exit with a skip in my step and adrenaline pulsing through my veins.

That felt so good.

I hang back, hiding out, waiting to see what Barbie does. She exits the bathroom with puffy eyes, messed-up blonde hair, and slumped shoulders. I expect her to go straight to Principal Cooper, but she veers in the direction of the cafeteria. She hesitates at the doors and Tish follows hot on her heels, asking her what's wrong. But when she turns to look at Tish, she spies me, and there's genuine fear in her eyes.

It almost makes me orgasm. Fuck me. That's amazing. I love it. I live for this.

I keep close watch as I enter through the other doors and sit back with Loki while she actually approaches Nok who tensed the second he saw her coming his way.

His arms fold across his chest as she speaks, and I shush Loki while I concentrate.

Barbie breaks down and starts sobbing but all Nok's friends are glaring at her. One of them says something to her that makes her cry harder.

And then Nok, who looks perplexed by the entire thing, looks up and finds me.

I smirk at him and lean back on my chair just as Barbie runs away crying, leaving Tish to stare after her with a gaping mouth.

I see Tish look at Nok and mouth something that looks like an apology, before she moves to a group of girls looking pasty faced and horrified.

Nok strides towards me, his boys behind him. He stops at my toes as I lean back casually against the table edge. He sees my arm, sees the bloody half-moon grooves in my wrist and gently touches them with the tip of his fingers.

"What's going on?" Loki asks quietly.

Nok, with his sparkling acorn eyes on me, grabs the front of my black T-shirt that says in bright yellow letters,

"If I don't say it with my lips, you'll see it in my eyes."

I got changed just in case I got blood on my school shirt. I'll change again before class.

He yanks me from the bench, and everybody stills. It was an aggressive move to an outsider. It was a pleasant one to me.

His lips descend, crushing mine in a powerful display that hushes the entire room. He yanks on my hair, deepening the kiss with his tongue, and holds my body to his with a hand on my back.

Fuck.

That was hot.

But it was also never supposed to happen.

People cheer, a chorus of claps and wolf whistles.

He pulls back, breathless and panting. Then he turns and walks away with his friends, smiling and talking about things I can't hear.

"You're with him now?" Loki asks.

I let out a laugh. "He wishes."

"So what was that?"

"The start of a dangerous game, Loki," I answer, sitting back down and watching Nok exit the cafeteria. "The start of a really dangerous fucking game."

"You're crazy. You know that?"

I grin at him. "You really have no idea."

CHAPTER 13

Willow and I spend a rare evening in with Mom. Though despite the fact she's here, she's not actually here. She's on her phone texting while we watch one of the Avengers movies. It's still nice getting to chill like this. It's such a rare thing for us all.

That coupled with the fact Willow is in good health tonight.

"You keep looking at your phone," Willow whispers, frowning at me from her end of the couch. "Expecting a call?"

I shake my head, glancing at my sickly mirror image. "Not really. I'm just..."

"You like him?"

I shake my head. "No. Not at all."

"Mm-hmm." She doesn't believe me, of course she doesn't. "Do you like him so much that you don't want to go through with it?"

"Hell no. I'm never wrong about this. You know I'm not."

She glances at Mom and whispers even lower, "What are we going to do if you are?"

I shrug and place my phone facedown on the arm of the chair. "Find someone else?"

She laughs sardonically. "We leave in three weeks."

"I've got this."

"No, you don't."

"I do."

"If you're so sure, then say the word."

I stand and stuff my phone into my pocket. "I'm not saying shit."

"I'm dying, Lilith."

I look at her frail form and resist the urge to sob. "I know."

"You're wasting time on him that could be spent with me."

"I know." I sit back down and curl into her side. "I know."

"Then stop this nonsense. Let me take care of you for once." Her cheek rests against my hair.

I shake my head slightly. "Let me be sure. Okay? I have a couple of weeks left. If I haven't figured it out by then..."

"Okay. Deal. But be home more. I need you."

She's right. I haven't been there for her at all since we moved in. I bet she's been feeling lonely and neglected. "I'll do better."

"You're the best already. Just fit in more time for me."

I look at Mom who is now smiling at us, a vacant, tired expression on her face. She gets like this when she misses Dad.

I sigh heavily. "What are we going to do about her?"

"Nothing. Just hope she gets laid and finds love again."

We share a smile and then we abandon our mom to go and paint our toenails upstairs. I need to invest in more nail polish. Neon pink is my sister's color. Not mine. But I ran out of my crimson red the last use.

"I've been chatting with locals in the school forum," Willow admits. "There are a lot of good people here."

"It's not all bad."

"They're terrified that they're going to be next on the School Sigil Searer's list." She's obsessed with watching the news these days so it's unsurprising she's getting local gossip.

I tense. "You know I saw a man in the woods yesterday."

"Oh?" Her eyes light up with excitement. "Was he naked?"

Laughing, I shake my head. "No, he was just staring at me, standing there. He had a similar body shape to Dad. It was beyond weird."

"Sounds it. What were you doing in the woods?"

I shrug and smile sheepishly. "Bonding with Nok."

"By yourself? Are you fucking insane?"

"I have to get him alone."

"What if he hurt you?"

I grit my teeth. I know she's concerned for me, but she doesn't have to be. I can look after myself. I don't know what it is about people suggesting I'm weak that has my hackles rising. I know that's not what she meant. It's just a deep-down feeling I can't shake.

I'm not weak. I'm strong and willful and fearless.

I need everyone to believe that.

"I've got this," I reply firmly. "Trust me."

"I do. I just don't trust your judgement. It's been sketchy in the past." She shuts down, her eyes lose their vibrance and her lips lose their sweet smile.

"We should get you out of the house," I insist, tugging on her hand. "While you're feeling good."

"What about Mom?"

"She doesn't want to be here, Willow," I implore, sighing at the end. "You know it. I know it. It's too fucking painful for her."

"I know." She pouts and I help her stand. "Why don't we go for a walk or something?"

"Let's do it."

We head downstairs and Mom is arguing on the phone with somebody. We both roll our eyes towards each other and slip out the back.

As we cut through the yard, our neighbor's head pops over the high fence. White hair and blue eyes and a friendly smile.

He smiles at us and Willow greets him with a wave which he returns. "Good afternoon, Mr. Miller."

"Good afternoon, Willow." He returns to his duties and I take my sister's hand.

"Let's go riding?" I ask, moving to the small garage where my bike is hiding.

She wets her lips, looking nervous. "I don't know."

"I'll go slow. We'll be able to go further together."

After a brief hesitation she nods. It's been a long time since I got her on the bike. She used to ride her own all the time but that ended when she got sick and her arms just don't have the strength in them to guide the bike anymore.

"This is going to be fucking awesome."

CHAPTER

14

"I can't do it," I growl, feeling frustrated when another fish gets away from me. "Can't I like stab it or something? This is boring."

Nok blinks at me slowly. "You mean like spear fishing?"

I nod. "Duh. Isn't that something your people do?"

"Not anymore but once, I guess. We'd need spears."

"Or just really sharp sticks with a kind of hook on the end."

He mutters under his breath about ungrateful women and their abuse of fishing and lack of skill.

"That's sexist," I point out playfully.

He grins at me over his shoulder as he finds a long enough stick for me to utilize. Meanwhile, I sit and enjoy the misty, cool air while sipping warm coffee he brought with him.

"So, do you know what I realized this morning?" I ask him and he grumbles, "What?"

"I don't know what you do for a living for you to have such a fancy-ass truck."

He raises his brows, clearly surprised. "I've never told you?"

"No, you have, I'm lying so you tell me again." My sarcasm goes over so well. Not.

He picks up a five-foot-long branch that's straight for the most part and tosses it my way. I sit cross-legged on the ground and balance it over my thigh before starting to carve at one end with my knife.

"You're very handy for a girl."

"Sexism," I singsong, concentrating on my craft.

"Whatever." He dips his hook back into the water, standing on the bank with parted thighs and a strong posture. "I take people out into the woods to hunt and do survival role-play for a place on the res. It's fun. I get to keep the truck so long as I look after it."

I yank on my collar to loosen it; it suddenly feels itchy around my throat. "Sorry about that."

"I deserved it," he admits with genuine sincerity for the first time since it happened. He has said it before but it just didn't ring true. This time, however, I sense, feel, and hear his remorse. I'm growing on him. He's starting to care about me. "I deserved worse."

"You're just saying that because I saved your reputation."

"You're going to be smug about that forever, aren't you?" I can hear the smile in his voice, he's clearly happy about what I did. He likes my psychotic side, so long as he's not on the receiving end of it.

He suddenly appears at my back and his legs open around me. The fishing rod is still in his hand, though he's holding it out of the way, so I don't accidentally cut the line while chiseling away at my stick.

"I wish we could just come out here every day," I murmur when his chest touches my back and I can lean into him.

"You enjoy it?"

"It's the most peaceful I think I've ever felt." I tilt my head back, stopping my whittling for a moment so I can look at him and not cut myself. "Minus the fact you're here of course."

"Oh, ha ha," he deadpans and presses a sweet kiss to my lips as though it's his right to do so. "You have the sweetest lips I have ever tasted, the sharpest tongue, and the evilest eyes— ouch."

I hit him for that last one.

"I don't have evil eyes."

I so do but that doesn't mean anyone else can say it.

"You have the worst case of resting bitch face I have ever seen in my life." His mischievous smile shows his perfect teeth.

"I don't have *resting* bitch face, Nokosi Locklear." I drop my knife and the stick and turn so I'm on my knees on the soft picnic blanket that has seen better days. "I simply have bitch face."

Smiling, I bite his lip, something I love doing. I decide, what with this being the second time I've done it and already I'm wishing for a third. If only to watch his eyes open and then narrow as my bite gets harder and harder, until he growls at me and his pupils expand beyond full dilation.

I just know he's hard, I can see the swell in his groin, but then he's always hard around me. Something else I take great pleasure in.

I'm sadistic.

When I free his lip, he nudges me with another kiss, and in one swift move, he flips me so I'm on my back and he's towering over me. I'm slightly winded but I don't have time to gather my breath or wits because he's kissing me so hard my head is crushed to the ground.

He consumes me greedily, the manly taste of him and a slight hint of coffee, tinged with passion, desire, and the kind of guy that even at a young age knows exactly what he wants and how to get it, it all sends me wild.

"How did you get so good at this?" I ask when he kisses down my neck.

"I've seduced a lot of women," he replies easily, and I feel a strange pang of envy and possessiveness. Something I've never felt, and I don't like it. "My first time was a mess, it was embarrassing. I taught myself to be better. What about you? How'd you get so good at giving head?"

I chuckle under my breath and try to look away, but he holds my face with his hand.

"Tell me."

"No, you'll make fun of me."

He arches a thick brow and trails his nose along the side of mine. "Since when do you care about that?"

He has me there. "I *don't* care."

"Then how?" He kisses me again, a gentle peck. Fuck me, this guy has a sweet side. I like it. I shouldn't like it.

"I practiced, like you."

His eyes darken and I wonder if he's envious too. "On men?"

"No, well... yes, but first my sister and I—"

"You practiced with your sister?" He drops his head to my neck when I nod. "Why do I find that so hot?" Then his head rises again, and his excited eyes search my face. "So, your sister can deep-throat too?"

My entire body turns to cement, and I push him from me. "I don't want to talk about my sister or deep-throating. I want to make my spear and fish."

"Yes, ma'am." He returns to his chair as I continue to whittle. Truth be told I'm not exactly sure what I'm doing but I figure so long as it's pointy and sharp, it'll kill a fish.

We sit in comfortable silence and I like it. Nok isn't one for words and neither am I. I don't want to gossip or talk about shit that doesn't need to be said. I'm not interested in that.

I just want to enjoy the silence and turn my stick into a fish-murdering weapon.

"You're nearly done," Nok comments, looking at my long pointy stick. "It looks good. Want to test it out?"

"Sure, stand still and I'll jab you through the foot."

He rolls his eyes, but his lips are twitching.

I move to the rushing water and follow it upstream to a shallower part where I can see the bottom. Fish swim through the crystal-like waters, kicking up sandy dirt, nothing too big and that's what I'm waiting for, *big*. If I'm going to take something I caught, it better be newsworthy.

I stand on the bank and stare down. I do a couple of practice jabs into the surface of the water, just to see how accurate the location of the fish is, as water distorts your view. It bounces the angle of the stick to the left somewhat, so I'll try to account for that.

"It's harder than it looks," Nok says, folding his arms over his chest.

I don't reply, I stop breathing, I wait. I see a fish coming and I hold the stick in both hands then I jab. And miss.

Though only by a fraction.

I hesitated in the last second, something I've always promised myself I'll never do. Never hesitate... never. It's my number one rule. Hesitation is weakness and people exploit weakness. You miss chances because of said weakness.

I don't say anything despite hearing Nok's laughter. I concentrate, zoning in to the sounds around me. Watching the fish and how they move.

I jab again, pinching my lips together when I miss again.

I'm dedicated now through my frustration. I can do this. I know I can. I'm good at this.

Sweat beads on my brow, I maneuver my sweater from my body, revealing my black lace bralette. I kick off my shoes and stuff my socks into them.

Nok whistles low and long and stands with his fishing rod, trying to hook the fish I scare away from the pole. "I want to eat your tits."

"Shush," I admonish and roll up the bottom of my jeans.

I wait for what feels like minutes, maybe more, but I wait patiently. Patience is something I'm good at when I must be.

"Just give it up," Nok says and I do it. I find the fish and it is huge.

I jab the stick and it crunches and pulls before hitting the muddy rocks beneath it, breaking the sharp point. For a moment I close my eyes, not daring to see if the large fish escaped.

It didn't.

I raise it slowly, hold it up to the light. The scales shimmer and shine like they've been slicked with oil or silver. Water runs down the jagged pole to my hands and I feel suspended in this moment.

Nok and I look at each other and just stare for the longest time and then the lifeless fish. A clean kill.

"No... fucking... way."

I jump and squeak and start cheering like a little girl who just got a new doll. I raise my stick in the air and do a bizarre laugh scream because words have escaped me. This is so exciting. I want to do it again.

"You did it."

"Just call me queen of the forest, catcher of fish, blower of men, ruler of Oregon!"

He catches me by the waist and swings me around, his arms banding around my creamy, smooth skin. I struggle to keep hold of the stick because the fish is heavier than I thought it would be and the rod bends, threatening to break under the exertion. "You brilliant fucking female you."

"Why thank you." My feet touch down and I skip with my kill to the empty bucket where Nok takes my fish off the spear and drops it in. "That's got to be a good six pounds."

"Definitely, it's a big fucker." He looks at his rod that he discarded during the celebration and sighs. "Can I try prodding a few?"

I nod and hand it to him, wondering what good it will do with a broken end. "Have at it. But take your shirt off, if you please."

Laughing, he obliges, yanking it over his head with one arm and throwing it at me. He kisses his solid biceps and hits a fist against his muscular chest.

I laugh too and hold his fishing rod while sitting in his chair and drinking his coffee. It's lukewarm now but it hits the spot.

He steals my knife too and tries to fix the end of the pole. The way his biceps bulge as he scrapes the blade over the end is so erotic.

Ugh... my phone vibrates with a text from my sister.

Willow: Having fun?

Lilith: Fuck yes. Wish you were here.

Willow: I'm with you in spirit. What time will you be home tonight?

Lilith: Don't wait up. That's what time.

Willow: Don't do anything stupid.

She should define stupid because it's subjective in my opinion.

"Everything okay?" Nok asks.

I nod just as my phone vibrates again.

Loki: Party at Pammy Shepherd's house on Friday, everyone's invited. Gonna be mega. You in?

. . .

I look at Nok who is cursing at the empty spike of my stick. "Party this Friday night at Pammy Shepherd's. You know him?"

"Her and yes, I know her."

I lick my lips to wet them and sip more coffee. "She good people? Will she mind if I go?"

"She's insane. She won't mind at all."

Well... good. "So are we going?"

He raises his brows. "You're asking me?"

"Should I not be?"

"Well, I already planned on going with Ethan and Payne. But I guess I could go with you instead."

I smirk and roll my eyes. "Don't do me any favors."

"I'm not. I might get laid if I go with you."

"You'll definitely get laid if you don't go with me."

He flashes his eyes at me. "You'll give in eventually. I'm persistent."

"Let's see how persistent," I mutter under my breath so quietly I know only I can hear.

"Huh?"

"Nothing. So, Friday. Pick me up at eight?"

He nods and looks back at the stream. He doesn't catch one that way and I don't try again.

Beginners luck and all that. I'm not screwing with my triumphant buzz.

CHAPTER
15

There's a bonfire and coal pits for the food. Elders sit near the ember glow, one of them is telling scary stories to the little kids who were running around but now no longer are, most are wrapped in blankets to keep the chill out. I have yet to be introduced as we got here late no thanks to Nok.

He decided it would be a good idea to go into Westoria to pick up a few bits, but realized he forgot his wallet. When he went back to the truck to find it, I walked out with the cart undetected. No way I was waiting for him.

His face was a picture when I started placing the groceries into his truck bed. But he didn't argue, or chastise me, he just snorted, rolled his eyes, kissed my temple, called me crazy, and then we drove away.

There is so much food. Everybody brought something but not everybody caught something. I feel pride over that fact.

"I feel like your dad tricked me." I motion to the buffet table full of foods from Walmart. I watch one guy dump a bag of cheese balls into an empty bowl.

Nok just laughs and gives me a playful shove towards the food table. "Eat. Mingle."

"Are you seriously about to leave me?"

His eyes flare that light shade of brown and the reflection of the fire in them just makes them so much more dramatic. "I have people to see. My dad invited you, not me."

And he's back to being an asshole. But he also has a point. I don't want him lingering around if he doesn't want to hang with me. He has his own family and friends here. I'm good alone. I've had enough of him today too.

"Fuck you then," I say with a shrug.

"Nokosi," Dasan calls and approaches us with Nash by his side.

I'm surprised when Nash hugs me like I didn't slash his brother's tires on Friday night. "Dad said you'd be coming." I keep my arms limp by my side for a moment because I don't want to hug Nash in front of Nokosi. Or at all.

But then I remember how Nok reacted to Loki and I return the hug with more fervor and give him my most seductive smile.

"How have you been?" I ask, keeping my hand on his arm when we part.

His familiar eyes, so warm and lacking the harshness that rest around Nok's, scan my face pleasantly. "Good. You didn't respond to my texts."

"I didn't get any texts."

He shrugs, a confused frown on his face. "I sent two on Monday. They said read."

I click my tongue and glance at Nok who is staring at my hand on Nash's arm. He doesn't like it. I can tell. I also have a feeling he has something to do with the missing texts seeing as I was with him that day.

"Do you want to go for a walk?" Nash asks and offers me his arm. "I'll introduce you to my grandmother. She's been eager to meet you."

"Why?"

"I'll take her," Nok insists. "She's my guest."

Oh, and suddenly I'm his guest again?

"It's fine, Nok. Your brother is better company anyway." I point to his group of friends that he usually hangs with on the track. "Go be with them. Tell *Vienna* I said hi."

A muscle ticks in his jaw, I see it before I turn to his father and thank him for inviting me. He nods and tells me to enjoy myself before moving on to someone else.

"Nokosi!" Vienna yells over the chatter of voices and the crackling fire.

"Don't worry, baby brother, I've got her," Nash assures him and hooks an arm around my neck.

I wind my hand around his waist and smugly grin at Nok. I know it's driving him wild. I love that too.

They stare at each other, unblinking, both a level height though Nok has more brawn than Nash, they're both so amazingly toned I have to wonder who would win in a contest of strength.

"Fight, fight, fight," I chant playfully and both glare at me.

Their glaring contest is broken when somebody moves towards us, her frame hunched. Two women flank her sides, holding each of her arms as she walks.

"Elisi." Nok steps forward to pay respects to his grandmother who is wearing the most magnificent crown of feathers and beads on her head, wisps of white hair peek out around it.

He leans in to kiss her cheeks and then so does Nash, releasing me first of course.

When she looks at me with eyes so blue they look almost fully white, I feel a chill run down my body.

"This is our grandmother," Nash explains. "Elisi, this is our friend Lilith."

Her eyes scan my face but I'm not sure if she's actually *seeing* me. Could she be blind? I don't want to insult her by asking. "Come to me, child. Allow me to hold your hand."

I glance at Nok, unsure, but he gives me an encouraging nod.

Stepping forward, I place my cold hand in her warm, satin soft yet wrinkly one and she curls her other hand over the top. I've never been one to believe in magic or spirits or anything of the sort, but when her eyes join mine, I feel as though she can see into my soul. Her grip tightens, her eyes lock me in place, and I can't move, or even blink. I can't look away. It's as though I've been cemented to this very spot and everything around me loses focus. I can't hear anything but the sound of my breath in my ears and my heartbeat in my throat.

It's disconcerting, disorienting...

"You poor child," the old lady whispers. "So much grief. So much death."

Like a plug in my mind is slowly lifting, water spills up from a drain that I had locked tight, and my eyes fill with tears. Real tears.

"No," I beg, trying to pull my hand free as feelings I've never allowed myself to feel suddenly bombard me like a tsunami of fire and ice.

"So much confliction. So much pain." She pulls me closer, her strength deceiving for her age and hunched stature. Her hand that covered mine now rests over my chest, flat against my skin. "You have a good heart, let it guide you, let it be your strength, not your weakness."

She lets me go and I stumble back into Nok's chest and his arms wrap around me. I don't realize I'm crying until I feel myself choke and feel the sting of tears on my cold cheeks.

The old lady walks away as though nothing just happened. Two women hold her arms to help her along.

Meanwhile I'm choking for air, trying to gather myself as an all-consuming grief blinds me to anything else. I turn in Nok's arms that are like steel bands around my body and bury my face in his neck. My tears soak his skin, they soak mine too. My mascara is likely now in dark rings around my eyes.

Nokosi lifts me, swinging my legs up with his arm. He walks

with me, not speaking, not stopping. He just goes and I'm too weak to breathe or protest. I just hold him, seeking his comfort in a way I've never sought comfort from anybody but my sister.

I'm a mess and I should be embarrassed but I can't get past this overwhelming sorrow I suddenly feel. As though somebody is in my head, screaming their pain so loudly it's all I know now. I feel as though I'll never be happy again. I don't want to feel this way. I need to let it go but I can't release it. It's tangled like thorny vines around my spirit. I don't know why it's there or how, but it hurts. It feels physically painful.

I hear a door open and shut and stop crying when the noises from outside no longer sound, and the cold air becomes warm.

He doesn't put me down until we're through another door and a bright light is shining overhead.

As soon as my feet touch the ground, Nokosi and I look at each other. My chest is still tingling with this lingering mourning I just can't seem to combat and right now all I can think of is one thing to get my mind off this sudden pain.

I look at myself in the mirror, my eyes are swollen, my lips too, and my cheeks are flushed with pink.

I've not looked this human in such a long time. I don't feel ugly or like I should apologize. In fact, I want to feel more human. I don't want this to stop.

I turn to face the man who brought me to this place and grab his collar before yanking him to me. His lips collide with mine, and at first, they're unresponsive, but he soon changes that when I lick the seam of his lips. Greeting my tongue with his own, he cups the back of my head, groaning and holding me tightly as my hand works on the button of his jeans.

I don't care what I'm here for. I don't care what I'm supposed to be doing. I want him. I need him.

I need to feel human. I need to feel pleasure and lust, and orgasms. I want to feel it all.

"Harder," I beg and he bites my lip, making it burn with delicious pain. The kind of pain I want and need.

My hands tug on his jeans and push them over his ass, and it has to be said as I grab it with both hands, it's the most solid, soft, incredible ass I have ever held. I squeeze as his hot length presses between us and he yanks my denim skirt up my hips enough to pull down my thong and back me into the wall between the sink and toilet. The tiles are cold through my sweater, but it only adds to all the sensations.

He continues kissing me, standing with his feet on either side of mine so his legs are parted and mine are shut tight.

I gasp when he pushes his solid cock between the apex of my thighs. The mushroom head parts my slick lips and rubs against my swollen clit.

My body almost collapses. I almost give up and die right here.

I've never felt something so incredibly tingly and arousing.

His lips move to my ear and then my throat. I legitimately can't breathe. There are too many things to feel. The burning in my womb, in my thighs, in my clit, in my feet, my hands... shit, even my eyes which are squeezed shut.

Nok groans, thrusting against me, fucking me without actually fucking me and I wonder why that is. If he just hitched my leg up his hip and pressed against my opening I wouldn't object. Hell, I'm salivating at the thought.

Though saying that, this is hitting a different sweet spot just fine and it won't be long until I'm coming all over his dick. Something I never thought I'd say about any man, especially not about Nokosi Locklear.

His thrusts get faster, his grunting louder. He's as close as I am.

Tears spring to my eyes for an entirely different reason this time.

"Nok?" Nash calls through the door and we both still, both looking at the door like it's about to catch fire. "You in there?"

Nok looks as aggravated as I feel. The tension around his eyes is likely mirrored in my own.

The handle starts to turn so I quickly call out, "Just a sex." I shake my head and start giggling. "I meant sec. Just a sec."

"Is Nok in there with you?" Nash asks, his voice muffled.

"I'm in here," Nokosi replies, buttoning up his pants and zipping up the fly.

I hear Nash let out a laugh but it's humorless. "Of course you are," he grumbles so quietly I had to strain to hear it.

I turn back to the mirror when I'm dressed again and wait for Nok to open the door and tell his brother that we'll be right out. Splashing water on my face, I ignore the pulsing in my core and hope it fades soon. I shouldn't have done what I just did. It was a severe moment of weakness.

I'm better than that. I know better.

Nok comes to stand behind me and kisses the bare side of my neck. His eyes meet mine over my shoulder and the blackness of them makes me shiver with need.

"What happened?" I ask on a breath as Nok looks at me in the toothpaste-splattered mirror. Tiny white dots mar our reflections.

"Elisi has magic," he sheepishly admits as his fingertips stroke the soft, flat skin of my belly, just over the edge of my skirt. "I didn't fully believe it until now."

"Other people don't react that way?"

He shrugs and smiles apologetically. "Not that I've seen, but it's been known to happen. She's really good at reading people."

I shake my head to clear it. "I felt like something in me snapped and I just... it's stupid right?"

"I wouldn't say it's stupid, you clearly needed the mental breakdown."

I turn, laughing, and slap his arm. "I did not have a mental breakdown."

"You kinda did but it's cool."

"Ugh." I shoulder past him. "You're such a dick."

"You like my dick though, so...?"

I roll my eyes but I can't stop the laughter that bubbles forth and releases.

Nash is waiting for us when we exit. "Food's ready. Edudu is telling stories."

Nok goes on ahead, clearly done with me now. Nash hangs back.

"He'll use you," Nash states, not looking sorry for stabbing his brother in the back at all. "He wants one thing from you."

His words still hit home because I know them to be true. "I haven't fucked him, Nash, and I don't plan on it either."

He doesn't look appeased, or like he even believes me. But I don't care. I'm hungry. I want food and then home.

Though thinking about it, I'm not entirely sure I believe it myself.

When we reach the bonfire again, Nok is sitting with his friends, and Vienna is to his right laughing about something he said. They're so close their arms are touching.

He really is a massive asshole.

"They're going to get married one day," Nash whispers in my ear, his hand on the small of my back. "You're just a fling for him. You'll never be his forever girl. He already has her. You're just how he sows his wild oats." When I don't reply because I'm too busy glaring at Nok and his forever girl, he continues, "You deserve better than my brother."

Nok slings his arm around her shoulder and I see red. Not enough to go over there and yank her hair out, but I'm pretty fucking mad.

"And what about you, Nash?" I ask, my tone biting and questioning. "What am I to you?"

"I think we have great chemistry."

"So... you want to fuck me, that's what you're saying?"

His lips part. I caught him off guard. He stammers for the right words.

"Would you still want to fuck me if I told you I've had your brother's dick in my mouth?"

His eyes flare but he doesn't say no.

"Is it because I'm new? Is it because I'm interesting? What exactly is it about me that makes you think we'd be good for each other?"

He grips my bicep and pulls me out of earshot of his family and friends. We stand in the shade of a tree by his home. I can still see Nokosi, which means he can still see me. "You're different."

"That's what they all say when they don't have a genuine reason, Nash," I reply, smiling a fake smile. "What do you want from me?"

His lips part, so soft and round. Kissable lips, just not the lips I want to kiss.

"Be honest with us both for once. Don't make this about your brother. You want to fuck me, don't you?"

He blanches at my candidness. "I respect you."

I blink twice and laugh once. "No, you don't. You know I'm trouble. You know we wouldn't last long term. But you're too much of a gentleman to be honest about it like your brother is. Say it, Nash. Tell me what you want from me really."

"I want to get to know you."

I pull him further around the tree. "You're a coward and a liar. You don't want to get to know me. You want to fuck me. Because you think I'm wild and I give no fucks about anything but what I can get out of my own life. And you like that because you live with generous, good people and that's what you'll have forever. A generous and good little lady. But not me... you need something wild, something fleeting to make you appreciate your future more. I wouldn't give you generous and good. I'd take everything good from you and give you so much bad."

His nostrils flare. His eyes darken. I'm so fucking good at bringing out the monster in people, especially men. We all have one, it's just some of us have a better handle on it than others. Nok and me, well, we don't have a handle on ours at all.

Nashoba, however, has repressed his so much he's too scared to bait it even a little. He has great self-control and a lot of respect for women and people in general. But that doesn't mean he can't be tempted.

"You've wanted to touch me since the moment we met."

He doesn't deny this either.

"Touch me," I breathe, pulling my pink hair over one shoulder so it's out of the way. "Treat me like the whore you think I am."

"I don't think you're a—"

"You either think I am, or you hope I am." I smile mischievously and press his hand against my breast, he makes a noise in the back of his throat. "You hope I am because then when you tire of my attitude it won't hurt to walk away and you know I'll jump onto the next dick without glancing back and you won't care because I'm nothing." I bring his other hand up to my breast and he squeezes gently. It tingles but I don't feel the same passion that I get with his brother. Although this does make it exciting, what with them being related. "Look at you, touching my tits meters from where your entire family are sitting, ready to eat their food."

"Fuck, Lilith," he gasps, stepping closer, pupils expanding.

"I'm using you," I breathe, standing on my tiptoes to brush my lips against his. "I'm doing this to make him jealous. How does that feel? Or do you not care now that you know that I'm nothing but a fucking whore?"

"You're not a—"

I grab his cock through his jeans, shutting him up. He groans and presses his forehead to mine. "I am. This is proof. Ten minutes ago, I was ready to make your brother come in my pussy in your bathroom, and now here I am with you, wishing you could fuck me against this tree."

He moans and pants when I rub him through his jeans, tempting him, testing him, but then he pulls away.

"I can't do this," he admits, shaking his head, looking me up and down. "I want to. I've never wanted anything more. But I can't."

"I know," I reply gently. "You're too good for me, Nash."

"No, that's not it." He shakes his head. "You're not beneath me."

"But I could be," I murmur and he laughs.

"No, I mean... you're just..."

"It's okay," I finish and pat his cheek. "I understand. Go back to the party. Maybe talk to Vienna yourself. Get to know her. Woo her."

"That'll never happen."

"It will if you use your charm. You were wrong when you said she's his forever girl. He's mine and I can't let him go." I look at the bitch sitting with him and then back at Nash. "She's going to need a shoulder to cry on when I take him from her forever."

His breath hitches and he watches me saunter away, straight to where Nok and Vienna are sitting together.

They eye my approach, him with his smug grin, her with an unsure one.

"Move her or I'm sitting on your lap," I tell him, completely ignoring the girl under his arm.

Vienna scoffs, clearly offended, "Excuse me?"

Her eyes narrow and then fly to Nok who is simply grinning at me, no small amount of excitement in his eyes. He's challenging me, to see what I'll do. Doesn't he know me well enough yet?

"Three," I warn, holding up three fingers and his friends cheer. "Two..."

Before I get to *one*, Nokosi shifts away from her and pats the space beside him. I claim it, forcing my butt between his and hers and then tilt my head up to his. He looks around the large gathering of people, hesitating for a moment before he brings his lips down to mine. I hum my appreciation and melt into it slightly.

"Until you tell me otherwise," I snap, changing from soft kisser to feral bitch while wrapping his long ponytail around my hand and tugging. "You're mine now. And if I find you sitting near or touching another girl, I'll paint your truck with her blood."

"Are you insane?" Vienna asks, gaping at me now as I rest back into Nok's chest. His buddies watch the exchange with avid interest.

"Yes," I respond flatly.

She looks at Nok. "Do something!"

"I'm good here," he states simply, holding me closer than he held her. How he holds me is possessive. How he held her was friendly, though she didn't see it that way.

"You can't seriously be taking her side? She just threatened me."

"I'm hers," he replies with a gentle shrug and an approving smirk. "It's not personal."

"You're hers? I can't believe this," she grumbles, her hands on her hips. But she knows that she can't get anywhere so she stomps over to where her own friends are sitting.

"I'm yours, hmm?" Nokosi whispers in my ear. "I thought you didn't want me."

"I don't," I reply and wink at Nash who is watching our exchange from across the lawn, by his father who is in the middle of a conversation with somebody else. "But I'm not letting anyone else have you either."

"Liar."

If only he knew how true it was.

I suppose he will soon.

"So... what were you and my brother talking about?"

"Ah, so you were watching," I comment, laughing gently.

Clearing his throat, he shifts behind me and replies, "He likes you. He liked you first."

"He wants to fuck me, there's a difference." At my words he growls in my ear, like an animal when you reach for its possession. "Don't worry, I dealt with it."

"Good." He kisses my temple, an odd display of affection, and plays with the ends of my hair as his friends talk to us. They introduce themselves and we get talking about the track, promising to meet there tomorrow so they can ride my pit bike. Fat chance on the latter, but I'll definitely meet them there.

We sit for two more hours, eating amazing food, praising people for their catches, though not the ones who brought Walmart goods. They're cheaters who caught nothing.

Everybody applauds when Dasan tells them that I caught my huge rainbow trout while spear fishing for the first time. That part was embarrassing.

But overall, we have an amazing night.

Until it's time to go, the people start dispersing back to their homes and Nokosi offers to drive me to mine. For the first time ever, I don't want to go home. I want to stay. I don't want to go home at all. I can't bear to look at my sister, or witness my mother ignoring us because she finds us too painful to look at.

So, I find ways to drag the night on and pull a large bottle of cherry-flavored gin from my handbag. I wasn't sure if I'd need it tonight but here it is.

Our small group of friends' eyes light up. All but Nok's.

"I'm driving," he points out, frowning.

"So? Just sneak me into your room later," I whisper and put the gin back. "I'll sleep with you."

He looks excited now and winks at me. "Fine, but no backing out now."

"Let's get wasted," Joseph cheers on a whisper so the adults don't hear.

"I like this chick," Bobby, their mutual friend, mutters.

"Let's go," Nok yells and we stand.

"Where to?"

"My shed," Joseph replies, grinning at me over his shoulder. "It has blankets, a light, it's really fucking cozy."

I raise a brow. "Is it now?"

When we reach the trees and wander out of sight, using our phones to guide us, I pull the gin from my bag and take a long pull. The others follow suit, passing it around, complimenting it on its sweet cherry flavor.

We race through the forest until the trees clear and another home comes into view. I love the privacy of their houses, no main roads, not too easy to get to so you can guarantee door-to-door salesmen aren't an issue.

The reservation is much bigger than this with its own shopping complexes and stores that eventually merge with Westoria, but this part of it is private. For the residents only. It's peaceful and it feels safe.

Joseph's house is a lot bigger than Nok's but we don't go inside to explore. We head around back to the very edge of his yard and past the first row of trees that form an almost uniformed line around his property.

"This must be it," I say motioning to the shed with its dark windows and rickety-looking exterior. It looks sturdy enough. It could just do with a paint job. And maybe a few replacement boards here and there.

Joseph races ahead, my gin in his hand, and opens the latch on the door with a flick of the handle. The door creaks and I laugh when a furry little animal comes scurrying out. Maybe a skunk. I sure hope not. My sister got sprayed by a skunk once when we were little. We'd been running around the yard playing tag with our matching dollies, in our little matching dungarees.

Mom had to bathe her in tomato soups and purees for about a week. I still joke now that the stench lingers to this day. My sister hates it.

It disappears into the brush and we all head inside, breathing a sigh of relief.

"It's been a while since we came in here," Joseph comments. "Being old enough to drink means I don't really need to sit in a shed and drink these days." He swigs the gin and I kick an empty can of beer across the floor.

Nok rolls out the blankets and checks them for damp. I sit on a checkered green and black one and lean against the wall, holding my hand out for more alcohol.

"Strip poker, anyone?" Bobby asks, laughing and throwing a deck of cards in between us all.

"No," Nok snaps, sitting beside me and resting his hands over his bent knees.

"We have to go around the room and say something bad that we've never told anyone before," Joseph suggests, waving a hand flippantly, "I saw it on TV. It looked like a great ice breaker."

"Sounds good to me." Bobby glugs three large gulps of the gin and then belches, doubling over as though about to vomit.

"Bobby's confession," I announce, cupping my hands to my face, "he can't handle his alcohol."

"That's kinda racist," Joseph jests.

I frown. "How is that racist?"

"Pale faces like to call us alcoholics and say we can't handle our liquor." Joseph is the one who explains this and my jaw hits the floor.

I look around them, waiting for the punch line but it doesn't come. "Pale faces are assholes."

"See? I knew I liked this girl." Bobby plays music from his

phone, not so loud that it's a burden on the atmosphere. "Right. Who's going first?"

"Joseph should," Nok states, smirking at his friend who has put the light of a flashlight against a glass bottle full of water. It makes the room glow a soothing green, highlighting everybody's features in a way that makes us all look kind of eerie and animated. "It's his idea."

"Fine, let me think." He sits and taps his feet on the floor. "When I was twelve, I stole twenty dollars from Elder Gray, because I needed to buy condoms for my babysitter."

Bobby starts howling with laughter. "You thought you were gonna fuck your babysitter?"

Joseph lifts a shoulder, looking proud of the moment. "She was so hot."

"I just can't believe you still had a sitter at twelve," I comment and Nok laughs in agreement.

Joseph flips me off and nudges Bobby with a foot to his bent knee. They're both sitting but Joseph is upright with crossed legs whereas Bobby is leaning back on his hands with his legs spread and bent at the knees.

"I once broke this ceremonial birthing jug and blamed it on my sister."

"That's a lie," I combat, raising a brow.

"Is not," he responds, raising his chin.

I laugh. "Did you get away with it?"

"Umm... yeah, duh."

Looking at Nokosi, I raise my nose a fraction, signaling that it's his turn.

"No, you," he instructs.

I cross my eyes and try to think of something, anything. But nothing comes to mind. In fact, not much of anything comes to mind. I look deep into the recesses of my brain for the memory of a birthday party, or a Christmas with my family.

My head starts to pound, like a battering ram is hitting it from the inside of the skull. The more I search for information, the worse it feels. How can I not remember anything?

But then my hand goes to my temple and the tender bruise still there beneath my skin.

Could the knock to my head have hurt me in such a way that I no longer remember my past?

"I held a group of men in a gas station at gunpoint and robbed them," I say quickly, simply to skim over my turn so they don't look at me so expectantly as I suffer this inner turmoil.

"No fucking way," Bobby breathes.

"She so did," Joseph states with pride and winks at me. "We were there."

"I kicked one of them in the face while they were already down, that's my confession," Nokosi adds and cringes after a swallow of the gin. The bottle is a quarter gone already.

"And you enjoyed it," I bait and his eyes flicker with the same thrill he felt that night. I see the same shadow in his eyes that I saw then. It's intriguing and so fucking sexy.

"How did that happen?" Bobby looks perplexed, terrified, but also impressed.

"It's a long story." I bring the bottle to my lips and pass it off.

"We have time," Bobby pleads, his eyes wide.

We let Joseph tell it because I'm not much of a storyteller and I'm still in turmoil. I shift away from Nok subconsciously, wondering the extent of damage that his tantrum has caused.

He notices my withdrawal and pulls me back with an arm around me. I lean into him and rest my arm along his thigh.

I'm being stupid, I'm just tired. It has been a long week... a long year.

"No fucking way. They just found and confirmed another body!" Bobby cries with excitement after his phone pings. He scrolls rapidly down the screen with his thumb, reading under his breath for a moment. He's a fast reader.

"That serial killer guy? The school one?" Joseph asks, moving to look over Bobby's shoulder as Bobby nods a yes.

"Bobby has a strange fascination with him," Nok whispers and bites the lobe of my ear.

"So does my sister," I mutter, feeling nauseous. "I don't like it. It makes me ill and anxious."

"Where did this one happen?" Nokosi asks, trailing his fingertips up and down my bicep.

I try to relax, but how can I? My memories are gone and they're talking about... I just can't even think about it.

"Denver, Colorado," Bobby replies, even more excited now. "That's really not all that far!"

"It's like a twenty-hour drive," Joseph says, laughing loudly.

"Road trip."

"You're vile," I state, shaking my head with judgment. "How can you be so blasé about death?"

"It's interesting."

"It could be you."

Bobby and Joseph look at each other, excitement evident once again. I roll my eyes but can't stifle a small laugh at their expressions. These are the kind of people who go looking for danger. We're more alike than I thought.

"Do they have any evidence pointing to who it might be?" Nok asks the question I too was thinking.

"Not that they've said. Apparently, suspects have been arrested and released." He clicks his fingers. "I personally believe that it's not just one person, I believe it's many."

"Many killers?" Joseph asks his enthusiastic friend, gulping the gin like it's water. I follow suit, cringing when the liquid touches my lips.

"Yeah, like maybe it's just a bunch of jilted girlfriends trying to throw off the cops?"

I roll my eyes at their conspiracy theories and drink more alcohol. I'm feeling buzzed already, but not so much that I can't control myself. Though I don't let Nok know that. I want him to think I'm thoroughly intoxicated.

I press my lips to his, eager to forget this night in his touch. He kisses me back, growling when I hold tight to the front of his shirt.

My sister comes to mind, her concerns that he might hurt me. She spoke of it again this morning and I know she's wrong. I know that I was wrong about him.

Sure, he's a bit of an asshole, but is he so much an asshole that he would hurt me if given the chance?

"I think," I mutter against his lips and hiccup convincingly, "that I'm a lil bit drunk."

He grins and holds out his hand for the bottle, closing his strong fist around the neck. "Then I should catch up."

I kiss his sweet, cherry gin lips and then taste it on his tongue with mine.

"What is that devious mind of yours concocting?" he whispers as his friends laugh and joke about murder mysteries and reservation police and how they'd all protect themselves like olden times. We shut them out, letting our eyes pass the communication between us.

"How we can get rid of them," I whisper and guide the bottle to my lips.

The drunker he thinks I am, the better.

"Boys," Nok yells suddenly, his eyes on mine, pupils dilated with arousal.

They both fall silent and look at us.

"Leave," he barks and sucks my lower lip into his mouth.

They laugh as they go, taking the rest of the gin with them, wishing us good fun and good fucks. *Little do they know.*

I fall backwards onto the blanket the moment the door closes and stretch like a contented cat.

Nokosi kneels at my feet, circling my ankles with his hands. It's a warming feeling and I moan when he starts to massage my calves, getting higher and higher with each stroke of his fingers. When he reaches my skirt, which stops above my knees, he drags it upwards baring my flesh and the triangle of my black thong.

His breath becomes ragged when I sit up slightly, letting my hair fall around my shoulders as I lean on my elbows and let my knees part.

"Rip it," I breathe, looking into his amazing eyes. The pupils expand, showing his arousal right as his hands grip the lace-covered fabric and pull it apart where my hip dips.

His smile is one of masculine approval and he makes quick work of the other side.

And then, when I'm free of the cloth that hides my sex, I part my knees again slowly and show him all that I am. The cool air hits my wetness making me shiver with excitement.

He watches as I push my own fingers between my lips and circle them over my clit. I have courage from the alcohol that I would not have otherwise. Well, that's not entirely true, but I wouldn't be so quick to part my thighs for a man I only like when it suits me and not because I think he's worth liking.

With eyes flickering from my gaze to my pussy, he lowers his head until I can feel his hot breath warming my sex. He kisses my thighs before he finally kisses me *there* and forces my hand away.

I breathe his name, not the shortened version. I want him to know that he's all I'm thinking about as his skillful lips and tongue dance me through a version of ecstasy that I have never experienced in my life.

He pushes a finger into me, just one as he dines on me so perfectly.

I almost squeeze his head with my thighs and have to force my hips to remain still. I want to buck against him, I want to press his face harder against me, but I fear I might lose what I'm feeling if I move even a fraction.

My back lowers to the ground and I stare at the shadows cast across the low ceiling of the shed.

My breathing is staggered and difficult to maintain the closer I get to the edge.

I hum and moan, letting him know I'm enjoying every swipe and swirl of his tongue as my sex holds tight to his finger. I almost wish it were thicker. But not *that*. Not tonight.

My orgasm shatters me.

Shatters me.

I cry out so loud, unable to control myself that I have to bite my hand to try and stifle it.

It pulses and burns, even as it dissipates, and he stops what he's doing to crawl up my body. His cock trails against my thigh, leaving a bead of precum as he goes.

I close my eyes gently as he ascends me. It's not hard to feign sleep when you've had a drink but all I really want to do is pull him on top of me and guide his cock into my throbbing sex.

"Hey," he whispers and laughs a little.

I let out a soft snore and feel him tense above me, resting on one arm as he pushes my hair back from my face.

"Lilith," he hisses, tapping my cheek with his fingers. I let it loll to the side. "Are you seriously fucking sleeping right now?" He taps me slightly harder. "LIL."

I let out a groan and let my leg drop. He lifts my hand and releases it. Dead weight. I'm good at this. I kind of want to laugh but I'm obviously not going to.

Although I nearly do when I think about it.

"Fuck," he breathes, and I feel his breath fan across my lips. But then he yells, "LILITH!" While shaking my shoulders. "Are you shitting me? Again? Fuck blue balls. *Fuck.*"

I feel him hesitate and I wonder if he's thinking about it. Wondering how easy it would be to just push his cock into my body, all open, wet, and ready for him. He drops onto me for a moment, taking most of his weight on both arms. I can feel him between us, trapped between his thigh and mine.

My womb quivers at the thought of him taking what he needs, and when he stands and yanks down his jeans I start mentally cheering. Not because I want him to do anything, but if he does, I was right all along and this will all be over soon. This game I'm playing.

I hear his jeans hit the floor; I hear him kick off his boots. It takes everything to not open an eye and watch him.

He's going to do it. He's going to rape me. Or he's going to try. I'll never let him get that far.

I wait a moment to see what he does. I'm not the type to jump to conclusions, I'll give him until the very last second before I stop him.

His hands pull on my ankles and then I feel soft fabric hook over my feet.

What the fuck is going on?

He tugs something up and up until he forcefully pulls it over my rear and it's covering me completely. His boxers... he's put me in his boxers. Because he ripped my thong... so he's covering me.

WHAT THE FUCK? This isn't right. This wasn't supposed to be how this went.

Then he pulls up his jeans and fastens them I assume because I don't hear much for a while.

"You absolute lightweight," he grumbles and then he's awkwardly lifting me into his arms. First in a cradle carry which I help with by wrapping my arm around his shoulders and sighing into his neck.

Ironically, because of how safe and comfortable I now feel, I pass out. I have no idea how he gets me home.

CHAPTER 16

The sun is shining from a tiny gap in the curtains, casting a strip of yellow light onto the wall that cuts down a calendar on January's model. A sexy woman with thick blonde hair sitting naked on a motorbike.

How teen boy of him. I smile to myself.

The quilt that protects me from the chill is dark green with black stripes, and the pillow is gray. It all smells clean and fresh like a flowery meadow. I smile and stretch languidly, sitting up when I hear a door downstairs close.

I'm still in yesterday's clothing, minus my skirt and thong as Nokosi put me in his boxer briefs last night. I check my body for injury but I'm otherwise okay, no worse for wear.

The room is empty, the space in bed beside me undisturbed, but then I notice a lump on the floor at the foot of the bed on what looks to be a futon mattress. Nokosi has his hair tied into a bun on the very top of his head and he's lying on his back, mouth open, eyes closed, breathing softly.

He was a gentleman last night in a way no man has ever been a gentleman to me before.

He helped me home, he helped me brush my teeth in the bathroom, he tucked me in and kissed my lips and then climbed into his own makeshift bed because he didn't want to take advantage, despite the fact I asked him to join me.

I thought I could entice him again, trap him again, put him in a position where he has to deny himself what I know he so badly wants. But he wouldn't even get in with me.

I really have gotten him all wrong.

I climb out of bed and sit on the edge of his. My knees sink into the soft mattress and my hand automatically goes to the tattoo that wraps around his bicep.

He's gorgeous. He could be a model he's so pretty to look at.

I touch his lower lip with my finger and feel the soft flesh twitch, then I trail it across the slight stubble of his jaw.

He hums a groan and shifts slightly, just enough for me to free the blanket and peel it down his body to his waist. I slide in beside him and press my cold feet against his.

He yelps and his eyes spring open to find mine.

"Morning," I whisper and circle his nipple with my fingertip. It tightens to a hard dark pebble.

He smiles lazily. "Morning, lightweight."

Giggling, I bury my face in his neck and hook my leg around his hips. "I'm so sorry about last night."

"Wait... what?"

"Huh?"

"Did you just say sorry?" He feigns surprise as I lean over him again to glare at him. "Can you say it again, just give me a sec to find my phone and record this moment."

I grab his dick and squeeze, but it only seems to excite him.

"What time is it?" he breathes as I move my hand over his hard, boxer-clad length. It's like steel and just the feel of it is making me drip with need.

"No idea." I kiss down his chest, startling him, and trace the contours of his pecs with my tongue.

"My dad will walk in, we have school," he hisses but his eyes are wide with lust and excitement.

I yank his boxers down and take him into my mouth, salivating even more when he cries out from the pleasure.

My head bobs, my lips tighten, I suck him deep and swallow around the head. He mutters curse word after curse word and his hand goes to my hair.

He starts bucking against me, desperate for release and even though I teased him last time and didn't let him come, he doesn't hold me down.

I release him, letting him pop from my mouth and his pleading eyes come to mine. He looks as desperate as I feel.

I push the boxers I'm wearing down, turning around so I can kick them off, then I straddle him.

"What are you doing?" he asks on a whisper as I hover above him.

"Fucking you," I reply and poise him at my entrance. I'm wet and ready but still have to roll my hips. He's got girth, a lot of it and I'm not used to it.

"JESUS... FUCK!" he cries out, squeezing his eyes shut and writhing beneath me as his hands grip my hips. He pushes up unable to control himself, sinking into the hilt, making us both cry out but me in particular because that stung a bit. I wasn't expecting that.

Still, no pain no gain. I don't waste any time.

"You okay?" he asks, panting, looking at where we're joined thigh to hip.

"Dandy." I wink at him and moan when we move together again, his movement an involuntary reflex when I clench him tight.

He guides me, helps me to move while I press my fingers against my clit as I ride him, holding his eyes and smiling every time he groans. His thumbs press into my hips so hard I just know I'm going to have little oval prints there for a while.

I start to rock aggressively, gripping his chest with both hands. The bite of pain dulls and, in its place, comes a wave of burning pleasure. I grab his hand and place it against my clit so I can do my thing without worrying about that. He willingly takes over, watching his cock disappear into my body, and tears burn my eyes at how amazing it feels. My body is tingling, searing, scalding. I want more... or less... I don't know. I'm on that precipice before the climax, desperately trying to tip myself over.

"Slow it," he begs, still rolling his thumb as I grind against him. "Slower."

"No," I argue, grinding faster and harder than before.

My nails bite into his skin and he groans, sounding desperate and almost delirious. I feel him thicken and it's enough to make me spiral with my orgasm. An orgasm I didn't think I'd be able to have.

He joins me, pulsing and throbbing deep inside, spilling all of himself into me. He moans with it so loud I cover his mouth with my own and we ride the wave together. Or more aptly I continue riding him until every trace of my orgasm has dulled to a low hum of pleasure and his cock has ceased its throbbing inside of me.

We stare at each other, my breasts gently touching his chest through fabric.

He cups my face with a shaking hand and smiles softly. Then he kisses me so tenderly my heart does this squeezing flip in my chest.

"Thank you," he breathes, sitting up so I can lock my ankles around his waist.

Our lips gently kiss again, our tongues softly taste, our bodies rock together, still joined. This is a good moment for me. For us.

I've never felt like this before. So at peace and warm. So welcomed and cherished.

We both startle when the sound of footsteps starts pounding up the stairs. I start to giggle quietly and he throws me off him and moves to the door, holding it shut with one hand while yanking his boxers up with the other.

"You're both going to be late to school if you don't move your asses," Nash calls through the door.

"What time is it?" I ask Nok who has just pulled open the door.

"Does Dad know she's here?"

"No, he left for work forty minutes ago."

Huh, I thought we had sex for longer than that.

Nash clears his throat. "There's blood on your hip dude, she bite your dick? The fuck?"

Nok looks down and slams the door when he too sees whatever is there.

I pull the blanket from my lap and chew my lip nervously when I see a few dry streaks of blood on my thigh.

"Did you get your period?" he asks quietly.

I shake my head. "Definitely not, there'd be a lot more blood if that was the case." I swallow harshly and stand. "Can I get a quick shower?"

"Sure," he mutters. "It's downstairs."

"I remember."

"Towels are in the closet."

"Thanks."

"I'll find you something to wear." He grabs my arm as I pass and pulls me into his body. We collide and then so do our mouths. "Are you okay?"

"Yeah. Umm... sorry about the blood. We must have just hit something at a funny angle." I feel a bit achy and sore, but nothing majorly bad. I don't feel like I've done any lasting damage anyway.

"Does it hurt?"

I shake my head. "Nothing a night of rest and some Tylenol won't fix."

We kiss again and then I escape to the bathroom to shower and freshen up, ready for the day.

"You were supposed to be here last night to look after your sister," Mom yells the second I walk through the door.

Thank God I convinced Nok to stay in his truck. At least he won't get to witness this dysfunctional family at its best.

I need my uniform; I can't really go to school without it.

"I texted her this morning, she's fine."

"She loses her will to live when you're not around."

"And you," I grumble, brushing past her.

"What was that?"

I turn to face her and stare into her frozen gray eyes that look so much like my own. "I said, *and you*. It's not fair that I'm constantly expected to be here. I'm eighteen, I have a life, I do everything for this family."

"You don't do enough. Your sister is sick..."

"That doesn't mean I shouldn't get to enjoy myself."

"But who knows how long she'll be with us?"

I rub my eyes with the heels of my palms. "Mom. Please. I'm always here when I can be. I'm doing this for her, remember?"

"Are you?" she spits back. "Because she's fading away, you're not around, and you seem to be shacking up with the guy you promised her."

"I'll find her someone else," I hiss and exit the kitchen, slamming the door behind me.

I head upstairs and don my uniform, grateful that it has been washed, dried, and hung up since the day before yesterday.

"Hey, I heard you and Mom fighting."

I sigh when I hear my sister's voice and turn to face her. She really does look deathly pale. "Oh... Christ. Are you okay? What happened?"

"Nothing, I'm fine. I just miss you."

"Yeah," I agree, zipping up my school skirt at the side. "I miss you too."

"I heard what you said to Mom."

I look at her and hesitate. This is my sister. My twin. My life. My best friend. "Can we talk about this later? I have to get to school."

"You don't *have* to get anywhere," she bites back, sounding and looking angry.

"Look," I say firmly. "I promised four weeks; it hasn't even been two. Both of you get off my fucking back."

"Five days," she answers petulantly. "I'm not waiting anymore. I'm giving you five days."

"What?" I breathe, feeling angry and shaky. "Do you think this is a fucking game, Willow? This that you're making me do."

"I'm not making you do anything!"

"YOU ARE BECAUSE IF I DON'T YOU JUST DO IT ANYWAY!"

We stare at each other, glaring, until she breaks down crying and falls to her knees. She's wheezing, she's weak and I immediately feel guilty. I move to her side and pull her frail body into my arms as she struggles for breath.

"MOM!" I yell. "MOM!"

Mom doesn't come. Of course she fucking doesn't; I bet she's gone already.

"Fuck." I help my sister get in her bed and tuck her in, placing her mask over her nose and mouth. "I'll be back, okay?"

"Okay," she rasps, holding the mask for dear life.

I race down the stairs and slip on my shoes, crushing the back of them under my heel. I yank open the door and run to the truck where Nok is waiting patiently.

"I'm sorry, Nok," I say after opening the door. "I have to stay with my sister. She's ill and my mom just fucking bailed."

He looks concerned. "You want me to stay with you?"

"NO!" I panic, feeling my heart race but when I see a flash of hurt in his eyes I quickly calm myself. "My sister doesn't like new people. You'll just distress her. You're hot and she'd hate for you to see her like she is."

"Okay." He climbs from the truck and pulls me into his chest. "I'll see you later?"

I nod and push him against the truck so I can kiss him. "Maybe. If not, it'll be tomorrow."

"Damn, I was really hoping for more of this morning," he jokes and grabs my ass with his hands. "I'll call you later."

I step back and give him a wave as he climbs back into his car. Then I head upstairs after searching the house for my absent dickhead of a mother and sink into bed with my sister.

"I'm all yours," I whisper, and we face each other. "What do you want to do?"

"Let's watch horror movies?"

"My life is one massive horror movie," I mumble and her smile fades.

"Seriously?"

"No, I'm kidding... kind of. But... I guess I just don't want to do this anymore."

She frowns, her dark blonde brows pull together. "You know we don't have a choice. I don't have a choice."

"Maybe we can stay."

"No, we have to keep moving... Mom..."

I roll onto my back and stare at the ceiling. "Mom can go fuck herself."

"We need her. I need her."

"No, we can get you help..."

"I'm beyond fucking help, Lilith, I'm dying, remember? Do you want me to spend the rest of my days locked away? You promised."

"But... we can't keep doing this. It weighs so heavily on me."

She glares at me and sits up, pulling the blanket from my body and letting it fall from hers. "We have to. I *have* to. And I'm not leaving Mom."

"Mom doesn't want to be here," I grit, climbing from the bed and stomping to the window. "We're tying her down. She's shackled to us and she's miserable."

She doesn't respond, because she knows it's true.

After a moment though, she sniffles, and I turn away from the rain-splattered window to find her crying.

"Hey," I murmur softly and rush back over to her. "What is it? Why are you sad?"

"You're going to leave me soon, for him, aren't you?"

I stare into her eyes, so full of longing, love, and sadness. "What?"

"You're falling for him. I can tell. I can feel it."

I roll my eyes and laugh a little bit, until her scowl forces me to stop. "I'm not falling for him. I hardly know him."

"But you want to stay," she points out, pouting petulantly.

Growling, I move back to the window and stare out across the street. "I'm fucking tired, tired of moving, tired of life, tired of school, tired of helping you do what you do."

"I need it. You know I do."

"You don't need it," I snarl, gripping the window frame. "We need friends. We need our lives back. You need to get out of this fucking house again and experience it all."

"I'm not ready."

"You never are," I reply softly. "Not until you do what you do and I just... I don't know how you find the strength."

"It's the only thing that keeps me going." My heart sinks at her admission until she adds, "Apart from you of course. You're the number one thing that keeps me going. But I need it."

"You don't need it. You're just angry. Understandably so."

She picks at the little lint balls on her quilt. "Fine... I'll try, for you. But you have to spend more time with me."

"Okay."

"You will?"

I smile. "I will. Maybe you want to meet Nok? We could all hang out together?"

"No," she snarls, sounding more animal than human. "No. No boys. I'm not ready for that."

"Okay. One step at a time."

"I don't know how you can be. After what happened."

I shrug my shoulders and scan the street below. It's empty. Everybody has either gone to work or school. "I don't want to talk about it. It doesn't feel real to me anymore."

"Feels real to me."

"Because it happened to you."

"It happened to you too," she whispers, so quiet I hardly heard her.

I daren't tell her I don't remember, that I think what Nokosi did with his truck caused damage to my head that scattered all my memories. I checked it out online, and apparently, it's common with a concussion which I had.

It'll right itself. My brain will unscramble, and I'll be better.

"I wish it didn't have to be this way," I whisper more to myself than to anyone else.

We stay like this for a while until my phone starts ringing, I expect it to be school, but instead it's a private number. I ignore it and climb back into bed with my coughing sister.

"We'll be okay," she assures me. "I promise. I'll get better and we'll be okay."

"I hope you're right."

"We just have to keep moving. We can't stop. Not for anyone. Especially not for a guy."

CHAPTER 17

Willow

I look at Lilith sleeping beside me, having taken one of my pills to help her fall under, and then brush her pastel pink hair from her face. Even though we're twins I always considered Lilith to be the prettier of the two of us and I still think that today. Especially while I'm so fucking weak.

I pad to the window she was staring out of earlier. The sky is black and the street dark and deserted. I stare at the space where her boyfriend's truck pulled up after school to try and convince her to go out with him. She refused. He returned an hour later with food and they ate it in the bed of his truck as the sun set.

He's going to take her from me. She's going to stay here and leave me to die alone with our vacant mother and the ghost of our dad looming over my head.

I've been patient, I've been trying to keep myself busy, but the urge is there. The thirst. The anger that consumes me.

What happened to me and Lilith was unimaginable, incomprehensible. Sick, twisted, vile...

I'll protect her until I can't anymore. I'll protect her until my last breath leaves my body. I'll protect her like I couldn't that night.

The night I let them into our house. The night we were no longer sixteen-year-old girls, singing crappy duets and dreaming of a happy future.

The night they defiled us, forced themselves upon us, took their turns on our screaming virginal bodies, passed us around like a bag of chips and then left us for dead.

Men, boys... arrogant, preppy, jockey, fucking popular school-boys. They're dangerous. All of them.

I can't let her get lured into his charm. He's not a good guy, he's not.

How can she be so blind?

How can she ask me to stay knowing it's because she wants to be with him?

"I'll protect you," I whisper, kissing her temple. "I won't let him hurt you."

I climb from my bed and cover her with the blanket. I get dressed and move to the mirror to adjust and brush my brown hair. It's a mess so I braid it and add a bit of gloss to my lips. I don't bother with other makeup, not anymore. I don't have the time or energy.

Lilith

"I am fucking exhausted," I say, dragging my ass into Nok's truck. He wanted to pick me up this morning. "I took one of my sister's sleeping pills last night and it has made me so fucking groggy."

He drags me closer. "Did you have fun?"

I nod and yawn. "Yeah, we just watched movies and ate junk."

"So..." He wets his lips and narrows his eyes. "You didn't come by my house last night?"

I give him a look. "Are you kidding? I swear I didn't even leave home last night. Why?"

"Dad said he saw somebody who looked like you just standing outside our house last night."

My heart stops. "For real?"

"Would your sister... no... stupid question. He was probably seeing things." He pulls me in for a kiss so deep it leaves me breathless. "How is she?"

"She's a lot better, thanks." I place my hand on his thigh and snuggle into his side. "So your dad saw someone outside your house? That's weird."

"He said she was just standing there, staring, this dark shape in the night."

"Y'all should invest in some floodlights."

"They scare the animals."

I quirk a brow. "You don't want to scare away bears and mountain lions?"

"It's their home too," he replies, smiling as he maneuvers the car with ease. "We leave them alone; they leave us alone for the most part."

"Coming from the guy who littered on our first date."

He pinches my thigh. "I was gonna clean it up. And... that wasn't our first date."

"It wasn't?"

"That night was a disaster."

"Yep."

"Maybe we can redo it?" I'm surprised he's even asking. "Don't look at me like that. I said I was sorry."

"You didn't, not really, but I forgive you anyway."

He raises my hand to his lips. "Forgiveness in my tribe is such a powerful thing. I appreciate you giving me that." We share this sweet moment in silence, but he ruins it by adding, "And I forgive you for falling asleep after I ate you two nights ago."

"I fucked you, didn't I?"

"You have no idea how painful my balls were."

I laugh loudly. "I fucked you though. I'm exempt from your ire based on that fact alone."

"You certainly did." His grin is devious and longing. I feel it in my core, just his smile turns me on. "Are we still going to that party later?"

I nod. "Fuck yeah."

"Your sister is okay with that?"

"Of course. I'll just spend Saturday with her." He kisses my hand again and then bites my wrist making me squeal, pull free, and slap him upside the head. "Dude, pay attention before we die in a car accident."

"That sucks though, I was going to invite you to work with me this weekend. I've got two survival role-plays booked in."

"Sunday?"

He nods. "Sunday it is then."

We head to school and I grin condescendingly at Barbie when we pass her standing by her car alone. Her friends have ditched her it seems. It's less than what she deserves for what she tried to do to Nokosi.

When he sees me staring at her, he hooks his arm around my neck and kisses my hair.

"Jealous?" I mouth at her and she looks away with a trembling jaw.

Stupid bitch.

She's lucky we haven't handed her in to the cops, but then something tells me Nokosi doesn't have a good relationship with them. And what kind of hypocrite would that make me anyway after all I've done?

People stare as we walk in together, intrigued by our relationship. Not that we care.

His best school buddies Ethan and Payne meet us on the way.

"So you're a thing now?" Payne asks, pushing his trimmed hair back with a dark hand.

Nokosi nods. "Yep."

"Well... welcome to the pack, Lilith." Ethan grabs me from Nok and holds me tight to his side, I know it's to wind Nok up but I don't like it so I dig him in the ribs with my elbow and stomp on his foot.

He cries out and staggers as I return to the crook of Nok's arm.

"Don't touch her, she doesn't like it," Loki comments as he passes and flashes me a grin. "Sup, Lil, lunch later?"

"She has plans," Nokosi growls aggressively and I realize that we're likely a match made in psycho heaven, also known as hell.

I tip back to look at him and accept his kiss. I really enjoy kissing him. It might be my new favorite thing to do.

"Sorry," I say to Loki but I'm not sorry in the slightest. I don't care about him or his feelings. Not that he's upset. He only hangs with me for the gossip.

"Not sorry," Payne adds, shouldering past him and sticking his tongue out.

I wonder if Payne is an asshole but swiftly push that thought from my head. I have to convince my sister to let us stay. Mom won't care. She can sleep in the office wherever she goes and leave us here, she can just send the money or something until I get a job that provides well enough. The main issue is my sister, not just her illness but also her other needs. I can't just deny her those and I doubt I'll be able to convince her otherwise anyway.

My phone rings in my pocket, withheld again. I ignore it as always and stuff it back in my bag.

"What's wrong?" Nokosi asks.

"Absolutely nothing," I lie and reach for my locker. "I'm happier than I've been in forever."

"Want to skip and fuck?"

I laugh and move my head to the side when he kisses my neck. "Don't tempt me."

CHAPTER 18

The party is heaving. It's insane but it's mostly outside so it's not so bad.

I watch somebody snort cocaine off the porch railing, and somebody else do a handstand on a keg and drink until beer spills into their eyes.

Nokosi and I stick together, hand in hand as we make our way around back to where the people he knows are waiting. I'm surprised to see Vienna here with Bobby and a couple of the other res kids. They all wave, all but Vienna who glares at me with dark eyes and pursed, thick lips.

I'd love to punch her in the face purely because that face has been kissed by the man I feel so entirely obsessed with. I hope this feeling never dies.

Nokosi grabs us both a beer from the cooler by the steps.

"Try not to pass out on me tonight, huh?" he says, smiling in the dark.

"Planning on sneaking me into your room?"

"Dad's not home, no sneaking required."

I wet my lips and grin. "And Nash is picking us up."

"Exactly."

"Well then, let's get toasted."

"I love toast!" somebody drunkenly shouts, and the house starts cheering.

The fuck?

"People are weird," I murmur.

"Yup." We reach his group of friends and I'm introduced to each of them, all but Vienna who won't look at either of us. She's really pissed off.

You snooze you lose and all that.

I'll admit it. I'm smug.

"How long were you two dating?" I ask Nokosi quietly when we sit across from her on wicker furniture.

"Two years," he replies, and I almost spray my beer everywhere. "On and off. We weren't dating, we were fooling around."

I gape at him. "Two fucking years?"

"On and off," he repeats, grinning at me. I shake my head, but he turns my face back to him. "Two years on and off and I didn't feel a fraction of how I feel when I'm with you."

"You mean horny?"

"Well, there is that." He grins, sliding his hand up my jean-clad thigh. "But I'm talking more about the passion and excitement. Whenever I'm with you, I feel like I never know what's going to happen." He winks at me and his smile broadens to one of mischief. "Such as, are we gonna murder someone today? Or maybe rob a bank? Or maybe you'll push me off a cliff? Who knows?"

I snigger into his shoulder and then rest my healing temple against it.

"I'm not that bad." Oh, but I really am. This past year isn't full of good deeds in the slightest. In fact, I can't think of a single thing I've done that's good. Does saving Nok and Joseph from those assholes at the gas station count? Or did I fuck up my good karma when I robbed them? I drain my beer and listen to the conversation. I've never been one to join in in conversations, I like to listen.

They go back and forth, bantering and chatting about things that don't interest me, until they finally find a subject I can't ignore.

"Aren't you a twin, Lilith?" Payne asks and I wonder how he knows that, but then figure Nok probably told them yesterday when I was off school looking after her.

I nod. "Yep. Why?"

"Do you have like a psychic link to her?" a girl beside Vienna asks. I think her name is Marla.

"Psychotic link maybe," Bobby puts in playfully. I throw my empty bottle at him which he catches with ease and a pleasant laugh, and I catch the new one he tosses back.

My hand aches as I try to twist the cap off. "We do sometimes, like I can usually tell when she's sad or hurt, even when she's not around. Not always... but when we were six, she broke her leg when playing at a friend's and I was at home and I started screaming. I just had this horrific pain in my leg. They had to x-ray both of us despite the fact only she was injured. I was fine but there was no denying the pain we were both in."

"That's so weird," Vienna mutters, rolling her eyes.

"Are you the same in most ways?" the girl beside her asks, seeming to be quite intrigued by us. Some people are. They love the idea of having somebody identical in their life. It's not always what it's cracked up to be.

"No, we're so different."

"How?"

God, she asks so many questions and I still can't get this fucking cap off the bottle. "Willow was always the bolder one of us both, super flirtatious. Sexy. Funny. I was always more withdrawn, sarcastic, less likely to join in at parties." That last part was a massive clue to get them to leave me alone.

"I'm sorry she's sick," Ethan says earnestly, leaning over Payne to pat my arm.

"Open this," I demand of Nok and thrust the bottle into his hands. He gives it one easy twist and it pops open, but it fizzes over from all the shaking.

I suck his thumb clean, making him growl and bring my lips to his.

We make out for a while, giggling and laughing together when the others tell us to separate. We don't separate. We don't ever separate. I never want to separate from him again.

Something changed between Nokosi and me. I don't know when. I don't know how. But it changed and here we are. I've never felt so happy and out of control.

"Why are we at this stupid party when your house is empty?" I whisper in his ear.

He tries to think of a reason but relents with a lusting smile touching his lips. "Let's go?"

"Let's go," I confirm, excited at the prospect of spending the entire night in bed with him.

"Nokosi, wait," Vienna calls when we stand. She glances at me and her lips turn up with a sneer. "Can I have a word?"

Nok glances at me as though seeing if I'm okay with it.

I don't care. So long as she doesn't touch him.

"Remember what I said about your truck," I whisper in his ear and he chuckles under his breath before following Vienna across the yard.

I watch her fold her arms, unfold them, fold them, unfold them, and then start waving them around. She shifts from hip to hip as she yammers on, face expressive and annoyed.

Not to be petty or whatever but she's said more than *a word*.

"Nok," I call impatiently, and she really glares at me now. I smirk back. Silly bitch wants to play, I'll play.

Nok holds up his finger and touches Vienna's elbow to get her attention. Oh hell no. I'm on the edge. He's touching her. Fuck. I'm so mad.

What is wrong with me?

But then when I think about it, it's always there. This rage at life, this anger that I keep suppressed the best I can.

Whatever he says to her has her looking at the floor with a sad expression on her face.

I move to him, figuring they're done and Nok takes my hand. "See you later, Vienna."

"Fuck you, Nok," she replies, and he hooks an arm around my waist to stop me from ripping her shit-looking hair out.

"Behave," he whispers against my ear and turns me back the way we entered.

"What did she want?"

He beams at me, smug satisfaction all over his face. "She wanted me to leave you and be with her."

I almost laugh. "Did you tell her that's not an option?"

"I offered her a three-way."

I smack his chest and bite his lip, squealing when he bends and puts his shoulder into my stomach and lifts me from the ground.

We enter his house attached at the lips, much to the annoyance of Nash who declares, "Guess I'll put my headphones in."

"Run," Nok whispers and I squeal as he chases me up the stairs and into the bedroom.

He pins me on the bed, holding my hands above my head as he devours my mouth and then my neck. I moan loudly, I can't help it. It tingles so fucking bad. I can't decide if I want to laugh, cry, or come.

My arms ache when he releases them to tug down my jeans.

He wastes no time. He doesn't eat me this time, doesn't do much foreplay at all. It's as if he can't wait to be inside of me and fuck it if I don't find that so hot.

After slotting himself between my thighs, he pushes inside and leans up only to help me remove my T-shirt and bra, freeing my breasts to his gaze for the first time.

He bites my nipple as his hand massages my other breast and his hips start thrusting in and out, faster and harder with each passing second.

It aches but in a really good way.

I wasn't lying when I told him that I'm tight down there.

I reach between us to find my clit and he helps me by pulling out and flipping me over, so my ass is in the air. I continue to tweak myself as he pins me by my shoulders to the bed.

My moans are muffled by the pillow, but they are still loud and so are his. This is amazing. My entire body is on fire, as though he just dropped a spark onto a puddle of gasoline. I'm lit. Well and truly.

"Don't stop," I beg, rolling my fingers around the sensitive bundle of nerves between my thighs. I can feel his cock pushing in and out, faster and faster as I stop breathing.

And then he sticks a wet thumb in my ass.

I squeak and try to lurch away but I can't move. "Dude, no, that's an exit not an entrance."

"Shut up," he responds harshly, his breathing ragged. "Shut up and fucking take what I give you."

Why does his command make my pussy clench?

"You're a dick."

"My dick is in you, baby, feel that?"

I laugh and then groan when he slowly starts to turn his thumb. Oh wow. That feels insane. If I thought I was tingly before I was so fucking wrong. I squeeze him with both holes, holding him tight as my orgasm powers through me.

I scream into my pillow, his name, a string of curse words... I'm fucked. Well and truly.

He hammers into me harder and harder, grunting when I find his balls between my thighs and roll them with a tender touch.

As I'm spiraling back from my climax, he's building up to his.

"I want to put it in your ass," he says, pulling out suddenly and pressing it against the *wrong fucking hole.*

"Dude, you're a lot bigger than your thumb," I complain, glancing at his excited face over my shoulder. "That's gonna hurt."

"You can handle a bit of pain," he whispers, spitting on his cock and smearing it there.

"Oh God," I whisper and hug the pillow to my face. "Have you ever done this before?"

"Nope. Have you?"

I shake my head, no.

"Fuck yes. I get to deflower both your holes." He presses on and the ache is immediate. It hurts a bit. No... *a lot.* "More lube?"

"Are you kidding me right now? This isn't fun."

"It will be."

"How do you know? You've never done this before."

His eyes cloud over and his lips twist with a look I can't decipher, anger perhaps, reminiscence?

"Whoa," I say softly, turning and stopping our *"fun."* "What was that look all about?"

"Nothing," he replies bitterly, "just get back on your knees."

"No," I answer, grasping his cock with my hand. "Talk to me. What's wrong?"

"I don't want to talk about it," he snaps, angry now.

"That means there is something," I mumble and roll my thumb over the head of his cock. He trembles and slots himself between my thighs. "You can trust me with it. I'm the least likely to talk about your shit."

"Stop talking," he whispers, sucking on my ear as he sinks back inside my pussy. "You really are so fucking tight."

Yep.

I wrap my legs around his ass and whimper when he sinks all

the way in. I circle my hips to meet him but we take it slower this time. It feels good again, so good, so tender and tingly.

I feel him come, his body shakes with it, his thighs tense with it, his hips buck with it and his face contorts with so much pleasure.

When he collapses on top of me, I push him to the side and catch my breath.

He rests his head on his hand and he stares at the ceiling.

"Are you going to tell me what happened to you? I know that look. It's the same look my sister gets in her eyes every time she..." I stop myself, letting my words drift off. I hardly know this guy and I'm ready to tell him our business? No. That's dangerous. He can't know about us and what we've been through. He might ask questions. Questions I can't answer.

"Every time she what?"

I kiss the space above his nipple. "If your secrets are yours, mine are mine."

"Fair deal." He sighs heavily, as though there's a weight on his body so strong. "I like you, Lilith."

My body tenses with glee as I search his eyes for any sign of a lie. "I'm not a likable person."

"I know, it's not an easy thing to do on my part," he jests, kissing the end of my nose.

"Fuck you," I hiss playfully and twist his nipple.

He rolls me onto my back and narrows his eyes. "I say something nice and you cause me pain. How's that fair?"

"Sorry, boo, did I hurt you? Let me kiss it better."

"Such a bitch," he growls and goes for my neck again. I kick and laugh and try to buck him off. I can hardly breathe.

"Stop," I beg, wriggling under him.

"You guys want pizza?" Nash yells up the stairs.

"Fuck yeah," Nok calls back, becoming distracted for long enough. I take the opportunity to wriggle my hips until his recently hardened cock is at my sex. He tenses and looks at me. "Again?"

"You can't handle it?"

"Oh I fucking can." He thrusts inside.

"Pepperoni?" Nash yells as Nok grinds against me.

"Ham and pineapple," I reply, trying not to moan because whatever Nok is doing with his hips is incredible.

"Ew," Nok says at the exact same time as Nash calls it. He looks down at me, disgusted. "Pineapple doesn't go on pizza."

"And dicks don't go up asses but who am I to judge?"

He laughs into my neck and his entire body shakes with it. Including his penis.

"Pepperoni is great, Nash," I say loud enough for him to hear. "I love a bit of sausage."

Nok laughs even harder and I smile triumphantly. When I'm with him, it feels different to when I'm at home. I feel different. I feel like I can be myself no matter what and he'll accept me for it all.

Well, maybe not for all of it. But most of it.

There are some things better left in secrecy.

CHAPTER
19

Willow

My sister is living my life and on one hand it feels really unfair, but on the other, I don't think I can be what she is now. I've seen too much, experienced too much. I hold so much anger inside that it's better for me to stay hidden. That and I'm so weak, so dizzy, so frail in comparison to what I used to be.

I've been watching her, all loved up, stealing kisses and holding hands with that... man, boy, whatever should he be named. It's disgusting. Apart from Saturday I've hardly seen her at all. She comes home to bathe and change and head to school so happy and I should be happy for her. She hasn't been so joyous in over a year since... the event that destroyed our lives.

Well, the sickness had already taken hold, and it was my eagerness to have us both live life to the fullest that put us in the path of those monsters who showed me how painful life truly is. Dying a slow and painful death is nothing in comparison to being trapped in a slow and painful life.

Five days have passed since my sister first stayed out all night and I can tell she has fallen too deep already. She can't see it and we fight over it. He's going to hurt her, and I can't bear it. My time is limited now. We were supposed to do one more before the end and she is taking that from me.

"Lilith, loca!"

I freeze at the sound of an unfamiliar voice coming my way.

"I knew that was you. Did you change your hair?" the darker-skinned boy asks when I turn to face him. I don't know who this is, nor do I care.

I'm not here for him.

"You're mistaken, I'm not Lilith."

He looks confused, his lips form an O and then something takes hold in his eyes, a realization occurs. "You're her twin, right?"

I nod and look past him for Nokosi. "Is her boyfriend with you?"

"Yeah, he's just filling up the gas tanks."

I steady myself on my walking stick, it hurts the palm of my hand but if I don't use it, I fall, and I can't fall. I feel so ill. But not to the extent that I can't be here to do this. To save my sister from these *men*.

"I'd like to meet him."

"No worries, I can introduce you."

"But..." I hold his wrist and bite on my lip. "Please don't tell her you saw me. She'll say I'm meddling, and she'll worry what with me being out when I'm not supposed to be." He looks unsure about my request, so I continue, "I never get to do much. It'd mean a lot to a dying girl."

"Fuck me, you're as savage as she is. Pulling the dying-girl card... how do I say no to that?"

I smile broadly. "You don't."

Laughing he moves to the door and holds it open for me, taking my arm as I hobble outside, back into the cold and drizzle. Although the drizzle doesn't touch me thanks to the roof overhead.

"Nok!" the man yells to get his attention; he then looks at me.

"I'm Joseph, by the way, Nok's best bud and funniest guy this side of Oregon."

"It's nice to meet you. I'm Willow."

Nok, the man I loathe, the man taking my sister from me is gorgeous, of course he is, they usually always are. His hair is thick, long, and different to any guys' I've ever seen, it's no wonder she fell for him. He's got muscles for days and lips so thick I bet he gives amazing head.

He looks surprised to see me. "You're not Lilith."

"Was it the hair that gave you away?" I ask playfully, twirling a strand of my brown mop around my finger. "Or the cane?"

"Neither," he mutters, frowning as he extends his hand. "You're just different."

"In a good way I hope."

He doesn't reply, he doesn't feel safe. I like that. Means his instincts are sharp. Means he'll be more difficult to get rid of. I like a challenge.

"It's funny that I bumped into you, actually. I keep saying to my sister that I want to meet the guy who is taking up all her time at the moment." I tuck my hair behind my ears. "But I can see why. She's got excellent taste."

He smiles an arrogant, charming grin that makes me want to wrap the pump around his throat and squeeze until his eyes pop out of his head. "I agree."

Ugh. Cringe. How can she like this?

"How are you feeling now?"

"A lot better today," I say as he looks around for his girlfriend. "She's not here. I kind of snuck out."

"Naughty." He's smirking again. "Why?"

I pull a Hershey's bar out of my pocket. "I wanted a snack."

"And Lilith wouldn't take you?"

"She got into a fight with Mom and took my sleeping pills again. She does that when shit gets anxious."

I'm surprised of the flicker of concern that shines through his eyes.

Joseph snorts. "Lilith gets anxious?"

"Only when Mom's involved," I mutter, crinkling my nose.

"Go pay for the gas," Nok tells Joseph who nods and does as he's told like a little puppy. "It's nice to finally meet you." He tucks his hands into his pockets. His biceps flex.

"Likewise, I'd like to say I've heard a lot about you, but Lilith keeps you to herself." I look him up and down, imagining him naked to really try and see what she likes about this guy. He's everything we bitch about in a man.

Again, he doesn't speak. She did say he's a man of few words. Another thing she must really like about him.

"How did you get here?" he asks after a moment, looking around the space.

"Dad's car," I point to the Prius parked across from the gas station.

"Your dad?" He looks perplexed. "Isn't he dead?"

"Yes, but his car didn't get buried with him." I laugh pleasantly, hoping it doesn't sound as forced as it feels, it's nice to joke a little about such a tragedy. It takes the edge off the grief we feel. "Well, anyway. I should probably get back. It was nice meeting you."

"Likewise."

"Umm," I place my hand on his arm but release it when a coughing fit takes over my body. It's a side-effect of the medication I'm on. My immune system is shot so I have a constant chest infection. "Sorry." He rubs my back, his eyes softer and sad now.

When I return to the more composed state I was in before my lung almost shot out of my mouth, I give him a mournful and imploring look. "Please don't tell Lilith you saw me."

"I don't feel comfo—"

"Please," I beg, sticking out my lower lip. "If she knew I snuck out she'd be so fucking mad."

"Well, if it's dangerous."

"Of course it's dangerous." I let my hands rise and fall. "Look at me. I'm a broken fucking mess. I'm dying. I don't know how much time I have and she's intent on keeping me for as long as possible." I step closer and put my hand on his chest. "Please don't tell her I was here."

"Fine," he concedes, but he still looks unhappy about it. "Maybe now you can hang out with both of us together? Your sister said you don't like to go out."

"That, mixed with how sick I usually am, I don't normally get the chance." I start walking to my car and he follows suit. "It really was so nice to meet you, Nok."

"You too." He opens my car door for me and takes my cane as I lower myself inside.

I wind down the window after closing the door and smile up at him. "She won't let us hang out."

"What?" he looks confused.

"She won't let us hang out," I half lie, "that's mostly the reason why I don't come."

He looks even more confused. "Why not?"

I shrug my shoulders and feign sadness. "I think she's embarrassed by me."

"Or me."

I drag my eyes down his body again, provocatively. He notices and shifts, feeling self-conscious no doubt. "Remember your promise, Nokosi. It was lovely to meet you."

I drive away, leaving him in my rearview mirror, and head home. Sneaking in as quietly as a mouse and climbing into bed without brushing my teeth. I really don't want to wake her.

201

Lilith

"You're so quiet today," I comment, looking at Nokosi who is on the opposite side of the bank. We're spear fishing or practicing at least. Both of us have carved new spears, these two better than the last. It's a lot harder than it looks.

His father wants to teach me how to grill a fish the right way but of course I have to catch it first. Dasan is so lovely and is just as charming as his sons, but he's all about those life lessons. It says something when you prefer a parent that's not your own.

"I'm concentrating," he replies, looking up at me for a moment. "You should be concentrating."

I lunge downwards and spear a fish through its body. I'd been concentrating just fine. "I was just waiting for you to go first so you didn't feel emasculated."

He shakes his head, looking aghast. "How do you do that?"

"I used to play hook a duck a lot. I don't know if that's related."

"Those are not the same at all." I love it when he smiles at me like this. I've done that. I've made him this way. I make him happy.

"Hurry up and spear one so you can fuck me up a tree and we can go to your father's and pretend I'm a nice and stable female that his son might one day marry."

Nokosi chuckles and lunges but misses. "What makes you think I won't marry you anyway?"

"I'm not the marrying type." My phone vibrates. Another unknown caller. I've been getting those a lot recently. I ignore it again and toss my phone onto our little pile of discarded clothing. "I'm the fuck-for-a-while-and-break-your-heart type."

"You couldn't break my heart if you tried."

I feel a jolt of pain, pain that's unfamiliar and unique. I can't place it and I want to deny it and what it might mean. "Why? Because you could never love me?"

He looks at me as though I'm crazy. "Uh, no. Because I'll never let you leave me."

"So... you think you might fall in love with me?" I really wish a powerful and treacherous stream wasn't separating us right now because letting him see all of me while we talk about something so important is making me feel open and vulnerable.

"I think I'd be stupid and broken if I didn't."

I smile down at my fish, unable to contain my glee. "Me too."

He lunges for another fish and this time gets it through its tail. I almost feel bad for it when he has to bash it against a rock to finish the job. But he finally has a fish.

"Well done," I praise and drop mine into the bucket. He throws his over and I move the bucket in its path to catch that one too. We walk along opposite sides of the stream, headed for the shack and the rocks that create a slippery path across. "So... I was thinking about staying."

His eyes are guarded, as though daring not to hope. "You think it's possible?"

"Well, I just thought... and it's just a crazy fucking thought... but..." I chew on my lip. "I want to stay with you. What if we do the adult thing? There are small cabins, trailers, and even houses for sale on the res. Maybe we can look into getting one together?" Before he can shoot me down, I add, "I know we hardly fucking know each other, but I'm all about the adventure and—"

"What about your sister?"

Right. My sister. "I don't know yet. I'd have to speak to her." I almost let myself be hopeful and human for a moment then. I almost forgot about all the things I've done and who I am.

How long until the police catch up to us? How long until I'm thrown into a maximum-security prison? Could Nok ever love me if he knew what I'd helped my sister do?

But what if they never figure it out and my sister dies of her illness and I'm left alone for the rest of my life? Do I deserve it?

Sure, I had nothing to do with it when she was doing what she felt she must to innocents for kicks, but I was an accomplice after that.

What do people get in prison for being an accomplice to that these days?

"I don't want to freak you out, so act natural," Nok says suddenly, his fake smile in place but his tone deep and dark. "Remember you said that there was a man watching us before?"

I nod once, also smiling.

"He's standing twenty feet away, watching us. Don't look. Not until I can get across and protect you."

Of course I look. I couldn't stop myself if I tried and sure enough there he is, the exact same guy as before, standing in the shadows, watching us from under a hood. My heart starts to race. A cold chill tickles my spine, putting me on the alert.

I can hardly breathe.

I drop the bucket and hold the spear like a weapon.

"For fuck's sake, you just couldn't wait, could you?" Nok hisses and I hear him start to run.

"Who the hell are you? You creepy bastard!" I yell, taking a step towards the faceless shadow man. "Come out before I come to you with my sharp pointy thing."

The man smiles, an evil grin that flashes a sharp white tooth and makes his eyes look as if they're glowing red.

My breath catches in my throat and fear unlike any I've felt before courses through me. But I've made fear my bitch in the past and this time is no different.

I stand my ground, staring him out, keeping my eyes on him so he doesn't evade me.

"I swear I'm going to jab you through your fucking eye, you pervert," I bellow and it echoes all around.

He raises his hand and wags his long, pasty-looking fingers. I glance at Nok when I hear his foot slip off a rock and splash in the water. He rights himself, but when I turn back, the man is gone.

FUCK!

Where has he gone?

Nok finally joins me, his own spear raised.

"Where'd he go?" he asks, panting.

I shrug and venture deeper into the trees, cautious of my surroundings. I'm not scared anymore, not really, I'm just pissed off. Unless he has a gun, he's got no chance against us both with long sharp spears.

How the hell did he vanish so quickly?

"I bet he just comes to watch us fuck," Nok suggests on a whisper. "I don't want to turn my back to the trees now. I feel like we're being watched."

"How often does he watch us to know when we're coming out here is what I want to know?" I sigh and lower my spear a fraction. We kick the ground around where the man was standing. "No footprints. Who the hell is this prick?" I cup a hand to my face. "You fucking scaredy-cat pussy. Run while you still can, asshole."

We look around, listening to the wind in the leaves, the running stream, the cries of animals in the distance. I don't pick up a footstep or a cough, or anything for that matter. Nothing remotely human.

"We should probably stop coming out here for a while." Nok takes hold of my bicep and guides me back to our things. I constantly look over my shoulder and so does he. "Does he still remind you of your dad?"

I shake my head. "Not even a little bit."

"Good." He kicks a rock across the ground. "Now we can't have tree sex."

"That's okay. I'll give you a blowy in the bathroom after dinner."

Hooking his arm around my shoulder he admits, "And this is why I would be stupid not to love you."

"I feel very privileged for a white chick."

"As you should."

We head to his house, mindful of our surroundings and lock the door to his house behind us. Nok's dad greets us and kisses both of my cheeks. He tells me how good it is to see me, and I return the sentiment. But then he and Nok discuss the man that Nok admits he thought was a figment of his imagination and to say the mood darkens would be an understatement.

"A flash of a tooth you said?" he asks me, frowning with thought.

I nod. "Like the light hit the point just right. He was far away but not so far that I couldn't see it."

Nok snorts so I punch him in the arm.

"Don't ridicule your friends, son," Dasan chastises. "They'll stop confiding in you."

"Oh heaven forbid she never tells me about pointy-toothed, disappearing men again," he responds with a heavy amount of sarcasm.

I punch him again and his dad chuckles.

Then I ask, "You were going to tell us something?"

He smiles deviously. "It might keep you up at night."

"I doubt it." I sit at the small round table after washing my hands and watch Dasan season another fish and double-coat mine.

I'm guessing I didn't do as good a job as I thought.

"Well, we have a scary story about these woods."

"Daaaad," Nokosi whines, crossing his eyes at me. He looks so young and boyish in this moment. "It wasn't like that. This was a real guy. I saw him myself."

"What scary story?" I ask with excitement and unwavering focus.

"Well, it goes something like..." He clears his throat and turns to give us his full attention. "In the depth of the brush and the thick of the trees, a demon of hellfire will come if one needs. He lives in the shadows, he hides from the sun, looking and longing

206

and waiting for one. One who is desperate, one who's not sane, one to die so they can live again, but it comes at a price, your life will be lost, your soul will be owned by the devil his cost. But then you'll have riches and all his gifts, a life of grandeur, but with shackled wrists. You will belong to the demon, you will belong to the fire, you will belong to the devil, now a slave to your sire."

I laugh loudly and give him a round of applause, laughing even louder still when he bows. I then glare at Nok. "How have you never told me that epic story before?"

"Because it's stupid. It's been said for years among our people and nobody has ever seen this demon."

"Perhaps because nobody needed him," Dasan suggests, a mystical flair to his voice. "Until now."

"Dasan, you rock," I say, grinning and look at my ringing phone again. I ignore it, telling myself if they call again, I'll answer it. I just don't want to take any chances. What if it's to trace me? Maybe I should change my number.

Damn I'm paranoid, rightfully so.

"Because of this man in the forest, though, I would like it if I could ride with you to your home. To make sure you both get there safe and my son returns to me in one piece."

"Trust me, Dasan," I say, grinning. "I'm the scariest thing on the reservation these days."

"And I do not doubt it." He cups my chin lovingly, like a father would a child, and returns to his duties. "Come. Now we must cook." He hands me a metal rack. "Oil it for me, please, otherwise the fish will stick."

"Yes, sir."

"I like this girl. You should bring her more often. She likes to listen to me."

"Dad, I promise that is something she will tire of soon."

I punch his arm again, making him hiss and lunge for me until

I wipe my oily hands on his face and he storms away from us to wash it in the bathroom.

"You are always welcome here," Dasan says around his laughter.

Nash walks in through the front door. "What's all the noise about? What have I missed?"

CHAPTER

20

Willow

Willow: I need a favor.

Nokosi: Who is this?

Willow: The evil twin, Willow.

Nokosi: What do you need?

Willow: I want to do something nice for Lily, but I need an outsider's help.

Nokosi: You call her Lily?

. . .

Willow: Not to her face. She hates it.

Nokosi: What do you need?

Willow: Did you know that she adores painting?

Nokosi: I didn't know that.

Willow: She can be quite the artist when she wants to be. It's not something she's done in a while.

Nokosi: Why not?

Willow: We move so much that it seemed pointless to keep getting out her paints. She doesn't do it the traditional way. She likes to paint walls, or huge canvasses.

Nokosi: Seriously? I don't see it.

I send him a few pictures from our past and wait for him to reply. Meanwhile Lilith is playing snap with Mom after cooking us an incredible lasagna. I didn't get to enjoy much of it thanks to the sickness, but what I tasted was amazing. My mouth is watering just thinking about it.

"You okay?" Mom asks, feeling my eyes on her.

I smile at them both. "I'm better than okay."

Nokosi: She's amazing.

Willow: Right? So... will you help me, in secret? You can't say a thing to her.

Nokosi: You need to tell me what you need first.

I laugh at my own stupidity and Lilith raises a brow, likely surprised that I'm laughing at all.

I flip her my middle finger and go back to texting her boyfriend.

Willow: I need your help clearing out the garage when she's either sleeping or not here... and then painting the walls a bright white... think it's possibly?

Nokosi: Sure, why not?

Willow: Epic! But she can't know... okay? It's a

surprise. She can't know a thing. We don't know each other, we've never met.

Nokosi: Until it's done?

Willow: Exactly. Until it's done and then whatever.

Nokosi: Fine. How bad is the garage?

Willow: It's not too bad. Nothing you can't cart out of here in that truck of yours. I'll give you gas money and whatever else you need.

Nokosi: Don't want your money, just let me know when and I'll be there. But if your sister catches me, I will sing like a canary. No way I'm risking her wrath. Got it?

Willow: Don't blame you. Bitch has a temper.

"Why are you smiling like that? It's creeping me out."

"Shut the fuck up," I say to Lilith and Mom's eyes swing my way, wild with annoyance. "What? She keeps bugging me."

"Language," Mom hisses, sounding more animal than human.

"I'm dying, you'd think cussing would be allowed."

"It sounds trashy."

"As opposed to Lily's pink hair?"

"My hair is not trashy, and don't call me Lily!"

I stick my tongue out at her and then pull a face at Mom when she's not looking. "I'm going to bed."

"Fuck that, you made me stay in so that we could spend time," Lilith snaps, looking annoyed. "If you're going to bed, then I'm going out."

"What about me?" Mom asks, looking between us both. "You both complain that I'm never here and here I damn well am."

"Damn is a cuss," I point out and she growls at me like a fucking tiger or some shit. I zip my lips with a shaky hand and grin at my sister who is grinning at me. We're joking together. Just like old times. I feel like we haven't been this way in so long.

"I'm going," Lilith suddenly announces while standing, and I feel irritated immediately.

"No," I declare, patting the seat beside me. "Stay. I won't sleep yet. Let's do something fun together."

"Like what?" she looks as irritated as I felt a moment ago, though I'm better at hiding it.

Truth be told I don't have anything to entice her with, nothing as new and as exciting as what Nokosi can offer her and I hate that. So fucking bad.

I hate him. I just don't get it. I don't like men anyway, but knowing she's fallen for the embodiment of everything we hate in a man is baffling to me. I'm not sure I'll ever get over it.

I'm not sure I'll ever get past it. Not until he's gone and she's all mine again. Where she's safe from hurt.

Lilith

213

I wag my fingers at Barbie as I pass her in the hall. I just love antagonizing her.

So does Nokosi. He winds his arm around my neck in a casual display of affection and possession and glares at her as we pass, his jaw moving as he chews on a wad of minty gum that he stole from me upon arrival.

We didn't ride to school together today because Nokosi has to work, which sucks. I can't go with him because I promised Mom I'd go shopping for groceries and run a few other errands. Nothing major but I have to make the long trip to Astoria because Westoria doesn't have what I need.

It's times like this that I almost wish I had friends outside of Nok and my sister.

Maybe I can consider it now that I'm thinking of staying. I just have to convince Willow.

"See you later," I whisper against Nokosi's lips when he leaves me at the door to my classroom. He'll be there to pick me up when I'm done too. I fucking love how involved he is and hope it never stops.

Lilith: Want to come to Astoria with me after school? If you're feeling up to it?

Willow: I dunno... my head is pounding.

Lilith: Please? If you get too tired, I'll bring you straight back. Promise.

. . .

Willow: Fine. But only because I could use some new makeup.

Lilith: And nail polish.

Willow: That too.

Lilith: And a bikini or something to swim in. Nokosi wants to take me to the beach on Saturday. You can come?

Willow: No fucking thanks to that. I thought we were chilling on Saturday?

Lilith: It's his only day off this week. I figured you wouldn't mind swapping to Sunday?

Willow: Whatever.

Lilith: Don't be a needy bitch. I deserve to have a bit of fun.

Willow: Do you? Do we? How long until our past catches up to us?

215

. . .

Lilith: I'm ending this conversation.

She doesn't text me again and I don't her. Instead I pay attention to the teacher and look around the class to scope out my peers. Maybe I can be friends with one of them.

But then friends ask questions and questions sometimes answer themselves.

No. It's better that I stay secluded, and when the school year ends, I can just vanish into the woods with Nokosi and stay there forever.

Right?

As expected, Nokosi is waiting for me at break. We make out for a while by the lockers, ignoring the disgusted groans of those around us.

"Did you speak to your mom and sister yet about staying?"

"No, I haven't really seen Mom," I reply, walking my fingers up the buttons of his shirt as he peers down at me with those acorn-colored eyes. "And my sister is too... fragile right now. But I'll bring it up soon, I promise."

"Make sure you do."

I smile at him and wag my brows. "You really want me to stay."

"That obvious, huh?"

Giggling quietly, I kiss him again, humming when our lips collide. "What if I stay and you get bored of me?"

"Then I'll throw you off the res to be with the rest of your white trash brethren," he jests, linking our fingers together and biting on my lower lip. "Don't worry about the future."

It's my past that scares me, I think but definitely do not say.

The future will always be uncertain, but my past is definite and there's no running from it. Not really.

"What happened to you, Nok? Will you ever tell me?"

He tenses. "What are you talking about?"

"I'm attuned to you in a way I don't understand, but ever since we met I just know there's something there. Something you're hiding from the world. Something you've never told anybody."

His smile fades entirely. "You don't know what you're talking about."

"Okay," I reply and shrug my shoulders. "But I do. And I can tell right off the bat when somebody is damaged. Let me help you."

"Stop sucking face," Payne cries and hooks an arm around Nokosi's neck, yanking him away from me. "It's disgusting."

I give him two middle fingers. "Your face is disgusting."

"Yeah, right, I'm prettier than this douchebag. You're just sad you didn't meet me first."

"Devastated," I mumble sarcastically and Nokosi winks at me over his shoulder, seeming to have forgotten the conversation we were having already. Or perhaps he's choosing to ignore. I think I might have pressed too soon and in all honesty I'm not sure why I think I'm worthy of his secrets when I hold tight to so many of my own.

"I'll be right behind you," I call after them as they continue to goof around on their way to next lesson.

"Miss Deville," Bromley yells, making me and many others turn to see what he wants. He pants as he catches up to me, ignoring the jibes coming from the other students about his weight. "I forgot to say that Mrs. Plumley wants to see you in the office."

"Why?" I cringe, annoyed.

"I don't know, nor do I care, but you're to head there immediately."

"Aye aye, Captain," I grumble, turning back the way I just came.

"Less attitude, Miss Deville, and maybe you'll make more friends."

"Less burgers, Mr. Bromley, and maybe you won't look eight months pregnant," I retort and watch his face turn beet red as students cheer around us, some laughing, some oohing, one even shouts, "ROASTED!"

I stomp past him, flipping my pink hair over my shoulder as I go. It could use another coat of dye. Something else to pick up during our shopping trip later.

"Savage," a boy from the year below me calls as I'm stomping past. He also smacks my ass making my right butt cheek sting like a bitch but raises both hands defensively when I glare at him. His smile soon fades when he sees something over my shoulder. I take in his face, putting him down as a potential— NO. No. I'm not doing that. Not anymore.

I grin, flashing my teeth when Nokosi grabs the boy by his hair, making him whimper, and throws him to the floor as though he weighs nothing.

"That's what you get," a nearby girl says to the kid who is curled into the fetal position on the floor. I recognize her to be Mackenzie, I share a couple of classes with her. She likes my hair. "Touching girls without their permission. Scumbag."

Nokosi spits at the guy and wraps me under his arm again. I lace my fingers through his that are hanging over my shoulder. "Can't let you anywhere alone," he whispers in my ear.

"Guess you'll just have to escort me everywhere then."

After he bites the ear he just whispered into, I squeal and pull away, giving a friendly nod to Mackenzie who is standing by an open locker. I'm guessing it's hers. I'm surprised to see the inside door full of article cutouts of the School Sigil Searer serial killer. She must be obsessed too.

"We should introduce her to Bobby or Joseph. They'd get on great."

Nokosi glances behind him to see what I just saw. "She's hot, they'd dig her."

"Don't call her hot," I admonish, frowning. "I'm the only hot girl you know."

"You're not *hot*. You're scorching. Roasting. Metal couldn't withstand your heat."

"Shut up."

"Yes, ma'am."

Laughing, I tuck my hand into the waistband of his school pants, grab his boxer briefs and pull them as high as they'll go. I have never heard Nok squeak so high-pitched.

I run all the way to the office, his footsteps close behind. By the time I get there I'm a mess of hysterics, tears streaming down my face.

"Miss Deville." Mrs. Plumley pushes her glasses up her nose and tips her head back so as to look at me better. "Thank you for coming."

"I'll be waiting," Nokosi says ominously so I shut the office door in his face, laughing when his glaring eyes continue staring at me through the glass panel in the heavy door.

I wipe my face with the back of my hands, using my phone screen to check for streaks of makeup. I'm good.

"Your attention, Miss Deville."

"You wanted to see me?" I ask, turning back to face her.

"I still don't have your records."

"Oh, those," I wet my lips. "I have them coming, I swear. I'll bring them in the next few days."

"You must, it's extremely important I have them."

"No sweat, Mrs. P. I promise. It's taken a bit of time because of how many schools I've attended."

She nods, her face softens with understanding. "It's hard being under the control of parents who have jobs that take us to many places. I was an army brat myself. We were always moving. You seem to be adjusting well enough to life at Lakeside prep."

I shrug both shoulders. "I do my best to fit in."

"Your schoolwork has been exemplary, and your teachers have no complaints."

"I'm glad to hear it, Mrs. P. It's nice to have you who understands too."

"I do." She looks honored, likely because she relates to me and she probably doesn't get that very often. "Well, off you go. Please don't forget your records."

I dip my chin and turn to pull the door open but Nokosi already has it pushed to a full ninety-degree angle.

He nods politely at the desk lady and takes my hand in his.

"When I said you should just escort me everywhere, I didn't mean it," I whisper, smiling wryly at him.

He ignores me and continues on his way, despite the fact he's now going to be late. His class is on the other side of the building.

We kiss at the door to mine, deep but brief, and I watch his ass as he saunters away, a dreamy smile on my face.

"Please don't take that," I whisper at Willow who is about to stuff the dark blue nail polish into her pocket.

She rolls her eyes to me and pouts petulantly, making her thick lower lip pointed and cute. "But it's so much fun."

"I know it is and I get it. You know I do. I'm not opposed to a bit of five-finger discount, but I've decided I want us to stay and can't have the cops sniffing around me over a shoplifting accusation."

She drops the bottle onto the floor, it doesn't break but it does clatter loud enough to draw the eyes of the bored-looking college student running the store while reading a magazine.

"Sorry," I say, bending down to pick up the polish and put it back on its plastic shelf. When I stand to my full height I glare at my sister. "Was that necessary?"

She ignores me and moves to the bags, touching the chain handle of one. "This would make a great weapon."

Anything can be a weapon if you're sadistic enough and my sister definitely is.

I watch her pick up a blue thong in the underwear section and stick it down her pants.

Groaning, I move around her, grabbing her arm as I go. We dump the foundations, nail polishes, and new eyeliners we've chosen, as well as a bottle of pink hair dye for me. My sister wants to stay a mundane brown. I don't care.

The girl scans our items and pops them into a paper bag with a handle. I carry them, and as soon as we're outside and out of eyeshot, my sister adds two bottles of nail polish, two new thongs, and a pair of socks with giraffes on them.

"You're incorrigible."

"And you're out of order making decisions for both of us without consulting me. As if I want to spend my last days on earth watching you suck face with that boy."

"He's not just any boy, Willow. I wish you'd be happy for me."

She narrows her eyes, making the jade green look as though it's glowing. "He's going to hurt you."

"And I'll have you to comfort me when he does. Just like old times, back before... before everything happened."

"You mean before we were raped," she replies on a hiss.

I look away, feeling my cheeks heat with rage that makes my arms and hands shake. "They got what was coming to them." I wet my lips and climb into Mom's car. "But we can move past it. I want to move past it. I want to live again, be happy, finish the school year and go to prom."

"And what about me?"

"Not everything has to be about you and the fact you're dying. If anything, you should want me to find happiness before you die, so I'm not alone when you go."

She stares ahead but I see something flicker in her eyes, a realization perhaps, compassion maybe. Who knows? When it comes to Willow, she rarely thinks about anyone but herself. She never has.

My memories have been coming and going, some things I can remember as though they happened yesterday, such as when Willow and I used to play pranks on our neighbor and steal pears from their tree in the garden. They didn't mind, they had way too many to eat anyway.

But a lot of memories, such as the rape and things since then, are hazy, foggy. It's like I know the details, I know they happened, but I can't quite recall the images.

"Would you at least consider staying here? Letting me be happy?" I ask my sister, placing my hand over hers on her lap.

She looks away and pulls her hand from under mine. "He'll dump you. Men like him never stick around."

"You're wrong. He cares about me. I can tell." Putting the car in gear I peel out of our parking spot and head home with a trunk full of groceries and the things we need.

And my bitch of a sister snoozing beside me.

CHAPTER
21

Willow

"Shhhhh," I say, giggling as Nokosi lifts the metal barrel and carries it out of the garage. He grunts with each step but that's unsurprising because it looks really fucking heavy.

"What's in here? A dead body?"

"It was here when we moved in so maybe," I reply, dragging my eyes from the top of his bulging shoulders to his ass. He really does have a great ass.

"Did you just check me out?" Nok asks, smirking at me over his shoulder. I fight the urge to grunt at him, sneer at him, grab his handsome face and push my thumbs into his eyes until he stops wriggling.

Instead I just shrug. "My sister has good taste."

He laughs and carefully places the barrel behind the garage. Only making a little bit of noise.

"What if she wants to use the garage before we're done?"

"She won't, I'll make sure of it," I state, looking around the near-empty garage space when we reenter.

I start sweeping the floor with a heavy broom, but apparently,

I'm taking too long because Nokosi snatches the broom from me and nods to a chair in the corner.

"Sit down," he insists. "I got this."

Chivalrous... a redeeming quality for the most part. Doesn't make me stop hating him though.

"What's it like living on a reservation?"

"Same as living in town, except we have more trees and less road signs."

I laugh a little. He's funny, even when he doesn't mean to be. "Do you get many wild animals?"

"Hell yeah." He stops sweeping and wipes his forehead on the bottom of his shirt. I blink when I catch a glimpse of his six-pack abs. I want to low whistle and ask him to strip for me like some skeevy guy in a strip club tucking dollar bills into a woman's G-string. "Bears, wolves, mountain lions, skunks, squirrels... racoons."

"I hate racoons."

"Feisty little fucks," he agrees and goes back to sweeping.

He turns his back to me and I consider how easy it would be to take the thin belt from my dated jeans and wrap it around his neck. It'd be so easy to kill him, well... not easy but not difficult either. He's let his guard down with me, sees me as nothing but a sick, weak girl. Probably thinks I'm attracted to him. If only he knew.

"So, what's wrong with you exactly? Your sister doesn't talk about it."

I'm surprised by his question, and the fact that my sister hasn't told anybody what I have. Though she has been acting strange lately. Is she embarrassed by me?

No. She loves me. She needs me. She'd never choose him over me. Still... I can't be too careful. It's better to remove the temptation from her path than to dangle it and take the risk.

"I have a brain tumor in the frontal lobe. It's been growing since birth so it's pretty rooted in there."

He stops, looking sad for a long moment. "That sucks."

"It is what it is."

"Does it hurt?"

I shrug my shoulders. "I get headaches sometimes and the medication I take can make me space out and sicky, but I'm good otherwise. It's the seizures that are the worst but they're very infrequent."

He leans the broom against the wall and crouches by the pile he made with a dustpan and brush. "And there's no cure? No way they can remove it?"

"No, brain surgery would kill me, it's surprising that I'm even alive while it's in there."

Almost-amber eyes search my face, a sadness to them that just intensifies with each passing second. "I couldn't imagine losing my brother. I couldn't imagine my brother losing me."

Something painful jolts in my chest at his words. Perhaps he understands me better than I thought.

"How long do you have left?"

"Months, maybe," I murmur, looking at the ground and frowning. I lose myself in my thoughts and memories, cherishing each one for a moment, allowing myself to feel them all.

My fifth birthday where I started to insist on having my own birthday cake because I didn't want to be the same as Lilith all the time.

When she looked after me after I broke my leg at six years old. How she was always good at hair and I was always bad at it, so she'd do my hair every day before school so I didn't feel out of place.

The time she beat up a kid called Adeline for being mean to me about my inability to read and write very well. My sister sat with me for hours teaching me to read after that. She said she'd never let anyone hurt me. She said she'd protect me, and she always did. We always protected each other.

We loved each other so much. I love her so much.

I jump when a hand lands on my shoulder. I'm about to bite it, sink my teeth through the flesh and rip, until I see Nokosi's concerned eyes on mine.

"You okay?" he asks softly, his demeanor and tone not matching his rough exterior.

I nod but don't shrug him off. His touch doesn't completely repulse me right now. In fact, I find it quite soothing.

"I lost you there for a minute. Where'd you go?"

I tap my temple. "Memories. Just cherishing them... while I still can." The last part was meant as a joke, but it falls flat, his frown is proof of that. "Lighten up a bit, Nok, tis all grand."

He doesn't reply, he just walks to the dilapidated shelving unit and starts to break it apart.

I join him, standing beside him and holding the metal rod that connects the corners as he kicks the shelves off. I do it too and it's therapeutic when my foot breaks apart the flimsy, aged wood.

I giggle, feeling free of pain and worries as I destroy something other than the people around me.

When it's rubble and garbage on the ground, Nokosi turns to me and we slap our hands together in celebration.

Then comes the cleanup and Nokosi laughs when I get a convenient headache and must sit down for this part.

This time when he catches me checking him out, I don't look away. I wink, mimicking the casual arrogant smirk that he often displays on his handsome face.

He rolls his eyes, a handsome and playful smile on his face, and continues with his job, leaving at midnight to go home and get some rest.

Lilith

"You keep yawning," I point out, resting my chin on Nok's bare chest as his fingertips trail lazily up and down my spine.

"Didn't sleep well last night," he mumbles, shifting slightly beneath me to find a more comfortable position. His other hand pushes my hair behind my ear. "I think I did a good job."

I agree, looking at the pink strands of hair that fall over my shoulder and tickle his chest, "You did. I'm glad I asked."

"Stinks like fuck, though. Dad's going to keep the windows open for a month."

I giggle. "Your dad loves me, he'll forgive me."

Nok holds his pink-stained hand up to the light and sighs. "If you ever tell anybody I helped you dye your hair, I'll shave your eyebrows while you sleep."

I look at his trimmed dark hair around his dick after lifting the blanket. "I'm still disappointed it didn't even slightly tint your pubes." His half-hard cock gives a little twitch as I assess it.

"If you ever tell anybody I let you do that I'll shave your hair as well as your eyebrows."

I laugh as I bury my face into his neck and drape my leg over his. "I still can't believe you let me do it."

I just wanted to make his dick look as unicorn as possible, but the pink didn't do anything but stain the skin at the base of it. I'm still in shock that he let me, but then I was sucking him and kissing him as I did it. Not an easy task in any shape or form. It's how he ended up with dye all over his hands because he forgot I had it in my hair and grabbed my head when he came on my tongue.

So fucking hot.

When he yawns again, I kiss his cheekbone. "You can sleep if you want to? I won't mind."

He blinks slowly, his eyes drifting closed before I even finished my sentence.

I watch him drift away from me, a longing in my heart to feel the kind of peace he's displaying. I'll never feel that kind of peace, there's a noose around my neck and a guillotine ready as a backup. I'm shackled to my past and the horrific things I've done. It'll catch up to me eventually, and when it does, I dread to think.

When I'm with Nokosi and he's smiling at me, looking at me, talking to me, touching me, I do forget. If only for a little while.

My eyes close too and I lose myself in the same slumber boat that ferried him away moments ago.

I've never felt safer than when I'm in his arms.

"Lily!" Willow calls. "Lily, come on. Hurry up."

I sit up, feeling clammy from the warm air.

"Lily, seriously, Mom's waiting for us, she's getting annoyed."

I climb out of bed in my nightgown and race to the window. My ottoman is beneath it, the fabric covering made from a dark green velvet, full of my toys and stuffed animals. I rest on it on my knees and peer out into the darkness. I swear Willow's voice came from the front yard. But why is she awake at this time? She's scared of the dark, there's no way she'd go out there alone.

"Lily," a hissed voice comes from behind me, breathing across my neck and across the back of my head.

I jolt and turn, pressing my shoulder blades to the windowsill.

My room is empty and still, there's nobody in sight but the shadows painting the pink walls.

"Willow?" I whisper, clearing my childish thoughts. "Willow, is that you?"

I step down from the ottoman, letting my toes wriggle in the soft plush rug on my floor. My heart rate spikes. I don't feel good.

I run across the room and dive into my bed, clammier now than before and I pull the blanket over my face, breathing harshly in the dark pocket of space between my knees and head.

Footsteps creak in the hall. Tapping sounds on the door. Tap.

Tap. Tap. Tap. Tap. Tap. A constant noise, like the point of metal hitting wood.

When my door creaks open, I cover my mouth and stifle my sob. I'm so frightened. So scared.

"Lily," Willow whispers, pulling black the blanket suddenly, showing me the room now full of angry eyes.

Men twice my size stand along the walls glaring at me, their bodies dripping blood, their necks snapped, their eyes lifeless.

I scream but she covers my mouth with her hand, stopping me from making a noise. I thrash as she climbs into bed with me and presses my face into her chest.

"It's okay," she soothes. "Just ignore them. Look at me. Ignore them. They can't hurt you. They can't hurt you. They're dead already. Ignore them."

I sniffle and sob, trying to keep quiet, terrified they'll get me.

"They're dead," she breathes. "They can't hurt you now. They can't hurt any of us."

I groan and roll onto my back, feeling sweaty and gross. My heart is pounding so loudly I can hear it over my ragged breath.

"What's wrong?" Nokosi asks, leaning over me to brush my hair from my sweaty forehead.

I bat his hand away and look around his bedroom, different to the one in my dream. "I need a shower."

"What is it? Talk to me."

"You don't talk to me," I point out petulantly and he doesn't argue with that. "Look, I just need a moment to gather myself. Okay?" Without waiting for an answer, I pull on his T-shirt and make my way downstairs. Nash is sitting on the couch drinking a beer with Joseph.

"Hey, pretty lady," Joseph calls but I ignore them both and lock myself in the bathroom.

I can't breathe. The dream... it felt so real... it's my paranoia speaking to me, telling me that my time here is limited. Nokosi will leave me when he knows what I've done.

I let the cold water splash over me, it's fucking freezing, but it helps to rid me of my nervous shaking, only to replace it with cold trembles.

Those I can deal with though.

Nausea roils my stomach so badly I have to fight the urge to vomit.

When I make the water warm, I'm feeling a little better though not much. It's not often I dream but when I do it's usually a fucking nightmare like that, or something equally as disturbing.

I hate it.

There's a knock on the door. "You okay in there?"

I don't answer. I just don't want to be around people right now. I need space to sort my head out.

Exiting the bathroom, I move past Nokosi, keeping my eyes forward, and head upstairs to get my things. Nok follows hot on my heels.

"What is it? What's wrong?"

"I just need space," I admit, hopping on one foot as I pull on my pants. "It's nothing you did."

"Hey," he coos softly, taking my elbow and turning me to face him. His eyes search my face for something... anything. "What is it?"

"I just... I need to go home."

I leave my bra and wifebeater that I wore here and race from the house with car keys in hand.

Nokosi watches me go from his front door and I feel guilty for a moment, but then the feeling in my chest intensifies again and there's nowhere I want to be than with my sister.

She's waiting for me, likely sensing my distress from the

second I park the car outside, and we curl into bed together as my anxieties crush my chest, making it impossible for me to breathe.

"We killed them," I whisper as she holds me tight. "We killed them, Willow."

She strokes my hair. "I know but they deserved it. They can't hurt us anymore."

I inhale her scent; she smells like sugarplums and vanilla. It's sweet and soothing and I don't want to ever be anywhere else ever again.

The memories resurface, awful memories of her lying beside me, reaching out to my hand as they forced a vodka bottle down her throat, chipping her tooth as they pushed it in. Her eyes were wide and bulging. She couldn't breathe.

I scream into her chest, scream louder than I ever have, scream until my throat is sore and tired and my voice nonexistent.

They defiled us. They ruined us.

They took everything from us.

"I'll always be here for you," Willow breathes against my hair. "I promise."

"No, you won't," I cry, hating myself for being so weak. I don't cry. It's not me. Willow was the crier, she was the baby, she was the weak one.

The sun set an hour ago, as I was driving home from Nok's, it took all my happiness with it, plunging it into the darkness as my fear and grief overwhelm me. It's not fair. I didn't ask to be attacked. I didn't ask for any of it.

When there's a knock on the door I'm not in the mood to answer it, but then I hear the sound of a radio and a deep voice I recognize but can't place.

"If somebody doesn't answer this door, I'm afraid I'm going to have to break it down."

I scramble out of bed so fast I trip and almost face-plant the floor. I stumble down the hall, down the stairs, and grasp the handle, all the while crying out, "Just a second!"

When I pull open the door a flashlight beams its brightness directly into my eyes.

"Shit," I curse, blinking and using my hand to shield myself. "Dude. What the fuck?"

"Sorry, miss," the officer says, lowering the light and looking over my shoulder.

I recognize him immediately and glance at my sister who is sitting on the stairs. She looks as tense as I feel.

"Officer Deacon, right?" I put on the charm, fiddling with my hair that's likely a nest on my head. I'm so not attractive enough right now to try and be charming.

"Ahhh, the little mud shark," he says and grins as his pale eyes creep down my body, stopping at my cleavage for a long moment. "I'm here to investigate a disturbance."

"A disturbance?" I ask, moving my body slightly behind the door for protection. I'm wearing nothing but a pair of Nok's boxers and his T-shirt. I'm not dressed enough for this. "What disturbance?"

"Somebody reported screaming coming from your house," he shines the light into the dark hall.

FUCK.

"Yeah... I'm sorry about that. It was my sister." The lie falls easily from my mouth and I see my sister slink upstairs out of eyeshot.

"Your sister?"

I nod and let my eyes fill with tears. "She's... umm... she has a tumor in her brain. It's terminal. It puts pressure on certain spots in her head and can make her a bit loopy."

His cautious eyes become sympathetic and he lowers his flashlight and his guard further. "I'm sorry to hear that, and while I sympathize, she can't just be screaming willy-nilly."

"It's a rare thing, sir, she gets hallucinations sometimes and..." My chin wobbles convincingly. "She thinks she sees things that aren't there." I let out a choked sob. "I'm sorry, sir. It's just been a long few weeks and she's spiraling and it's hard to watch."

"Maybe she should be in some kind of hospice..." he mumbles, looking uncomfortable by my display of emotions. "Am I okay to come in and look around? It'd give me peace of mind."

"You can," I pull the door but then stop. "But please, be quiet, if she wakes up again now... I can't medicate her again."

He hesitates, looking over my shoulder again. He displays kindness but oozes something else, something more ominous.

I don't like him. I don't feel protected by him.

"Where are your parents?"

"Mom's at work, Dad's dead."

"Wow, you're a real tragedy, aren't you?"

I lift my shoulder. "You could say that. I promise I'll be quicker with her meds this time. I'm not the best at it. Mom will be so mad if she hears of how loud I let her get."

"Ah, parents can be hard on us, especially when they're under pressure. I imagine having a sick child can make us a bit snappier than most."

I smile as sweetly as my inner bitterness allows. "Do you have any kids, Officer Deacon?"

"I do, a son just a couple of years older than you."

"You must make him so proud," I comment; really I don't give a fuck.

The light dims in his eyes as he loses his gentle smile to some kind of pain that I'm really good at seeing in people. It looks like grief, regret, anguish... so much of all three.

"Well... I suppose there's no reason to keep you." He shines the light over my shoulder once more and then takes a step back, his posture more slumped now. What just happened? "Have a good night, Miss Deville."

"You too, Officer Deacon."

He turns away and lifts his pants by his belt, making them rattle while shifting them into the correct place.

"False alarm, it's all good here," he speaks into the radio attached to the front of his left shoulder. When dispatch replies a muffled something, he turns back to me and smiles that faux kind smile that creeps me out. "Be careful while out and about."

"I will."

"You didn't hear it from me but..." He glances around, smiling now as though he holds the key to all the world's secrets and whatever transpired before between us no longer does. "This place could be next on the Sigil killer's list and there have been a few sightings of an unknown man wandering around."

My breath catches in my throat. I hope he's wrong, I really do. "I'll be sure to carry my mace spray with me."

"Good girl." He starts the long walk down my drive to his car, giving me one last wave before driving away.

I close the door and press my back to it.

Why does he think this place could be next? What does he know?

I look at my sister who is sliding down the stairs on her bum.

"I hallucinate?" she asks smarmily, raising a pointed brow.

I laugh but it's forced. "I said the first thing that came to mind."

"Ooookayyyy." She slides the rest of the way down and I help her to her feet. "So... the killer could be in town huh?"

"Seems like it."

"I'll look into it."

I nod, frowning. "Me too. I know a couple of people who might know more about it. See what local cops think they know."

She claps her hands with excitement. "I love a good mystery."

"There's nothing good about any of it," I snap, stalking past her and into the kitchen.

"Your voice sounds sexy," she tells me, totally ignoring anything else I said, "it's all husky from the screaming I did with your throat."

Flipping her off, I down a glass of water and slam it onto the counter, ignoring the darkness around me. I don't often turn on the lights when I'm home at night. I feel safer in the dark. The dark hides the monsters and a monster is exactly what I am.

I pad back upstairs and go into my sister's room to grab my phone. I have a few missed calls and a single text. I like that Nok has given me space, though I think I might have pissed him off. I did leave there abruptly, but I had to. My anxiety was... it was too much.

I was worried he might follow but he's not an overbearing person. He likes my attention when I want to give it, he doesn't beg for it in between. I'd like to say I'm the same but if I want his attention and he's not listening I'll turn his face towards me or stand in his line of sight until he looks at me.

Just like today, he said he was going to stay at home with his brother for a while, so I showed up and rubbed up against his dick until he took me to bed, and then I woke up from that horrific nightmare.

He didn't seem to mind. Not in the slightest.

Nokosi: You left your bra here.

Lilith: Your moobs need it.

Nokosi: I do not have moobs.

. . .

Lilith: Sure.

Nokosi: Want me to drop it by?

Lilith: Not tonight. You should rest. I'm taking a pill and going to sleep.

Nokosi: I wish you wouldn't do that.

Lilith: Sleep?

Nokosi: Keep popping your sister's sleeping meds.

Lilith: Don't start. Not with that.

Nokosi: I'm just worried about you.

Lilith: I don't need you to worry. We're not about that. That's not us.

Nokosi: Noted.

. . .

I've annoyed him, I know I have but I can't deal with him bitching at me for my choices too. Mom gets on at me enough about it but how else can I sleep? Nokosi helps me sleep, he helps me rest... or he did. Until today. Until the nightmares took place in our haven too.

CHAPTER 22

Willow

"What did she do?" I ask Nokosi as he angrily rolls the white paint up and down the garage wall. I work on the edges with a brush, feeling woozy from the smell, but I felt woozy anyway.

He doesn't answer, so I keep painting for a bit longer, silent and patient.

When he huffs again, I cross my eyes and blow out my cheeks.

"What are you, a middle-aged wife whose husband forgot their anniversary?" I throw my paintbrush into the tray and look at him with a frown. "What's wrong? What did my sister do?" He glances at me out of the corner of his eyes. "You can talk to me. I'll take it to the grave... which is coming sooner rather than later."

His lips twitch with a faint smile and he finally stops his aggressive rolling and drops it on top of my brush. "Do you always joke about your death?"

"Should I always cry about it?"

He scratches his jaw with paint-splattered fingers. "I guess not."

"So... you want to tell me what my bitch twin did?"

He wets his lips. "She just... it's hypocritical of me to say."

239

"So? Say it anyway."

"She shuts down whenever we talk about..." He throws his hands up in the air and sits on an upturned bucket. "Anything. Be it in regard to you, her past, her future... and now she's being *off* with me. She ignored me all day in school today to talk to this girl that she has never spoken to before."

I nod to show him I'm listening. "Mackenzie?"

"That's the one."

"Is it so bad that she wants to make friends?" I question, smirking at him and his jealousy. "Is it because it takes her away from you?"

"That's not what it is," he grumbles but even I know that's exactly what it is. Maybe we are more alike than I thought.

"What is it you want from my sister, Nok?" I ask, sitting cross-legged on the concrete floor, dancing the tip of my finger in a splatter of paint beside me. My bum is going numb.

He clears his throat. "Excuse me?"

"Do you love her?"

"I hardly know her."

I grit my teeth and repeat with force, "Do you love her."

"If I do or don't... that's a conversation I'll have with her when the time is right."

"But you think she's special?"

He groans and wipes his face on his T, lifting the hem so I get to see what lies beneath. I love it when he does that. I'm not so much of a monster that I can't appreciate a handsome male when I see one. "Let's just drop it."

"Not a chance." I bum shuffle closer to him, stopping when I'm within touching distance. "Is she special to you? Or is she just your step on the way to finding the right woman?"

His hazel-ish brown eyes shine in the dim light, flickering as he thinks on it and I'm curious as to what's going through his mind right now. "I'm only eighteen—"

"So? Age is—"

He raises a hand to cut me off. "I always thought love was a pussy excuse for losing your game in the dating world." His eyes don't come to mine, they close for a moment as though daring himself to speak and when they reopen the fiery determination there sends a thrill through my body. "And yet here I am, finding myself terrified that your sister might just suddenly decide she's bored of me."

"If only you knew," I mumble under my breath, feeling almost sorry for him because his feelings replicate my own so well. "She's ignored you for one day. Not a year. It's not a big deal."

"Has she said anything to you?"

I shake my head, wishing that she had, wishing that she would tire of him so we can go again. "Nothing."

"But even if she had, would you tell me?" His charming yet annoying smile returns.

Laughing, I pick up his roller and stand with it poised and ready for action. "Definitely not."

"I'll look after her, you know that, right? After you're gone. I'll protect her."

My heart thuds painfully in my chest. I want to scream at him. I want to tell him that it's not his job to. I want to tell him she's mine and always will be. But I find myself thinking of my sister and how happy she has been lately. Am I so selfish that I can't allow her one young love?

"Thank you," I whisper and start rolling the white onto the dirty gray wall. "We probably should have cleaned the wall better before adding gloss."

"I did say that."

I put my finger to my lips and shush him, making him laugh under his breath.

Nokosi Locklear isn't a bad guy... but he has the chance to

derail our lives. I can't let him do that. No matter what, my plan still stands.

He's going down, it is as it is.

But I can allow her a little more time. It would be a kindness she deserves.

"Don't hurt her, Nok," I say firmly, and his brows hit his hairline, "you'll regret it if you do."

Lilith

"How did you get all of this information?" I ask Mackenzie, awed by what's laid on the grass between us. Two binders full of laminated pouches that hold sheets upon sheets of information on the School Sigil Searer and their victims. "It's insane."

"Too right," Joseph mutters, also as awed as me.

I brought Mackenzie here on my dirt bike, much to her despair. I let her use my sister's old helmet, somebody may as well. She was shocked to say the least but there's no way I was getting my dad's Prius to the fucking track.

She clung tight to my body and screamed most of the way here, her heavy backpack weighing my turns down.

This all got planned yesterday at school when I hung around with her for the day after learning of her obsession with this killer. I'm so glad I did. This bitch has FBI files on it that have never been released to the public. She won't tell me how she got them, just that, if she gets caught with them, she'll go to jail.

My lips are sealed, and she trusts that much of me.

"It took a lot of time, but I had this thought that I might be able to figure it out myself. I mean there's a fifty-thousand-dollar reward for any information leading to this dude's arrest." She is so animated and chatty in a way I've never been. She's like Emma Stone whereas I'm more Billy Eilish.

She's nice enough but I reckon I'll tire of her soon.

Bobby whistles a long low note. He's impressed. "You've even got some of their fucking dead photos. That's just creepy."

"Totes," Mackenzie replied. "I had nightmares for days the first time I saw them. I felt like I was doing them a disservice and violating them in some way, so I don't look at the pictures anymore."

"Respectful," I state, nodding softly.

"Where's Nokosi?" Nash suddenly asks, appearing from the tree line with his friends.

"At work," I reply without looking up from the paper.

"What are you doing?" he asks as he gets closer.

Mackenzie looks at me for confirmation of trust.

"That's on you," I tell her. "These seem like good people, but I don't know them well enough to vouch for their loyalty."

"Ouch, Lil, what a burn," Joseph jokes, giving me a playful shove.

Bobby cuts in, "So, what we know so far is this psychopath has killed twenty-seven guys aged sixteen to eighteen?"

"Twenty-seven and counting," I add, wagging my brows.

Bobby grins at me, showing slightly crooked teeth and dimples in his chin. "I thought you didn't like talking about death."

"I don't, with my sister being so close to it, it's upsetting... but I figured I better start making friends before the school year ends and who better to entice than you freaks to my weirdness?"

Mackenzie laughs and shakes her head, Joseph pushes me again, and Bobby throws a stick at me.

"In between sucking Nok's dick, and looking after my sister, I haven't had much time."

"Gross," Nash baulks, standing and moving to my dirt bike. "Can I?"

"Where's yours?" I frown, throwing him my keys.

"In for repair."

He pulls on my helmet, straddles my beast of a bike, and kick-starts the engine. Then he peels away, showing off on the track like he always does.

"Why don't you ever let me on your bike?" Joseph pouts, disappointed.

"Because you're shit."

Bobby falls backwards laughing and I grin wryly and unapologetically as I always do.

"You're such a bitch, Lil," Joseph jests good-naturedly. "What the hell Nokosi sees in you is anyone's guess."

"His penis," Mackenzie answers flippantly and freezes when we all look at her. She gulps the orange down that she just placed on her tongue and adds, "He sees his penis in her."

I laugh, it starts as a slight giggle that bounces up from my chest but then becomes full-body laughter. I clutch my stomach and pat her on the back. "That was good, Mack. That was really good."

Mackenzie beams with pride.

"Anyway," Joseph says clearly and flicks through the blue binder. "So, we know the last victim found was a month ago."

"Found a month ago but died over two," Mackenzie puts in.

Hands tip my head back and lips touch my forehead. I smell him before I see him. Nokosi. Just whispering his name in my brain sends a shiver down my spine.

"Hey, gorgeous," he whispers, sitting behind me and pulling me into his crotch. "What's this about my penis being in you?"

Laughing softly, I turn my head and touch my lips to his. We deepen it for a moment and the others let us have it. Normally they moan at us for the display, not that we care what makes them uncomfortable or not.

I softly suck on his lower lip for a second before looking into his eyes and breathing the words, "I'm sorry."

He knows what I'm apologizing for, I don't have to elaborate, and he won't make me.

His tired browns soften and his hand cups my cheek tenderly. When his thumb strokes the skin beneath my eye, I kiss him again. We share this private moment in this crowded place and then look at the binders.

"Where can I get me some of that passion?" Mack cries and scrunches her nose up at me. "You two are so hot you have no idea."

"I'm passionate," Bobby declares, raising his hand.

Nok groans into my neck and Joseph clips his friend upside the head.

"Well, I am," he grumbles and Mackenzie sighs dramatically while uttering the word, "Boys."

"So, what do the FBI know so far?" I ask to change the subject.

"Well..." She glances at us all and lowers her voice as an evil, excited smile stretches her pretty face. "They think he might be here."

I tense and look at Nokosi who shrugs. "I'll protect you."

Snorting, I roll my eyes back to the binders as Joseph is stuffing things back inside. "He's after boys, remember. Last I checked, us women are safe." Mackenzie and I fist-bump.

"Don't worry, boys, we've got your backs," Mackenzie cries, raising her pale fist high.

I pull my knife from my boot and flip out the blade with a click. "Or are we going to stab you in it?"

"That's not funny, don't freak me out," Joseph whines as I tuck my weapon away, cackling like a witch.

"Stay with me tonight?" Nokosi asks. "Just in case the killer tries to get me in my sleep."

The sky is getting gray which means our little gathering must end soon.

"I don't see why not," I murmur, climbing to my feet just as Nash comes skidding to a stop before me. "But we need to give Mackenzie a ride back into town."

"No problem, we'll take my truck."

"Nash," I call, and he pulls off his helmet which is actually my helmet. "Can you take my bike back to your house when you're done? I'm gonna hang with Nokosi for a while."

"Sure, I'll fill her up too."

I flap a hand at him. "Don't worry about that. Just leave me enough to get home."

Nokosi wraps an arm around my neck as Joseph and Bobby rush to help Mackenzie pack away.

"So," she asks, catching up to us after a moment. "Why the sudden interest in the serial killer?"

I sigh heavily. "Truth be told I need the distraction."

"Well, hit me up if you want to go through it all again."

"Definitely." I grin at her genuinely. "It was cool hanging with you. You're not like the other girls I've met at prep."

"You mean because I don't want to conform to society's standards on makeup and boys and shit?"

"Pretty much."

"I'm glad you've seen it and approve."

We fist-bump again and make our way through the trees to where Nokosi parked his truck.

"I can't believe I'm hanging out with the cool kids," Mackenzie comments, climbing into the front seat after me.

I laugh, she's quite funny. "We're the cool kids?"

She nods rapidly. "You've been here a month and already you've been voted most unapproachable and the person people want to hang with."

Nokosi laughs at that. "They got the unapproachable right."

"Yeah," I agree, wiping my dirty hands on my jeans. "I don't like people."

"You're not going to punch me in the face if I bug you, are you?" Mack hides behind her fingers playfully peeking at me from between them.

"Only if you try to fuck my boyfriend. You're safe otherwise."

She leans forward to look at Nokosi suggestively. "I mean..."

I know she's joking but when Nokosi wags his brows at her I dig my fingers into both their thighs until they both yelp. Mackenzie thinks it's hilarious.

I'll be keeping a close eye on them from now on.

When we get to town and drop her at her house, I turn to Nokosi and declare, "If you fuck anybody while we're together, I will genuinely run you both over and throw your bodies off a cliff."

"Why the hell would I?" he asks, smiling from ear to ear at my jealousy. "Have you seen you?"

I narrow my eyes on him until I'm confident he's received the message loud and clear and then he touches me intimately, uncaring who sees, and devours my mouth until I too fully accept his message.

Which was what again?

CHAPTER 23

Willow

I look at the white walls. They need a second coat, maybe even a third.

I'm stalling for time.

"Looks good," Nokosi says around a loud yawn. I know how he feels, these days I constantly feel as though I'm fighting to stay awake.

"It could be better."

"Does it matter? She's painting over it soon anyway," he grumbles and yawns again.

I look at him, it's only ten but he's clearly exhausted. "You can go."

He raises a brow. "Are you dismissing me?"

"Could you maybe take me to the store first? I've got a major craving for some Hershey's."

Hesitating, he seems to think about it for a moment before looking around the room. It's pure brilliant white though you can't tell in the dim lighting. We only have an old lantern that was left behind by the prior tenants. "Sure, why not?"

"Yes!" I cheer and take the arm he offers. "Thanks, Nok."

"No problem, I figured that the nicer I am to you the more likely you are to stay."

Laughing I slap his chest and shake my head. "Everybody has an agenda I guess."

"Of course, life would be shit without one. Can you imagine not having a goal in life?" He shrugs his shoulders. "I bet you have an extensive bucket list."

He has no idea. "There's just one thing left on my list." Pulling open the truck's passenger door, he grips my hips to help me inside and for the first time ever I don't feel repulsed by his touch. I don't fully welcome it either but it doesn't make me feel sick.

"What's that?" he asks after rounding the truck and climbing in.

I tap my nose and look ahead.

"Maybe I can help you achieve it? Maybe we all can?"

"I doubt it," I mutter and check my pocket for my wallet. "How are things with my sister now? She's hardly been home for the past couple of days."

"Good. We got past whatever happened, she's happy again." He looks me up and down when we stop at a red light. "Are you happy? You can always join us."

"One step at a time," I say, placing my hand on his for a few seconds, until he clears his throat and pulls his away.

Well, he's definitely loyal to my sister.

I start coughing, I can't stop. It's not so much that anything is on my chest it's just what happens sometimes. My chest feels so tight. I stagger on a breath that I try to pull in and pain pops in my throat.

This sucks.

"Fuck, Willow, are you okay?" He rubs my back until I've calmed myself, his eyes shining with concern.

I nod and sit back. "Fuck this illness, man. I'm done. I feel like I'm fading away."

We don't speak for a while. What is there to say? I'm dying. There's only so many times one can tell me how sorry they are as I suffer through the symptoms and side effects of my ailment, and the drugs I have to take for it.

"I have an idea... it's unconventional and it defies the laws of modern medicine... but..." He suddenly pulls over, startling me and I tense, not liking being taken by surprise. But then he taps on his phone screen and puts it to his ear. "Auntie, is Elisi awake?" After a pause where he listens to a feminine voice reply, he starts speaking in another language and at the end he's smiling.

"What's going on?" I ask weakly, trying not to cough again.

He puts the car in drive and makes a U-turn. "How'd you like to meet my grandmother on the res?"

My breath catches in my throat. "I don't know... I'm not good around people."

"She's a healer," he insists gently. "Not the kind you know but she's saved lives. I don't believe in it more than a placebo but if it can help you then isn't it worth a try?"

"I guess," I mutter, suddenly feeling like a lost little girl again. I don't have a weapon, or mace spray, or even my phone. "Will you... protect me?"

"Protect you? From what?"

"Everybody?"

His brows pull together with confusion and his hand goes to my thigh. "I promise, nobody will hurt you while I'm with you."

Resting my forehead against the cool glass, I take a deep breath and mutter, "Okay. I'll go."

"Did somebody hurt you before? Is that why you don't go anywhere?"

I consider telling him to fuck off. I consider berating him for prying. But something inside of me screams to let it out, to trust somebody with just a tiny part of me. It begs me to. It begs me to feel human again.

"Not just me, but my sister too."

He tenses, his body becomes cement. "Somebody hurt Lilith?"

I nod once, trying not to let the grief I feel overwhelm me and trigger my own anxiety. Lilith isn't the only one with issues.

"What happened?" he asks urgently. "Who hurt you?"

"It doesn't matter... they can't hurt us anymore."

His urgency becomes concern and confusion. "Willow... what did you do?"

I don't reply and that in itself is reply enough if one is smart enough to read into the silence. Nokosi is definitely smart enough to do that. He's also smart enough to let it end there. He doesn't push or pry and I respect that.

No more questions are asked, and we drive through the trees to the woodsy part of the reservation, away from town by far. It's quiet in the truck for the longest time. Nothing but potent pain swirling between us, making the atmosphere thick and heavy.

"Still like me?" I ask, unable to control myself. For some reason the thought of him not liking me makes me feel things I don't want to feel. I don't care what he thinks. I don't care what anybody thinks. Or at least... I didn't.

"Somebody hurt me once too," he confesses quietly. "So whatever you did, or whatever you wanted to do, I get it."

Somebody hurt him too.

We share a look in the darkness when we pull to a stop, lighting up a dark house with strong headlights.

"Wait here." Pushing open the door, he jumps out of the truck landing steadily on both feet. The door to the one-story home opens as he crosses the distance with powerful strides. I spy an older lady with a hunched back and white hair pulled back into a tight bun. It's difficult to make out her features.

Nokosi speaks to her for a moment as another woman appears behind the older one. I'm guessing it's his grandmother and aunt, but I can't say for sure.

He comes running back after a long moment of me scanning the dark area with tired eyes. There are more homes in the distance, all different shapes and sizes to this one. I wonder if they were built by them.

"Come on," Nokosi urges after opening my door. He takes my hand and helps me down, then keeps hold of me as we make the journey to his grandmother's home. I approach cautiously. I don't feel secure anymore. I feel on edge and guarded. Like I'm being watched and judged silently by devils in the trees, ready to take my soul to the underworld and torture me for an eternity.

It's a silly thought but it's a true one and I almost can't breathe.

"What is she going to do?" I ask quietly.

"You'll see," he replies.

"Hi," I greet meekly as we make our final few steps, crossing what felt like a long distance in no time at all.

"Sorry it's late, Elisi," Nokosi says, kissing her cheek.

The old lady's eyes don't leave me, she looks as cautious as I feel. Her pale eyes, so light it makes them fade into the white, scan me up and down. The woman beside her urges her on, a cigar-like object in her hand and a matchbox in the other.

"Elisi," she utters and finally the old woman holds out her hand to me.

It's trembling visibly, shaking like beads in a bowl during an earthquake. She hesitates and so do I.

"I don't think..." I whisper to Nok, pulling back but the old lady moves quickly and snatches my hand before I can go anywhere.

Her other hand closes over the top and her eyes hold mine.

I wish I'd run because the noise she makes has my heart racing and my palms sweating. She screams into the night startling us all and then she glares at me.

"DEMON!" she bellows, her voice croaky but strong.

"Elisi," Nokosi tries but she throws my hand back at me and grabs her grandson, clinging to him desperately.

"Evil!" she hisses as Nok battles to free his shirt from her grasp. She yells at him in her native tongue, throwing around words I don't understand all the while keeping him in a tight grip. They argue back and forth loudly as I back away to the truck, feeling shaken and mad that I ever let Nok bring me here.

He promised me he'd protect me.

"No! You mustn't be alone with her," Elisi begs, clinging to him for dear life. "She is death. She is evil. She wants to harm you!"

"You're being silly, Elisi, it's Willow, Lilith's sister... you love Lilith," he tries, looking at me sadly. "Please try to heal her..."

"No," the old woman snarls and spits at my feet. "The sooner this one dies, the better."

"Elisi," Nokosi gasps and so does the woman by her side. He says something else in his own tongue and then turns to me after prying her from his body. "Come on, let's get you home."

The woman shrieks after us but his aunt guides her away, soothing her with kind-sounding words and a soft tone. But the despair and panic that I can hear in the old woman's voice is genuine fear. She really is magic. She was so right about every-thing she said.

Maybe she could have healed me if I were a better person.

Maybe I do need to die. Maybe she does for speaking to me like that.

He guides me back to his truck, both of us visibly shaken, and helps me inside. He even leans across me to strap me in and I get a strong whiff of his hair. It smells like coconut and pineapple. So sweet.

"I am so sorry; I don't know what came over her. She has never done that before."

I don't reply, I just want him to drive us home so I can forget this ever happened. He drives and we sit in the dark silence for a while, not even the radio crackles in the background.

"Maybe... I mean... I don't know," he stammers for the right thing to say but at this point, what can be said? "I wish I'd never taken you. I should have left it all alone and just taken flowers to your funeral like a normal person."

Despite my racing heart and confusion, I laugh because that was a bit funny. I love dry humor and Nokosi comes with barrels of it.

His hand closes over mine on my thigh and my skin beneath it quivers and tightens at his touch. I remain impassive, trying to deny the fact that his hands can make me feel anything.

I hate men.

I hate him.

He pulls over at the side of the dirt road we're on, the head-lights highlight the trees and I see the eyes of animals in the far distance, glowing like the tiny demons I feared back at his grand-mother's house. Really, I'm the scariest thing in these woods, and both I and the old lady know it.

"I'm really sorry, Willow," he whispers, squeezing my hand tighter. "I feel... I'm not one to feel bad usually but I feel fucking awful right now."

I turn to look at him in the truck, chewing on the corner of my mouth.

"I know you are," I breathe and place my hand over his, holding him in place. "Old people are crazy... but... maybe your grandmother was right."

His light brown eyes scan my face in the darkness, and I wonder what he sees in the shadows of my profile.

"I've done bad things, Nokosi, when I die I know I'm not going to heaven and I've made my peace with that." My voice is but a whisper in the silence.

"I'm sure you did what you had to do, Willow."

I shake my head sadly. "I didn't. I did a lot that I never had to do."

"Maybe you can redeem yourself before... before you go?" His hand is still on mine, on my thigh, and I'm still coiling inside. I've never felt like this before.

I shift in my seat and feel his fingertips brush my inner thigh. My entire body shivers, my soul lights a fire that hasn't burned for so long.

This isn't okay. I don't want to feel this way. Not about *him*, not about anybody.

He has his hooks in my sister, but not me. No...

I could do it now. I could end him and take my sister away forever... but she'd never forgive me, would she?

Because I'm finally starting to understand what she sees in him.

"There's no redeeming me..."

He wets his lips gently, eyes still on mine. "Was she right?"

"About?"

"About you wanting to hurt me?"

I laugh lightly and look ahead again. The silence stretches between us endlessly. "Do you love my sister?"

"I—"

"Do you love her?" I demand, my lips a flat line. "Would you protect her with your life?"

He takes a moment and clicks his tongue against his palate, then he sighs and rubs his face with both hands, releasing my thigh to do so, making me feel cold and alone again. "Love is... not something I understand... or something I ever understood. I get familial love for my sibling and father. I get loss love for the mother I never knew but even that's shadowed by guilt over the fact I killed her as she birthed me. But soppy love between two people that hardly know each other, it's not something I ever believed in or wanted. When I met your sister I thought..."

He laughs gently and looks away.

"I thought she was a pain in the ass, and I'd take what I could while she let me. But I don't know... now I feel like if she ever walks away from me I'll be a shadow of the person I am now. I'm young, I get told this by Anetúte a lot. But not so young that I can't feel a connection to her and know what it means." He smiles at me, slightly embarrassed. "And I know without a doubt that I would die for her before I ever let anybody take her from me. And I know that as much as she'll deny it, she'd die for me too. There are only a handful of people in my life, even less so, that I would trust with my very soul, your sister is one of them. She was made for me, I don't care how fucked up that sounds. She was made for me and she is mine."

Fuck...

"So," he continues, grinning at me now, pink tinging his cinnamon-colored cheeks. "Was Elisi correct in thinking you want to hurt me?"

I stare at him, openmouthed like a fish, eyes brimming with tears. His words affected me more than I'd ever like to admit. My sister is safe. My sister is loved. My sister loves.

This is the moment I'll remember forever, until my body is no more and my memories are all I have in the abyss.

"Willow?" he urges, looking nervous now.

I wipe away a stray tear that trickles down my cheek. "I don't want to hurt you, Nokosi." He looks relieved by that fact. But then I finish, "I want to kiss you."

Lilith

I hold back my sister's hair as she vomits into the basin. She's deteriorating at a rapid pace and Mom is worried. She wants to take her to a hospice to live out her final days, but I just can't bear it.

"Go," Willow tells me when she's stopped puking and is feeling a bit better. "Mom's got me. Just go."

"I'm not leaving you."

"You've been planning this beach trip for days. Please just go," she gives me a strong shove and grins at me. "Please... it would make me happy if you would go."

"Let me get you comfortable first."

Mom takes her other arm and we guide her to bed where I set her up with her laptop and phone.

Mom sits by her bedside, not looking at me, unspeaking. She's not taking this well.

"I should stay."

"No!" Willow yells and I can tell I've annoyed her. "Just go. Be with Nok. You've abandoned him enough for me lately."

I'm surprised she's suddenly on his side, up until now she has only ever spoken about him with animosity. I wonder what changed. Maybe she's finally willing to stay?

"Besides, I've got shit to figure out. I don't need you breathing down my neck."

"What shit?"

The look she gives me has me raising my hands in surrender. "Okay, okay... sorry I asked." But then I panic and swing back around. "Wait... please don't tell me you're going to..."

"No," she replies, frowning. "Nothing like that. It's just something I need to know about. Something unrelated."

Satisfied with her answer, I head out. My sister has never been a liar, not with me. She evades the truth but she doesn't lie. I trust her that much. That and as selfish as it is, I really want to go to the beach.

It's cold, I mean, it's February so of course it is, but they like to build a bonfire with driftwood and some of them surf while the rest of us watch. Though I can see myself surfing if we can rent a wetsuit. I've never surfed before and I love a thrill.

He's outside, leaning against the side of his truck waiting for me, looking at the invisible watch on his wrist.

"Impatient," I admonish, leaning into him to kiss his lips.

Grinning, he wags his brows, opens the door for me, and smacks my ass as I climb inside.

I love it when he does that.

"If only we had bikini weather." Nokosi sighs heavily once in his own seat. His eyes linger on my breasts which are hidden behind two layers, my white top that gets floaty at my stomach, and my thick bra that makes my tits look a bit rounder.

"You see me in my underwear all the time," I point out, helping myself to his soda in the cup holder below the stereo.

He snatches it from me. "It's not the same as a bikini."

My head hits the headrest as I laugh. "It's exactly the same thing."

"Agree to disagree," he declares with extra elongation of each word. His hand goes to my thigh. "How's your sister?"

"Not good today, but I think it's because of all the sneaking out she's been doing." His hand on my thigh squeezes harder for a moment. That's weird. Is it a reaction to what I'm saying or is it meant to be comforting?

"Sneaking out?"

I think she's up to something, which worries me, but I also don't want to start questioning her if she's getting herself back into the world. She's been so afraid of connecting with people for so long. Could this finally be it? Could she be healing? Or is she continuing the legacy I was hoping she'd leave behind? "Yeah, she's a hermit... she's terrified of people."

"Why?" he asks gently, giving my thigh a different kind of squeeze this time.

"Not today, Nok. I don't want to ruin the day."

"But you'll tell me?"

I think about it for a moment, considering it. It'd be nice to speak to somebody about it, but then it'd lead to questions I can't answer. Questions that could put my sister in danger.

"If I tell you," I say, looking at him. "At any point... do I have your word, on your life, that you won't ask me any questions."

He frowns, his eyes ahead as he navigates the car with ease. I love driving with him. I just love being near him. He's an anchor to my calm. He helps keep me grounded.

"Because if I don't have your word, I won't give you even one."

"No questions? Not one?"

"No. Not one."

"That's going to be a hard promise to keep."

I nod with understanding. "Trust me, I know."

The beach is fucking cold, the water colder. I don't get to surf but Nokosi does take me on a bit of a hike which I enjoy. We come to the top of a cliff and stand looking over the harsh waves hitting the face of it. I love standing on the edges of cliffs. It gives me a certain rush because of how dangerous yet beautiful it is. It's deceptive.

I suppose it's the closest thing I can think of to compare myself to.

"I am this cliff edge," I say to Nokosi who just raises a brow. "I'm beautiful..."

"You are."

"I'm dangerous."

"You're that too."

"I'm deceptive."

He hesitates. "Not with me, I hope?"

I look at him in the eyes and then spread my arms as the wind whips through my hair and caresses my body. Closing my eyes, I let my foot hang over the edge out in front of me. It would be so easy to die here today, to hit the water and drown, or to hit the rocky decline and break my neck, or perhaps it'll be slow, and I will beg for death... or for life.

"What are you doing?" Nokosi snaps, grabbing the back of my shirt and yanking me back.

"Tempting fate," I reply when my butt hits the grass as he falls to his knees in a bid to protect my body from my twisted soul.

"Why?" He's seriously mad, his eyes are aflame with the anger coursing through him. "Do you want to die? Are you suicidal?"

"Suicidal is a subjective word."

"It's about as fucking subjective as a potato!"

My lips twitch into a smile. "A potato?"

He tightens his ponytail. "Nobody can say a potato isn't a potato."

"This is true, but suicidal is more of a condition of the brain, like depression, a chemical imbalance, your body warring against you. I don't have that. I'm not suicidal. I don't *want* to die. I just know that I'm going to and I'm ready for it."

"So, what... you're some raging adrenaline junkie?" Standing, he yanks me to my feet and watches me shrug my shoulders with dark eyes. "Can you maybe think of somebody else when you're finding your stupid thrills by tempting death and testing your lifespan?"

"Like who? You?" I ask, raising a brow. "Are we at that part in our relationship? Do you care if I die, Nokosi?"

"Is that a serious question?"

I place my hand against his racing heart. I scared him. I kind of like that, as fucked up as that sounds. I like that I have the ability to terrify him, that he needs me in his life so desperately. "*Deadly.*" I play invisible drums with my hands. "Bad-um-tss."

He turns away from me, but I see him trying to stifle his smile.

I wrap my arms around his waist and press my cheek against the space between his shoulder blades. "I'll stay with you for as long as I can, Nok. I don't want to be anywhere else. Dead or alive."

"Your sister..."

"I'm starting to work her over I think, she's starting to see things my way. If I can just get her to see that life here could be good." I blow out a breath and he turns until both of his arms are around me too.

"Your mom?"

"My mom's a cunt." I can't remember the last time I had a conversation with her. "She just looks at me with these judgy eyes and then fucks off to work, usually leaving me notes telling me how proud she isn't of me."

"She's not proud of you?"

"I'm not a good person, Nokosi. She knows it. I know it. We accept it and move on. I'll never be the daughter she wanted."

"You sound just like—" His lips thin to a white line as his words cut off abruptly.

"Like who?"

Thunder rolls in the distance, seconds after a flash of blinding white light over the sea. I smile and move towards the cliff edge again but Nokosi pulls me back.

"Let's go make camp."

I look around us. "Can't we camp up here?"

"Away from everybody?"

Nodding, I try to move to the cliff edge again.

"I want to watch the storm, Nokosi."

"Can we stay on one topic? My brain is fried."

I look at him and think about us staying up here, alone. But then I see him glance over his shoulder, his body language telling me that he wants to be back with his friends as much as he wants to stay with me. I need to stop selfishly taking up all his time.

"Let's go back," I state, deciding now is as good a time as any to turn over a new leaf and relieve my body of its selfish ways. For the most part. Some things are better left kept as they are.

"Good, because I have a surprise for you..." he mumbles, taking my hand and leading me back down the cliff towards the others.

"What is it?"

"You'll see."

It takes thirty minutes, but we greet the others with enthusiasm, relieved to see tents up and crates out.

"What are we thinking about the storm?"

"It should stay out."

Both Bobby and Joseph speak amongst themselves as I lift myself into the bed of Nokosi's truck as he builds the tent upon it. He has a truck bed tent. That's so fucking cool. When he said he had it handled he really meant it.

"Did you have fun?" Nash asks, pulling himself up beside me. "You were gone a while."

"I was testing my ability to fly," I joke and Nokosi grunts and starts grumbling under his breath about crazy bitches, meaning me. My smile only gets brighter. "Your brother worries about me. It's cute."

"Everyone worries about you," Nash replies, nudging me with his shoulder. "You're a headcase."

"I am not."

"I bet if I told you to swim to that buoy and back, you'd do it."

"Nash," Nokosi warns.

I shake my head. "Even *I'm* not that dumb. Those waters are feral, man. I'd sink faster than the Titanic."

"The Titanic didn't sink fast," Bobby argues so I throw an empty can at his head. "Ouch."

"Your surprise is here," Nokosi whispers in my hair and kisses my ear.

I turn, looking around him to see a car pulling up. My excitement rises. But then Mackenzie gets out of the car and with her comes another girl I don't know.

I can't even fake a smile. "You shouldn't have, Nok. You really shouldn't have."

"Hey!" Mack cries, waving animatedly. She races over to me and hugs me like we've been friends for years.

The evil shit chuckles under his breath like he's hilarious.

Nash grabs my hand because I'm legit about to rip her head back by her hair.

"Be nice," Nokosi warns but his tone holds his amusement. Nash releases my hand but he looks as entertained as Nokosi does. "I thought it would be good for you to socialize with your own species."

"I'm going to kill you," I mouth at him, eyes narrowed and hands gripping the truck, so I don't stick my thumbs in his eyes.

He just whistles casually and gets on with making the truck tent while Mack chats excitedly about being a part of something awesome in senior year. I only perk up to her chipper arrival when she tells me she has more FBI intel.

Bobby who had already sidled up to her looks as excited at the news as I feel. Nash helps Nokosi finish the tent and the rest of the people all put plastic sheeting on the ground between the few tents standing in the small clearing. They pin it all down with heavy rocks and put lanterns on top of those. These people don't mess around.

"Tell us then," Bobby begs, looking at Mackenzie with round, lusting eyes. He's like a puppy eyeing a juicy bone. I resist the urge to roll my eyes. "What's new that we don't know already?"

"Well... they think they found the killer," she whispers excitedly, her eyes as round as saucers.

"Who is it?"

"I don't know for sure, I couldn't get that info, but..." She wets her lips and bounces from foot to foot. "The killer, if it's this person, has already been declared dead. They found the body in Vegas a few weeks ago but only just connected it with the murders."

"Vegas?" I ask, frowning with confusion.

She nods, her eyes still wide. "Yep. I've been trying to figure out a timeline while checking over everybody declared dead that month but there are *so many* to go through. It's a needle in a haystack."

"You're determined."

"Duh. And that's not even the craziest part..."

"Tell us," Bobby demands, and I can taste his excitement in the air.

"They found two more victims. Students of Saltwater High or something. I forgot the name. Both teen males."

"Whoa... that's twenty-nine, right?" Bobby breathes, looking on edge now and freaked out. As am I.

Mackenzie nods, looking sad. "All those lives lost. So sad."

"Do you know anything else?" I ask, chewing on my lip. "Are they closing the investigation?"

"No idea. I doubt it. They still haven't identified who this person is or why they think it's this person and their security systems are getting harder to crack." She slaps a hand over her mouth. "Forget I said that."

"Said what?" I ask, smirking.

Bobby shrugs his shoulders. "All I can hear is thunder."

"That'll be my beating heart from all this excitement," Mackenzie jests and then slaps Bobby around the face when he takes this as an invitation to put his hand over her chest, directly over the swell of her breast.

"Ouch," he murmurs but doesn't argue the fact he deserved it and more.

"Don't touch titties without permission, dude," I admonish playfully and pat him on the shoulder.

"Understood," he replies, rubbing his cheek dramatically, "I still love you, Mackenzie."

"No," she states simply, shaking her head. "Just no."

"I'll win you over eventually with my charm and serial killer knowhow."

"So attractive." I laugh under my breath and move to where Joseph is keeping Mackenzie's guest entertained.

I get annoyed at her laugh and walk away before Joseph finishes introductions. She has one of those nervous giggles that sprout at any fucking time and I can't deal with it.

"S'up?" Nokosi asks as I approach.

"Can we go back to our cliff to get away from Giggly, Chatty, and everyone else?" I ask but I'm only half-joking. "I want to smoke weed and have sex."

He groans into my neck and hardens against my thigh. "Why do I get hard whenever you mention sex or anything pertaining to?"

"Because you find me really attractive and devilish in the sack?"

"You're not very humble these days."

"I'm dating you... have you seen you? Imma gloat for the rest of my life at the world."

Laughing, he guides me around the finished tent and lifts me inside where the mattress is ready and covered. My bag is stuffed to the side behind his and I'm happy to see two flashlights and a lantern. Within reach.

I take the biggest flashlight but Nokosi snatches it from my hand. "Mine."

"Okay, Seagull," I mutter petulantly, taking the smaller one which actually feels nicer in my grip but I won't admit that to him. "So... who has the beer? I'm ready to get this party started."

Nokosi cups his hands to his mouth and howls at the sky. I do the same, trying not to laugh as the entire camp joins in. It's his thing and I fucking love it.

We drunkenly hit the mattress giggling... yep... both of us. Even Nokosi. He's so wasted but so am I so who cares? The tent interior is spinning so I cover my eyes with my arm. It's cold. Not so cold that I'm shivering but I just want to bury myself under the blanket.

He takes a gulp of his beer after fumbling with the tent zip and goes to lift his shirt over his head.

"Too cold," I whisper, rolling onto my front. "I don't want to get naked anymore."

"Whatever," he breathes and yanks my pants down just over my rear. I squeak, then laugh, then yelp when his cold hand creeps around my front and finds himself between my legs. He nudges his way into my warm sex, stretching my skin in a nice kind of way as his girth struggles to fit. My legs are stuck together so I'm not much help, and his chest is against my back so I can't raise my hips or anything to meet him.

I relax, wriggling to help him find his way, sighing when he pushes into the hilt and starts thrusting wildly, grunting in my ear with each powerful jerk of his hips. I swear the truck bed moves but I'm too drunk to care.

It's so fucking tingly but I'm too drunk for it to be more than that. Or at least I think I am. I soon find I'm wrong when the hand that guided him in starts playing with my clit.

I groan and bury my face in the blanket as he kisses my neck and grinds into me.

"So tight," he whispers, getting harder and faster. "Fucking love your pussy, Lilith."

"Shhh," I hiss, giggling when he cries out louder just to be an ass.

"Take it in the ass, Lil!" he yells, still pounding inside of me.

"Oh my God, shut up!" I try to roll over, still burning with need, still laughing my metaphorical ass off. "I swear on all that is Satan I will shave off your beautiful hair while you sleep."

He snickers, tipsy and happy and stops thrusting wildly so he can kiss me softly, forcing me to crane my head at an unnatural angle to accommodate it. Then he slaps my bare ass and keeps going, working me to orgasm before I even realize what's happening. I almost scream... it surprises me that much. It feels incredible and I can hardly breathe when he's done.

He holds his hips against my body until his own orgasm subsides and then pulls out immediately, finding wet wipes in his bag which we both use to clean up.

"I WANT THAT PASSION!" Mackenzie yells and Nok and I look at each other wide-eyed.

"I'M STILL PASSIONATE!" Bobby replies and I have to clutch my stomach to stop me from choking on my laughter. Oh it hurts. My sides are splitting.

Nokosi and I undress in record time, getting into our matching onesies that his father purchased for us specifically for this trip because he thought it would be funny. We both look like teddy bears but now I'm under the blanket in his arms, fur on fur, I'm so happy Dasan did. I'm so snug and warm in a way I never would have been in normal pajamas.

He also gave us a talk on sex education... reminding us that sex equals babies and disease and all that stuff. It was really funny. Nokosi didn't think so. I couldn't stop laughing into my shirt.

I told him that I got the implant over a year ago, so he didn't have to worry about becoming a granddaddy just yet. He called me smart then asked when he could meet my mother. Nokosi promptly removed me from the house before his father could start talking weddings next.

In Nokosi's culture they aren't supposed to have sex before marriage, but his father isn't as strict as most. He understands his son's needs to explore life a bit before settling down. But I also think he's convinced that Nokosi will settle down with me. Apparently Locklear men marry young and usually always pick the right woman for them. I can't say I'm completely opposed to the idea. Especially if I'm now off the hook with my past.

That would be fucking amazing.

"Remind me to thank your dad."

"Uh-huh," Nokosi drunkenly mumbles and relaxes when I trap my thigh between his.

CHAPTER 24

Lilith

Bobby throws a napkin at Nokosi's head, so I throw a butter knife at his face. He ducks and screams like a little girl. It misses by a mile, but it was never meant to hit him anyway.

"Pussy," I comment, grinning at him as he rights himself and kicks the knife across the floor. It scrapes along the tiles before coming to a stop at Nash's table leg. Nash who is currently on his phone with a serious look on his face.

We're in a diner just off the route home after a long day and night and morning of camping. We had to leave first light because the storm changed course and by the time we packed up it was ready to rain hellfire down on us. The clouds are so thick and gloomy they look almost black. But overall it has been a great morning and now I'm treating them all to pancakes and whatever else they order. Because everyone is poor right now and I'm desperate for greasy food slathered in butter and syrup.

"How can you afford to pay for everyone's breakfast when you don't even have a job?" Mackenzie, who decided to sit opposite me, asks.

"How do you know I don't have a job?"

She looks away for a moment, embarrassed. "Do you have a job?"

"Do you?"

"I do. I work for—"

"Didn't ask, don't care," I respond, and she laughs around the word, "Bitch."

Then she sobers and adds, "You didn't answer my question."

I tap my nose and sip my coffee. It's not the best but it will do.

"You're super evasive," she comments, her smile fading now. "In a bad way not a good way."

I stare her down, wondering what her deal is. "And you're super nosy, in a bad way... *not a good way.*"

She looks away, out of the window, and chews on her lip. After a moment she apologizes but it sounds insincere and forced. "I'm not the best company in the mornings. I don't like not knowing things."

"I can tell," Nokosi says, having my back as always.

She ignores him and continues. "I just find it all a bit weird."

"What?" Bobby asks, looking at the girl who is sitting to his right.

Joseph and Mack's friend, the giggler, are sitting opposite Nash on the other table looking over with inquisitive gazes.

"That a new girl rolls into town and throws actual cash at a fancy school that costs thousands per semester, a furnished house in the richer side of town, yet no job to speak of." She shrugs her shoulders.

"Have you been putting your nose in my business?" I ask, suddenly seeing Mackenzie in a darker light, one more threatening. I completely underestimated her.

"It's what I do. I can't help myself."

"Don't go down this road, Mack," I warn, gritting my teeth. "You won't like what you find."

"Is that a threat?"

I shake my head to clear it. What am I doing? Mack is obviously good at getting information. The last thing I need is her poking around where I don't need her poking and provoking her isn't going to entice her to stay away. "It's a private matter, one I don't like talking about."

"I can tell," she rebuts, shrugging her shoulders like she doesn't give a fuck.

This bitch... she's starting to piss me off. But she's dangerous. She asks all the right questions. She'll be an excellent detective one day. "You want to know where and how I have money?"

"Yes," she replies, and I take back what I said about her being pretty. She's fucking ugly and I hate her. But I also need her off my back. I don't like that she's not intimidated by me.

I start to lie, "My mother—"

"Your mother the environmentalist that nobody has ever met? Your mother who doesn't work where you said she does or if she did it's under a different name and also... *if she did*, she wouldn't be earning nearly enough to throw the amount of paper bills you threw at the school to get a place."

I decide at this juncture it's best to tell the truth. Maybe it will make them all so uncomfortable they'll never talk to me about it again. Dad always said the most convincing lie is one based on the truth. Well... let's hope he was right. Although this one is all true. Sadly. Such is the tragedy that is my life.

"My twin sister and I were assaulted..." Nokosi tenses and everybody's eyes swing to me. I'm not being loud but I'm not being quiet enough so that nobody hears. Luckily her smug face starts to fade into something a bit softer, more understanding. "It was brutal, it scarred us both for life. The money we have is the *compensation* from the assault. They were loaded. They paid well to make us disappear. End of conversation."

"You said *they*..." she points out and I want to reach over and punch her in the face. "There was more than one?"

I nod bitterly. "There were five of them and two of us. Happy now?"

The glass of OJ in Nokosi's grip cracks and then shatters. That took some serious strength. Orange juice spills over the edge of the table and between his legs but he doesn't see it. His eyes won't leave me.

He looks devastated, angry, upset. All of them swirling around his eyes.

"I am so sorry," Mackenzie breathes as Bobby rushes to clean up the OJ. "I should never... I feel terrible. I can see I've made you... I've made us... I do this, okay? This is why I don't have friends. I'm not a trusting person. I'm too paranoid. I hate myself for it, but I live for it. I'm sorry. So sorry." She reaches for my hand, but I pull away. I'm not taking comfort from this bitch who put me on the spot in front of people I consider friends. "If there's anything I can do to... I just..."

"Stop," Bobby tells her softly. "Stop talking."

The waitress places our food down, but nobody starts to eat. Suddenly everybody has lost their appetite, everybody but me.

"Get the fuck over it, guys." I stab a piece of bacon with my fork and pop it into my mouth. "At least now you all know why I'm a fucking psycho. And let me just tell you, if you breathe a word of that to anybody, I will pluck your eyeballs out and feed them to the person beside you."

Nobody knows what to say. It's awkward now. I made it awkward.

No... Mackenzie made it awkward.

I look at her again. "Satisfied?"

"No. I wish you'd robbed a bank to be honest."

At that I laugh lightly and wag my brows at her. "Maybe I did."

Willow

"We need to tell Lilith about this," Nokosi declares.

We've put three coats of white paint over the dirty garage walls and I don't have anymore excuses to keep him to myself. That's so bad isn't it? Wanting my sister's boyfriend all to myself...

I think he knows that's my game too because he's been keeping his distance ever since I told him I wanted to kiss him. It's crazy thinking that was almost a week ago. He's been around twice since. Not nearly enough.

"I know," I murmur, looking at him with puppy dog eyes. "But not yet. *Please*. I just need more time to think. If she knows we've been hanging out, one, she'll get insanely jealous and two, she'll think that means I want to stay."

"Why don't you want to stay?"

I raise my hands and let them hit my thighs with a slap. "Because I want to see more of the world before I die."

His head dips. "I get that. I respect that too."

"It's not like she can't come back when I die."

He nods again. "I totally understand that too. Have you told her that?"

I walk away from him and play with the end of my braid. My hair feels so dry these days. Another symptom of the meds, perhaps? Who the fuck knows anymore?

"We just end up arguing about it."

He blows a raspberry. "Siblings fucking suck sometimes. But... I can't keep hiding this from her because you're worried about the fallout."

"I know," I agree sadly.

"You need to tell her about this."

I look at him, the narrow points at the edge of each eye, the heavy lids that make him constantly smolder, the creases around his thick, heart-shaped lips, the striking dark ring of brown that circles his light brown iris. "She won't let us hang out anymore."

He chuckles under his breath and murmurs, "Maybe that's for the best."

I laugh with him, not denying the fact I want more from him than I know he will give. "Promise me you won't tell her until I do?"

"I'm not making that promise."

Of course, he's not. He's too fucking loyal to her.

I groan and punch him playfully in the chest, it doesn't bother him in the slightest. "Then can I ask a favor?"

"You already asked me about a million and I'm still working on them," he jokes, smirking at me now in that very way that used to infuriate me.

"Can you use this last time alone with me to make your confession?"

His smile fades as I knew it would. A sad sight.

"What?"

"Your confession. I told you mine, my sister told you too, so now you tell me yours."

He looks dumbfounded, almost terrified. Suddenly this strong, handsome man that my sister is bedding looks about nine years old, wanting to hide from monsters that don't exist. Or perhaps they did for him.

"I don't want to talk about that."

"I know, and that's exactly why you should."

He frowns. "Why?"

"Because damaged people understand damaged people. I'm about as damaged as it gets. Lay it on me. Let me take it from you for a while. I know you want to tell somebody."

He shakes his head. "If that's so true why won't your sister talk to me about what happened to her? I want to ask her about it, but I gave her my word I never would."

"What do you want to know?" I ask, and we both sit on upturned buckets facing each other. "Ask me anything, I'll answer if I can."

"I'm almost scared to," he mutters and rubs his eyes with the heels of his palms.

I wait expectantly and I can tell by the look in his browns and the way he's biting his lips he's really thinking hard about the questions he wants to ask.

"What happened? How did it start?"

"Are you sure you have the stomach for it, Nokosi?"

"No."

I laugh through my nose. "Well, you better line it with lead in preparation." I rub my hands on my thighs. "Growing up, my sister and I were good students, great daughters, good friends. We weren't bullies or bullied, we had stable lives and a happy-ish home."

"That's good to know."

"But..." I continue, smiling sadly. "We found out I was sick. I had a seizure and collapsed during a school trip, they did a brain scan and six months later I was being pumped full of medications to stop the growth of this tumor. A tumor I've had unknowingly since birth."

His lips part. "I'm sorry... that sucks."

"Yes... well... anyway. So, treatments failed, and I was told I had maybe two years left to live. The chances of me reaching my nineteenth birthday were slim then and even slimmer now." I raise my hands to show him all I am.

"You don't look skinny and frail like I imagined you would," he admits softly, and I laugh.

"You've been imagining my body, have you, Nok?"

He rolls his eyes.

"Anyway, I decided that we needed to live a little, me and Lilith. We didn't really party or do much other than take our bikes out, and I really didn't want to die a virgin but not many people wanted to date the new girl with no hair."

"I'm sure you were still beautiful."

"What's worse is... I lost my hair for nothing. The chemo failed to stop the tumor's growth, so it was all pointless." I flap my hand at him. "So, me being me I decided to make friends with all of the wrong people. I started dabbling in drugs because you only live once, right? I started drinking and partying and then finally I met this gorgeous eighteen-year-old guy. He was so fucking hand-some, really preppy, rich, like Bill Gates rich."

"Sounds like a dick."

"He was, but he wanted to party, and I wanted to lose my virginity. He said he knew what he was doing, that he'd make it good for me. I believed him, but my sister didn't want me to party alone. Of course, she didn't. She never did. She followed me around, making sure I got home safe, loving me and looking after me..."

"Lilith is good like that."

I nod slowly. "She really is. She's amazing. So, we go to this guy's house and he's having a gathering with his friends, right? Just him and a few buddies, but that's cool, they're all snorting coke and drinking tequila, we're all just there to have a good time."

His back stiffens. "I don't know if I want to hear this."

"I'll spare you most of it but let's put it this way... one minute I was awake and grinding up on him, the next I'm on the ground and my head is foggy. But I hadn't done any drugs or drank much. I wanted to be mostly sober for my deflowering."

Nokosi buries his head in his hands for a moment, his thigh is bouncing. "I really don't know if I want to hear this."

"My sister, who was saving her virginity for somebody she cared about was on the floor next to me but too far for me to reach. Some asshole was peeling down her pants as another kept trying to get her to drink. She'd been saying no to their offers for drinks all night and they didn't like that. They pushed the bottle into her mouth... it broke her tooth, her incisor. She rolled over and vomited, I saw it floating in the bile between us."

"Fuck... what the fuck?" he breathes, looking as sick as I feel telling this story. This truth of mine that I've never once told anybody.

"They raped her, I watched them lift her legs, spread them in her dazed state and one by one they fucked her, coming inside of her, laughing with each other and chatting like they weren't committing a crime. She screamed. She wasn't one of those who lay there and just took it like I did. She screamed, and begged, and fought, and they wouldn't stop. They didn't care. These were not men, they were fucking animals and they took something from her that she'd never get back."

Nokosi places his hands on mine and squeezes. "You don't have to continue if you don't want to."

"I felt my sister's pain more than I felt my own, that's crazy right? I felt sadder for her than I did for myself." I turn my hands over and grip his tight.

We're bonding, sharing this moment with him is bringing us closer together, I can feel it.

"What happened to them? What happened to you?"

"Well, there wasn't really any hiding what they'd done, we were a mess, I felt sure they were going to kill me but everybody knew where we were because the fucking idiots had posted all over social media with pictures of us partying with them." I sigh, thinking back to that night all the while trying not to vomit and lose my mind over it.

"The rich one, he was an arrogant son of a bitch. He didn't care who knew what he'd done because it turns out his father was... let's just say an important man. It became clear to us by the morning that nobody was going to help us. The father of said prick was as sadistic as his son... he told us he'd have us institutionalized and accuse us of trying to rob him to pay for our medical expenses. Blah blah blah. It was all bullshit. He paid us off for our silence and we took the cash, of course we did, we weren't stupid. Or I wasn't... My sister wanted nothing to do with the money." I laugh coldly. "The fucker even paid for our medical care, made one of his doctor buddies take care of us. We were so badly brutalized that we needed stitches down below... that's how fucked up that night was. Trust me when I tell you that I'm sparing you the gore."

"I believe you. You don't have to. I can handle it."

"No, you can't. You love my sister. It'll keep you up at night." I relax my hands in his. "The man had us followed for weeks, making sure we didn't go to the police. He had our clothes that we were wearing that night burned and any other evidence. We had not a leg to stand on even if we did go to the cops. We knew it was pointless and to say that felt frustrating is an understatement. We couldn't handle how unfair it felt. But we told our parents, of course we did... though I wish we hadn't."

"I bet they wanted to kill them."

"Oh yeah, my dad couldn't handle it either. The animals that did it to us, he approached them, he asked them why and they goaded him. Bragged about it. He lost his mind, he couldn't speak to us, he felt too guilty. He blamed himself. And then... he killed himself. My mom is a shell of the person she was, Nokosi. She can't even look at us."

He's mirroring my sadness. "I'm so sorry, Willow."

"Me too," I reply, keeping hold of his hands when he tries to pull them away. I shuffle closer until my knees are between his parted ones. "Now it's your turn."

"I don't think I can, not after what I just heard..."

"You should. Or you never will."

He shakes his head. "I feel like I'm trying to take away from your moment."

"I'd rather you did."

He groans and rubs his eyes with both hands. "I used to be best friends with a kid called Conner. Our moms were friends once upon a time, but then she died giving birth to me. Conner's mom kept in touch and often took us on days out together, which turned into sleepovers as I got older. Conner's father was an officer of the law, so my dad thought this was a great idea. Officer Deacon was an excellent role model, he'd say." Laughing bitterly, he clings to my hands like I'm his lifeline and I almost wish I was. "Officer Deacon is a pedophile who started grooming Conner and me from around age three. He used to make us do things together, things that..." His eyes cloud over with shame. "It felt good, okay? And we were young, so we didn't know any different."

My heart rate begins to rise. I'm not sure I can hear this, I keep telling him he can't handle my past but the truth is... I don't think I can handle his.

"And then one day, Conner was walking funny. He was in pain. We must have been about seven at the time and we had this secret that only each other knew. It made us close because we had to be. So, Conner had no issues with telling me his father had... anally *penetrated* him the night before."

My lips part. I feel sick.

"His father touched us, of course he did but it felt good, we liked it. We wanted more of it. We didn't know it was wrong. We'd fool around together; we'd fool around with him... and then it was my turn. He didn't fuck me for the first time until I turned nine. I guess he was worried I'd be in too much pain and he wouldn't be able to hide it. I just remember him holding me... while he... and he kept telling me I'd enjoy it eventually." He closes his eyes, unable to look at me while he speaks the words. "And I did. He was right. I wanted more of it. And he kept saying that I was as depraved as him, that he was helping me... It hurt at first but then it became normal. But then that normal became weird because we started getting into girls and we did sex-ed at school and were told

281

how wrong it was to show our privates." He rolls his shoulders and bites his lip. "I was confused. I started puberty and my orgasms made a mess now which was embarrassing. Conner started to withdraw. He stopped talking to anyone, myself included."

I shuffle closer, the bucket scrapes on the ground.

"He didn't want to do it anymore and to be honest, neither did I. Age thirteen I wanted to fuck girls, not men. I wasn't into that. Officer Deacon stopped but not without begging, it was messed up. He used to try and bribe us with new games until we just stopped hanging around at his house at all. Conner's parents had divorced by now and he moved in with his mom. Things were great for a while. We were happy. We were still best friends. I managed to get him back from his darkness but then it all changed.

"I don't know what happened but Conner, at age fifteen, didn't come to school for a week and he stopped talking to me again, like before, but worse this time." His eyes mist over, tears fill them and my heart breaks. "They found him hanging from a tree in his back yard the following Sunday, while everybody was at church, Conner killed himself. I should have done something to help him, but I didn't know what to do. He wouldn't even look at me."

"Do you think his dad got him one last time?"

He nods. "I think that's exactly what happened."

"Why didn't you tell anybody?"

"Officer Deacon became sheriff. A bit like you, he's a powerful guy. I've got no evidence that he molested either of us and if I stirred that pot it would be my family who suffer."

I shake my head. "Animals. All of them."

"Agreed," he whispers. "I've never told anybody that before."

"Not even Lilith?"

Shaking his head, he admits, "Not even Lilith."

I reach a hand to his face as his eyes hold mine. What we just shared is such an intimate... heart-wrenching thing that I believe will bond us forever.

I have to have him, if only once. It's not fair that my sister gets him. I like him too. Maybe he'll like me more than her?

"I really want to kiss you, Nok," I whisper, leaning closer. "Just once."

He places his hand over mine that cups his cheek. "I can't do that. I couldn't hurt your sister like that."

"She wouldn't have to know."

"I'd know. And I live with enough secrets already."

My lips pinch together. "Just one time. It wouldn't have to mean anything to you. Just once."

"Willow," he mutters softly, his tone pleading but in a different way to mine. "It'll hurt her."

"If she ever finds out, which she won't, she'll understand." I've never begged a man for his kiss before, but then I've never kissed a man willingly before. "Please, Nokosi." I lean into him, grabbing the front of his shirt. "This could be the last kiss I ever have."

"Way to lay it on heavy," he jests as I slide my hands up his chest to his neck. "I just can't, Willow. I'm sorry. I can't betray Lilith like that."

I've never been a very calm person; I've always been a little bit bitter. And as it turns out, I don't handle rejection very well either. The more he says no, the more I want him. As fucked up as that is.

"If you don't kiss me, I'll tell Lilith you instigated it, and then she'll never want to stay."

He blanches, staring at me with wide eyes after lurching back a step. "What the fuck, Willow? You really want to force me into kissing you after everything we just spoke about? I said no."

"Don't act like you don't want to kiss me, Nokosi, I'm my sister's image in every way and you're fucked up enough to find that a massive turn-on." I grab his bulge through his pants, but he rips my hand away. "What's the big deal? It's just one fucking kiss."

"You're insane. I thought we were becoming friends."

"I can't be your friend, Nokosi," I admit, shrugging. "I want you too badly." I wave my hand to the bucket he was just sitting on. "Sit back down, kiss me like you kiss my sister and I won't ruin your relationship with her."

"You know that if you make me do this, I'll never forgive you. Right?"

"I'm dying soon, Nok. I don't care about forgiveness. I want you and if this is the only way I get to have you then I'm okay with that."

He glares at me but I can see the excitement in the depths of his eyes. As much as he hates this, it's a thrill for him too. His girl-friend's sister is pining after him, I loathe to admit it, and he loves to know it. It's good for his ego.

"She won't believe you," he argues unconvincingly.

"She won't only believe me, Nokosi, she'll smash up that pretty truck of yours and never speak to you again."

He grits, his jaw clenched, his teeth bared. "And if she walks in on us, or finds out, she'll do that anyway."

"Sit down," I order.

"I'm not doing this." His willpower is wavering. He really does love my sister.

I shrug my shoulders and smooth down my skirt. "If you walk out of that door, I swear I'll tell her. I'll say you came on to me. I'll say you showed up at our door asking to meet me, then lured me out here and tried to seduce me." I'm serious too. I'll tell her that. I don't want to hurt her, but I want to feel his touch more. "It's just a fucking kiss, Nokosi. It doesn't have to be so dramatic. Just sit down." I'm surprised when he does so, his eyes murderous. "And there's one stipulation..."

"Seriously? You're making me kiss you *and* giving me rules?"

I laugh a little and smooth my braid. "I guess so."

"What is it?"

"Don't touch my hair," I instruct, staring him down. "I don't like my hair being touched, not while it's in such atrocious condition."

"Whatever," he murmurs and parts his knees so mine fit between them.

I blow out a breath and wet my lips. "Just kiss me."

"I'm never coming back here. You know that right?"

I click my fingers and grin. "How about this? Kiss me and I'll never make my sister leave. She can stay and be yours forever... or don't kiss me and I'll take her away. We both know I have the power to do that."

He wets his soft-looking lips. "I have your word?"

I nod. "I'll tell her we can stay. For a kiss I'd say that's not a bad deal. I'm trading the rest of my life for just a minute of your lips on mine."

"She can't know," he states.

"Duh."

He grabs my arm and yanks me towards him. I squeak when his lips hit mine, crushing them painfully.

Ouch.

He pulls away just as suddenly, his eyes wild and angry. Does he really think that's enough?

This time I yank him, and his hands grab my biceps, squeezing hard but not so hard that it hurts. I lick the seam of his lips, tasting him and he opens his mouth. *Finally.*

My tongue touches his. He tastes of cola and something else, something that's strictly him. It's exactly how I imagined but also so much better. He growls as his lips move against my own. This isn't passionate, this is anger. It's incredible.

It's exactly what I need. I have a feeling he needs it too. Especially after that conversation.

I deepen the kiss, grabbing the back of his neck so he can't escape but he bites my bottom lip so hard my eyes ping open and I taste blood.

"That's enough," he snaps, leaning back to glare at me.

My hand connects with his cheek and his head flies to the side. A welt the shape of a handprint appears on his face, bubbling across the surface of his smooth, bronze skin.

We stare at each other for a beat as blood drips down my chin.

"I decide when it's enough." I grab his hair and kiss him again, diving deep into his mouth. I can taste him, myself, blood... *fuck.*

This is my game. I get to decide when this ends. I get to choose. Not him.

I climb onto his lap, my lips still attached to his. He doesn't stop me. His eyes are squeezed closed as our mouths assault each other, his hands by his sides. He won't touch me. He doesn't want to. But I want him to. I *need* him to.

I want this. I *need* this. He needs this. I can give him what my sister can't. I can be an outlet for all his anger, and I can tell that he has so much of it. Maybe as much as me.

I reach between us, pulling down the elasticated waist of his paint-covered sweatpants, and before he even realizes what I've done, I have my hand around his cock.

His eyes spring open, and he pulls back. "Wait," he breathes, panicked, but it's too late, I've already worked my skirt out of the way, yanked my panties to the side and have poised him at my entrance.

"WILLOW, STOP!"

My back hits the floor so hard my head bounces off the concrete. Ouch.

Nokosi stands above me, eyes blazing as he pulls his pants back up. "Are you fucking insane?"

"Probably," I reply, smiling at him. "That and horny." I hide the rejection I feel, the burning anger and jealousy that he still chose my sister after that kiss.

He needs me I can tell.

"You're so uptight."

"Stay the fuck away from me," he barks, grabbing his truck keys off the ground and heading towards the door.

"It's just sex, Nokosi... I know you want it."

"Not with you."

My hands fist by my side and I punch him in the back between his shoulder blades. "What does she have that I don't?"

"My heart," he replies, slamming the door closed so hard a piece of wood splinters from the frame and falls to the floor.

Just his heart? I could win that too. I could own that.

I'm worthy.

I pick up the shard of wood and hold it so tightly in my hand my knuckles turn white.

The way he kissed me... I know he wants me... it's just my sister got to him first.

CHAPTER 25

Lilith

"We need to talk," Nokosi whispers, taking my arm in his hand.

"I'm playing soccer," I whine, looking at Mackenzie who I hate but am choosing to stay close with because she knows things and I need to stay on top of what she knows.

Nokosi kicks the ball away from me and all but drags me to the edge of the field.

"I'll be back," I call, ignoring my teacher when she blows the whistle at me. I investigate my lover's pointed pupils and then up at the sun in the sky. It's a really nice day, he better not be about to spoil my mood. "Couldn't this have waited?"

"Probably," he answers, grinning and pulling me into his arms to kiss me. His hands cup my rear making me squeak and shove him away.

"Will you stop?"

"Never."

"Is this what you pulled me out of class for? To grab my butt and kiss me?"

"Well, that and... Dad just called." He pulls out his phone and I shield it with my hand so I can see the screen. "He said that one of our neighbors is having another kid and have bought a bigger place. They're selling their old one. It's a ten-minute walk from Dad's at most." He scrolls through the pictures of the log cabin-type house that's like his own. "Dad said he'll loan me the money for the deposit because my savings aren't enough... but I don't want to get it if you're not going to do it with me."

I can't stifle my smile as I take the phone from his hand and look through the pictures that show the small, cozy home that's big enough for a family of three. Or in our case, us and maybe a big dog.

"You're asking me to move in with you?" I mutter as his arms come around my waist. He nods against the side of my head. "We hardly know each other."

"I know that I love you and I don't want to lose you."

I close my eyes to stop them from burning. "You love me?"

"Stay with me. I'm not going to college, my job pays well enough to keep us happy, you have no plans for college... and I know you love this life. I know I can make you happy."

"You do make me happy."

"Then stay with me."

I hesitate. I want to scream yes at the top of my lungs more than he knows, but I have obligations.

"Please say yes and we'll sign the papers this week."

I turn in his arms and press my cheek to his chest. "What about my sister? I can't leave her."

My teacher blows her whistle again. "You have five seconds, Lilith!"

"We'll talk later," I say, kissing him once more.

"Say yes," he orders, backing away from me.

I wave at him and get back to my game.

"What was that all about?" Mack asks, kicking the ball to me and catching it with her hands when I return it with a little too much power. "Not the face, come on..."

"Sorry." I try to balance it on my foot, but soccer has never been my game. I'm more into baseball.

"Tell me," she insists, tightening her ponytail with both hands.

"Nokosi just found us a place. He wants us to move in together."

She grins. "That's so fucking cool!"

"Right?"

"But...?"

"Huh?"

"You look ready to say but."

"My sister," I say as a reason and shrug my shoulders. "She's dying."

"I get that... but you're not." She's such a bitch, but I really respect that about her. She's not fake. Even though she asks all the right questions that piss me off immensely, she doesn't pretend to be something she's not or try to spare your feelings. "How long does she have left? Can't she live with you while she dies?"

"You're so crass," I tell her but I'm chuckling too. She's only saying all the things I'm thinking. "I'll speak to Nok about it, and her... we'll all figure something out." I bite my lip and kick the ball a little too hard again. "He told me he loves me. He's never said it before."

"He strikes me as the type that's never said it to anyone before."

I nod my agreement. "I don't think he has." We kick the ball back and forth silently for a few beats. "Any news on SSS?"

We abbreviated the serial killer because saying School Sigil Searer each time was getting too much. Especially since it's mostly the focal point of all our conversations.

"They're pretty sure that the body they found is of the killer, every update is just further evidence pointing to this person."

I feel my relief soar. "This is good. Maybe it'll all be over soon."

"Yeah, exactly." She grins wryly at me. "You know, for a while there I thought it might be you. New girl, new town, sketchy history, tons of cash, dating the nastiest guy in a prep school. You totally fit the MO and Nokosi for the most part fits the victims' profile."

I knew she suspected me. Not that I care. "Only fifteen percent of all serial killers to date are female... roughly. What a find that would have been. Not only a female, but just a kid, killing over thirty boys across the States."

"Yeah, I know, you're totally not savage enough for that. You've got to be really fucked up to have killed all of those people and still be able to interact with the world afterwards."

I laugh even though I shouldn't find it funny. It's just the situation. If only she knew how close she was to my own truth. "Well, let's hope I'm actually not the killer because the next person on my list would definitely be the smartest girl in school with the wrong suspicions."

"Not funny," she retorts but she's laughing too. "If you kill me, make it quick, yeah? And at least let me pop my cherry first. I don't want to die a virgin."

"Have you met Bobby?" I jest, knowing full well she has and how irritating she finds him. "He's passionate, remember?"

She kicks the ball at my face, but I duck at the right moment and it sails over my head.

Laughing still, I run after it.

Willow

Willow: Can you come over later and help me out again?

· · ·

He doesn't reply. I really pushed him too soon. Fuck. If I'd bided my time and been patient, I'd be able to hang out with them and seduce him that way. Maybe then he'd see how good we are for each other. If I'd given him more time he might have fallen for me too.

He should be mine. Not hers. She's got a lifetime to find someone like Nokosi. I only have a few months.

Willow: I'm really sorry for what I did. I feel terrible. If there's any way I can make it up to you, let me know.

Nokosi: Stop texting me. This has gone too far.

Willow: Can you blame me for it though? Really? You've seen you right? No girl in her right mind could spend all that time alone with you and not fall for you.

Nokosi: I love your sister. You're sick for wanting what she has.

Willow: You're right. I'm sick. I have a tumor in my brain. I'm dying. Try to see this from my side. All I wanted was one night. What's wrong with that?

. . .

Nokosi: I'm not texting anymore. I'm done with you, Willow. Leave me alone.

Willow: You're losing the best thing that has ever happened to you. I'm everything you need. I can make you happy. Just give me a chance.

Now I know how loyal he is... I want him until I physically can't have him anymore. He's one in a million. He's loyal, fun, sweet, kind, gently, loving, sexy, yet stable... he's all the qualities in a man that I never knew I wanted. And now that I've found him, I can't let him go.

Lilith

"What's troubling you?" Willow asks.

"I had a fight with Mom this morning," I answer, throwing the bouncy ball at the wall and catching it when it comes back. Willow lies next me, our heads on my pillow. I throw and she catches. I've been playing with a lot of balls recently.

"I heard some of it, sounded gnarly."

I nod. "It was."

"Want to talk about it?"

I shake my head, no.

"Please? Let me unload your burden."

"She thinks I'm being selfish," I whisper, thinking back to the past few months of my life where I have sacrificed everything to be with my family. How am I selfish? "She called *me* selfish because... well... it doesn't matter why."

I'm not telling her yet that I'm moving out. She's not ready to hear it. I'm not ready to say it. Especially not after the mom thing. I don't know why *she* can't stay and take care of Willow. I'll still be here all the time. I'll just be living with Nok. It's what I want. I've never wanted anything more.

"You're not selfish," Willow breathes, sounding confounded. "You're anything but. You deserve the world. Mom is a cunt."

"Agreed." I sit up and slip my feet into my shoes. "I have to go and meet Nokosi."

That and I have to get away from her until I can talk about everything. I feel terrible sitting so close to her and lying to her face.

She pulls a face, it's a curious one that I can't read. It looked like anguish, or something similar... I don't know.

"Say hi to him for me," she breathes as I leave her room.

"Sure," I mutter back, frowning with confusion. Suddenly she's acknowledging he exists? Last I checked she despised him. Although come to think of it, she hasn't really mentioned him at all recently, not even in ire.

She usually blames him and thinks he's stealing me away. Maybe she's finally calming down and seeing reason.

———

I wake, covered in sweat, the lingering images of my nightmare still flashing in my eyes.

It's pitch-black and I don't like that. I feel like the nightmare creatures are still lurking, staring down at me with their blank gazes. Dead... Dead because of...

"Nokosi?" I whisper, reaching beside me in bed. "Why's it so dark?"

I feel a cold hand. It doesn't belong to him.

It doesn't belong to him.

My heartbeat rises as I realize I haven't yet left the land of nightmares. I daren't look. Whoever it is is dead, I can tell. Their skin is waxy and holds no warmth and there's a funny smell emanating from them. Not yet putrid but something bad with an overflow of a scent that is almost sweet.

I sit up, holding the bedsheet tight to my chest. Light finally glows from the moon through the windows. I'm not in Nokosi's room... nor am I in mine. I don't know where I am.

The coldness of the body beside me seeps into my bones and soul. I feel a chill. I feel nauseous.

Turning my head, I look, my breathing staggered and harsh. I've never felt so much dread and terror.

I don't want to look at the face.

"Nokosi," I whimper, begging for him to come to me. "I need you. Where are you?"

I gather the courage, too scared to move in case the body reanimates and grabs me, but still I manage it. I look up and up and up, dragging my eyes the smallest fraction at a time until her face comes into focus.

"No," I breathe, sobbing now. My chest twists with agony, my heart burns a hole in my chest. "No... please... no. Not yet. My sister. Noooo." I pull her limp, lifeless body into my arms, holding her to my chest. "I'm not ready to let you go. I need you. Please. Don't die."

Her head flops, her body a deadweight against mine.

"Not yet," I beg, trembling and crying. Feeling a grief so overwhelming I can't breathe.

"You did this," a voice whispers in my ear. A croaky, whispered voice that echoes from somewhere not in this room. *"You did this to me."*

"No," I sob, holding her away from me so that I can tell her that she's wrong. "I didn't. I love you. You know I do."

She sits upright suddenly, bones clicking and cracking, her jaw hanging open, maggots feasting on her tongue, eyes rotting, hair falling from her scalp. A scream gets stuck in my throat when her hands wrap around my neck and squeeze.

I kick, thrash, and claw at her face, fighting for a breath so I can scream.

"You did this!" she shrieks, showing black teeth only an inch from my face.

I dig my nails into the flesh of her cheek and her skin melts over my nails. She laughs in my face, a demonic sound that hurts my ears.

"WAKE UP!" she yells, different to before. "WAKE THE FUCK UP, LILITH!"

A new light reaches my eyes and my sister's demon fades from existence, bringing Nokosi into view. But not just Nokosi, his father and Nash too.

Nokosi's handsome cheek has nail-deep gouges in it, blood trickles from his jaw.

"Did I do that?" I whisper, feeling tears spring to my eyes.

"It's okay, you didn't know what you were doing," he says gently. "Are you okay? You were screaming."

I look at Dasan and Nash. I shouldn't even be here. Nokosi snuck me in. Dasan is going to be so angry.

"Is it just me or is the room spinning?" I ask, trying to climb from the bed. "I need a water or something." As soon as my foot hits the floor and I try to put weight on it my body buckles. I hit the deck, smacking my head on the side of the floor.

My body seizes with pain, every muscle cramps and freezes.

"She's having a seizure!" Nash yells.

It's the last thing I hear before that dreaded darkness takes me again.

CHAPTER 26

Lilith

I've never felt so groggy in my entire life. My head is pounding so hard I daren't open my eyes. My mouth is so dry, and oxygen is being pumped into my nose.

"Nok?" I whisper, feeling the sunlight on my eyes. I'm not in the darkness anymore. Thank God.

"I'm here," he replies, squeezing my hand.

Opening my eyes, I finally see him, his front a shadow, the sunlight casting a warming glow on his back giving him such an angelic aura.

"Hey," I say, reaching up to cup his cheek. There's an IV sticking out of my wrist. He has white gauze on his face and I have blood under my fingernails. I let my hand drop. "I'm so sorry, baby. I swear I didn't know it was you."

"I know," he whispers, bringing my hand to his mouth and kissing it. "I know you didn't." He rests his forehead against the space he just kissed. "I thought you were dying, Lilith."

"What happened?"

"You had a seizure," he replies, looking up at me again with tears in his eyes. "You collapsed and just started bleeding from your nose, your eyes, your mouth... it was fucking horrific."

I touch my upper lip but find nothing there. "Why?"

"That's for me to explain." It's the kind doctor that gave me the CT scan after my accident in Nok's truck. He looks at Nokosi. "You should step outside now."

I grab Nok's hand, I don't want him to leave.

"We need to talk, in private, Lilith."

I sigh and nod. "Go on."

Nokosi grumbles his way out of the room, muttering about getting a coffee.

"I've been trying to contact you for weeks," the doctor states gently. "You haven't answered your phone. I even called the schools in the area, but you've hardly been attending."

"I'm sorry, I've been busy looking after my sister and getting laid," I jest despite the fact this is not a time to be joking. "What's wrong with me, Doc?"

He sits on the side of my bed as I pull myself further up, feeling sick and dizzy.

He places his hand on my knee as his calming blue eyes make me feel at ease. "When we gave you the scan before, it showed something *alarming*. A mass on your frontal lobe and deeper into your brain, as though your brain had simply grown around it."

My lips part and my already dry mouth becomes lead. "That can't be right."

"I know, I checked, I thought maybe there was something wrong with the machine because I can't fathom how you're still alive with something so huge and dominating beyond your skull." He gives my knee a squeeze and wets his lips before reaching for something on the table beside the bed. I sip water that he offers, trying to wrap my head around this... no pun intended. "I didn't want to take any chances that I could be wrong so the moment you arrived I did some more tests. A more in-depth scan of your brain."

"This has to be wrong," I breathe, feeling my chest constrict with pain and panic. "My twin is the sick one. She has the tumor."

"Your identical twin?"

"Yeah, Willow," I reply.

"We've been trying to contact her and your mother since you arrived five hours ago. I have the police locating them both now. Your friend out there said your mom works for LEG Energy? The police will track her down I'm sure."

"Thank you," I whisper, needing my sister beside me, though in all honesty, I'm craving Nokosi more. "How does this happen? How do I have the same thing as my twin?"

"It could be that you were both born with a tiny seed of mass in your head and it has just grown with you over time. It has been known to happen with identical twins but nothing like this from what I know of."

Fuck. This isn't happening.

"So... am I the same as her? What does this mean?" Tears fall down my cheeks and my lower lip trembles. "Am I dying?"

He looks as devastated as I feel. And then he nods. "Yes. I'm afraid there's nothing we can do. Removing the mass will kill you for sure. What we can focus on now is keeping you comfortable in your final weeks, until your brain just shuts down and your body with it."

"Weeks?" I choke, suddenly feeling dry again. "No chemotherapy? No radiation?"

"At this point it's already too big. They'll stop its growth, but the side effects will kill you. You don't look it, or feel it, for whatever reason, but you're very weak. Your blood pressure, heart rate, nothing is quite as it should be."

The door swings open, the same one Nokosi left through. Tears are falling from his eyes, leaving shining trails down his dark cheeks. "So you're just going to give up on her?"

"Nok," I say, reaching for him as he glares angrily at the doctor.

"You're going to do nothing and just what? Watch her die?"

"Nokosi," I snap, trying to keep myself composed. "Please, stop shouting."

He looks at me, his eyes distraught. "What about the cabin? The money you gave me today to pay for it for our future." His voice cracks and he wipes his eyes with the heels of his palms. "What fucking future?"

I hold out my hand to him but he doesn't take it. *"Please."*

He doesn't meet my eyes, as though he's incapable of looking at me.

"I have sent your scans to colleagues of mine who are going to give a second, third, twentieth opinion," the doctor assures me, standing and putting his hand on my shoulder. He looks at Nokosi. "She needs support right now. Not this. I know it's hard—"

"Hard is running sixteen miles without a break, not saying goodbye to the love of your fucking life at age eighteen," Nokosi grits bitterly. "That's not hard, it's impossible. I can't watch this."

"Nok," I whisper, pleading for him to come to me. "Please. Not now. Don't do this now."

He rips a hand through his hair that has fallen out of its tie. "I can't be here. I need to leave."

"No," I beg. If he'd just hold me, tell me that it's going to be okay. "I need you to be my rock right now."

"AND I NEED YOU TO BE MINE FOREVER!" he bellows, his nostrils flaring, spit flying from his mouth. "I need you forever... not for a handful of fucking weeks."

With that parting gift he turns and walks away, slamming the door behind him and yelling a roar of anguish as he goes. My heart is breaking.

"I don't want to die," I admit quietly. "But I probably deserve it."

The moment the doctor leaves after filling my broken head with more shit than I can handle about waiting on blood results and responses from neurosurgeons and whatever the fuck else, I yank out my IV and exit the hospital, stealing somebody's jacket on the way out.

I need my sister. I need my mom.

Willow

"Can I help you?" I ask, smiling at the man on my doorstep in his beige uniform, a badge clipped to his chest, a gun holstered at his hip. "How can I help you?"

"I've been trying to contact you and your mom for the past few hours. Is she home?"

I shake my head. "Mom's at work."

"Where does she work?"

"LEG Energy," I respond.

"Funny," he replies, looking behind me and into the house. "Because I checked at LEG Energy and they'd never heard of her."

"I don't know what to tell you," I reply, eyeing him warily.

"It's probably an error." He looks around me again and into the house. What is his deal?

"Is there a problem, officer?" I snap, feeling guarded. I don't like this guy; he gives me the creepy vibe.

His demeanor softens and his smile becomes sad and sincere. "No problem, little lady, it's your sister."

"What about her?" I ask, feeling my heart rate elevate.

"I'm afraid she's had a bit of an accident that landed her in the hospital early this morning."

Sounds like her. Probably fell off her bike. "Is she breathing?"

He nods.

"Is *Nokosi* with her?"

"He sure is. Don't like him?"

I grunt, "You have no idea." Sighing, I wipe my hands on my nightgown and blow a raspberry. "Well, if he's with her I'm sure she's fine and doesn't need me."

"She does need you," he responds, and I hear the sincerity in his voice and see it in his eyes.

"Fine." I step back. "I can't drive, I've had my meds, can you give me a ride?"

"Sure can."

"I'll just get dressed then," I say, smiling and allowing him into my home, motioning to my tatty pink nightgown. He steps inside, looking at the lack of furniture and pictures on the walls. "What did you say your name was, officer?"

"I didn't, sorry, long day." He holds out his hand and I take it. "It's Officer Deacon."

"Officer Deacon," I repeat, feeling my heart thrum with excitement. "I have heard a lot about you from my sister."

"All good I hope."

"So good," I lie, "I feel like I'm in the presence of a hero. Please, follow me and sit while I get dressed."

Officer Deacon

My head hurts. I've never felt so hungover. Did I drink last night?

No... it hasn't been last night yet. I was talking to that girl... the one with the weird green eyes. The mud shark. The nigger fucker. I was pouring her a drink... she was upset... worried about her sister... and then...

Now I'm here.

Where is here?

I blink open my eyes, surprised to see a blinding light pointed directly at me. I hear groaning and try to find the source, but my head keeps lolling.

I think the groaning is me.

Fuck it hurts so bad.

"Hello?" I try to speak but it's muffled. There's something in my mouth. Fabric. It tastes bitter, like it's been used to clean and hasn't been rinsed properly.

My hands are pulled tight behind me... My shoulders ache. My entire body aches. It feels like I've got the flu. Am I dying? Bleeding? Wounded?

I look down. I'm only wearing boxers and a white wifebeater. I was dressed. I was in my uniform. Fuck. *My gun.*

"Shut the fuck up," a feminine voice hisses at me and yanks my hair back. Her fingers grip my cheeks painfully, her nails digging into my flesh.

It's her. The one with the freaky green eyes like her twin.

"What do you want from me?" I ask but I can't speak properly. This fucking rag in my mouth.

My eyes adjust. I'm in a white room. Plastic sheeting lines the walls and floors.

Oh my God.

I'm going to die.

Willow

Willow: I know we're not exactly speaking right now, but I need you to meet me in our spot ASAP. It's important. Come alone. Don't tell Lilith.

. . .

Nokosi: I have been calling and texting you all fucking day! Where have you been?

Willow: I've been busy. Come around and you'll see.

Nokosi: I'm only coming because I have to tell you something and not because you've asked.

I pace back and forth, twisting my braid around my hand as I go.

It takes him a while, but he gets here. I greet him at the door, blocking the garage behind me from his view. Man, I'm so fucking excited. If this doesn't show him that I love him and I'm worthy of him, I don't know what will. If this doesn't earn me his love and trust, I definitely don't know what will.

"Okay, before you say anything," I state as Officer Deacon thrashes in the chair and screams around the gag in his mouth. "I just want to tell you that I know what I did to you was wrong, so I want to make it up to you." I yank him inside as his eyes find Deacon and quickly close the door behind him. "Tada!"

"Willow... what the fuck?" he gasps, eyes wide and on the cop that abused him growing up. "What have you done?"

"I'm going to kill him for you."

Nokosi swings around to look at me, his eyes still wide but now full of disbelief.

"Unless you want to do the honors yourself?" I motion to the spread of weapons on the floor by the far wall. I didn't have a table, so I had to make do. "There's a screwdriver, knives, pliers, if you want to pull out his teeth or something. Or... I have his gun?"

"This isn't right, Willow, you're not thinking straight," he whispers, gripping my biceps. "You don't want to do this. He's not worth the prison sentence."

"Prison? I'm not going to prison, I'm dying. By the time it goes to trial I'll be dead." I place my hand on his chest as Deacon screams louder, even more scared now that he knows I've got nothing to lose by killing him. "Isn't that awesome? I can do whatever the fuck I want."

Nokosi looks at a loss for words, understandable. This is a lot to take in.

"Oh my God... this day just won't fucking end," he whispers and gulps audibly. "Look, Willow... your sister is sick. She needs you."

"I DON'T WANT TO TALK ABOUT MY SISTER!" I yell at him, annoyed that he's even thinking about her after what I've done for him. "My sister has everything. She has her life, money, the guy I *want*, friends... well, that last part is debatable, strength and energy to do things every fucking day."

"Is that what this is about?" he asks, shocked. "You want me? You did this because you thought it would make me love you?"

"He abused you," I yell, pulling the gun from the back of my pants and pointing it at Deacon. "He abused you for years. Don't you want revenge? Look at this room. Nobody will ever know what we did."

"Willow, I don't want to kill anybody. I just want a long and quiet life. Okay? I don't want this on my conscience, I don't have the stomach for it. If you truly love me, you won't force me into this."

Okay... I suppose he sort of has a point.

"Fine, turn around," I say firmly with a shrug of my shoulders. "I'll do it. He's not leaving here alive. He's a pedophile and I'm sort of what you call a... vigilante, rapist-pedo hunter. Cool, right?"

"What the fuck are you talking about?" Nok asks, gripping his head with his hands, looking at me with wild eyes. "Let's just put the gun down and go and find Lilith. She's really fucking—"

I push the barrel of the gun against his mouth, enraged at the sound of that bitch's name.

"DON'T SPEAK ABOUT MY SISTER!" My teeth are bared, I'm really fucking mad. I need to calm down.

Nokosi raises his hands but shows no fear. He's so brave.

"You love her so fucking much, but you don't know what she's done or why you two met to begin with," I hiss, taking deep breaths. Officer Deacon screams for help again so I hit him around the temple and scream, "SHUT THE FUCK UP!" He immediately goes silent with a whimper.

Much better.

"You think she's so innocent?" I ask Nokosi whose hands are still raised, and eyes are on me. "Yep, sweet Nokosi... you were scouted by my sister for me. Do you recall her trying to entice you to do things to her that could be considered rapey?" He doesn't answer. I don't care. "I'll take that as a yes."

I press a kiss against his unresponsive lips, standing on my tiptoes to do so. The plastic sheeting crackles under my movements.

I then walk over to Deacon who flinches, and I lift his wifebeater, showing the star-shaped burn on his rounded beer gut.

"Oh God," Nokosi chokes. "No."

"I normally heat a knife, or something sharp and burn draw the sigil into their flesh, but I just held his badge over an open flame and pressed it against his skin. Cool, right? He screamed and screamed. Not good when you have neighbors. I had to hit him a few times, but we managed it in the end. Look at it."

"You're dying, you're weak... you couldn't have killed all of those innocent people."

"They were rapists and murderers and disgusting arrogant

PIGS!" I sneer, pressing the barrel of the gun into the blistering burn on the older man's stomach. He cries.

I love it when they lament as I torture them.

"You don't know that, Willow. Arrogance doesn't mean they were bad."

"Male means bad," I respond darkly, turning again to look at him. "All men are vile fucking pigs. You have no idea what they did to us." I laugh lightly. "Or maybe you do? Because that's what he did, isn't it? He fucked you, made you think you were enjoying it when really it was destroying your soul."

"I'm not destroyed," he insists. "I'm strong. I survived. I'm okay. Look at me. I'm not damaged."

"Yes, you are," I say, raising the barrel of the gun again and pointing it right at the sobbing officer's eye. "And I'm going to end your pain by ending him."

"Don't, Willow... Lilith is dying, she has the same tumor as you. She needs you!"

My lips part as a new wave of pain floods through me. "What?"

"That's why she's in the hospital," he explains, taking a step towards me. "She collapsed. She's really sick." His eyes fill with tears despite everything I just said about her.

"You really do love her, don't you? Even knowing what she did? What she came to do?"

He looks away, at the man behind me who is still shouting for help through the rag. Or trying to. He's not very smart.

"Shut up," I snap at him again and he does so, looking at Nok for help. "Don't you look at him, you fucking pedophile." I raise the gun. I'm not even enraged anymore. I'm dead inside.

My sister was always supposed to live after me. It was my one saving grace. And now I'll never get Nokosi because he'll choose the dying sister that he loves. He doesn't care what I've done for him.

"Well, if she's dying, I guess I really have nothing holding me back." I pat Deacon's cheek. "Sorry, dude. You fucked up touching him. Any last words?" Yanking the fabric from his mouth, listening to him yell for help for a little while, I twist the silencer onto the end of the pistol. I got that from the twelfth guy I killed. His daddy was a hunter who promised me over the news that he'd find me and kill me. He hasn't yet and I'm glad of it. This doohickey has been a great tool to use for my little hobby I've got going here.

Nokosi moves closer and starts to speak, "Maybe we should—"

POP.

My elbows almost buckle when the gun fires and the bullet soars through the air, hitting Deacon in the eye.

The splatter of blood across Nokosi's face shuts him up and he becomes deathly pale.

Deacon is slumped to the side, a hole where his eye was, the bullet passed through and took a massive chunk of brain and skull with it. They're on the floor by the wall over there.

Nice splatter pattern.

"He's dead," Nokosi breathes, eyes wide and full of fear. "You did it. You actually killed him."

"What? You thought you were being punked?" I laugh and blow on the end of the gun like an old western movie. I wipe the blood from Nokosi's face using a white rag and kiss the tip of his nose. "You're welcome." I tuck the gun into the back of my pants, it's hot but not so hot that it burns. "Can we kiss now? I deserve that much at least."

He turns and vomits onto the ground, so I rub his back instead.

"It's hard the first time. My first time were the guys that raped me and my sister. I took them out one by one. It was so fucking satisfying."

"You're insane," he breathes, wiping his hand on his mouth and standing. "I can't deal with this. I need to go."

"Go? You're not going anywhere. We need to get rid of the

body." I move to it, throwing a towel onto the blood pooling on the ground from Deacon's head. I kick him back in his chair and start cutting through his bindings with a knife from my boot. "Help me then, don't just stand there."

"I want nothing to do with this."

I stand and point the gun at him again. "You need to have something to do with this, so I don't have to kill you. Please don't make me kill you."

"If you love me..."

I raise the gun; he's overestimating how strongly I feel for him. "Help me get rid of the body."

"Do it yourself. How did you do it before?"

"I had the strength then."

The door opens slowly.

"Did you tell anybody?" I hiss, raising the gun with my heart racing. I point it at the door as a hooded man steps through.

"Sweetie, put the gun down," the man says, his voice is so familiar. Pain slices through my chest as he raises his hands and pulls down his hood revealing dark blond hair and familiar eyes. "Put it down and we'll fix this. We'll get you the help you need."

"Daddy?" I whimper, feeling grief from the loss of him hit me. "You're dead."

The garage metal shutter door slowly starts to open so I turn and shoot bullets through it. They hit the metal and somebody curses on the other side. Holes litter the metal, tiny holes but no blood.

"Sweetie, it's just Nash and his father, Dasan." He then calls out, "You all good, guys? Anybody hurt?"

Nash responds with a disgruntled, "Yes and no."

"How are you alive?" I whisper, feeling my heart break and pain slice through me. "You killed yourself. You couldn't handle what happened to us."

His jade green eyes, like mine and my sister's fill with tears.

"No, honey, I didn't kill myself. Remember? I abandoned you, I was in a dark place, but I didn't die. I ran away like a coward. I should never have done that. I know it was wrong."

Hot tears stream down my face as I point the gun at the chest of my father. The man who taught me how to ride a dirt bike, and tie my shoes, and kissed the grazes on my knees.

"But Mom said…"

"Mom's not here anymore," he breathes, choking on his sorrow.

"I saw her this morning."

"No, sweetie…"

"Where's my sister, she'll tell you. Where's Lilith?"

Nokosi looks at me and then at my father, realization dawns in his eyes. "No… how is that…"

My dad cuts him with a look and shakes his head. "Sweetie, I want to speak with Lilith now. Can you call her for me?"

"Call her yourself," I bite back, feeling angry. "Isn't she at the hospital?"

My head is pounding, my wave of energy is fading. Fuck.

"Honey, what do you remember about that time. The time you were assaulted and the years that followed?"

"Why?"

"Just tell me, I never listened because it was too painful, I put my own feelings before yours. I just want to know. What happened? What do you remember?" He stays calm, still smiling gently, his eyes wary and on me.

I let memories wash over me. "I got sick…" I blink rapidly, my head is throbbing. "Why do we have to do this?"

"Please, for me, for Nokosi, so he understands."

I lower the gun slightly. "I got sick. I wanted to enjoy what was left of my life. So I… umm… I partied and then we were raped." He flinches, so does Nok, so do I. It's still painful to think about,

312

even now. "And I spiraled, I wasn't myself anymore, nobody was. And then... I killed them and we moved and nobody knew. Nobody, not Lilith, not you, or Mom."

"Lilith didn't know you killed them?"

"No," I whisper. "She found out in umm... I don't know... my head hurts."

"That's okay," Dad whispers, putting his finger to his ear and scratching it. He seems to whisper to himself, *"Not yet."* Who is he talking to? "When did she find out?"

"I don't know," I cry, feeling my throat constrict and burn as bile forces its way back up. "Vegas."

"Right." Dad looks excited now. "And when was Vegas?"

I shake my head and almost drop to my knees as more pain thumps under my skull. "I don't fucking know."

"Think. What school did you go to last, who was your last victim?"

"I DON'T KNOW!" I scream, pointing the gun at him again. "STOP! STOP MAKING ME THINK!"

"Why don't you want to think? Tell me? Why can't you figure out your memories? Is it because you're trying to place pieces that were never there?"

"What?" My hand is trembling, my teeth are chattering.

"When was Vegas?" Nokosi asks me gently. "When did you kill your last victim?"

"Maybe November?"

"Yes," Dad pushes, "and what happened in Vegas, sweetie? What happened in Vegas?"

I grip my temples with the heels of my hands, gun still gripped tight.

I can see my sister flashing in my vision. She's doing something, she's stabbing somebody in the stomach but no... that's not right that was me. I did that.

"I killed him... but Lilith killed him... but she hasn't had brown hair in so long... who is that? Did I do that?" I look at my father. "Daddy... I don't understand what's going on." A sob tears its way up my throat. "My head hurts."

"You're sick, baby, you're very very sick and it's not your fault. None of it is your fault."

My hands are squeezing her throat. I'm choking her. But I love her.

"I didn't kill my sister!" I screech, falling to my knees now. "I didn't kill her. I wouldn't do that. I loved her."

"Your sister was beyond help, Lilith."

"NO! I'm Willow."

"No, you're not," Dad says, sinking to his knees in front of me. "You're not Willow, you're Lilith."

"What the fuck?" Nokosi breathes, stepping back away from us both.

Dad reaches up, cupping my cheek, and then he rips my hair from my head forcing me to almost fall to the side.

"NO!" I scream and hit my dad around the face with the gun, he falls and the gun leaves my hand, landing on the floor by the brown wig.

I scramble for it but so does Nok. I'm faster, I grasp it and put the barrel against his forehead. The safety is off.

My hand goes to my head. I should have nothing but a layer of wispy hair and scalp but instead I find a knot of hair at the base of my skull. I pull it free and let the pink hair hang over my shoulder.

"What's happening?" I cry, tugging on the hair to make sure it's real.

"Lilith?" Nokosi breathes, his face a mask of devastation.

"This is all your fault," I hiss at him. "If Lilith hadn't fucking fallen for you, you'd be dead already and we'd be gone."

"No, he wouldn't be," my dad yells, nursing the bleeding gash on his head with his dark sleeve. "Because you didn't kill those people, Lilith. Willow did."

"I AM WILLOW!" I remove the silencer and shoot at the ceiling to frighten them but all it does is make my ears ring and make me see things that didn't happen.

CHAPTER 27

Lilith

I climb from my bed, feeling lethargic and weak. I don't remember how I got here or how many pills I popped this time. My head is spinning.

I check my phone, but I have no messages... but then... my phone fades. What the fuck? I better not be in another nightmare again.

"I AM WILLOW!" Somebody yells and it echoes around my room.

The fuck is that?

Is my sister having a meltdown again?

"Will?" I call and exit my bedroom then cross the hall into hers. "Willow, you okay?"

She's not here, her bed is empty. I need to talk to her, to tell her that she's not going to die alone. That's the one silver lining that I can take from this, my sister won't be alone in death.

My vision splits for a second and I see plastic walls, blood, Nokosi... Dad?

I shake my head and I'm back in Willow's room again.

Fuck, this tumor is fucking fucked.

My head. Ugh.

I go back into the hall and sit on the top step as the plastic room flashes back into view again. I almost fall down the stairs trying to lean to avoid this weird room that seems to be spinning out of control yet not moving at all.

"Brain... please... stop." I rub my temples and slide further down the stairs on my ass. So unattractive.

"WILLOW?" I shout but still no answer.

"What did you do?" Mom screams at me all of a sudden, and when I blink, I'm... in a red room faced with furniture I don't recognize but then I also do. It's familiar, a memory perhaps. "Oh my God... Oh my God... my baby, my sweet little girl." She's sobbing, holding something on the bed.

I shake my head and I'm back again, in my house in Westoria. WHAT THE FUCK?

It feels like I'm walking through syrup. My legs are lead.

I head to the kitchen, maybe she's in there? But that's empty too.

"I wouldn't kill my sister, I love her," Willow's broken voice floats around me... or is that my voice?

Sometimes even I get confused.

"WILLOW?" I shout, opening the back door.

Mom grabs my arm and pulls me into a hallway. "We need to go," she whispers, tears streaming down her face. "We have to get you somewhere safe. Somewhere they won't find you."

I pull against her. "What the fuck, Mom? Let me go. Where the hell are we?"

Falling to my knees, I'm back in my kitchen again, holding on to the door handle for dear life.

Jesus. I think I should go back to bed.

"LILITH LOVES NOK, IF YOU DO THIS IT'LL DESTROY HER!"

Dad? Was that my dad? Is he gonna appear too? Fuck me what a trip. What have I taken?

My body lurches backwards. I'm in a car, Mom is speeding down the highway, still sobbing.

"She was bad, Mom. She killed all those people. I had to." My mouth is moving, and words are coming out but I'm not saying them right now.

Scenery blurs by, a mess of black and white patches fading out of existence.

"You could have called the police!" she shrieks at me. "We could have gotten her help!"

"She was in so much pain. They'd have locked her away for thirty years and then killed her anyway. She's at peace now."

I look down at my trembling hands and my tears fall onto them. Is this a memory? It feels familiar.

The pain I'm suddenly feeling feels all too familiar. Both mental and physical.

The car lurches to the left, through a metal barrier and down a steep road. I'm tossed around in the car. So much pain.

It hurts so bad.

I'm back in the kitchen again, still on my knees.

"WILLOW?" I yell, scared now. I need my sister to help me get through this.

I need my mom.

"I'm here, baby," a warm hand touches my shoulder. Thank God. I turn and bury my face into her stomach. "I'm right here."

"I don't know what's happening," I whisper, crying now. I just want out of this nightmare.

She strokes my head. "You're very sick, Lilith, but none of this is your fault."

"I'm dying."

"You are. But you always have been."

I peek up at her and she helps me to my feet. Her eyes shine with tears too. She's so beautiful, even when she's crying.

"Help me," I whisper, and she pulls me into her body. "Help me fight this."

"Don't fight it. Accept it. Remember. Let it in. Just relax and let it in."

She kisses my eyelids and wipes away my tears with her thumbs.

When my eyes open, I'm standing in my garage which has been cleared of everything, is now covered in plastic, blood and... holy fuck I'm holding a gun and pointing it directly at Nokosi.

I click on the safety and lower it.

"What the fuck is happening? Is this real or am I having another weird dream?" I ask, murmuring the words. My mouth is so dry.

"Lilith?" Nokosi asks, his eyes swollen and red, his cheek still covered where I clawed him. "Please tell me that's you?"

I glance from him to my father and mutter a curse. "This is a dream. It's great to see you, Dad, but please go. Mom's fucked with my head enough already, dragging me to cars and driving us off fucking cliffs."

I tremble and shiver when somebody taps at the inside of my head.

"Can I have the gun?" Dad asks.

I shrug my shoulders. "What the fuck ever, I'm going to wake up in a minute anyway."

I start to hand it over but my vision goes black and pain like I've never felt attacks the inside of my skull. It feels like my head is going to explode.

I fall to the ground in pain, screaming and seizing, bleeding from the nose. No. No. No. What the fuck is going on?

I can hear Nokosi yelling my name, telling me to fight it.

FUUUUUCKKKKK

This hurts.

It feels as though something, or someone is peeling away from me. My skin is on fire, my body an aching entity no longer under my control.

I writhe on the ground, resisting the urge to vomit and then I feel a slap around my face and the pain stops. I open my eyes and find the eyes of my sister.

"Get up," she barks and I do so, confused and unsteady. She has a gun in her hand, the gun I took from those racist fucks at the gas stop. I still have a gun in my hand too, where is this one from? "Look what you did."

I look around and scream when I see the body of Officer Deacon on the floor. My heart thumps against my ribs and I fall backwards onto Willow but she shoves me away from her. "I didn't do this."

She points at me with the gun. "You made *me* do it."

"No. I didn't. I swear. I would never..."

"You promised me blood."

I look at Nokosi. "I couldn't let you hurt him."

"YOU FUCKING KILLED ME!"

"No... you're standing right there." I look at my dad who has his hand on Nokosi's chest, holding him back.

"Remember?" Willow asks, tears falling down her cheeks. "It was YOU who made me go to the fucking party. It was YOU who wanted to live before you died. YOU KILLED ME! You made me a monster and then you slipped your pills into my drink, wrapped your hands around my throat when I was asleep and strangled me until I could no longer breathe."

The memory surfaces, coming to life.

"What happened in Vegas?" my dad asks me.

With chattering teeth I reply, "I followed her, I suspected her for a while but I didn't want to believe it and I saw her stab that boy in the stomach." I look at Nokosi. "She was in so much pain and she told me... she told me how many she'd killed, what she'd done to them, that she *needed* it." I wipe my eyes on my arm. "I didn't know what to do. I couldn't stomach what I'd seen. I was so angry. She'd ruined everything. I was dying and my sister was dangerous. She wasn't Willow anymore. I remember drugging her warm milk and waiting for her to fall asleep. And then I squeezed her throat... I thought it was mercy. I didn't want anybody to know what she'd done. I didn't want that to define our family but then Mom came home."

I did. It was me.

I look at my dad and then Nokosi. "What's going on, how is she here if I killed her? I don't know what's happening?"

"She's not here," Nokosi answers softly. "It's all in your head, Lilith. It's been you this whole time."

"We found your mother's body in her car deep down a steep decline just days after we found your sister's and I've been looking for you ever since," Daddy whispers, smiling with so much sorrow and anguish my lip trembles. "Your blood was in the passenger seat. We knew you'd been in the wreck and knew you must have been hurt, you saw your mom die less than hours after your sister. You couldn't handle the trauma of losing your family, so you created a new one. A replica. You became both Willow and Lilith, and Willow took on your sickness so that Lilith could be strong. Think about it. Look at your memories... they're Lilith's memories—"

"No," I look at my sister who is standing beside me, as solid as my father. "You're the one who's dead."

"Look at me," Nokosi orders, stepping closer but not close enough to touch me. "I'm not dead. I'm telling you; your father is alive and your sister, whoever or whatever you're seeing right now, isn't there."

I reach out a hand and so does she. Our fingers touch.

But she's cold.

I stagger a sob. "Are you dead? Did I kill you?"

When she nods, I break down. My body is pained with hysterical tears and agony. It's too much. It comes flooding back so quickly and violently that all the grief slams into me, buckling my knees. I can feel my hands around her throat, squeezing the life from her limp body.

I'm sorry, Willow. I'm so sorry.

My dad takes the gun from my hand and Nokosi pulls me into his arms.

"I killed my sister," I breathe. "I killed her. And my mom... she'd be alive if I hadn't... I killed them. This is all my fault."

"Shhh." Nokosi strokes my hair as I cling to him. "It's not your fault."

"I'm sorry, I'm so sorry, Willow. I'm so so sorry."

The door opens and people enter the room. I hear their footsteps and their voices but I'm too deep in my hysterics to hear them.

I'm a monster.

"No," Nokosi begs. "Don't... don't take her. Please."

"We have to," somebody replies softly as I sob into his chest, soaking his blood-stained shirt with my tears. "She's sick. We're going to help her get better."

He holds me until he physically can't anymore. Muttering promises that he loves me and that it's all going to be okay.

How can he still love me when I'm not good?

CHAPTER 28

Lilith

"*It has been six months since the discovery of the School Sigil Searer in Las Vegas and two years since she claimed her first victim...*" The TV goes blank.

"How does that make you feel? Seeing all of those families rejoicing over their justice?" Doctor Geraldine, my therapist, asks.

"It makes me feel... justified," I respond honestly and the handsome doctor scribbles that down in his notebook.

I twist my hands in front of my lap and look at the window where Willow is standing, staring out over the grounds. I wave at her, flapping a hand as though wafting away smoke and she vanishes.

"Was she here just now?"

I nod and then ask, "Will she always be here?"

"Most likely," he replies gently, smiling sadly at me. "But you're in control now."

I nod again and reach for my tea, sipping it after blowing on it. It's good tea. Reminds me of Dasan's. The only other place I've had tea in my entire life so maybe that's why I immediately think of him.

"Why'd you kill your sister, Lilith? Do you want to talk about that?"

I know why I killed her, I remember wrapping my fingers around her throat as I sobbed and screamed, and she didn't even move beneath me due to the drugs. I couldn't leave her here alone. I couldn't stomach it. Not when she was going to continue killing innocent people and I was dying. I couldn't hand her in and leave her to face prison and her lingering rage and pain without anybody left to love her. Mom was useless, Dad was gone.

It was just us. I had to stop her. I had to.

"It was the nicest thing I could have done for her."

He scribbles that down, eyes sad. "It must have been hard."

"Harder than you'll ever know."

I look away, trying to repress the memories to a darker place. They haunt me, what I did, what I caught her doing, what she asked me to do for her, with her. I couldn't, I'm not a good person but I couldn't kill those men, I couldn't trap them into death. But when she died, my brain somehow let me believe that that was exactly the path I chose. I rationalized it in my grief-stricken, fucked-up brain that she was doing the right thing and I had been helping her. I suppose as a way to take back the fact I killed her.

The guilt weighs on me so heavily there's little room for anything else these days. I understand why I repressed it. It's too painful to bear.

"Do you want to discuss..." He points at my stomach with his pen. "Because it can't go undiscussed anymore. You might very well pass away before..."

"I know," I say, biting my lip. "But we have to ignore it for the most part. She can't know. I can't trust her to do something that might hurt it before I can give it a chance to live."

"You think you can keep it hidden from her?"

I nod again. "She only sees what I let her see. She only knows what I tell her."

"And when it's born?"

"Send her to her father."

He reaches over the table and takes my hand. "You're a very, very brave young woman, Lilith. You have been through so much. You don't have to do this, there's still time to end the pregnancy, have the surgery..."

"No," I respond, pulling my hand away. "It should be this way. I'm not a good person, I'll never be a good person and I have this *demon* inside of me that will forever put those I love at risk. Regardless of whether or not my inner *Willow* is my sister, she believes she is, and she believes she's the School Sigil Searer. If she gets control. If she beats me... I'm terrified of that ever happening, and the weaker I get, the stronger she gets."

He dips his head with understanding. "I'll look after you until the end." When he smiles kindly at me and holds out a tissue, I take it to wipe the tears I didn't realize were falling.

"I just want to leave one good thing behind." My hand strokes my rounded belly again and she kicks me, comfortable and happy in her cozy little bubble.

"Have you written to Nokosi? Have you replied to any of his letters?"

"Not yet, it's better that he doesn't know. Not until it's too late."

"You don't think he should get a say?"

I allow myself to think of Nokosi for a fleeting moment and of how it'll hurt him if I even consider telling him about the pregnancy, just for me to die before the baby is viable. Not to mention the fact that we have to be extremely careful. I have control of Willow for now, but I dread to think what she might do if she knows we're pregnant. She's unstable now more than ever.

Or I am...

I shake my head. "I can't risk him talking about it. *We* should stop talking about it."

How I want to talk about him and to him. How badly I want to love him, hold him, return to the forest with him and catch fish and live a simple life, just us. That will never be. Not anymore. It's impossible.

"Is she coming back?"

I nod and remove my hand from my stomach. "Like you said, she always does, and she always will."

"What did I miss?" Willow asks, grinning and sitting on the empty seat beside me. "You look so intense. What's going on? Damn, that doctor is a hottie. Don't you think, Lil?"

It never fucking ends.

Nokosi

I raise the axe and bring it down, it splinters the wood into three pieces. They're a bit dry this time of year. Great for burning. I drop the axe and wipe my face with the T-shirt I've hooked over the waistband of my jeans.

After taking a gulp of water, I place the bottle back on the ground and pick up the axe again, letting it stall in mid-air after chopping another block when a truck I recognize pulls down the driveway over a hundred yards away.

"Stay there," Anetúte yells at me as he bounds out of the house. I've not seen him move that fast in years.

What the fuck is Shaw doing here? Lilith's father.

Nash suddenly appears at my side and places his hand on my chest as I wipe my hands clean.

Anetúte and Shaw speak sometimes, but apart from asking him how Lilith is, we don't personally have fuck all to do with each other. It's not personal, I just fucking hate him for abandoning Lilith when she needed him the most.

If he hadn't left, maybe she and Willow might not have suffered their pain so much.

I watch them talk in silence. Nash and I don't say a word. But then Shaw starts sobbing, his head falls onto my father's shoulder who hugs him with one arm.

My eyes burn.

Nash holds me under his arm.

She's gone. She's gone and she never replied to one of my fucking letters. I never got to say goodbye.

"Fucking bitch," I hiss, gritting my teeth and turning back to the block. I put another piece on it and whack it with the axe, letting all my anger out. "I'm glad she's dead. She can go to fucking hell."

Nash squeezes my shoulder and I turn to him, hating that I want to hate her, but I can't. She was the fucking light of my life. She was everything to me. She consumed me. Her kisses, her touch, her smell, her smile.

I never accepted that I would actually lose her until now.

I shove my brother away after a moment and he puts another log down for me.

THWACK.

And another.

THWACK.

And another—

There's an ear-piercing screech from far away and Nash and I turn to watch Shaw's truck reverse and peel out of here faster than if flaming cops were chasing him.

"Coyote?" Nash asks when the sound gets louder.

"Doesn't sound like any coyote I ever heard."

Dad makes his way towards us, his arms cradling something pink and fluffy. His cheeks are shiny with trails of tears and his eyes are swollen with grief and sorrow but then they hold something else... something akin to joy.

"Son," he says to me, beckoning me closer.

"Is she dead?" I ask, crass and guarded. I don't want to cry over her anymore. I've allowed myself to do so too much.

"She passed away this morning at five fifteen," he breathes, and my chest tightens. "She passed in her sleep, gently."

I'm never going to see her again. I'm never going to see her smile and she had the most beautiful smile. Her evil-as-sin eyes, green and fucking weird in a sexy and seductive way. Her laugh... so mischievous.

Gone. No more.

The lump in my throat gets bigger.

"She's at peace now, son, she was in a lot of pain."

I look down trying to compose myself.

"But..." He takes a final step towards me and holds out the pink fluffy thing. "She left us a gift. A very precious, generous, beautiful gift."

I pull down the edge of the fluff, it feels soft like rabbit fur.

A gasp gets clogged in my throat when I see a tiny little nose, fingers clutching a chubby little cheek, teardrop eyebrows above soft, closed eyelids and thick lashes.

"She gave you a daughter," he whispers, gently guiding her towards my chest.

I look down at the girl almost in my arms and one of my tears falls onto her forehead. She cries, it startles me, so I push her back.

"I don't know what to do with a fucking kid. I want Lilith... not a baby." I walk away, from them, from a child that's supposed to be mine.

"Wait!" my father calls, handing the girl to my brother who is more than happy to take her. He can be her dad. I don't want this. "There's something else." He grabs my ponytail, something he did to us as kids but not adults. Then he slaps a large envelope to my chest. It's thick and heavy and it has my name on the front in her handwriting. Or at least I think it's her handwriting, I didn't get her for long enough to ever fucking know.

I carry it up to my room and lock the door, ignoring my brother's coos to the child.

How dare she just leave me a fucking baby I never asked for and then die?

I punch my door, and then punch it again, and then again until my knuckles start to bleed and red stains the oak.

"FUCK YOU!" I scream at her picture that I pinned there. My body hurts. My soul.

How could somebody I hardly know have the power to destroy me like this?

She meant to kill me. She never said she loved me. She never even really told me she cared except for when she was jealous or bouncing on my dick unprotected. Because turns out her sister— the not dying one—was the one who had the birth control... or so I gather.

What a mess.

Lilith was a mess. She's made me into a mess.

I hold the large letter again and contemplate ripping it up, but I just can't.

It's Lilith. Apart from a few photos of her, it's all I have left.

Nash and my father enter the house. The kid is squawking.

I don't care.

I rip open the large envelope with the same amount of care I have for that kid downstairs. ZERO. More, smaller envelopes fall out, one of them is so thick and heavy I wonder if it might be a book. I push that to the side and go for the one that says, **READ ME FIRST OR BE HAUNTED FOREVER**.

I tear it open with a little more tact this time and hold it level with my eyes.

Nokosi, I have started and stopped this letter around

fifty times. It's the hardest one I will ever write in my life… and the last one. (That was a joke. Maybe one day you'll laugh.)

I know you probably hate me, or maybe you've forgotten all about me and have moved on already. But I just need you to know that those few precious weeks that we spent together were the greatest, most fucked-up weeks of my entire life.

I fell for you so hard and so fast my head is still spinning… or maybe that's the tumor.

I didn't ignore your letters. I consumed them and I replied to every single one. They follow this, but you need to read this one first because it's the most important.

I'm dead now. Not right this second but by the time you're reading this I'm dead and I am entrusting you with my greatest achievement.

My beating heart. The only part of me that is not tainted and never will be.

Our daughter

I have yet to meet her myself but I love her so unconditionally it hurts to think that you might not want her. I'm hoping you've already seen her and have fallen in love, faster and harder than you did with me. Because fuck it if we didn't fall fast and hard and my biggest regret is never having the chance to tell you just how much you mean to me.

That's my gift to you. My undying, unconditional love. It just comes in a completely different package.

You will make a kick-ass father. I trust nobody else with her but you.

Get Nash to teach her how to ride a dirt bike because you suck, and you teach her how to fish with a spear, and climb trees to the top, and fear nothing.

I wanted her so badly and you. I wanted to see you one last time, but I left you with an awful memory as it was. I can't bear for you to see me now. Not in the condition I'm in. I'm dying and I look like I'm dying. I can't put you through that or myself.

*I've stuck a photo to the back of this letter, my favorite photo of you and me together from the camping trip on the beach. I hope you might use it to show our girl how much love created her.
I also hope you might look at it one day and think fondly of me and not just that psycho bitch you screwed around with once or twice.*

I love you, Nokosi Locklear, and I am so sorry for everything I did that ever hurt you and your family. And I know you struggle with what happened to your mother during your birth but as a woman, giving up her life to save her daughter, I can tell you right now that it is worth it and your mom would be so proud of you.

Just as I will always be proud of our daughter.

This wasn't a sacrifice. This was the greatest decision I ever could have made.

Forever yours,
Lilith Locklear

I scrunch the letter up to my chest and growl a quiet, painful scream. Then I drop it and rip open the rest. Sure enough, there they are, the responses to my letters and also two huge wads of cash.

Well... at least she paid child support.

I almost laugh to myself; she'd have loved that joke. Her humor was so dry and witty.

I pick up the scrunched-up letter and peel away the photo. It's a bit crinkled but I can see why it's her favorite. It's a stupid selfie photo, we're in our truck tent and I'm sleeping, my head is tucked under her chin and she's smiling at the camera. She looks so beautiful and happy.

"I'll remember you like this forever, baby," I breathe, touching her face.

Then I stand up, open my door, go and wash my hands and head downstairs to meet my daughter.

"I'm calling her Lily," I say firmly, taking my fluffy pink bundle from my brother. "Because Lilith hated being called Lily."

Nash snorts, my dad sighs, but neither of them argues.

"I have no idea what to do with you," I say to the most beautiful girl I have ever seen in my entire life. "You're going to have your momma's smile so I don't ever lose it."

She hiccups softly and purses her tiny love-heart-shaped lips.

I kiss them twice.

"You're not alone," my dad assures me.

But I already know I'm not. I'll never be alone again.

EPILOGUE

6 years later

Nokosi

"Lily?" I call, scratching the scruff of my chin. "Where are you? You little beast."

I hear her giggle quietly from somewhere in the trees and chuckle to myself.

"Lily?" I call again softly, standing tall so as to try and catch a glimpse of the top of her black hair. "Come out, come out wherever you are."

She giggles again and I see a flash of her pink jacket as she runs away from me.

"Come on, Lily," I whine. "Dinner's ready. I'm hungry. I've been working all day."

"Gotta find me first, Papa!"

I race around the tree I saw her blur past.

This is getting tiresome.

"Lily," I snap, feeling irritated now. "If you don't get your butt here right now..."

"Okay, okay," she grumbles, crawling out from under a bush. "Bossy boots."

I grab her and lift her over my shoulder. "Who are you calling bossy boots?"

"You, Mr. Stinky."

I swing her down into a cradle carry and she laughs, looking up at me with light brown eyes, just like mine, Nash's, my father's, and grandfather's. To say they're a dominant eye would be an understatement. Her hair is long, sleek, and black but braided into two perfect braids. She looks like me, but as promised on the day I got her, she kept her mother's smile.

It's my greatest joy each day seeing my heart smile and she is so easy to amuse.

"I love you." I tell her this often because once upon a time I didn't say it often enough.

Suddenly Lily gasps and scrambles out of my arms and onto her feet. "BINGBONG!" She races back towards the trees.

"Come on, Lily," I push my hand through my hair.

"I'll be one second, I forgot BINGBONG."

Bingbong is this ridiculous-looking purple caterpillar stuffed animal that Nash brought her back from England. It's funny because he was the homebody that never wanted to leave and he's the one that has travelled the world. I, however, have stayed here with my daughter and father and I don't regret a single second of it. I never want to be anywhere else.

Lily screams, it's loud and sudden and not a scream of joy.

I don't think, I just react, racing towards the sound, thinking the worst.

"LILY?" I yell, terrified. My feet hit the dirt, my legs carrying me faster than they ever have before. "LILY!"

No answer. Where was she hiding before? THINK, DAMN IT!

I look around, feeling my breath come out in quick, short bursts.

"LILY, PLEASE!" I beg, pushing on, deeper into the trees. She knows these woods; she wouldn't have gotten lost. She couldn't have gotten so far that she can't hear me when I call.

WHERE IS SHE? I can't lose her. No.

"LILY!"

"Right here, Daddy," she says from my right, strolling from around a huge red alder tree without a care in the world, the purple toy under her arm.

I grip her shoulders and check her for damage. "What happened?"

"I slipped down the slope," she replies, smiling, eyes shining with innocence and happiness. "But I'm okay, Mommy saved me."

She has fantasized about her mother before, of course she has. She's a little girl with only my aunts, and Mackenzie, Lilith's sort of frenemy who stepped up to help after she found out about Lily.

I don't know what I would have done without her to be honest. She's been a constant, despite her busy life and crazy journalism job. I always thought she'd be a detective.

Lily is always obsessing over her mother and asking about her, and a few times she has claimed to see her. Usually on her birthdays.

It's all wishful thinking of course.

"Did she?" I ask, raising my brow.

"Yeah," she implores, nodding her head excitedly. "She told me to be more careful."

"Well then, she's very smart."

"And beautiful."

I laugh and pinch her nose. "The most beautiful woman in the world."

She catches my humor and scowls at me. "You don't believe me."

I cup her cheek and smooth away her frown with my thumb. My hand is so big compared to her perfect little head. "I believe that you love your mommy so much, that you want to see her wherever you are."

"She knew you wouldn't believe me too, she said all you have to do is howl and she'll howl back."

I chuckle nervously, because that's a bit eerie.

We still do the howl like I did as a teen, but it's rare, and it's mostly just something my family shares with Lily. She enjoys it.

"She did, she said she'll howl so you know she's okay and she's happy and so you'll know I'm not telling tales."

Her imagination is insane. I just hope not as insane as her mother's.

That was a joke Lilith definitely would have found funny.

"Come on." I pick her up and prop her on my hip and we exit the trees in silence.

We get to my little cabin, the one Lilith and I were supposed to have, and I push open the heavy door then place my daughter on her feet.

I turn back to look at the trees, so thick and beautiful and peaceful.

Then, on a whim, and because *why not?* I cup my hands to my mouth, tilt my head back, and howl loud and long at the setting sun. Lily joins in, her little voice not carrying as far as mine, but it still lingers in the following echoes.

She giggles and holds my hand when I let it drop and I wait forever, watching the sun set for a few minutes, eyes scanning the trees, hoping she'll maybe come back to me.

Nothing comes back to us, not a sound, not a shuffle, not a whisper, so with sadness we turn to go inside.

But then...

It happens.

Something howls back. A long, high note. It sounds just like Lilith. Exactly how I remember. Or maybe now I'm the one with the insane imagination.

It makes me feel emotional, even now after all these years I still wish she could be by my side.

"See, Daddy?" Lily asks, tugging on my hand and grinning with excitement and wonder. "That means she's safe and happy."

With tears blurring my eyes, I pick my daughter up and hug her tight. "It sure does, Lily-bug."

I close the door behind us, saying goodbye for the last time.

ENDING NOTE FROM THE AUTHOR

Thank you so much for reading Lilith and Nokosi's story, I really hope you enjoyed it. I'm adding this note to explain a couple of things to you that I couldn't explain before you started the book because *spoilers*.

As you might have noticed, this book has been written by both A. E. Murphy (me) and Xela Knight (Me). Both are my pen names and the reason for the crossover is because this story is a sort of villain's prequel to Xela Knight's works in progress.

Xela is my pen name for all my future paranormal/fantasy works. At this point in time, 23/07/2019, I haven't released any under Xela Knight except for this.

This is purely because I'm building a massive collection of novels under that pen name and I want to make sure most of them are done before I release them so that you guys don't have to wait too long for each installment.

To follow Xela Knight, simply like her page on FB.

Thank you so much for your time.

Much love,
A. E. Murphy
Xela Knight

HAVE YOU READ...?

STEPDORK

A. E. Murphy

Available on KU

"I hate him. I hate him like a rash. I want him to leave before I have to leave." I roll onto my back and sling an arm over my eyes. My feet press into the soft mat of the lounger I'm on.

We're supposed to be decorating my bedroom, but the sun is shining and I really need to bake my tan a little bit more. Plus, Cella got bored and Molly got hungry.

Bris is swimming laps in the pool. Or trying to. She's not the most graceful swimmer. I've never seen somebody splash so much. She swims like she's trying to break through ice.

It's a nice spray of cool water as she goes by us though.

"Is this about what he said the other day?" Molly asks around a mouthful of bread.

Oh carbs, how I miss thee.

"Oh no, it gets better," Cella says, having been the one to suffer my grumblings this week.

We haven't seen much of Molly this week because she's been sick and Bris has been with Parker sucking face every chance she gets. So gross.

"The little fucktard is like majorly OCD and we have to share a bathroom, right? So he is constantly organizing and bleaching and shit like that."

"Doesn't sound so bad," Molly says, still eating.

"Close your mouth, skank." Cella grins at our mutual friend. "Nobody wants to see that."

Bris swims to the side of the pool closest to us. "What's going on?"

"Well." I sit up, straddle the sun lounger and look at them all. "He decided to mop the floor like a weirdo, and instead of picking up my clothes and dropping them in my room, he pushed them with the mop, so *hello, bleach stains.*"

"Oh no, he didn't," Molly gasps, her mouth now wide open and showing a mixture of sloppy bread and ham.

"Close your dick-sucking mouth," Cella yells at her, throwing a small towel directly at her face.

"Why didn't you put your clothes in the hamper?" Bris asks and I shoot her a glare.

"I usually do, okay, but I was high, I forgot! He could have told me to move them and I would have." We haven't spoken at all since that night in the kitchen, we actively avoid each other at all costs.

Bris cringes. "What a snake."

"Right?" Cella agrees.

I fake sob for a moment. "It was my Beatles shirt, the one we got from that greasy bridge guy on the strip."

"Oh no, I loved that shirt." Molly pats me on the arm, leaving breadcrumbs behind.

"Ew," I murmur and brush them off with the side of my hand.

Cella pulls out a cigarette and pops it between her lips. She lights it with her favorite dolphin-shaped lighter and relaxes back on her lounger. "He's such a loser."

"Oh my God, he's at the window upstairs!" Molly hisses, without pointing or drawing too much attention. Cella and I both look up, over the pool and above the kitchen window. There he is, standing at his window though I can't tell if he's looking at us or not.

"Probably batting one off to our sexy bodies," Cella comments and flips him off. "Look all you like, perv, you'll never have this!"

"Closest he's getting to a vagina is the moment he exited his mom's," Bris states and we all burst into a fit of laughter.

ACKNOWLEDGMENTS

To PamPammy Shepherd, thank you for taking the alpha copy of this book and guiding me to the next stage. You're a crazy AF lady that I adore. I can't wait to share more alcoholic slushies with you.

Jami Kehr, you are still a goddess and I will be forever in your debt for all the amazing things you do for me and so many other authors. You deserve a medal.

Judy Zweifel of Judy's Proofreading, I don't thank you enough for your hard work and epic editing. I highly recommend this editor.

Danielle Dickson, a cover-creating legend, I couldn't imagine working with anybody else. Your design skills just match my very vague visions so entirely. You outdo yourself every single time.

Graphics by Tammy, the lady who formats my books to get them ready for eBook and print. You're amazing at what you do and so helpful and patient with me despite some of my errors in the past.

To everybody who accepted an ARC of A Little Bit of Guilt (Little Bits #5), my last release, thank you kindly. Lori Lynagh, Scarlett Emily Phillips, Charlotte day, Jami Kehr, Addi Willock, Magdalena, Monika Raun, Nikki Jones, Savanna Miller, Charlena Barclay, Natasha Gutierrez.

Thank you to all the above and everybody else in my life who are constantly there for me. I hope I haven't missed anybody. You're incredible and I know how fortunate I am to have you all in my life.

ABOUT THE AUTHOR

A. E. Murphy is the queen of sarcasm and satire, she likes long walks in the park, as much as ice cubes like to chill in a roasting oven. She's effortlessly independent and so good at adulting it's unfair on the rest of the world. She only napped twice today and has only avoided the dishes for three days before making the child slaves do them this morning. Winning! Her favourite hobby is writing, her worst hobby is reading through that writing. Also, she has three cats that carry toys to the top of the stairs and drop them down so they can chase them. They do this repeatedly in the middle of the night. Who cares if she has work the next morning? Not the cats, that's for sure. And if it's not the cats doing the waking, it's the toddler crawling into bed with her and pulling individual hairs from her scalp with pudgy little fingers for comfort.

This is likely why she's in a constant state of grump unless there's chocolate and coffee. P.S. Please leave feedback, if not on the book then on this ridiculous bio she wrote herself. It's the least you can do seeing as she'll forever talk in the third person now. Alex loves her readers. Alex says thank you. Alex smiles.

Contact

Website
aemurphyauthor.com

Twitter
twitter.com/A_E_Murphy

Facebook
www.facebook.com/a.e.murphy.author
www.facebook.com/XelaKnight

Email
a.e.murphy@hotmail.com

Connected

Forever

A Broken Story

Disconnected (Dillan)

Sweet Demands Trilogy

Lockhart

Lockdown

Unlocked

Made in the USA
Columbia, SC
20 November 2023

26823710R00196